The Unexpected Human Problem

To all my wonderful readers.
Your continued support and excitement
drives me to create and finish my tales.
Never underestimate what your comments
and support means to writers!

CONTENT WARNINGS

Discussions and later depictions of domestic abuse.

Discussions of contentious divorce proceedings.

Kidnapping and alien abduction.

Off-screen body modification without victim's consent.

Non-consensual touching (no penetration) due to language and cultural barriers.

Dubious consent scene.

Physical altercations, blood, and gore.

Sexually explicit scenarios.

Transphobia, including deadnaming.

CHAPTER 1

It wasn't supposed to be like this.

Rayelle's chest heaved as she careened through the alien landscape, two moons dolefully watching overhead. Behind her, the raucous crashing and thumping stomps of something large broke branches behind her, growing closer. As she raced through the trees and half-tripped over unseen things in the underbrush, her brain worked tirelessly to make sense of the world around her.

The trees weren't a solid trunk of bark and wood nor were the leaves flat and green. Instead, the trees — in orange and red and magenta hues — were like huge, braided vines, smooth and slippery looking with drooping branches and spheres that were presumably fruits or leaves. Rayelle wasn't sure which. The flora around her shared the same deep purple hue of the globules on the trees, which *implied* leaves to her. Here and there, she spotted a nocturnal bloom. Usually glowing with some sort of phosphorescence.

If the flora wasn't disorienting enough, the sounds of the world were worse. The noises of life bubbled up around her, mostly in the distance. Buzzes and chittering and sounds that *almost* sounded familiar but weren't.

Oh, they very much weren't.

Shadowy silhouettes scurried or flew away from her, but she couldn't stop to make sense of them. Too many legs, too many eyes, too much of an odd shape that didn't fit her mental encyclopedia of animals.

And still there was the ever-present pounding footfalls and crashing behind her. No matter how she zigged and zagged or tried to lose her pursuer, they always sounded just a few steps away from snatching her up.

Every time she thought they were close, that she was about to feel the large, clawed hands wrap around her and yank her back, flashes of blood splattered through her brain.

Bright red – and inexplicably green and purple – liquid splashing, the squish of meat rending, the crunch of broken bones and cartilage, agonized screams and sobbing. All while she was cowering in that damned cage. Then, from the flickering darkness of the broken spaceship lights, a tall and broad figure appeared. Dripping in multi-hued blood, dressed in black armor.

Chaos ensued after they broke open the cage and snapped her chains. In the flickering lights, she threw something at the figure – her water dish, probably, but she wasn't sure – and hurtled from her prison. Everything was a blur from there. She just ran, barreling her way down halls and ignoring the carnage underfoot until she found an exit and burst into cool, oddly heavy, night air.

It had taken her a few seconds to realize she was somewhere *completely* alien. The creaking of the spaceship as that armored thing followed her startled Rayelle into another mad dash.

They were still pursuing her, through foreign terrain and mud and underbrush. Never a pause or a stumble that made them lose ground on her. Perhaps the landscape wasn't so unfamiliar to them. That thought made Rayelle's stomach drop.

No matter how painfully her lungs ached and her muscles cried, Rayelle could not stop running. Survival instincts drove her forward, pumping her full of adrenaline as she wildly looked for somewhere safe to hide or somewhere the hulking thing couldn't get her.

Before such a salvation graced her awareness, her worst horrors became fact.

A clawed hand snatched at the back of her shirt. A scream tore from her lips as her arms and legs flailed, making contact multiple times to something hard and fleshy but not having any effect. Her back slammed into the cold damp ground, the air escaping her sore lungs as a warm body dropped atop her.

A single hand clamped around her wrists, pinning her easily to the ground.

She threw herself forward and twisted in the creature's grip. Her back arched, her feet kicking out to gain purchase on the ground, anything to slide herself away. She might as well have been doing nothing. Her captor showed no signs of struggle in keeping her down.

The thing's free hand went to her chest, their claws easily slicing the thin fabric. Rayelle jerked as she felt the cool air on her chest. Her desperation renewed as she violently thrashed against the alien, escape was the only thing on her mind.

Her heart stumbled as a vibration reverberated from the figure above her. A growl?

For the first time since being caught, she turned her eyes to the figure's face. She stared, wide-eyed, into the mask of whoever — *whatever* — had caught her. An evil little voice reminded her they had killed her abductors earlier, too. Not a small feat. Even though she couldn't see any copious amounts of blood any longer, the iron tang still clung to the stranger. It made Rayelle's stomach lurch.

She almost forgot what the thing was doing — her brain filled with the blood-drenched memories — before she felt her shirt shift. The thing pushed away the sides of her torn top, baring her fully to the air. A whimper died in her throat as the alien's clawed hand trailed down her front. The pinpricks of those dangerous fingertips traced firmly from her clavicle to her stomach, almost hard enough to scratch her.

It made her skin prickle in a confusing way. A harsh gasp sliced down her throat, her back involuntarily arching under the touch.

The thing seemed to be appraising her, which was nothing new. Rayelle had seen hundreds of aliens since being stolen from her home. Whatever the aliens were looking for, it seemed she couldn't provide. Thankfully.

She hoped that would still be the case now. They were assessing her. Briefly, a miserable hope bloomed that they weren't seeking to use her. Maybe they looked for injuries.

The longer the thing's palm stayed on her, the more that hope dwindled. It stroked over her breasts and her eyes wrenched shut, still trying to convince herself it meant nothing. They were just checking her over, she lied to herself.

All the while, she ignored how her body responded to the touches. Gooseflesh crawled over her skin and her nipples hardened and her stomach churned with a confusing heat.

A large, clawed thumb ran over a puckering nipple and Rayelle choked back another whimper. Disgust fizzled in her stomach as she felt a growing heat, a telltale dampness start between her thighs. Traitorous body, Rayelle thought as she instinctively pressed her thighs tightly together. But the creature caught the gesture, inclining their helmeted head toward the movement. They nudged their knee between her thighs.

The hand moved lower until it traced along the elastic waistband of Rayelle's underwear. Her eyes snapped open, her upper body attempting to jerk forward, to break free as fresh terror bloomed in her head. But she barely moved. Its hold on her wrists was too strong.

Her sudden action caught the thing's attention, their head cocking slightly. Its clawed finger slowed, its point catching on the fabric. There was a brief second when Rayelle *knew* what was coming. Before she could even shake her head or issue dissent, the sound of tearing fabric shrieked through the air. It had yanked her underwear off with ease.

A jolt shot through her body, suddenly aware of the strange planet's ambient temperature and this thing's too-close presence. Bare and vulnerable, a tremble arched through Rayelle. Her eyes wrenched shut as the thing — the alien, the creature — raised its hand to its mask. There was a hiss and it shifted, likely taking off the covering.

She braced herself for teeth and tongue, unwanted touches, rending flesh. She didn't know what to expect other than the worst, which was a tossup between being devoured or being violated.

Then it spoke. It was a series of clicks and guttural gnarls, reminiscent of the snarls and croaks of crocodiles to Rayelle. With effort, she swallowed before forcing her eyes to open.

She wished she hadn't done that.

The thing, the alien, was nothing she could have imagined, even as her brain scrambled to make sense of their features. Their skin ranged in color from a light yellow to burnt orange, textured like thick leather or tortoise flesh and speckled. Their nose was flattish, pressed tight to their face and ridged from brown to nostrils. Long feather-like structures, black near the head and fading to red at the tips, grew from their head like hair. Horn-like growths protruded at their forehead and at the crest of their cheeks.

It partly reminded Rayelle of a dinosaur until she saw its mouth.

Oh, the mouth was the worst! Four pincers — mandibles, maybe? — with sharp curved ends guarded a lipless maw filled with sharp teeth, ready to bite into flesh.

A whimper tore from her throat, her body instinctively pressing away from the strange creature and further into the gunk beneath her. Dizziness swept over Rayelle, the alien world around her spinning. Fear, shock, her breaking point. She wasn't sure what was happening.

Once more, her eyes closed and the alien clicked at her. The sounds echoed through her head, sickeningly. Pain ached through her temples.

It nudged its knee against her sex again. Rayelle wildly wondered if it could feel the preparatory slick, the heat, and misunderstood what was happening to her. It took her brain another second to realize a warm bulge pressed against her thigh. What her brain understood as an erection pulsed against her leg and Rayelle gave another pitiful, choked sob. Tears burned at her eyes, forcing their way through her eyelashes until droplets dribbled down her cheeks.

She had cried so much in the beginning when she was first taken. When had she last cried? Days ago? Weeks? There was no way for her to tell. There had been no way to differentiate the minutes, the hours, the days.

She had thought she'd run out of tears, having to deal with life in a cage until the next horrific living situation met her. Being poked and prodded, watching strange creatures come and go. Being fed tasteless slop and offered tangy tasting water. Most had stared. Some had touched her curiously, with touches ranging from gentle to unnecessary to carelessly harsh.

None had seemed interested in fucking her, which had been a relief.

It turned out the tears had welled inside her, frozen beneath a layer of shock and exhaustion. And here, with Rayelle partially stripped and vulnerable under this massive beast of an alien, was when the surface broke and her tears came silently flooding out.

Another round of clicking growls issued, heavy on the gnarl. She didn't answer. Didn't even consider answering. Her heart just pounded and the hot wet streams slid over her dirty cheeks. Rayelle choked as she felt the creature shift again.

Thankfully, it was getting off her. It still kept a firm hold of her wrists, pulling her up with it as it stood. Rayelle continued to whimper, unable to stop the flow of tears as she trembled. Enveloped by distress, she didn't notice how the alien remained slightly bent, so as not to haul her feet off the ground when it got to its feet. With its other hand, it once again affixed the mask to its face, before hefting Rayelle bodily over its shoulder.

Strong arms locked against her lower back and behind her knees shook Rayelle out of her misery. Desperation once again gripped her chest. Her shaking fingers balled up, slamming against the creature as it began to move.

Through her tears, she pounded at the creature's armored back with her fists as her feet wildly kicked at its front, and she sobbed, "No!"

It was no use. Just riding along on its shoulder, Rayelle could sense how solid the creature was. They were a bulk of muscle. The armor added another protective layer that made her strikes laughable. Any hint of somewhere weak to strike would be fortified. Not that she could've caused any damage, in the state she was in.

She continued to flail, her begging cries becoming screams. Her shrieks echoed through the foreign world, disturbing unknown creatures from the brush. A small part of her hoped that, maybe, if she made too much of a fuss, they'd just leave her. If she was too much of a hassle, they'd just leave her to die on the planet.

It was better than any alternative she could think of.

A brief window of hope opened as the creature stopped. She felt its shoulders rise and fall in what she took as a sigh. Maybe it had worked. Maybe it was going to drop her and stride off into the night. It moved its arm away from her knees and foolish hope bubbled up in Rayelle as she craned to see what it was doing.

Her heart sunk as she watched the creature's free arm shift, the hand going to about where a belt would be. There was clicking, a beep, the hydraulic hiss of something opening. Something metal glinted in the moonlight.

Rayelle didn't know what it was, what it would do to her. It was a cylinder of clear liquid with something metal on the end. Intuition told her it was like a syringe, a shot, a tranquilizer. She savagely squirmed and tried to shove away from the thing again, but the arm around her middle held tight.

"No! Don't!" Her scream came out involuntarily as she felt cold metal press against her thigh. A sharp pain sliced into her skin, aching and hot. She could *feel* the liquid invade her vein, cold and harsh. Her shriek became a wordless howl and, for a few seconds, she hysterically fought.

Suddenly, the world started to melt around her. Her movements became sloppy, uncoordinated, before falling slack. Her screams dwindled into slurred yells, then drooling complaints, before she fell silent. She thought she felt the world shift under her. A barely coherent thought believed she was moving; no, *it* was moving, carrying her away.

Rayelle wondered what was going to happen now and if she would ever wake again as darkness swallowed her whole.

CHAPTER 2

After dressing the human in a shift left by a previous mate and depositing them into the brig, Tai'dqei tromped his way back to the cockpit. He wanted to suit out and shower first, but he needed to figure out what to do about this new development. After setting the drop-off location for his bounty into the navigation system, Tai'dqei sat back in his chair.

Finding a human among the targets hadn't been expected. He supposed he should have been more careful, given his bounty had their fingers in an array of sticky trade. Though Tai'dqei hadn't heard of them pushing into trafficking. But if opportunities arose, that gang was sure to swipe it. It was a small solace that their heads and spines were now in his cargo hold, waiting to be presented as trophies to his employer.

Tai'dqei's mandibles tightened against his mouth and a small, frustrated rumble vibrated through his chest. Still, this predicament caused concerns.

Where had the human come from? Earth? One of the colonies? Tai'dqei doubted they'd been born in captivity. There were a number of aliens that abducted humans – among other species – for the novelty of it. That had resulted in generations of humans completely unaware of Earth and needing a rehabilitator.

They had been well-fed, from Tai'dqei's assessment. His hand flexed, remembering the feel of them beneath their palm. Soft and warm, no bones on display through the skin. Their flesh felt weak, easily pierced. That was just how humans were, he thought.

He wasn't sure what someone attracted to humans looked for in one. This one had large round pecs, too soft to have housed muscle. There was a slight cinch in their middle, though they still had plenty of softness there before they widened again at their hips.

After touching them, Tai'dqei supposed he could see the appeal in a tactile way. He hadn't seen many humans in his life, but most weren't quite as cushiony as this one. Their scent as he touched them had grown increasingly… curious. As if they liked his touch, though their expression and reaction to him suggested otherwise.

Tai'dqei's fingers curled into a fist as a sudden thought struck him. Had this been a blackhole job? The damned Thrittens had been advertising time travel via blackholes recently and a couple had been on this bounty's payroll. Wanton time hopping had caused an uptick in temporal crimes.

If Tai'dqei couldn't drop the human off just anywhere before, that was doubly true now. With his mandibles twitching, he considered the likely options calmly.

A human born in captivity needed rehabilitation. Otherwise, they would be taken advantage of or trafficked easily at a station.

A human from the other side of the universe – even simply across a solar system – could have completely different tech-translators than what was needed in the quadrant.

An Earth-bred human was even more underprivileged. They usually only had tech-translators for their planet's languages, not space travel.

A human displaced from their own time? Unaware of technological advances and without something to translate alien language? Not even aware of historical developments?

Tai'dqei wasn't even sure if there *was* a rehabilitator – or anywhere – equipped to deal with that. He had yet to hear of such an occurrence.

All of that aside, there was another annoying thought biting at his mind for attention.

He'd taken their scared fleeing as a mating initiation. In his trade, it wasn't rare to find someone who wished to show their appreciation in carnal fashions. Not to mention humans were some of the most pliable and enjoyable sex partners if rumors were to be believed. And there were plenty of rumors swirling around humans.

Tai'dqei wasn't one to pass up recognition, either. Yet, he hadn't even taken time to consider why they'd been there.

Removing his mask, Tai'dqei let out a growling sigh. A minor ache throbbed at the side of his face, a reminder of what caused his own mistake.

As soon as the human slammed that metal bowl against the side of his head and fled, he had misinterpreted. His body had shot out of the spaceship, instinct driving his muscles and lurid excitement in his thoughts. He had given in too easily to the instinct, it was utterly shameful.

A violent action followed by a chase was the mating custom of *some* ja-tau, Tai'dqei included. Grab a potential mate's attention, make them chase you – *hunt* you – and then they could claim their prize.

That was not necessarily the same for everyone, let alone other segments of his own species. Tai'dqei *knew* that. The high of a hunt accomplished – knowing the human had seen it and believing they had to be impressed by his skill and power – had blinded his logic.

He wasn't even sure if the human knew what he was. Even though they displayed such horror at Tai'dqei's face, that didn't translate to much. Many who knew what the ja-tau were capable of would, obviously, feared them.

Irritation coursing through his veins, Tai'dqei shoved himself from the chair. He stalked to his training room, grabbing a spear as his tangled thoughts fought for attention.

As he went through his forms, he tried to disseminate the problem. The first step was figuring out where the human came from. But wherever the human came from, they didn't know how to communicate with Tai'dqei. No translator, no learning, nothing. He couldn't communicate back, since he relied on a Straux nano worm to translate.

It wasn't rare for some of the more isolated colonies and

outposts to not know or not possess translating mechanisms concerning ja-tau language, either. They often had out-of-date models with only the most prevalent languages.

Which meant Tai'dqei first needed a form of communication. From there, he could determine what the best course of action would be. Options branched out in his head, but before he could explore too many, he slammed the butt of his spear to the floor. Closing his eyes, Tai'dqei took a deep breath.

There was only one other person he trusted enough to buy the correct translator *and* to put it in the human's head. The option made dread and anticipation swell up in his insides.

Tai'dqei made a low clicking growl, his eyes squinting open. Meeting with Ah'ke with mating instincts unsatiated was going to cause complications. He really shouldn't wait, though. He didn't know if the human could withstand the life support of his ship, didn't know if they'd had any modifications made to them. For all he knew, they could have been altered to eat inorganic material and breathe iodine. The sooner he got this over with, the better.

At least, that's what he told himself.

He sent a communication to Ah'ke before placing his spear back on the rack and heading to the showers. Hopefully, cold water would cool the mating fire in his loins. Tai'dqei doubted it, but he could hope.

◊ ◊ ◊

Heavy. Groggy. Dark.

Those were the first things Rayelle noticed when she came back to consciousness. It was like she'd clawed her way out of one darkness and into another. With a brain full of fuzz, she pushed herself into a sitting position, trying to remember.

She realized this wasn't "her" cage. Although it was definitely a containment area of some sort. It was much larger than her previous hold and, she suddenly realized, it was equipped with a cot that she currently sat on. Looking down, Rayelle noticed the shirt she wore was even different. Dark grey and made of heavier, perhaps nicer, material than her previous covering. And it was huge on her, which was a feat. She wasn't particularly slight.

Suddenly, it all came back to her. The blood and screams. Running until a heavy weight pinned her down. Leathery skin in warm hues. The mandibles and sharp teeth. Claws tearing fabric.

Heavy footfalls startled Rayelle out of her horrified recollection. Slow illumination bled into the room and bathed the area in a yellowish light. With new brightness, she realized the room and her cage wasn't simply dark. It was made of dark grey metal and a strange white mist crept along the floor.

Her eyes flickered around her surroundings again, taking in the additional details. On the opposite side of the cage something akin to a toilet squatted. For the most part, the hold was simply a box with bars on the open face and a solid door. Faintly, Rayelle wondered if the bars were electrified.

With such a bare area, it didn't take her long to turn her attention to the creature in the doorway.

It was as massive as she remembered. Perhaps more so in the better lighting. She also realized it was far less dressed than she initially assumed. Previously, it had been dressed in full dark-grey-nearly-black armor, save for its hands.

Yet the only metal armor appeared to be a chest plate with heavy shoulder guards, bracers on their wrists and heavy metal boots. Under the armor, it wore something akin to skintight bicycling shorts, though they were probably made of a technologically superior material. There were also additional accessories. A belt laden with pouches and fishnet material glimpsed between each piece of armor. It had decided against wearing its helmet.

Swaths of their leathery red-orange skin was left bare. Faintly, she wondered if it was hubris that made the creature bare so much skin or if the fishnet material had some sort of protective abilities she was ignorant of.

Perhaps she was misremembering last night and this *was* what they'd been wearing. Between terror and the darkness, maybe she was mistaken. Or *perhaps* the thing had changed out of full-body armor to specifically indulge in other activities.

Wariness lit through your brain at that thought. She sat straighter on her cot, her eyes narrowing on the figure. Its mandibles flexed at her sudden stiffness, but they closed the distance from the outer door to the cell. She watched as the alien opened a grate and slid a tray in. Silently, she stared at the offering of presumable food.

It looked like coral-colored mashed potatoes with flecks of darker red *something* in it.

The meal looked and smelled better than the gruel she'd been given previously by her other abductors. However, suspicion kept her from edging toward the meal. Her gaze flicked from the tray, up to the creature on the other side of the bars.

Unsettling pale-yellow eyes watched her intently. It nodded toward the tray of food, making a series of chittering sounds. When Rayelle didn't move, the creature made a sharp motion with their hand. The next round of clicking was laced with a growly undertone. Still, Rayelle refused to move closer even as hunger clamped through her stomach.

Once more, the thing motioned to the food, snarling something at her. Evidently they were getting annoyed. Good, Rayelle thought, her eyebrows lowering into an angry vee. She didn't feel like cooperating. If she starved to death, all the better.

Her captor seemed to have different ideas.

Rayelle watched as the thing typed something into a wrist gauntlet and the door to her cell shifted open with a hydraulic hiss.

It entered, prompting Rayelle to immediately stand and back away as it picked up some food from the tray. Turning to her, it raised the mush to its mouth. She watched as its tongue came out, pulling mush into its maw and overemphasized swallowing. Indignation flared inside her, realizing it thought she was ignorant on how to eat.

From the corner of her eye, Rayelle noticed the alien hadn't closed the cell door.

As the creature issued another series of clicks at her, her attention returned to its face. It insistently held out the tray to her, making motions for her to accept the meal and to eat. She only edged further away from the creature, moving slow and keeping her gaze locked to its face.

Why didn't it get the hint? Why didn't it just leave her alone?

Her refusal to eat made the creature give a gurgling displeased growl. It scooped the mush up in one hand, tossing the tray aside with the other. Momentarily distracted by the tray clattering across the floor, Rayelle barely had time to react to the alien's charge.

The sudden movement had her instinctively pressed back against the wall, which only benefited the alien. Using its broad body to box Rayelle in, it used its clean hand to grasp at her jaw.

"Let go," she snarled, her hands shoving at its arms as the thing tilted her head back. As expected, they were too strong, they didn't even budge as Rayelle violently jerked. She felt like an obstinate cat refusing medicine as she pushed and fought. The alien's beefy fingers held her firm, surprisingly refraining from using their claws.

Its other hand — the one that had scooped the food into its palm — shoved its hand closer to Rayelle's mouth, while trying to squeeze her mouth open. It was only when the creature's hold threatened to bruise that she opened her mouth.

She *did not* intend to eat.

As it shoved the food toward her mouth, she pretended to accept it. Her glare pinned to its face as her tongue licked their hand clean, faintly registering a citrusy taste to the mush. Some tension eased from the creature. Though its own gaze watched her mouth, a heat other than frustration now in their eyes.

That look made Rayelle's stomach turn, but she decided to use its fascination against it. Her tongue drew one of its fingers into her mouth, sucking on the digit. A sound, something like a cross between a growl and purr, vibrated from the creature.

That was enough. Rayelle's teeth clamped down on its finger, biting as hard as her jaw would let her.

A startled screech left the creature as it jerked its hand away, only to have Rayelle's mouthful of food spat out all over its chest armor. The stare the alien gave her now was one of angry bafflement. Their pale-yellow eyes flickered from her face to the mess on its chestplate.

Taking advantage of their surprise and loosening grip, Rayelle lurched from their grasp. She made a beeline for the door, but with each step, she knew it was a useless attempt. Where would she go? If this was a spaceship – which she assumed it was – and they were in transit through space, she was stuck. If they just happened to be docked somewhere, how did she know she wouldn't just be dragged back to this thing? But she just couldn't stop, she just couldn't so obviously change her mind after biting and spitting at them.

It was almost a relief when the thing grabbed her, its claws digging into the fabric of the borrowed top but not tearing into it. The alien hauled her back and up, tossing her onto the cot. A surprised shriek left her lips as she flailed mid-air before her body landed with a thump.

She didn't even have a chance to yelp when it descended on her. One arm braced against her chest, pushing her flush against the mattress as the other hand removed something from its belt. Rayelle's own hands grappled with the forearm, her nails digging into its bare skin as her feet kicked out, determined to cause some impact.

In a swift movement, the hand not pinning Rayelle down snapped something heavy and cold around her throat. Then, just as quickly as it had descended on her, it pulled away. As the creature stormed through the open doorway, its booted feet pounding on the floor, Rayelle's hands fluttered to her neck.

Her fingers traced the metal collar, her angry glare darting to the creature's back. But the door had slid back into place, obscuring the thing from her view.

Without thought, riding on a wave of adrenaline and rage, Rayelle pushed off the bed and barreled toward the door. Her fists pelted the metal, an animalistic scream drawn from her throat.

Why was this happening to her? Why had she been taken from Earth? Why was she being handed off from one awful alien race to the next?

Why couldn't she catch a break?

Her thoughts completely stuttered to a halt as the thing, still on the other side of the door, slammed its fists against the metal and gave a bellowing roar in return. Instinctively, she ducked into a crouch, covering her head with her hands. Ice ran through Rayelle's veins, her pounding heart skipping a beat, the longer the howl went on.

Eventually, the bellow petered out, but Rayelle heard its panting breaths on the other side of the door. Had she already worn its patience thin?

Part of her hoped so. Perhaps she'd be released if she proved to be too difficult. Another part of her flinched at the thought, though. If she was too much of a pain, wouldn't it just be simpler to kill her? It could just jettison her out into the oxygen-less void.

Whatever the case, the alien on the other side of the door gave one last half-hearted thunk of fist against metal, before she heard it retreat. The door to the rest of the ship hissed open before solidly closing behind her captor.

As Rayelle's hands dropped from her head, she realized she was alone once more. Her body still trembled, adrenaline still pumping after that thing's roar. Temptation returned her attention to the meal they offered. The food was mostly splattered on the tray but at least not on the floor. The tangy citrusy taste the alien had forced into her mouth lingered on her tongue.

It had not been an unpleasant taste.

Stubborn rebelliousness tore the observation from her head. No. Absolutely not. The food could have been laced with something like a sedative for all she knew. It could have been an aphrodisiac. Or it could have made her placid and agreeable.

Rayelle didn't trust it.

Getting to her feet, she stumbled back to the cot, where she promptly flopped down. She glared at the wall with her back to the food. If the thing came back, she wanted it to see her snubbing the offering.

◊ ◊ ◊

After his last interaction with the human, Tai'dqei needed yet another shower. He leaned against the wall, forearms bracing himself as the water ran down his back. He tried to focus on the cold streams and the way the droplets slid over his skin, but his thoughts circled back to the human no matter how hard he tried to avoid the subject.

The little shit had made an aggressive display before attempting to run. *Again.*

Tai'dqei had barely gotten the mating urge out of his system before attempting to feed the little ingrate. Here they were, riling him up all over again.

They didn't understand, Tai'dqei told himself. It wasn't their fault and he should be capable of controlling his instincts. At least, this time he didn't strip them. No, instead he clamped a monitoring collar around their throat. It would allow him to keep an eye on their vital signs from a distance and even track their location if they did manage to escape.

Given how easily they provoked his mating instincts, tracking this human himself would only exacerbate the issue.

Though, as he thought back over what just happened, perhaps he shouldn't have forced food into their mouth. If the human was captive-bred, Tai'dqei thought perhaps it didn't know how to feed itself. Or maybe their lack of familiarity with the dish made them wary. He tried to illustrate its safety.

It did not help.

A mixture of concern for the creature and his own annoyance had him forcing food into the human's mouth. Which led to Tai'dqei feeling their warm soft tongue on his palm and watching as they suckled on one of his fingers, their gaze intense on his face. At the time, he impulsively wondered how that mouth would feel on other parts of his anatomy. The memories made his fingers flex, the clawed tips digging into the shower wall as heat rose in his loins.

Even their bite on his finger – which startled Tai'dqei more than hurt – only served to tempt him.

An annoyed growl caught in his throat as he shifted his position slightly, leaning his head against his forearm as his other hand reached down. His fingers curled around the shaft of his erection. It flexed at his touch and Tai'dqei began stroking. Heat stoked hotter in his loins, his hips jerking every so often to the stimulation.

His brain fed him the usual images of Ah'ke and other previous mates, the memories of their frenzied carnal sessions, the way her claws would rake down his back or how he'd struggle to make her submit. The thrill, the adrenaline, the drive. The memories made his heart pound, desire flaring through him. Heated breaths caught in Tai'dqei's throat, his chest gently heaving as excitement sunk into him. His hand moved faster, the slap of his palm against his thigh adding to the memories.

All the while, thoughts of the human weaseled their way in. The sensation of their tongue, their softness, the enticing snarl they'd made when pounding at their cell's door. Vaguely, he understood why others would find the soft fleshy things so appealing. There was something hard to describe that lured one in.

He squeezed harder at his cock, hand moving desperately as the crest quickly overtook him. Tai'dqei threw his head back, letting loose a snarl as the orgasm clamped into him, ropes of seed splattering against the shower wall.

Tai'dqei closed his eyes, allowing the embers of his release to simmer at his skin as his cock emptied itself with a few more spurts. He took a deep breath before opening his eyes again. For now, his dick had fallen soft, but Tai'dqei could still feel the desire, the need, clawing at his core. He needed more than his own hand.

It would have to do for now, he decided, as he shut the shower off. If the need to mate hadn't left him by the time Ah'ke was done setting the human up with a translator, then maybe he'd broach the subject with her. The thought made embarrassment and uncertainty flame through him.

Ah'ke and he were no longer mates, for particular reasons. Yet Tai'dqei could not ignore the feelings that still lingered from their committed time together.

He shook the memories from his head as he stepped out of the shower. It wouldn't be long until they arrived at Ah'ke's outpost. He needed to get dressed again and check the logs to make sure the human hadn't hurt themself during his shower.

At that thought, Tai'dqei's mandibles tugged downward. He wasn't sure what he'd do if the human had managed to hurt itself. It was evident enough they had an inherent ability to rile him up. Whether they meant to or not.

A small dose of shame, having pictured the human briefly during his masturbatory session, flickered through Tai'dqei's head. They really didn't know better. His teeth gnashed together and his mandibles pressed tight to his maw. It wasn't common for a mating ritual to sink its claws into him so deeply, but here he was, being goaded by a human.

Once more, he shook his head and headed to his quarters. He'd have to control himself a little while longer, that was all there was to it. No matter how the human played into his instincts.

Although, it was becoming clearer that requesting Ah'ke's aid to extinguish this heat was necessary. If only to give Tai'dqei a fresh equilibrium while solving this unexpected human problem.

CHAPTER 3

It was the jarring thump of the ship that awoke Rayelle. Pushing herself upright on her cot, she stretched her arms over her head and arched her back. There had been a few more feeding attempts since the first. After the second attempt – throwing the tray at the creature and trying to grab their gauntlet, which seemed to control the door, through the bars – there'd been sparser contact. It would just place the food in the slot and retreat.

Later, it'd retrieve the tray and replace it with a new one. Rayelle couldn't help but notice they had kept to self-contained foods, like whatever constituted space-veggies or space-fruit. No more mash, nothing messy.

Though she didn't eat any of it, she occasionally snagged one or two from the tray. Just enough to not be noticed. She had considered collecting enough to flush down the toilet in an attempt to get her captor in and have the door opened. The plan was nixed after she realized she didn't know how the toilet got rid of waste. Maybe it just zapped it into oblivion, in which case clogging it would be useless.

Rayelle decided she wanted *something* to wing at the creature if it chose to enter again so she quietly collected a small cache of hard projectiles.

Now she wondered what her damn captor was doing. There was a slight shift, as if something had gotten ahold of the ship, and now she heard further hydraulics hissing and the chunk of something possibly locking into place. Then nothing.

Her eyebrows furrowed, trying to make sense of the sounds and the sensations. Rayelle's first thought was they had landed – or perhaps docked – somewhere. It would explain the mechanical whirring and thunking and vibrations, she figured.

But where? Was she about to step onto yet another alien planet, this time full of the same massive, mandible-faced creatures as her current captor? Or was it going to be a station of some sort?

As Rayelle considered her chances between a single-species planet or outpost versus somewhere with more diversity – and fighting the dissociation that sheer absurd thought caused her – the door to the hallway opened. Her stomach sank as two pairs of footfalls entered the room. As the lights brightened, she half-turned to face the front of her cell, glaring through the bars at both the familiar face and the newcomer.

Her red-orange captor stood next to a different colored version of the same species. They were chittering and growling away as they approached Rayelle's cell, giving her a chance to scrutinize the newcomer.

It was a blue-green hue with black speckles. Their head ridge striated, like a washboard, and their feathery hair reminded Rayelle of a peacock with blues and greens. Even the way the feathers were pulled back into a ponytail, pieces sticking out wildly in all directions, stirred thoughts of a showy peacock tail in her brain.

The blue-green one was also taller than the red-orange one. Not by much, but enough for Rayelle to notice. They also didn't wear dark grey armor like the other currently wore. Though they did wear a silver chest plate and a matching gauntlet that seemed tech-based. Other than the scant armor, they wore sleeveless grey coveralls and a sleeveless dark blue lab coat. That same odd fishnet-like mesh was used to cover their arms.

A particular gurgle of a growl from her red-orange captor caught Rayelle's attention. She glanced toward them, not moving from her cot. As the other responded, her eyes narrowed.

She had a suspicion they were discussing her. No surprise. But if the blue one was wearing a lab coat, did that make them a doctor or a scientist? Rayelle pressed her lips together in a tight line, trying to determine which option was worse.

Rayelle jumped as the door to her cell slid open. She scrambled to her feet, grabbing one of the hard fruits she had swiped from a prior meal. Her shoulders tensed as she backed away to the far side of the cage. The blue one entered first, while the red-orange one lingered in the open entrance.

It approached slowly, carefully, with a hand extended and fingers splayed to show they weren't a threat. It also clicked and gave gurgly growls by means of communication. Though Rayelle felt it was gentler, more level than how the red-orange one vocalized. With its free hand, it slowly withdrew a silver boxy object from the pocket on its coat.

Rayelle nervously watched as it held the object up to its own arm, crouching to give her a better view. Light blue light fanned out from the silver box, moving over the alien's arm. Once the machine beeped, the blue-green alien turned the box around to show a screen where alien language flashed and scrolled upward.

She glanced from the machine up to the alien, still having no clue what was going on. Something in the blue alien's eyes seemed hopeful. For some reason, the whole situation reminded Rayelle of a doctor showing a young child that a stethoscope didn't hurt.

Her attention flickered across the room, where the red-orange creature tensely stood. It appeared ready to spring into action should something happen. Whether it was to keep the blue one safe or herself, Rayelle wasn't certain. Once more, she glanced warily at the blue alien before sidling to the side, toward her captor and, more importantly, the exit.

She kept her eyes on the blue alien, her shoulders stiffening as it trilled something. From the corner of her eye, Rayelle saw her captor's eyes flicker to their comrade, replying to whatever the blue one said.

Tightening her grasp on the alien fruit that she hid behind her back, Rayelle decided it was time to test her luck.

The Unexpected Human Problem

◊ ◊ ◊

"Hm, they must be more comfortable around you," Ah'ke observed as the human edged closer to Tai'dqei.

Tai'dqei was not so certain of his former mate's assessment. Preparedness tensed along his muscles, ready to chase and snatch the human up if his own presumption proved correct. He shot a look at Ah'ke, keeping partial attention trained on the human. "They're going to try escaping, just watch."

"I don't know." Ah'ke stood up from their crouch, straightening to full height. "They seem—"

Before Ah'ke could even finish their statement, an orange chemond came hurtling at Tai'dqei. He instinctively caught the flying projectile with ease and swore to himself for not counting the amount of fruit or vegetables he'd given the human.

As expected, the little thing bolted for the door, reaching for the frame as they got close. With a snarl, Tai'dqei lunged and grabbed them. As soon as his arms latched around their middle, they squirmed and yelled. They kicked their feet out as they tried to throw themself to and fro, thrashing with every ounce of their strength as Tai'dqei lifted them up. It was like trying to keep a hold of a feral bozeak.

Tai'dqei threw a dirty look to Ah'ke, who had been chittering with amusement over the scene. His mandibles clicked in irritation. "Going to help or just stand there and laugh?"

"On it." Ah'ke continued to chuckle, but pulled a tranquilizer injector from her belt, quickly approaching the struggling human and Tai'dqei.

The human in his arms struggled harder, howling as Ah'ke neared. They recognized the injector, considering how similar it looked to the one Tai'dqei had used that first night.

They even went so far as to attempt to bite Tai'dqei, leaning their top-half over his forearm and sinking their dull little teeth into his flesh. A growl rumbled out from Tai'dqei's chest, unbidden and not exactly out of anger. The human tensed, braced for Tai'dqei's retaliation. Whatever the human thought he'd do, it didn't happen.

Instead, Ah'ke swept in during the temporary – and likely very short – calm. She pressed the tranq to the human's thigh, eliciting a startled gasp of a whimper as the needle punctured their skin.

Their violent struggles resumed, tears pooling at the corners of their eyes before dribbling down their cheeks. The human's angry yowls turned to quieter wailing as the force of their fighting dwindled. Even when they slumped in Tai'dqei's arms, they continued to warble obvious dissent, weakly shoving at his arms.

A small part of Tai'dqei admired the persistence, in spite of how troublesome they'd been.

"I managed to get a hold of the most up-to-date Straux nano-translator worm for you two." From yet another pocket, Ah'ke withdrew a small case. "These were designed with all dated and modern Terran languages as a specialty."

As she popped the case open, Tai'dqei saw the two yet-to-beactivated earworms. He nodded, relieved that he'd soon be able to communicate with the human. "It's appreciated."

"Move them to the cot and I'll get everything done," ordered Ah'ke, taking charge of the situation. Tai'dqei gave a grunt of acknowledgement, adjusting his hold on the human so they were carried more comfortably in his arms.

After he deposited the inert form on the bed, Ah'ke pushed him out of the way. As she knelt by the human, she held the second translator device out to him. "I trust you can insert your own."

Once more, Tai'dqei gave an affirmative grunt and took the worm.

"You should move them somewhere more hospitable," Ah'ke said as she waited for the translator to boot up. She fiddled with the settings, focusing on calibrating the worm Terran languages and ja-tau. She gave a little chitter of a laugh. "I would not be pleased myself, if I awoke in a brig like this."

"It was necessary," Tai'dqei growled, making the same adjustments to his own worm. Over the decades, one got used to upgrading translator tech. He was just thankful the Straux had figured out a way to get the nano worms to absorb previous versions, rather than having to yank old ones out. "I didn't know what they'd do to escape. For now, they get the brig."

The blue metal worm soon came to life, its hundreds of little legs tickling his palm, and he held it up to his ear canal. Tai'dqei braced himself as the thing skittered in and grunted as the harder part of the process began. Through bone and cartilage and tissue, the technological bug burrowed. In its wake, it repaired the damage it wrought.

As efficient as it was, it was not painless.

That was evident as the human, even unconscious, cried out. Ah'ke held them as they jerked on the bed, tears once more streaming down their cheeks. The sedative eventually dealt with the pain and whatever straggling string of consciousness still clung to them finally dissipated.

Tai'dqei didn't realize he had moved closer, watching the human struggle, until he heard himself ask, "They will be okay?"

"They will be fine," Ah'ke answered with a sigh, as if she'd been asked the same question many times before. She stood up from her stoop, pinning a serious look on Tai'dqei. "Once you're able to communicate, will you move them to the guest quarters?"

"We'll see." He bristled, not looking at Ah'ke as he crossed his arms. Her stern tone stirred something in his core. It was the same something that had been exacerbated multiple times by an unwitting human. He tried not to think about it. "It depends on how they react."

Giving the human free reign would have made all of the efforts to get them somewhere appropriate useless. They could run straight into a dangerous situation, get themselves killed, and be none-the-wiser. Worse yet, they could crash his ship and kill them both, perhaps taking out others in the process.

No, it was better to lock the human down until he could assess their cooperativeness and mentality.

"Go easy on them. From the way you describe it, they may have a lot to adjust to." After wiping blood from the human's ear, Ah'ke got to her feet. Tai'dqei had turned his attention back to the human, considering what preparations should be made for when they awoke.

Ah'ke interrupted his mental checklist as she added,, "And about your other issue."

The change in subjects sent a confusing burst of tingling heat up his spine. Tilting his head toward Ah'ke, Tai'dqei hoped he didn't appear too excited. "Yes?"

She reached out to touch Tai'dqei's arm and he hesitantly hoped she'd help him. It was a gentle touch, her claws ghosting over his arm. Memories of their past dalliances flooded into his brain, but Ah'ke's words doused whatever soft heat filled his chest. "There's a brothel on this station. Check them out."

Tai'dqei's mandibles flared in agitation, a hiss escaping his mouth as she laughed heartily at him. "I've never been into men. You know that."

"I just thought it could be different with me. If it was something purely physical." Tai'dqei shifted his stance, arms crossed over his chest. He could feel Ah'ke's knowing amusement and it only made the agitation in him churn harder. Once more, he turned his attention from Ah'ke to a middle distance, unable to meet her gaze.

"We tried that when your change began." From the corner of his eye, he watched Ah'ke cross her arms over her chest as well. Her own mandibles twitched downward. Guilt dribbled into his stomach.

Tai'dqei grunted before falling quiet at the mention of his change, his arms tightening over his chest.

In the course of his relationship with Ah'ke, they both had shifted sexes and, subsequently, genders. Though Tai'dqei found her just as appealing as before, the feeling was not mutual. She only liked women, no matter her own presentation.

He could have chosen hormone modifiers to reverse the changes, but he hadn't wanted to. It was a difficult feeling to put into words.

Thus, their romantic relationship ended. Not without some complicated feelings, mostly on Tai'dqei's part.

"I need to return to the clinic," Ah'ke announced after consulting her wrist gear. The words drew Tai'dqei from memories. It struck him as odd how unaffected Ah'ke appeared. "I'll check back in soon, okay?"

"Alright," he replied, his tone unintentionally dipping into deep dour octaves.

"Tai." Ah'ke's hand brushed against his arm again, eliciting prickles along his flesh. The softness in her gaze made something in his chest involuntarily swell. With a reassuring squeeze of his bicep, she softly said, "I still care very much for you, even if we're not mate compatible."

"I know, that's why I trusted you with this," he answered just as quietly, raising a hand to indicate the sleeping human. There was a beat of silence, unsaid things mounting in the air among the weight of responsibility concerning the wayward being. Unable to take the heaviness, Tai'dqei heaved a sigh and gave a careless shrug as he added sardonically, "Sorry, I had to go and turn into a smelly aggressive man."

At that, Ah'ke gave a gurgling growl of her own, swatting the sides of Tai'dqei's face with both hands. He gave a yelp as mild pain throbbed through his skin. "I was joking!"

"It was not funny," she hissed, grabbing tight to the sides of his face and pressing her forehead to his. Annoyance faded out of him at the touch. His eyes closed, briefly allowing himself to pretend reality was different. Maybe a world where Ah'ke did find men appealing or where he agreed to hormone adjusters.

The fantasy only lasted a moment before Ah'ke pulled away. Her palms tapped the sides of his face as she teased, "Behave until I get back."

She was already heading out the cell's entrance when Tai'dqei opened his eyes. He watched her go before glancing back at the human. Other than the even rise and fall of their chest, they were still.

After retrieving a blanket for the human and a chair for himself, Tai'qdei locked the cell door again. This time, with him inside the bars alongside the human. He watched them sleep as his own thoughts roiled and rolled, trying not to focus on the upsetting stillness in his own chest. Or the aggravating heat simmering in his center.

◊ ◊ ◊

When Rayelle woke, feeling the now-familiar cot under her body and seeing the dark grey metal of her cell, she briefly thought she had dreamt up her last escape attempt. As consciousness slowly dawned, she realized there were some differences from when she laid herself down to sleep.

Her thigh ached from where the tranquilizer had been injected and she had a blanket, something her captor hadn't given her previously.

She sat up, wondering what the hell the aliens had done to her this time. The last few times she had been sedated – other than the first time with her current red captor – she always awoke feeling as if there was something different with her. Rayelle never could figure out what changed.

Tai'dqei watched as consciousness returned to the human. Their eyes fluttered open, pupils dilating and contracting to adjust to the lighting. They didn't seem to notice him as they sat up, obviously taking stock of themself.

While Rayelle was still trying to shake her stunned brain into operation, someone spoke beside her, their voice intertwined with that damnable clicking, "Good, you're awake."

Her attention snapped to the source, her eyes widening as she saw her red-orange captor sitting at her bedside.

There was a brief second, as the human turned its attention to him, when Tai'dqei realized he should have allowed the human more time to adjust. Shock drew a scream from their lips and they sent a fist flying at his face.

Torn between catching the hand or simply dodging, Tai'dqei ended up allowing the strike to land.

The smack of her knuckles landing right between their eyes rang out before she scrambled off the cot. Shock vibrated through her, realizing her punch had made contact. Not that there had been any reaction. She only received a throbbing pain in her knuckles. Her alien captor drew back, muttering swears to themself.

Hyper-aware and with adrenaline coursing through her veins — while fighting the groggy drugged sensation weighing down her limbs — her eyes fell on the cell door. Without thought, her feet ran for it. It had been opened earlier. Perhaps it still was.

Like all her other attempts, she didn't get far. There was a shriek of metal on metal and clattering as her captor's chair skidded across the floor. A single thump of their boot hitting the ground was followed by an arm looped around Rayelle's middle. She yelped as the arm clamped tight, pulling her back as a large hand splayed over her middle. Her back hit something hard and warm. Her lungs and heart pulsed overtime, pumping hard and making her chest heave.

Tai'dqei knew grabbing them was a mistake the moment his arm locked around them. They had struck him and they had run. Now he had them in his grasp, *caught*. A short hunt was still a hunt. Especially when compounded with all the other failed attack-and-run tactics this human had used. Triumph swarmed his thoughts, heat blooming in his center and his loins.

For a long moment, a battle waged in his head. Considerations of what to do next fought against salacious imaginings. Then his senses registered the squirm of the smaller body crushed against his chest.

The human's struggles were oddly enticing and their skin soft against his palm. He itched to feel more of the human, skin-to-skin, like that first night.

Rayelle's hands went automatically to the arm, trying to push against the flexing muscle. It was no use, as a small part of her expected. Still, she tried. She had to, otherwise she definitely wouldn't find a way out of this.

Tai'dqei clenched his eyes shut as the human's writhing caused friction between their bodies. His free hand, braced against the wall of the cell, curled and tightened around a bar as he fought the urge to throw the human back onto the cot. It took more effort than he cared to admit to speak. "Stop. Running. From me."

As it spoke, the fingers against Rayelle's stomach flexed, curving into the fabric of her shirt and the softness of her stomach. The words strangely didn't sound mad. They sounded strained and tired. From the corner of her eye, she noticed their hand was braced on the front of the cell, fingers curling around a bar. The sight made her heart race harder.

"Why should I?" Rayelle tried to yank herself away, tried to squirm out of the hold. Heat soaked into her back from the alien while her own body ran hot from adrenaline and aggravation. She twisted in the thing's arms, trying to pin a heated glare on its face. "And when'd you learn English?!"

"I didn't," Tai'dqei answered, without thinking.

"*What?*" The word came out as a bite and Rayelle craned her neck to look at the alien. Other than it learning English, what other fucking way could they be talking? She certainly didn't know whatever it spoke!

She reminded herself of the sedation, the inability to gauge how long she had been out. The lurching realization that anything could've been done to her in that span of time barreled into her. It wasn't a new thought. She'd grappled with it so many times in the past, since her first abduction. Maybe a small part of her wanted to believe this alien was different from the others, but if they'd done something to her while she was unconscious, how different were they?

"If you promise not to try escaping, I will explain," Tai'dqei's words came out as calm as he could manage. He took care to not allow his irritation at himself to ooze into his tone. The human would assume the frustration was directed at them. When the human didn't respond, he added, "If I meant to harm you, I could have done so many times over."

Rayelle narrowed her eyes at that response. Her frustrated, if fruitless, struggles began once more as she hissed, "You got pretty close that first night."

His hold on the human tightened as they began squirming once more. Or maybe his muscles simply stiffened, annoyance at himself over the prior situation making him tense. "That was a... misunderstanding."

"A *misunderstanding?*" Incredulity burst from Rayelle and she could only let out a bitter laugh. A misunderstanding. Sure. That's what human men on Earth said all the time too. Her lips curled into a sneer, caught between the disgusting familiarity of it all and the surreality of thinking aliens had behavioral similarities with human men.

"Yes, I—"

"Oh, our patient is awake!" Before Tai'dqei could finish explaining, Ah'ke burst through the hall door. She tilted her head, eyeing the position the red-orange ja-tau and the human were in. Her eyebrow ridge raised as she closed the distance. "Getting to know one another already, hm?"

"They punched me and tried to escape. *Again.*" Tai'dqei growled, embarrassed heat creeping across his face. At least Ah'ke's appearance caused the human to still. Slowly, almost unsure, he loosened his grip on them. Not enough for the human to have freedom, but enough to not be squeezing them so tightly against him. "I was just trying to get them to calm down, so we could talk."

"They are certainly putting you through the ringer, aren't they?" The tension in Ah'ke eased, hearing that the situation was just another repeat of previous interactions. Tai'dqei was simply trying to keep the human contained.

Rayelle looked between the two aliens as a frown curved at her lips. Escaping was less likely now. The blue one gave a chitter of a laugh, their mandibles pulling upward and eyes squinting in something akin to a smile.

"Well, a good place to start is introductions," the blue alien said as they approached Rayelle. Their grey eyes caught her gaze and they motioned to themself with a hand to their chest. "I am Ah'ke, she/her, medicine woman."

Rayelle eyed this *Ah'ke* suspiciously. Her brain's understanding of what the alien said did not match up with the way her mouth and mandibles moved. It was like watching a dubbed movie. Which meant these two aliens did something to her after they knocked her out. That thought made Rayelle's stomach churn, but whatever they had done bridged a communication gap.

Ah'ke waited patiently, a pleasant squinty-eyed look on her face. Rayelle became increasingly aware of her captor's hold on her and the heat of them against her back. She needed space and behaving would likely grant her some iota of leeway. Grudgingly, Rayelle forced herself to say, "I'm Rayelle. She/her or they/them."

"Now it's your turn." Ah'ke nodded to Rayelle's captor.

There was a moment of hesitance from the red-orange alien. A tension throbbed from him before, against her back, Rayelle felt the alien's words. "I am Tai'dqei. He/him."

A pause entered the conversation as Rayelle considered his name. She glanced up at him, awkwardly craning her neck once more. Around her, she felt him nervously adjust his footing. Wondering what he had to be nervous about, she turned her attention back to Ah'ke. "Can you tell *Tai'dqei* to get his hands off me? He seems to have a problem with that one."

To Rayelle's surprise, Ah'ke gave a far-too-knowing chuckle-like titter. She nodded at Tai'dqei, whose arm muscles tensed briefly. "Well, you heard her."

He gave a grudging hum, not ready to let the human go. As inconsiderate as it was, and likely fueled by mating instinct, Tai'dqei enjoyed the feeling of someone in his arms.

Rayelle assumed he didn't trust her, didn't want to release her lest she run again. She waited patiently as he came to terms with the new turn of their situation. Though she kept remembering the first night and how he had touched her. She shifted in his hold, disconcerted as the heat reignited at her center. How much of a traitor could her body be? Or maybe it was a stranger at this point.

Finally, Tai'dqei released her.

As he stepped back, she turned to look up at him. Her narrowed gaze made him stiffen once more. Rayelle's gaze reminded him of being sized up by potential mates. Obviously, that wasn't the case. She probably was trying to find weak points, to aid her escape. Although, perhaps comparing her to a discerning ja-tau wasn't too far off.

Still stuck between two aliens, Rayelle wasn't sure what to do now. There was a tenuousness in the air mingling with Ah'ke's amusement, though Rayelle couldn't imagine what the blue alien found so funny. Likely, Ah'ke and Tai'dqei had history. It reeked off the two.

She could've been amused that he was stuck with a human for a number of reasons. Maybe he always brought home strays or he never liked humans. Maybe it was something Rayelle didn't even consider. There was really no way for her to tell. Or maybe Rayelle's actions entertained Ah'ke. Such a small thing, acting so tough and big when it was comparatively tiny and weak.

Crossing her arms, Rayelle tried to hide her bristling uncertainty. Assessing the situation with further questions seemed the best course of action. Giving her best unimpressed glare, she eyed Tai'dqei and grumbled, "So, now what?"

CHAPTER 4

'Now what' turned out to be talking. The three adjourned to a more hospitable room, which ended up being the mess. It was a smallish square room with a kitchen on one side and a table with six chairs on the other. It was better than the brig area, Rayelle grudgingly admitted.

Being flanked by two massive aliens didn't really brighten her mood. Between their hulking bodies and the closed doors, it was difficult to gauge escape potential via other routes. She'd just have to wait until she was more familiar with the ship.

Rayelle's obvious attempts to scan the ship hadn't passed unnoticed by Tai'dqei's awareness. It didn't give him much confidence in her ability to cooperate.

As they entered the mess, he took a seat at one end of the table. Quietly, he nodded at Ah'ke to take a seat further down so Rayelle could sit between them. He suspected Rayelle felt more comfortable closer to Ah'ke and wouldn't mind being on the same edge of the table as her.

"Before we get too far, how did you end up on that ship?" Ah'ke took the seat her friend indicated, tone polite and curious. It didn't escape Rayelle's attention that the two aliens had positioned themselves in strategic places to keep her boxed. Especially as Ah'ke pulled out the seat between them, offering it pointedly to Rayelle. "Tai'dqei tells me you were caged."

Maybe she was overthinking this or maybe it was understandable for both to keep her boxed in. She had tried to escape on Tai'dqei's watch many times. It wasn't like this was some convoluted ploy by her original captors since those fuckers were dead.

She didn't know anything particularly important and didn't have skills or power that would make anyone fight over her. A small hope in Rayelle's thought that these two monstrous-looking aliens might help her get back home.

With uncertain movements, she accepted the seat and slowly sat down. With her head slightly inclined toward Ah'ke, and away from Tai'dqei, she answered, "I was kidnapped."

"From where?" Ah'ke pressed, leaning forward a little.

From Ah'ke's interest, Rayelle felt her stomach flip. Wasn't it obvious? Humans were from Earth or whatever the greater galaxy had decided to name it. "From my planet, from Earth. Where else?"

Ah'ke and Tai'dqei shared a concerned look as Rayelle's answer tipped their problem to the more complicated end of the spectrum. There were plenty of space-born humans. Between space stations and colonies, there were likely more humans dispersed in the universe than on their home planet. Most humans knew and acknowledged that fact.

Rayelle did not.

◊ ◊ ◊

Something was not being said. Maybe even a lot of somethings. Rayelle narrowed her eyes, looking between the two aliens. She felt like there was an obvious answer that she was obstinately overlooking. "Where else would I be from?"

Tai'dqei asked quietly, "What year was it, when you were abducted?"

The softness of his voice felt wrong. Rayelle fought the sinking feeling in her stomach as she turned to him. A somber air, one she hadn't seen before, draped over him. Tension strung along her muscles. "2024."

"How long were you with your captors?" Again, his voice was soft like someone speaking to a scared, injured animal.

Rayelle was about to say 'ongoing' after a meaningful glare at Tai'dqei, but his tone and body language dulled her agitated edge. It was a good question, she realized. How long had she been with her initial kidnappers? Her eyebrows furrowed, trying to recall any passage of time.

The days had bled together. One long stretch of fear and uncertainty punctuated by little pockets of mind-numbing boredom with nothing to do. There were occasions when they'd shoot her up with something. It happened a lot in the beginning but became rarer near the end. "I'm not sure. Time ran together and I'm pretty sure they sedated me a lot."

This time, Tai'dqei didn't say anything. He gave a growly hum, his gaze flickering to Ah'ke. Rayelle couldn't shake the feeling he was looking for guidance. Both aliens remained silent for a beat. Their mandibles clamped tightly to their faces, reminding Rayelle of lips pressed tightly.

"What?" Her body braced, but for what she wasn't sure.

"The Earth year is currently 2372." Ah'ke answered, unflinching even as Rayelle turned to her. She pulled something up on her wrist tech, displaying it in a holographic form above the table.

The hologram was an image of Earth with text scrolling alongside it. Rayelle stared at it, the alien script flickering and unreadable to her. "You've been away from home for 348 years."

Rayelle's thoughts fizzled as her eyes widened. With a sharp turn to Ah'ke — ignoring how Tai'dqei jerked in his seat at her movement — incredulity had words shooting from her mouth, "What? There is no way!"

"Temporal crimes are a new phenomenon," Ah'ke explained, trying her best to break down the problem. "Authorities are not entirely certain, but they seem to target historical, already-missing persons. It helps to mask their activities."

"I…" Rayelle began, her eyebrows furrowed. The memories of her kidnapping, her abduction, were chaotic and muddied. Even if she thought of the hours or days before that incident, it seemed foggy. What she did remember were core things. Life with her family, time spent with friends, snippets of being in school decades earlier. One thing rang out over all of her other memories, though. "I have kids."

"What?" Tai'dqei breathed, not quite following Rayelle's thought process. Realization quickly clicked when he noticed the pained expression and strained tone.

It wasn't a continuation of the conversation. It was a realization. Raw and aching and agonizing. Apprehension had his muscles flexed, waiting for tears or screams or even a swoon. On the opposite side of Rayelle, he could tell Ah'ke was preparing for the same.

"If it's been over 300 years, they're dead." Images flooded Rayelle's head. Her two kids, Elliot and Skylar, one on the brink of graduating high school and the other in their first year of high school.

She was supposed to go to prom shopping with Elliot in nine months. And she had bought a new computer for Skylar, for their birthday. It was one designed to let them play games and stream.

Her nails dug into her thigh, wondering how her kids did after her disappearance. A number of stomach-churning scenarios played out in her head. From simple things like struggling grades and toxic friendships, to larger problems like dangerous relationships and facing bigotry in society and more.

Did they manage well without her? Who would have raised them, if not her? At that thought, sudden realization skipped through her brain. "I was in the process of divorcing their father. He called one night, asking to talk and I agreed."

As Rayelle paused, blinking rapidly, Tai'dqei and Ah'ke remained silent. He could tell from watching how glassy her eyes became, tears were on the brim of erupting from her. The mention of her children had him on edge. The addition of a father, presumably Rayelle's mate, made something hot pierce at his center. Whatever a 'divorce' was, it did not sound good, but he held his questions for another time.

"We met at a fast-food place," Rayelle closed her eyes, not sure if the aliens would understand. Heat rose against her eyelids, threatening to spill out. Ignoring the unshed tears, she heard herself explain as her voice cracked a little. "It was a cheap place to get food and it was open late. Like until midnight or whatever."

Tai'dqei watched her intently as she swallowed. She seemed strangely still, but from the way her arms shifted, he could tell her hands were moving, flexing. He silently shifted a little, catching a glimpse of her hands on her thighs. Red little half-moons dotted her legs from where her fingers had dug into her own skin.

Rayelle was too focused on visualizing what had happened to notice Tai'dqei move. She could remember the smell of stale fries and sugary syrup of the soda fountain, the stickiness of the floor on the bottoms of her sneakers.

There had been Evan, dressed in his nice slacks and button-up shirt, smelling of some sort of cologne that made her nose itch. He'd tried to talk her out of the divorce, once again. Said that further pursuing it would tear up their family.

But she couldn't stop. For the sake of her kids and herself, she could not let Evan remain around them. Her stomach lurched, realizing Elliot and Skylar would have gone to him after her disappearance. Rayelle continued forward in her memories, needing to understand.

"Evan, my ex, told me 'take care' after we talked. It struck me as strange, but I was tired and wanted to go." Once they were done in the restaurant, Rayelle had gotten up to leave. Evan had followed suit but claimed to need to use the bathroom.

She left the restaurant without a second thought and headed out into the parking lot. It was oddly dark, like the streetlamps in the lot hadn't been turned on. Not paying attention to her own instinct, she just trudged to her car and rifled through her purse for her keys. "I was unlocking my car when…"

The memory of an engine roaring to life made her stomach clench. The lights of a van blinded her before pulling up alongside her. The door rolled open with a hiss of metal against metal. Hands grappled at her arms when another pair covered her mouth. She screamed, but it was quickly muffled by the gloved palm.

With all her strength, she had fought and kicked as her attackers hauled her into the van. Someone yanked her purse from her arm and she heard it clatter to the pavement of the parking lot. She faintly heard miscellany clatter from her open bag before her eyes caught something else.

Evan. Standing outside the restaurant and watching everything play out.

"He watched these masked people take me." Rayelle slammed to her feet, her chair screeching behind her as it was pushed out of the way. Adrenaline and outrage swarmed through her, residual and fresh.

With wide angry eyes she stared blankly at the table as tears crested her cheeks. "He was smiling and even gave a wave."

"Then what?" Ah'ke asked, eyes glued to Rayelle.

She didn't like Ah'ke's tone and threw the blue alien a dirty look. To Rayelle, it felt like the alien was too excited for further details and it made her own stomach churn angrily..

She only eased when Tai'dqei stepped back into the conversation. "Were your kidnappers the ones from the ship I took you from?"

That question recalibrated her perspective. These two were *aliens* trying to understand and help her. They weren't delighted by her misfortune. They weren't hungry for sordid details. They simply needed as much information as possible to fully understand.

If they were to be believed, she was not just displaced physically but temporally. The rage in her suddenly dampened, a chill settling over her skin as she forced herself to sit back down in her chair.

It had been 348 years. Evan was dead. Her kids were dead. This was ancient history. *Insignificant* ancient history.

Numbness climbed over Rayelle, settling deep into her bones as she hollowly answered Tai'dqei, "No. They were humans, but…"

"But?" He leaned toward her, his deep voice soft and the clicks less prominent.

"I don't know. They had a sack over my head," Rayelle flatly recalled as she hunched over the table, staring blankly at its surface. A cold dissociation oozed through her body. She was having a hard time clinging to reality, so she simply relayed the memories flickering her thoughts. "We were driving for a long time. Then there was a loud bang and some confused yelling. I think the car broke down. Then chaos."

Once more, Rayelle closed her eyes. Sounds and sensations returning to her, making her heart pound and her stomach knot unhappily. Hands previously on her, restraining her, suddenly gone. The rough rope that bound her wrists and ankles. Frantic yells as a *whum-whum-whum* filled the air, not exactly loud but something she felt in her bones. "Doors opened, guns fired, people screamed. I got yanked out of the van to some strange sounds and then… nothing."

Everything had gone black.

"When I woke up next, I was in that cage surrounded by aliens." A throb went through Rayelle's temples as she pinched the bridge of her nose. remembering all that had opened a floodgate of residual feelings and an ache in her head. The burn at the back of her eyes had also returned, spreading to her sinuses. Rayelle pinched her nose harder, hoping to stave off tears.

"I'm sorry." Without thinking, Tai'dqei reached out to her hand where it lay on the table. He reconsidered directly touching her, though his claws did ghost over her skin in the faintest touch possible. Many others wouldn't have noticed, but Rayelle did.

Her eyes snapped open, staring at where their hands lingered near each other. It was only pure stubbornness that kept Tai'dqei's hand close to hers. He wasn't going to be scared off by a human's glare.

"What are you going to do with me now?" Her question came off more like a demand, her eyes not averting from their hands.

"I don't know yet," he answered honestly. There were still so many unknown factors. Some of it would have to be left to the Temporal Authority Council, the authorities on crimes involving time travel. Then it was a choice between returning her to her time, which would be a feat in itself, or finding her somewhere to go in the present.

His answer had Rayelle pinning him with an angry look a breath away from being hostile. "What do you mean, you don't know?"

She wanted to scream, but she kept her voice even. If only barely. She was finally in the hands of aliens willing to communicate — not kick her or leer or make disgusting sounds at her — and they didn't know what they would do with her.

A return to Earth, to familiarity, seemed the most obvious. Part of her knew that wasn't going to be easy, but her anger ignored it.

Tai'dqei struggled to find the words to answer her. He was still processing and parsing her story. Her life, her children, a lover. Albeit one she had been separating from but still.

To have it all ripped away. First by humans likely hired by this Evan, then by off-worlders. Tai'dqei could only imagine how the temporal jump affected her those first few days. Hallucinations, fatigue, nausea, and a long list of other effects. If they'd been sedating her, perhaps she slept through the adjustment period.

"We'll have to talk to the temporal authorities. They need to investigate your case in the present and the past." Ah'ke surprised Rayelle by being the one to answer.

Turning to the other alien, her brows furrowed. Ah'ke didn't flinch under the human's intense look. The frustration and anger Rayelle felt toward Tai'dqei was beginning to leak into her own feelings toward Ah'ke and it was hard to hide. " *Why?*"

It was apparent to both Rayelle and Tai'dqei that Ah'ke chose her words with supreme care. "Like I said earlier, sometimes missing persons cases are targeted in these temporal crimes."

"I don't understand." Rayelle frowned, wondering what exactly stood in the way of returning her to her own time. It wasn't like she'd tell anyone of this foray. No one would believe her. If they returned her to the correct time, talking about aliens and time travel wasn't going to help her divorce case.

"It sounds like your former mate orchestrated your abduction." Still, Ah'ke spoke carefully. The hint of a wince echoed in her body language. "The temporal authorities have to determine if your missing persons case has greater ramifications."

Rayelle stared, still not understanding.

Helplessly, Ah'ke looked to Tai'dqei, hoping he could explain to the human in a way that would be clearer. His mandibles flexed, hesitant considering how Rayelle obviously didn't like him. Even her gaze on him felt hot and unforgiving. Heaving a sigh, he tilted his eyes toward her. "If your case inspired someone to create an important piece of technology or if your absence in their lives inspired your kids to do something particular..."

He trailed off, making a motion with his hand as if he were sorting through the air for more words.

Realization finally clicked in Rayelle's head. The words echoed around her head, before dully leaning her lips, "Then it's better if I stay missing to them."

"I didn't mean it like that," Tai'dqei rushed to say, holding his hands up as if he could stop Rayelle's interpretation of his words. Between her eyes drifting from him and the way something crumpled in her expression, he doubted he could salvage the situation. Still, he tried. "Time is very complicated and causing a rift could be—"

"I've seen sci-fi movies, I get it," Rayelle snapped, the entirety of her situation sinking in. From the corner of her gaze, she saw both Ah'ke and Tai'dqei straighten in their seats. They were on alert now, hearing the unmitigated rage in her voice.

She was too consumed by her own thoughts to care. Even if she couldn't return to her time due to temporal anomalies or whatever they called them in sci-fi movies, would she find familiarity in her home planet? So much time had passed. Would she recognize anything?

Would it be worth it without friends or family?

The thought made the room spin and her head felt too light. Without a thought to how the aliens would take it, Rayelle gave a groan and pressed her forehead to the table.

Over the human's lowered head, Ah'ke and Tai'dqei shared a concerned look. Gently, Ah'ke put a clawed hand on the human's shoulder. When Rayelle didn't flinch away, Ah'ke gently said, "You should eat and drink something."

"I don't think I can." Her head was too full of thoughts, she doubted her brain had the capacity to also manage consuming anything. As another pang shot through her head and she mumbled, "I just want to sleep."

At that, Ah'ke made a sound and gained Tai'dqei's attention again over Rayelle's slumped form. She gave him a meaningful look and he recalled what she had said earlier.

"I can show you to the guest quarters," Tai'dqei said as he stood from his chair. He straightened, realizing how small Rayelle truly appeared slumped on the table. She seemed larger when throwing stuff at him and struggling against him.

Rayelle looked up at him from her spot on the table. Faintly, she wondered why such a fearsome alien would take *any* guff from a human. Especially the amount she had unleashed on him.

Whatever Ah'ke and he were, they appeared formidable and gave off an inherent air of 'taking no shit.'

Perhaps she was wrong though. Tai'dqei waited for her answer, shifting from one large foot to the other. If she didn't know better, he seemed nervous under her gaze. As she pushed herself to a more upright position, she remembered the weight around her throat.

"What about this?" Rayelle motioned to the collar around her throat.

"I'm sorry, but that stays." Tai'dqei's answer was met with a glare from not only Rayelle but also Ah'ke. Both women looked about ready to say something, but he cut them off with a sharp look. "Humans can be a commodity to other races. I don't want to risk you being taken again."

From Ah'ke's sudden stance, Tai'dqei knew she was ready to fight and remind him he was technically her most recent abductor, but Rayelle's tense shoulders slumped.

After spending who-knew-how-long on that first spaceship, being evaluated like a cow on an auction block, Rayelle could guess the varied usages other races had for humans. Not to mention Tai'dqei's initial interaction with her. Which he had yet to explain, she realized. She wasn't sure she wanted to hear his excuses.

"Fine." With a sigh, Rayelle pushed herself away from the table, the chair scraping mournfully along the floor. Her body ached from exhaustion and her head continued to pulse with a headache. Somewhere dark and quiet and alone sounded splendid.

As Rayelle stood, another wordless exchange shot between Tai'dqei and Ah'ke. She made it clear with her eyes she didn't agree with his decision, but his posture never sagged under her silent judgment. Even if he could trust Rayelle to not run away, that trust didn't extend to others. While not all humans were subjected to such incidents, she was too vulnerable given her lack of knowledge.

"Follow me," he told Rayelle, ignoring the increasingly heated look Ah'ke gave him as he turned to lead the human down the hall.

Rayelle rolled her eyes as she shuffled after him. "Like I have a choice."

When he stopped abruptly, she almost ran into his back. She backed up a step before her body registered his radiating body temperature. She wasn't fast enough to keep her eyes from noticing the musculature along his back, beneath the mesh and partial armor.

Flashes of the first night popped into her head, remembering how easily he hauled her up onto his shoulder even as she struggled. The thoughts were soon joined by more recent memories. Especially the one where Tai'dqei had caught her from behind, his arm wrapped around her and his hand splayed across her middle.

"You have a choice," he told her with a glance over his shoulder. Rayelle swallowed, trying to shoo the thoughts away as she turned her attention from his back to his eyes.

"You can follow nicely or I can haul you there myself."

Something in Rayelle's expression hardened. Tai'dqei mentally winced. His attempt at joking had been a misfire. The air between himself and the human weighed heavily, made all the worse when he remembered Ah'ke's eyes on them.

He was about to continue walking when Rayelle retorted, "Or I could run."

The way she said the words was like a threat. He remembered all too well the strained demand he'd given her earlier. Tai'dqei's hands flexed at his sides. The ghost of her warmth and softness teased along his palms. "You could, but I would advise against that."

"Yeah yeah, I know," Rayelle snorted, rolling her eyes again. She crossed her arms, leveling an unimpressed look up at Tai'dqei. "You haven't told me why."

Even from a distance, Tai'dqei could feel Ah'ke's surprise bordering on disappointment. He turned to face Rayelle, rushing to answer, "Becau—"

"I don't care, I want to rest. Just show me to my room," Rayelle interrupted, raising a hand to cut him off.

With his mandibles tight to his face, Tai'dqei shot an uncertain glance at Ah'ke. His former mate seemed amused more than anything as she tilted her head and raised her eyebrow ridges tauntingly. It was as if Ah'ke was telling him it was his problem to solve, his decision to make. And she would be correct.

Instead of replying to Rayelle, Tai'dqei simply nodded and led her down the hall. He tried not to think about how, though he had been joking, he'd have been happy to carry Rayelle to her quarters.

Followed by tossing her onto the bed and climbing atop—

With a forceful mental push, he shoved the image from his head. A trip to that brothel was in order, he decided as his fingers punched a code into a wall panel a little too forcefully. The door beside the panel hissed open, unlocked and now freely accessible to his unplanned guest.

Tai'dqei stepped to the side, motioning toward the room with one hand. Rayelle looked from him to the room. At a glance, it was certainly more comfortable looking than the cell, she decided. She entered slowly, taking stock of the room. It was small with drawers built into the walls and scant decoration. The bed, she guessed, was a human full-size equivalent, though it looked plenty big to her.

Behind her, she felt Tai'dqei watching her. It made the hair on the back of her neck rise and squirming sensations flood her stomach.

Her eye caught the panel inside the room beside the door. It mirrored the panel in the hall, she realized. Intuitively, she reached out and pressed the largest glowing button.

Rayelle watched the door hiss shut with Tai'dqei on the other side. If he was waiting for an ounce of gratitude from her, he would be waiting for a long time. Numbly, Rayelle turned to the bed and laid down, leaving the lights on for the time being.

CHAPTER 5

Tai'dqei stared at the closed door for a beat. While he assumed Rayelle wasn't going to re-open it, whether she meant to close it experimentally or intentionally, he thought it best to wait. Just in case.

As expected, the door did not re-open.

Turning back toward the mess, Tai'dqei considered what to do next. There was still a lurid itch in his loins. The thought of tossing Rayelle onto her new bed had reignited hormonal impulses. He decided he *would* hit up the brothel Ah'ke had mentioned.

Beyond that, he needed to restock on food and minor necessities. Then there was the question of collecting on his work. After finishing the cleaning process on the skulls and spines of his bounties – accomplished sessions of monitoring Rayelle – he had sent a request for a change in meet-up location. Hopefully, his employer would agree to meet at this particular outpost. If not, that was yet another stop to be made at some point.

As he entered the mess, spotting Ah'ke still seated at the table, Tai'dqei realized there was another snag he hadn't thought of. He couldn't very well leave Rayelle alone on his ship. Ah'ke glanced up from the holoscreen her gauntlet projected as he approached her.

Tai'dqei gave her holo a cursory look, noting it was a search for the few organizations that aided humans displaced from their time, before inclining his head to Ah'ke. "Can you stick around while I get some errands done off-ship? Might be awhile."

She gave a little titter, her mandibles pulling upward with amusement as she turned the holoscreen off. "Going to that brothel after all?"

There was no point in denying it, he decided, but that didn't mean he was happy about it. He rolled his eyes and gave a resigned sigh, his mandibles twitching down. "Among other things."

Ah'ke's eyebrow ridges raised with curiosity. "Such as?"

"Resupplying. I'm low on med sprays and I need some replacement filaments," he replied as he gathered a bag and checked his account via his wrist gear. Mentally, he tabulated a rough estimate as to how much he'd be spending.

Well… he vaguely budgeted what he'd spend on the supplies. He was too embarrassed with himself to consider just how much he was preparing to blow on carnal relief. "I should probably get food Rayelle will eat, as well."

His friend made a humming sound, the leg crossed over her knee bouncing a little. "You should consider getting some things for her, too."

Tai'dqei stared woodenly at Ah'ke, unsure if she was being suggestive or sincere. Maybe it was the hormones infesting his brain, but he could only think of adult toys or contraceptives. Either way, he had no clue what she realistically meant. "Like what?"

Ah'ke leaned back in her chair, motioning with her hand as she spoke. "Some clothes, toiletries, things to enrich her mind."

For the most part, the suggestions made sense and Tai'dqei acknowledge that, yes, his brain was just far too infested with hormones to think straight.

He doubted Rayelle would abide by wearing his clothes, so her own her necessary. Providing items for self-care and hygiene seemed reasonable, as well.

Though perhaps he should just get her some clothes and have her shop with him. There was no telling what her preferences were or if she had food restrictions or allergies. The last thing he wanted was to buy her something she couldn't use or, worse, would cause her discomfort.

But there was a phrase that Ah'ke used that he couldn't let go.

"Enrich her mind?" Tai'dqei snorted, his eyes noticing for the first time that his friend had painted her claws a violet color. The last few times she had done so was when she was trying to get a non-ja-tau's attention. His gaze re-focused back on her face. "You're making her sound like a pet, Ah'ke."

"You know what I mean," she said with a huff, waving her hand to dismiss his wry statement. Her voice softened as she went on, "She went from one cage to your brig to your guest quarters.

She's had nothing to do."

Tai'dqei couldn't help the way his mandibles twitched upward. Being bored was tantamount to torture to Ah'ke. He supposed the amount of mind numbing nothing-to-do that Rayelle had been forced to go through was a sort of torture.

While that was true, Tai'dqei knew it wouldn't always be so. No matter her circumstances, she was going to have to learn about her current environment. Which might mean Rayelle would have a lot of reading and adjusting to do. "She'll have plenty to do soon enough."

Ah'ke seemed to read his mind. Her mandibles pulled up a little in a ja-tau's version of a smile, though a somber one. "Yes, she will. Maybe give her something so she can mentally escape a little."

"I'll consider it," was all Tai'dqei could bring himself to say. He wasn't certain how many credits he'd be burning on these errands. Especially if he was going to be sexually serviced.

"In sector C, there's a little general store run by a Haaloidian. You might be able to find her some fun stuff there." Ah'ke had chosen not to pick up on the ambiguity of Tai'dqei's statement. As she often stubbornly did. If he read her tone correctly, it almost seemed a done deal that he'd be purchasing things for Rayelle. Or perhaps she had other reasons for the suggestion. "Tell Khimiel I sent you. She will give you a discount."

Haaloidians, the merchants of the universe. As expected, they were often very friendly and, in most cases, eccentric. At least, in Tai'dqei's experience.

"Khimiel." Tai'dqei raised a brow ridge, though his tone dipped into mild amusement, "Is she the reason for your painted claws?"

"You noticed!" Ah'ke laughed as she held up a hand, wiggling her fingers. The claw polish shifted colors in the changing light and had specks of glitter in it. Around her extended hand, she shot him a teasing look and fluttered her eyes at him, "Don't be jealous."

"No promises, but I'll let *Khimiel* know you sent me." Tai'dqei shook his head but couldn't help the slight way his mandibles pulled up. As much as he was envious of this Khimiel for gaining Ah'ke's attention, it wasn't like strict monogamy was present in ja-tau culture. Even if they were still together, Ah'ke would have been free to pursue other lovers. As he turned to leave, waiting for the door to the exterior to open, he couldn't help but add, "And I'll be sure to put whatever I buy on the tab you inevitably have."

"Don't you dare!" Ah'ke bolted to her feet so quickly, Tai'dqei had to stifle a laugh. His old friend likely had a long tab already, especially if she were trying to get this Khimiel's attention.

Ignoring her outburst, he continued out the door. "Thanks for staying, Ah'ke. Appreciate it!"

She did not bid him farewell. Dogging after him, the clicking in her voice became more pronounced as she hissed, "Tai, if you rack up a huge bill, I swear I'll wear your skull as a purse!"

"You've used that threat before and I'm still not an accessory," he called back over his shoulder as the door slowly began closing in his wake.

He caught a very unamused Ah'ke watching him go, her arms crossed over her chest. Offering a cheeky wave, he chuckled as his former lover made a rude gesture before the door fully closed.

◊ ◊ ◊

Tai'dqei sat nude and awkward on the overly lush bed, the mattress sinking under his weight. The pink sheets, made of a high-quality thread, were more delicate than he was used to. In fact, everything in the room seemed fluffy or velvety or, well, *soft.* From the faint yet comfortable lighting to the carpet to the bed and furniture.

With his back ramrod straight and his arms crossed over his chest, Tai'dqei felt like the roughest and most haggard thing in the room. He doubted he looked like he was there to enjoy himself either. He wasn't even sure he wanted to be there.

Located in the station's patrolled and regulated red light ring, House Euphoria was one of the outpost's homes of carnal delights and desire. It came with Ah'ke's recommendation.

He had stood a while outside the bawdy house, staring at the two large display windows that flanked the entrance. One window had some of the scantily clad workers, lounging in a comfortable looking sitting area and flirtatiously batting their eyes or making lewd gestures to those who passed by. The other window had a screen, rotating between testimonies of happy customers, various upcoming events, and some base pricing options.

Tai'dqei was swept up the instant he stepped over the threshold. The offered profiles of available companions, the different bundled services, the dizzying array of add-ons. It had all been a lot for his already impaired state of mind. He honestly thought he blacked out at one point.

"You look kind of tense, sweetie." A nude Ankushian slid from behind a room divider. Tai'dqei's frantic thoughts wheeled through the offering catalog, trying to remember their name. His brain managed to bring up her profile: Saisha, she/her. She smiled at him, coming closer with a sway to her movements. "Has it been awhile for you?"

She was a pretty array of purples. Her violet jelly-like skin and long lavender 'hair' – like lighter colored wax-like drippings adhering to a candle – almost glowed in the dim light of her workspace. Dark purple antennae poked up from the crest of her head, the rounder ends bobbling with Saisha's every step.

Tai'dqei swallowed, his eyes trailing over the curves of her large breasts, soft stomach, and wide hips. He tried not to think how her form was similar to Rayelle's own.

Had that been intentional or coincidence? He didn't want to know the answer.

When he didn't answer, the smile on Saisha's plump lips took on a teasing edge. "You know, as an Ankushian I can tell your mating instincts have been roused."

"How can you tell?" He already knew how. Her antennae sensed pheromones and chemicals in the air. After little over three cycles in his current state, even with the frequent showers, he was invariably marinated in his urges.

"Your chemical signature leaves a taste in the air." Saisha's antennae wiggled a little, smug in answering his question. She dropped herself into Tai'dqei's lap, her arms languidly wrapped around his shoulders. Like most others, she was shorter and smaller than him. Though she was currently solid, she had a texture that made Tai'dqei think of liquid contained in something malleable. Like a waterskin.

As Saisha spoke, she fiddled gently with the plumage of his hair, sending tingling sensations across his scalp. "I'm curious to know who could have stimulated such a reaction from big surly you. They must be particularly impressive."

"No— I mean, I don't know about that." He shoved the brief mental image of Rayelle away. If she kept infesting his thoughts, he'd never find peace.

Turning his attention fully to Saisha, Tai'dqei wondered if it was true that Ankushians changed color when fucking. He vaguely recalled something about their near-invisible nerve endings glowing and shifting color when a litany of stimulation arrested their senses. He swallowed, trying to focus on answering her, "It was an odd series of events and a misunderstanding."

"Oh well, their loss." Saisha's hands had gone to his shoulders, kneading into his muscles. A soft sound escaped him, heat bleeding down his back. He grunted as she suddenly rolled her hips, pressing against his slowly rising arousal. "I find ja-tau particularly fun."

"Is that so?" Tai'dqei huffed as her mouth found his throat. Her teeth grazed over his skin, from neck to shoulder. He shifted, every spot where their bodies touched tingled as her cooler body and his warmer temperature mingled.

"Yes," she purred as she slid further down his front, her liquid soft lips trailing hot breaths and kisses down his chest.

His knees instinctively tilted open, giving her access to his growing erection as she hit his midsection. With a grin, she slipped to the floor between his feet. Her words whispered over his shaft, her mouth barely touching him, "The sheer power. The rippling muscle. The absolutely desperate horniness."

Her words teased over his pulsing flesh and an excited growl tangled in his throat. One of his clawed hands went to her scalp, cradling the back of her head and nudging her face closer to his cock. Tai'dqei's hips rolled, eliciting a giggle from the Ankushian.

As her mouth opened a series of soft excited clicks left him, and her tongue — so long and dripping with viscous purple — coiled twice around his shaft. Something in him snapped to attention. An insatiable prickling heat clawed at his insides.

His cock pulsed as her tongue worked up and down his length, squeezing tight around him. Her tongue was moister than the rest of her, but the cool temperature coaxed a hiss from him as his hips jerked against her ministrations.

Without thought, both of his hands grappled at the sides of her head. Saisha gave a little breathy, excited gasp. He needed her to be warmer and the first solution was to heat her up himself. With that thought, Tai'dqei thrust his hips forward, landing his cock square in her mouth. Like her tongue, her mouth was wetter than her skin, but still a lukewarm sort of cold. Her moan vibrated around him, reverberating through him from his dick and into his bones.

Tai'dqei's body moved on its own. Hips rocking back and forth, harder with each passing thrust as he leaned over the sex worker. A growl bubbled in his throat, the Ankushian's body warming to his friction. The sounds she made were sweet and sinful to his ears. A balm after such a long stint of aggravation.

Something still agitated his senses about all this though. It was all manufactured. A script, a delightful farce. Saisha wasn't sincerely entertaining his strength or capability. She was just feeding into some instinctive desire of his own. Which was her job, he knew.

This wasn't genuine. This was just to alleviate the libido pounding on his insides. Nothing more. And that dulled the pleasure somehow.

Annoyed with his own thoughts, Tai'dqei yanked Saisha off his cock. She made a startled little sound as he swung her onto the bed, onto her hands and knees. Pinning her squirming form down, his clawed hand at the back of her neck, he realized Saisha was losing consistency. She felt stickier, more liquid than earlier.

For a brief second, Tai'dqei worried he'd gone too far and gotten too rough with her until she wriggled delightedly. "Yes, that's the desperate horniness I love."

Apparently Ankushians literally became wet when excited, Tai'dqei mused as his claws pricked into Saisha's neck. A mewl of pleasure escaped her at the almost piercing touch.

"I'm not desperate," he growled, arching over her back and sliding his cock between her thighs. She gave a whiny purr, rolling her hips and rubbing herself against his throbbing excitement. His free hand reached under her, his fingers tracing her slit with his claws. Saisha writhed and her hands fisted into the silky sheets of the bed.

"That makes one of us," Saisha giggled, her breath hitched.

"Yeah, you're desperate for ja-tau cock, aren't you?" Tai'dqei snarled, his mandibles close to Saisha's head. A guttural rumble echoed through his chest, vibrating through Saisha's liquid self. He watched as little flashes of lights lit up her back and near where his mandibles clicked, roughly where her ears would have been had she been human.

"Very much so," she whined as her hands twisted harder at the sheets, her body wriggling under him. She pushed herself down and back against Tai'dqei, his cock still stubbornly between her thighs and lining her lower lips. Unlike the tepid temperature of the rest of her, heat was growing at the crux of her legs.

Experimentally, Tai'dqei flexed his cock against her, sliding himself back and forth to coat the top-half of his shaft. Her reaction was almost instantaneous. Saisha keened, reciprocally moving against him the best she could with his hand still on the back of her neck.

Heat snapped along his own body, through his muscles, scouring his veins. Tai'dqei's hold on her neck tightened, eliciting a sweet whimper from the Ankushian. Lining himself up, he could feel her excitement swelling, her writhing intensifying as she tried to rollick back against his knob.

Tai'dqei held her still, his hand under her trailed his claws along her stomach and over her breasts. Tiny wakes followed his tips, quickly disappearing as Saisha's liquids shifted back into place. Sharp little gasps and moans left her. Her back arched and bowed, seeking some sort of relief from his pleasuring touch.

He didn't like doing what others expected. And Saisha thought he'd mindlessly fuck her, hard and rough. Like any other ja-tau man hard-up with a mating fervor would do. While it would be hard and rough, Tai'dqei wanted to make her squirm and cry out and beg for his seed. Until she was a sloppy, sopping mess on the bed.

Her slowly warming core called to him, making his dick throb and flex. The spark of her excitement ran through her body, making her body fade from a lush purple to a pleasant magenta pink.

Saisha's whines had taken on an impatient tone, her minute squirming becoming more insistent. He slowly dipped the thick tip of his cock into her, the flared ridge of his head catching against the sides of her opening. With a moan, Saisha tried to raise her rear up and roll back for deeper penetration.

He didn't let her though. As slow as he entered, as sweet as her extra moist heat was, he pulled out quickly. He ignored his own body's rage at himself and Saisha's distraught cry.

The two continued like that. Tai'dqei, disciplined and measure, delving his cock only an inch deeper with every pass. Saisha mewling and arching and crying out when denied deeper satisfaction, growing more desperate.

Tai'dqei's fingers flexed on Saisha's neck, gaining her attention as her writhing became more demanding. "Tell me how much you want it."

"So much," she sobbed, rolling her hips erratically to ease him further in. But he went no further than what he deemed appropriate.

"Describe it," he demanded, his mandibles spreading and a hiss leaving his mouth.

"I want to feel you deep in me, stretching me, churning up my insides. Hard and relentless," Saisha gasped and arched her back up, pressed flush against Tai'dqei's chest. The once coolish purple skin was now heated with a gentle sort of red glow, little sparks lighting up her body as pleasure coursed through her. "I need to feel your white-hot seed bathing my insides. All of it, Tai'dqei. Give me all of it."

Through her pleas – in spite of the fact it was all rehearsed script – a pleased growl grew in Tai'dqei's chest. It crested into a snarl as she demanded all of it, everything.

With a forward slam of his hips, he buried his dick into her. Liquid warmth trembled around him as she threw her head back. Automatically, Saisha tried to swing forward and back, wordlessly needing continued penetration.

His hand adjusted to the front of Saisha's throat, claws digging into the sides of her neck as his other hand braced on the bed. Tai'dqei fell into a fast, hard pace.

His knees smacked against the mattress, making it vibrate with every thrust. His cock cleaved through her folds, hitting Saisha deeper and deeper with every passing strike. Her whole body lit up brightly with every full-force impact, ripples bubbling along her form.

Burning excitement swelled in him, his cock pulsing. Saisha was warm and wet and malleable. In waves, her form rhythmically hugged around his thick cock, her body jostling as she frantically attempted to meet his thrusts. Pressure pounded at his core as he snarled and panted, frenetic lust pushing him toward his orgasm.

The heat became unbearable and finally, *finally,* Tai'dqei threw his head back with hiss of satisfaction. White-hot ropes of heat surged from him, painting Saisha's insides and making her glow all the more vibrant as she cried out. His hips drilled haphazardly into her, even as her body pulsed around him.

Saisha wobbled and trembled, oozing between his claws as she gulped down a lungful of air. Even though Tai'dqei's own chest heaved with heavy breaths, he still eased himself from her quivering folds and stepped back. Beads of cum oozed from the tip of his cock, still obviously erect and ready for more.

"Oh dear," Saisha tittered, still trying to catch her breath. She had rolled over onto her back, as much as someone who had turned half into ooze could roll, and eyed Tai'dqei with his proud cock. He stood tall, shoulders back and breath slowing to something manageable. He leered down at her, not entirely satisfied and knowing he'd need more than this to be remotely satiated. "I better call in reinforcements, hm?"

"You do that," he growled before descending on her. His cock easily slid home into her wet core as she gave a squeal of mingled delight and surprise. Even as Saisha's moans bubbled up around him and her body happily accepted his thrusting ruts, Tai'dqei could feel the itch, the hunger, for more continue to gnaw at him.

At the back of his head, behind the lust and pleasure, thoughts of Rayelle still frustratingly lingered.

CHAPTER 6

It was six hours before Tai'dqei returned. Half of that time had been spent catering to his baser needs while the other half had been spent trekking around the station for supplies.

Tri'ken Outpost was a decently sized trading station where spacefarers often stopped to replenish goods and trade, among other things. That said, the place was rather large with plenty of shops and even more merchants and hawkers attempting to upsell. Which honestly exhausted Tai'dqei more than the carnal romps.

Perhaps that was why he bristled when Ah'ke cooed as soon as he stepped back onto his ship. "Oooh, you must have *really* enjoyed yourself. It's been awhile."

"Shut up," he growled, dropping the bulging sack of supplies and miscellany he had acquired over the hours. He tossed a small wrapped package at Ah'ke with a bit more force than necessary. "Khimiel wanted me to give you this."

The blue ja-tau caught the projectile with ease and wasted no time in tearing into the packaging. Before the paper even hit the floor, she trilled in delight. "Veruvian delights! I've been waiting for these to come in!"

As she sampled her sweets, Tai'dqei went about dumping the supplies on the table. He sorted through the items, separating things based on where they needed to go. Med sprays to various med kits onboard. Food and drink for the pantry. Filaments and new tools for the secondary cargo hold.

He picked around the items he had bought for Rayelle, not quite wanting to see the smug look cross Ah'ke's face.

"In all seriousness, how was your jaunt to the lewdy house? Get it all out of your system?" Her question came suddenly, around a maw full of her sticky Veruvian delights.

"I—" Tai'dqei started to answer, but movement in the corner of his eye made him pause.

Rayelle had sidled from the hallway, a tray in her hand. He couldn't help but notice the residue of food and the peel of a chemond. Faintly, Tai'dqei wondered if it was the same fruit she had thrown at him earlier.

"Oh, yes, Rayelle woke about two hours ago. Said she was hungry, so I made her some tep and gave her some fruit," Ah'ke informed as she re-wrapped her box of sweets. "I also gave her a quick check-up and got her vaccinations up-to-date, so you're welcome!"

Tai'dqei only gave Ah'ke half of his attention, nodding and muttering thanks to his dear friend. To say Rayelle's expression was icy would have been an understatement. He thought the freezing vacuum of space would be more hospitable. She'd undoubtedly heard Ah'ke's teasing questions.

And she certainly had. Something weighed in her chest, unhappy and spiky when registering what Ah'ke had asked Tai'dqei. If a lewdy house left anything to the imagination, Ah'ke's repeated question drove all question away.

"Get it all out of your system?" The words echoed in her head, making Rayelle want to gag. Was Tai'dqei so perpetually horny that he had to make frequent stops at such places? Is that why he tried to accost her? It apparently was often enough that Ah'ke teased him about it.

As she passed him to deposit her tray into what seemed to be the sink, she couldn't help but throw him a sidelong glare. She wanted to make her stance on his libido well-known.

"Anyway, it's been fun playing babysitter and offering you my expertise for free," Ah'ke chattered after checking the time on her wrist gear as she quickly gathered her things. "I really need to get back to the clinic. It's probably a mess in my absence."

Tai'dqei hadn't really been paying attention to Ah'ke's words until she said she had to leave. That made his stomach drop as his attention swerved from Rayelle to Ah'ke. "Do you have to go?"

As Ah'ke shot him a mixed look of infuriating sympathy and fondness, Tai'dqei already knew the answer. His stomach lurched while he fought the urge to nervously glance at Rayelle.

"Yes, Tai'dqei." His friend's tone took on that of a parent chiding a child. It made embarrassed heat climb up his face and his shoulders hunch a little. His shame at his own juvenile actions only intensified as Ah'ke went on, "My clinic and colleagues need me. You can handle this. She's only one human."

"A temporally displaced human," he hissed as Ah'ke gave him a reassuring pat on the shoulder. To himself, he mentally added '*And she rightfully despises me.*' Judging from the sympathetic look his former mate gave him, Tai'dqei guessed Ah'ke already knew what he was thinking.

He watched sullenly as Ah'ke bid goodbye to Rayelle before exiting from the ship.

Rayelle, too, watched Ah'ke go. A strange sensation churned in her stomach, realizing she was alone with Tai'dqei once more. They hadn't been alone together since before the nano-translator procedure, which Ah'ke had explained to her in his absence. It sounded like nothing more than a cybernetic centipede had been coaxed into her ear canal, but Rayelle tried not to think too hard about that.

Being alone with Ah'ke was less unnerving than being alone with Tai'dqei. For obvious reasons.

Once the quiet had dragged on just a little too long, with no evidence Ah'ke would reappear, Tai'dqei steeled himself. Motioning toward the still half-sorted pile of recently bought items, he told Rayelle, "I got you a few things while I was out."

She glanced at the things with a critical eye. At a cursory glance, it all appeared like decent offerings. Clothes and food and just stuff.

Nothing suggestive. But Rayelle couldn't forget what Ah'ke and Tai'dqei had been discussing before she entered. "Before or after you visited the sex workers?"

"After," Tai'dqei answered, her disparaging tone completely lost on him. "Not sure why that matters."

Not sure why that matters? *Not sure why that matters?* Rayelle's nose wrinkled at his response. Had he completely forgotten how he pinned her in the mud and stripped her? Was that just his average Tuesday night? Fighting against a swirl of nausea, considering this horndog alien was who she was stuck with for the time-being, Rayelle crossed her arms over her chest. "In that case, anything you got me should be washed."

"Why?" Taken aback, Tai'dqei finally looked up from his continued sorting. Confusion made his eyebrow ridges furrow, realizing that Rayelle seemed angry.

"I don't want your after-sex stench on anything near me." To emphasize her disgust, she made a gagging face. As if the idea of Tai'dqei's smell could actually make her vomit. Perhaps it could, she thought. She was doing her best not to pick up on any sort of scent from him, considering where he'd just been.

"Fine." Her antagonization was still lost on Tai'dqei. With a shrug, he returned to his task of sorting supplies from items meant for Rayelle. "It's called musk, by the way."

Confusion joined Rayelle's repulsion. "What?"

"My arousal scent. It's called a musk," he explained, faintly wondering if humans didn't emit an aromatic indication of arousal.

That seemed strange, considering the biology of humans and similar species. The second he considered excitement and humans, however, his thoughts turned to Rayelle. Imagining her in a situation that would give her that sweet heady scent of interest.

Mentally, he shoved the image away and tried to keep his tone level and conversational. "I showered before leaving House Euphoria, so you shouldn't smell any of that on your things."

Rayelle stared woodenly at Tai'dqei, uncertain of how to process his answers. He didn't rise to her anger. In fact, he seemed oblivious to it which somehow made the agitation writhing in her chest all the worse. Utter obliviousness was just as bad as simply not caring, wasn't it?

The longer Rayelle remained silent, her stare slowly melting into a glare, the more Tai'dqei shifted and fidgeted. He could feel her eyes on him and it made his skin itch. It got to the point where he realized he must have said something wrong but he had no idea what. He replayed their conversation thus far in his head. It all seemed rather benign, he thought. He'd even gone out of his way to be informative.

They needed to focus on a different conversation, he decided.

"I bought you more than clothes. Food, hygiene supplies, some…uh," Tai'dqei's eyebrow ridges furrowed again, holding a small box of miscellaneous plastic toys. He'd been told by Khimiel these had been historically popular in Rayelle's time. "Fidgets?"

"Fidgets," Rayelle repeated, incredulity lacing her tone.

"The merchant I bought them from said they were popular in your time," he said as he awkwardly held the box out to her. She stood at the far end of the table, but she edged closer at his gift. Rayelle eyed the box before her gaze pointedly slid to Tai'dqei's hands and up his arms to his face.

Receiving the hint, Tai'dqei set the box down on the table between them and shuffled back to the supply piles. The movement sent small things rattling and plinking inside the box.

"Yeah, fidgets were popular," Rayelle muttered as she grabbed the box and pulled it closer to her instead of venturing closer to the alien.

Inside were an array of colorful plastic toys she remembered as allowance drains for Elliot and Skylar. A fidget cube, a circular pop-it with various smaller inverted hemispheres, a squeezy stress ball, and a few other things she recognized but didn't have a name for. Her kids had buckets of these little stress-relievers, mostly pop-its and squishies and spinners. Their teachers and therapists even had an array of the plastic anxiety soothers.

As she picked up a black fidget cube, the burn of tears started at the back of her eyes. Skylar had been so excited to get their first cube after months of always coming across sold-out displays. Rayelle only managed to click the light switch side once before a tear crested down her cheek.

As Rayelle hastily swiped at the tear, Tai'dqei was quick to reach out for the box of fidgets. Uncertainty razed over his back, realizing how her features crumpled. Obviously the fidgets weren't something she wanted if she was crying. "If these cause you distress, I can retur—"

"No!" She grabbed the box possessively, turning wild eyes to Tai'dqei. He paused, his clawed hand hovering in the air between them. She rushed to explain, more out of habit than to help the hulking alien to understand, "Elliot and Skylar, my kids, they had toys like these. It's just…"

Memories. Everything she ever knew only existed in memories now. Rayelle pressed her lips tightly together, unable to finish her sentence. Her gaze fell to the table, unable to meet Tai'dqei's eyes.

She could only imagine how she seemed. Crying one second and then clinging to a box of toys the next. Two sides of her battled it out in her head, seesawing between her own self-consciousness and her own disregard for whatever Tai'dqei thought of her.

He stared, watching as Rayelle's expression change from distraught to a stiff sort of sadness that mingled with something else. Some sort of inner turmoil he could only imagine.

His eyes fell to the toys in her grasp. Rayelle held the box tightly, as if she was afraid they'd be snatched away. He lowered his outstretched hand. "They're yours. If you want them, I won't take them."

When she hazarded a glance up at him, he couldn't ignore the conflicting mess of emotions painted over her face. Relieved, but not trusting. Thankful, but not wanting to show it. A superficial sort of hostility, but deeper down? He didn't thinks he hated him down to her very bones.

Tai'dqei turned his attention back to the purchases, ignoring his own mess of thoughts. "As I was saying, food and clothes and soaps and the like. Use what you want."

Distracting herself from the sadness, and with the box of fidgets placed next to her on the table, Rayelle surveyed the other offerings.

Of the food, there was dried fruit, what appeared to be trail mix, some fresh vegetables, and packets of chips. Her eye caught on something pleasantly surprising wedged under a bag of dried banana chips: Three chocolate bars, stacked atop one another. She never thought she'd see such a thing again, let alone be allowed to eat it.

But she tamped down her excitement at the small grace, her eyes moving on to the other purchases. All of the toiletries — shampoos, soaps, conditioners, and so forth — were basic, generic scents. It was the clothing that caught her curiosity.

Holding up a pair of jeans, she checked the tag before holding them to her waist. From both the printed size and the way they laid against her, they *seemed* like the right fit. Rayelle turned a suspicious eye to Tai'dqei. "How did you know my size?"

Until that point, he had been silently putting away the other supplies. He marched back and forth from table to pantry and cabinets, seemingly paying her no heed. Though he always kept Rayelle in the very corner of his attention. The careful way she looked at the items, picked them up, studied them drew his curiosity. Once more, he felt at a loss for what she could be seeking.

Was the style abnormal from her era? Had he overlooked some sort of flaw? Or did she simply not like the colors?

At Rayelle's question, Tai'dqei perked up and his head inclined to her. He made a motion to her neck. "The collar on your neck scanned you."

"Including my body measurements?" A frown made her lips curve downward, her tone dry and unyielding to his explanation.

It sounded far-fetched to her. Yet any other answer made her squirm. Either he memorized her body's size from their time together *or* he'd measured her when she was unconscious. She didn't much care for either alternative answer.

He gave a helpless shrug, closing the distance from the kitchen area back to the table. "If none of it is to your liking, you'll have to come with me next time."

"You trust me to tag along with you?" Her eyebrows inched upward, surprised at the offer. It almost made her uncertainty take a backseat. If Tai'dqei was so worried about her running off, why risk giving her such freedom? Ah'ke had stuck around the ship to effectively babysit her while he ran around getting his dick wet and do shopping. Rayelle knew that.

Despite himself, Tai'dqei could feel his mandibles pulling downward. A calculating light edged into Rayelle's eyes and he didn't quite like it. He didn't want to open the floodgates to her attempting plan after plan to escape him. Given how persistent she had been to this point, he honestly didn't think he'd have the fortitude to put up with it. Especially if she roused his more salacious instincts again.

Crossing his arms over his chest, he couldn't keep the apprehensive click out of his growl, "Don't give me a reason not to trust you."

His guttural rumble made a shiver run down her spine. It wasn't necessarily a bad feeling but Rayelle didn't want to focus on that. Something hot and uncomfortable scraped through her veins and she dropped the jeans back on the table.

Don't give *him* a reason to not trust *her*? What had he done to garner *her* trust? Sure, maybe Tai'dqei had given the two of them a way to communicate and he had bought her an array of things, but that didn't absolve him of anything.

The memories of that first night remained though. The way he had chased her down and pinned her to the ground. How his claws had so easily sliced open her shirt and panties, baring her to an alien world. The way he touched her, despite her obviously distraught body language.

With narrowed eyes, Rayelle sneered, "You're such a hypocrite."

"What?" Staring the human down, his own eyes hooded at the accusation.

Rayelle became aware she didn't even have the safety of a table between them. There was only empty air separating them.

He was very aware of that, as well, and his arms pulled tighter across his chest. An itch of temptation played along his fingertips and crept down his palms. He wanted to touch her.

"I'm not supposed to give you a reason to distrust me, but you nearly raped me that first night." She jabbed a finger at his chest, taking a bold stomp forward. With her other hand, she grabbed at the metal secured around her neck. Giving the collar a pull, her voice rose a little as she snarled, "And you've collared me against my will."

Only the slow deep breath Tai'dqei took kept him calm. His chest expanded, straining against his crossed arms, as the desire to grab Rayelle billowed up more intensely. This was becoming more than just an instinctive issue, he worried.

Was it her stature and clear lack of strength when compared to him that agitated or aroused something in him? Part of finding adequate mates wasn't simply brute capability. Intelligence and personality played into it too. Strength meant nothing if you didn't have the relentlessness or savviness to utilize it to its full extent.

There was always something to be said for pure, vicious tenacity. Rayelle certainly didn't lack in that trait. That only spelled trouble for Tai'dqei as he tried his best to not ruin what little progress he made with her.

With the human staring him down and no other feasible excuse to put it off, Tai'dqei grudgingly decided taking this confrontation head-on was the best tactic. The longer he avoided it, the worse it'd be.

"I misinterpreted the situation," Tai'dqei admitted, his mandibles flexing awkwardly. He attempted to stifle the nervous tic as Rayelle glanced at the movement. Whatever she thought of his mandibles, he could only imagine. Non-ja-tau had told him more than once his mandibles were unsettling.

"How do you misinterpret that situation?" She felt the hysterical edge crackle through her·voice, making the her words rough. Her attention was still transfixed to those pincers on Tai'dqei's jaw. They couldn't just be for show. A prickle crept up her back, wondering if it was agitation that made his appendages fidget or something else.

A muscle flexed in Tai'dqei's jaw as he considered how to answer her. She was a human with no experience or knowledge of aliens. How did one even begin? He wasn't even sure what a normal human mating ritual was like, so he couldn't even draw comparisons.

Which meant he should start with the basics, he decided.

"I am a ja-tau," Tai'dqei began after a breath to gather his thoughts. Judging from the annoyed expression that crimped Rayelle's face as she turned her eyes to his, Ah'ke had already introduced their species.

He trudged on before she could interrupt him and derail his minor progress. Doing his best to keep his tone level and non-condescending, he continued, "The instinct to hunt is strong in our blood. When a hunt goes well, like my bounty job that led me to you, the adrenaline and euphoria are high."

At that, Rayelle scoffed. This was beginning to sound like the plethora of other excuses she had heard in her lifetime. "*It's not my fault, emotions were high!*" "*Can you really blame me for having fun?*" "*That wasn't me, that was the alcohol.*" Etcetera etcetera etcetera.

"So your sense of accomplishment makes it okay t—" Her words abruptly halted as Tai'dqei grabbed her by the arm, pulling her closer to him and pressing his warm palm to her mouth. The movement had been so fast that Rayelle's heart barely had a chance to stutter. Her eyes flew wide with rage, instantly trying to pull away from his firm hold.

"Let me finish," he said quietly, hunching over her. The heat of her skin and her breath against his palm did little to still the sudden fire at his core. If she was going to interrupt him every other sentence with biting remarks, he'd never get through this explanation.

It didn't help that every confrontational word out of her mouth or her every infuriating action razed at his insides. He didn't want his romp at the sex house to be completely undone as soon as he returned to his ship.

Rayelle's eyes flickered over his face, searching for something that was even a mystery to herself, but she stilled. Something — an unspoken sincerity maybe — gave her pause. Or maybe she was a fool, she didn't know it.

Though she did squint in displeasure at him, hating how warm and gentle his unwavering hold felt. It scraped at something raw inside her. It was only that sensation that kept her from planting her hands on his chest and shoving. Additional points of contact, she feared, would just further frustrate and confuse her.

As Tai'dqei resumed speaking, he slowly lowered his hand from her mouth. "In that state of mind, I had no intention to touch you like I did. Until you threw something and ran."

He paused experimentally to see if she would cut in again. She remained quiet, her demanding gaze on him as she waited for further explanation. "One ja-tau mating ritual is meant to assess the capabilities of a mate by gaining their attention and then running. Challenging them to a different sort of hunt."

As he spoke, his mind's eye replayed their initial meeting clearly. Him approaching the small cage she cowered in, her eyes locked to the sight of him. The tang of blood in the air, the smears on his armor, the adrenaline still clawing delightfully through him.

Tai'dqei could only imagine what terror she felt when she saw him — with his blood-covered armor and intimidating stature — but his brain was pumped up on success from a job well done. Though he knew she was staring warily, part of him wondered if there was a bit of admiration in the look. She had to acknowledge his strength, his fearsomeness, if she was wary.

Then she threw that damn water bowl at him and he completely lost his sense.

When Rayelle next spoke, her tone only solidified Tai'dqei's own annoyance with himself. "Excuse me?"

Now she writhed out of his hold, jerking herself from the hand that had gone lax on her shoulder. It took all of Tai'dqei's discipline to not grab at her, clutch her tight, just to touch her.

Heat bled into her face and down her body, embarrassed and angry. "You're saying because I stared and threw something at you and ran, you thought I wanted you to fuck me?"

Between the memories and the slowly kindling heat, it was easy for Tai'dqei to recall how he felt and thought during their first meeting. Even now, he could feel the burn of temptation gnawing at his hands. "Yes. I thought you were inviting me to pursue you, to catch you. As gratitude for helping you."

Rayelle took a step further away from him, taken aback by the straightforward answer. She stared wide-eyed up at Tai'dqei while her brain scrambled to understand. What was his play? He didn't sound remorseful but he didn't sound agitated either.

"When I realized you were not enjoying yourself, I stopped." His voice softened as he bowed his head. Rayelle watched as the feather-like hair shifted with the movement, catching the light above. "I cannot apologize enough."

Her thoughts completely escaped her. She could not find anything to respond with. The only thing Rayelle could do was stare at the alien — a ja-tau, she reminded herself — and attempt to process his words.

She wasn't sure if she believed him. It would be so easy for him to lie to the naive little human, wouldn't it?

Part of her didn't think he was lying. If so, he could have come up with a million better excuses. She couldn't think of any at the moment but she was still trying to parse his straightforward attitude when it came to answering her.

At the very least, he seemed genuine. There was no balking and no excuses, just an explanation why things had happened the way they had. Even if he could have hidden behind instincts driving him, he chose not to.

Tai'dqei knew he did wrong. Something inside her wailed about how he was still doing wrong by keeping her captive and collaring her. If he truly wanted to do right by her, wouldn't he give her freedom?

Another part of Rayelle reminded herself this wasn't her home, her time, her planet. She managed to get into this trouble without playing an active role, beyond pursuing a divorce. What other trouble could she get into out of ignorance? Tai'dqei already said the collar was for her safety. But was it really?

Though she knew he was waiting for a reply, her brain spat out static amid the chaos.

Instead of reacting or replying, or doing *anything* to acknowledge his apology and explanation, Rayelle turned and walked away with a blank stare on her face. A million different thoughts tumbled around her head but she couldn't make sense of a single one.

An alien took her vicious bid for freedom as a flirtatious invite. An alien that had, with daunting strength and precision, bloodily dispatched a whole squad of other aliens. And that same alien had bought her fidget toys and chocolate.

It was too much for Rayelle. Once more, she had to lay down as her sense of reality wobbled.

Tai'dqei let her go, watching as she ducked back into the guest quarters. It was for the best, he told himself as he went to put his supplies in their appropriate places. The expression on her face reminded him of the haunted looks older ja-tau back home would wear when recounting countless battles and hunts. It spoke of pain and grappling with a reality that continued to upend itself.

He was part of what pained her. The least he could do was give her space while her mind settled with all this newfound knowledge. Better yet, he should be figuring out who would be better at caring for her than himself.

Even if that thought left a bitter taste on his tongue.

CHAPTER 7

Over the course of the next couple days – or cycles as Rayelle was learning, since there was no sun or 24-hour segmentation – she and Tai'dqei avoided one another. She did the bulk of the avoiding, if she was being honest. Tai'dqei would offer a greeting and small talk, letting her know they'd be staying docked until his employer arrived at the station, but she never responded. She'd only take the food he offered or look at him when he spoke, but beyond that, their interaction was minimal.

Well other than the one time she needed his help operating the shower. Whenever she thought about that moment, as short as it was, her face warmed with embarrassment. Which only served to further annoy her. It was no different than asking how to operate the shower anywhere else!

Except it was a little different.

She had asked someone who had taken her assault on him as

a flirtation. Who pursued her and almost raped her due to misunderstanding, if *that* were to be believed. Who had, thus far, given her a way to communicate and provided her with food and new clothes and entertainment. Even if the damnable collar remained on her throat.

Thinking about Tai'dqei made her suspicions, hope, and logic fight. It was like a pack of dogs chasing cats.

It was simply easier not to think about him.

For Tai'dqei's part, he felt like her efforts to ignore him were for the best. Especially after she asked how to work the shower. Just being in an enclosed space, knowing she'd soon be naked in the area, taunted his thoughts. He had given her a straightforward rundown on how to use the shower and retreated as fast as he could to his training room.

He would have liked to say he was trying to redirect the energy elsewhere. In reality, he just chose to work up a sweat to excuse his need for the shower later on. Once in the shower, he'd get a little dirtier before getting clean.

After three cycles, something new transpired.

"I'll be heading out today. My employer finally came in to finish up our contract." He informed her as he peered into her room, holding his breath to not inhale her scent. Her presence was becoming exceedingly distracting.

Rayelle was sitting up on her bed, alerted to his entry seconds earlier by his knock before her door slid open. The antique paperback she had been reading rested on her lap, her finger marking her spot.

Her irritation at his sudden entry was somewhat mollified by his announcement. Curiosity lit up in her eyes when she noticed his full black armor, including his helmet. She hadn't seen him in it since the first night. Faint memories flickered in her head, although most of the first half had certainly been a blur.

"Is Ah'ke going to babysit me again?" She posited the question with a heaping dollop of sarcasm. Hopefully she was sardonic enough to get through any language or cultural barriers.

"No, she's too busy." Tai'dqei pointedly ignored her sharp tone. Ah'ke had reminded him enough times through their frequent communiques that Rayelle was still adjusting. Rising at her mere tone would accomplish nothing.

He hefted the container that held the bounties' heads onto his hip and shot Rayelle a look which she likely couldn't see beyond the mask he wore. "Stay here until I come back."

"I don't have much choice," Rayelle retorted, tugging at her collar pointedly. She critically eyed Tai'dqei in his whole set-up, realizing portions of his arms and legs weren't entirely covered by the dark armor. Between plates and under the mesh material, his rusty red-orange-to-pale-yellow colorations peeked through.

Tai'dqei stood still for a breath, watching her through his visor. She returned his steadfast leer with a raised eyebrow and a slightly mocking shake of her head. "Well?"

He pointed to the floor, emphasizing each word with a downward motion to the floor. "Stay. Put."

While he worried about her safety were she to run away, another concern lay with the hormones that had consistently remained simmering inside him. Tracking her down through the station would only whet that unwanted appetite.

Rayelle's frown deepened, her glare heating unhappily as she crossed her arms over her chest. She wasn't about to agree with his demand. Heaviness settled in the air between the two, growing heavier when she didn't respond.

After another moment to consider, Tai'dqei set the container down and input a command into his wrist gauntlet. Rayelle tilted her head curiously at him. When he retrieved the container, once more settling it on his hip, he turned to leave. Before he moved beyond the limited visibility of her door, he stated, "When I go, the ship is going on lockdown. *Stay. Here.*"

With as much scorn as she could muster, Rayelle snorted. Tai'dqei ignored her and continued down the hall, her door closing behind him. She sat back on her bed, returning to the book. Or attempting to, at least.

No matter how she tried to force her eyes to the words, her mind was focused on listening. She heard Tai'dqei's heavily armored boots thump down the hall, the sound gradually becoming softer. When it sounded as if he had exited the ship, additional mechanical sounds shuttered behind him. Rayelle could hear the extra security measures, whatever they were, clunking into place.

Setting her book down in her lap, she eyed her own door. It was likely her collar was tied to some sort of system or program that would alert Tai'dqei to movement outside of a certain range. Perhaps the ship. Perhaps the docking port. Rayelle's eyes narrowed, wondering how long she had until Tai'dqei returned.

Tai'dqei would presumably be too busy collecting his payment to pay attention to every notification. That meant, if she timed her escape right, she could get out of the ship without him immediately realizing it. Gradually swarming questions began to spin across her mind.

How far could she even get? Should she even bother trying to find someone to remove the collar? Or maybe just slumming it onto a ship, getting out of the presumed range, was a better option? If the Time Council, or whatever they were called, were such a big deal, Rayelle could probably find them on her own. She was capable, after all.

Her gaze flicked back to the book in her possession. Her mind lolled over the other things Tai'dqei had gotten her, his concerns for her well-being, the lengths he'd gone to get them capable of communicating.

Should she even try to leave? Her alien abductors had intended to do something with her. Maybe it had been extremely good luck to be found by Tai'dqei. Who knew how others would treat her? What if the temporal authorities weren't so easy to find?

And what if it all had been a lie? How'd she even know the difference? What if Tai'dqei had made it all up, just to keep her subservient? At least, as subservient as he could manage. Rayelle swallowed at that thought, considering how Ah'ke would be an accessory to the lies if that was the case.

Her hands tightened on her book until the spine creaked in her grasp.

She gave Tai'dqei thirty minutes of peace while she haphazardly collected a bag's worth of supplies, before working on finding a way out.

◊ ◊ ◊

Roughly forty-five minutes after he left, Tai'dqei's gauntlet pinged. He glanced at the notification, barely holding back a frustrated curse. He'd gotten a notice of the ship unlocking, quickly followed a notification of Rayelle on the move.

"Something wrong?" Tai'dqei's employer, Zav, regarded the ja-tau with an entirely dark green gaze. The green Florizian sat far more elegantly than necessary, given the transaction currently happening between employer and hunter. With one lithe leg crossed over the other, his body leaned sideways against the only table in the rental space. The container of skulls sat on the table, already perused by Zav.

"A delayed shipment of parts," lied Tai'dqei, already on edge with Zav's inquiries before the notifications interrupted them. He didn't like how the Florizian watched him, especially as the vine-like hair shifted atop his head. Shoving aside his own discomfort and annoyance, Tai'dqei nodded to his employer. "You were saying?"

Zav stared unblinkingly at Tai'dqei. Behind the Florizian, others stood at the ready. Mostly they were beefy four-armed aliens that often found jobs as bodyguards, but the ones that concerned

Tai'dqei were the other Florizians. They, too, watched him with dark eyes and hard-to-read expressions.

"This particular contingency of cretins," Zav motioned to the skulls atop the table, "Were rumored to have valuable cargo."

"You didn't request cargo retrieval," Tai'dqei returned with an unyielding tone. It wouldn't have been rare, had Zav requested such a thing. When one employed a bounty hunter, sometimes it was a matter of getting something valuable back along with the heads of the bounties.

"No, I didn't since I thought it'd be a long shot. They likely already pushed this particular valuable out," Zav sighed, his posture slouching further as he rested his elbow on the table and cradled his chin in his hand. "But humor me, Tai'dqei. Was there anything of worth I should be made aware of?"

"No, sir. Just the crew, some counterfeit goods, drugs. The usual." Tai'dqei gave a stiff shrug. A suspicion mounted in his head, but he didn't want to acknowledge it lest he made it a reality. After all, Rayelle was a person, not a thing. Zav was talking about a thing.

Zav's expression didn't falter or change. Other than their writhing vine-hair, he didn't move a muscle as he stared at Tai'dqei. "I see. Well, I do hope you aren't lying."

Tai'dqei offered no verbal response, though an annoyed growl rumbled deep on his chest. At his snarl, the bodyguards and Florizians behind Zav tensed, prepared to protect their leader.

"Point taken." Zav's thin lips twisted into a smile, serrated teeth flashing in the dim lighting. His calm tone soothed his posse behind him, tension sagging away with the unspoken stand down order. With a bored little wave of his hand, Zav airily added, "You may go now."

"My payment?" Tai'dqei's eyebrow ridges rose even though Zav wouldn't be able to see his expression change behind the mask.

"Already wired to your account. You may check if you like." The Florizian waggled his fingers idly.

Tai'dqei proceeded to do so, not one to simply rely on an employer's word. He made that mistake during one of his first assignments, being left with roughly three-quarters of the agreed upon price and a promise to receive the rest through 'exposure.' Thankfully, Tai'dqei's request for an impromptu Hunt was approved by the elders in his clan and *that* former employer wouldn't make the same mistake twice. Or any mistake ever again.

After verifying that the full amount and a decent gratuity had been applied to his account, Tai'dqei gave a curt nod and turned to leave.

He tried to keep his movements slow and fluid, as if he had nowhere else to be. When he, in fact, had to track down that damned human. His mind was already racing with possibilities as to *where* Rayelle would try to go first. Most likely, she'd try to hitch a ride out of the area, trying to break the signal emitted from her tracking collar.

Less likely, but more to Tai'dqei's hopes, she'd seek out Ah'ke if only to prove to him she had the right to freedom.

He just barely kept from growling to himself before Zav's voice rang out again, causing the ja-tau to pause. "If I do find out you kept something valuable from me, I'll be very cross."

After a breath of waiting, Tai'dqei continued on his way out. There was nothing more to say to the Florizian, though the ja-tau felt the stare on his back the entire way out.

Once the bounty hunter left, the crew scurried to lock the door of the rental office. Zav plucked up a skull possessing one eye socket from the container, staring at it in a bored fashion. A human-cyborg assistant scuttled up to his side. Without looking at them, Zav asked, "What were his notifications about?"

"S-security event. His ship was unlocked and there were alerts from a tracking program." The assistant held out a holo-tablet to Zav. One of his tendrils relinquished it from the cyborg, who flinched at the touch.

Sucking air in between his teeth, Zav considered the chances of someone daring to break into a ja-tau ship *and* something of enough value to require a tracker. As he scrolled further, he realized it was a tracker that could measure biological vitals.

Though his assistant hadn't managed to hack further into the logs, Zav was willing to bet those particular files would affirm his suspicions.

"Home in on that tracking signal and follow it," Zav commanded, shoving the tablet back to the cyborg.

They took the tablet, instantly tapping commands into it as they turned to the others. Zav let his assistant deal with assembling a team and orchestrating a plan as he turned his attention back to the skull in hand. He flexed his fingers, the bone cracking under his grip.

He wanted that human.

The Unexpected Human Problem

◊ ◊ ◊

Getting out of the ship had been easier than Rayelle expected. The ear worm didn't extend to written words, so she was out of luck just looking for a plainly labeled escape hatch. Using context and intuition, she soon found an emergency release lever for the door that led outside. She presumed it was used in cases where the ship went up in flames and the system malfunctioned or some similar misfortune happened.

Of course, getting the damned door open was another story. It took her a solid fifteen minutes of hauling on the lever before the heavy entryway divided enough for her to squeeze through. Once she got her ass and packed rucksack out of the ship, freedom tasted sweet.

Well, metaphorically.

Rayelle's initial presumption she was in a sort of docking sector for spaceships proved correct, so the air tasted like oil and electricity and metal. Among a number of indecipherable or unnamable smell-tastes, as well.

Steadying herself and trying not to look like some naive space tourist, she marched her way down the ramp and into the docks. It was hard not to stare. Whether it was at the ships – a variety of designs and shapes and materials that she couldn't even begin to understand the engineering behind – or the variety of people. Skin colors, textures, solidity, feathers, scales, furry, large teeth, mandibles. Her brain overloaded, drinking in the new details and marveling at the sheer diversity of sentient life.

Rayelle didn't realize she'd even left the docking sector until her ears registered the familiar sounds of salespeople.

"Two for the price of one! This cycle only!"

"Try our new fragrance! Made from the nectar of the luscious and rare zelu flower!"

"Fresh gth'uk! Get it fresh, get it hot!"

Bright white tiles blanketed the floor. Storefronts lined the walls. A little to her right, she found a large window looking out into the inky expanse of space. A reddish planet slowly rotated nearby, which was likely what the station orbited. There were tables set up in front of the window and it seemed a number of aliens – and even human or human-looking people – were enjoying their lunch break there. Or whatever meal it was for them.

It was like a mall or airport, Rayelle realized with a start. Albeit filled with non-humans and glimpses of unfamiliar tech and a literal stellar view. Still, it felt like a mall or airport. Then again, maybe that was just her mind trying to equate it to something more familiar.

Adjusting her hold on the rucksack she had stolen from Tai'dqei's storage, she tried to figure out where to go. Ideally, she wanted to get the collar off but she had no clue where to go for that. A tech shop? A welder? The authorities?

She skimmed the signs around the entrances of the shops. Unfortunately, she couldn't make heads or tails of anything.

If she couldn't find someone to help, Rayelle feared she'd just have to hitch a ride outside of the collar's range. It couldn't report her position to the ends of the universe, right?

As that thought crossed her mind, she paused. Suddenly thrust into this world of unfamiliarity, part of her had to admit that Tai'dqei had a point. She had no clue where to go, who was friend or foe. She couldn't even read the store signs! Could she make it much farther than this? Did she *want* to?

At least with Tai'dqei she was reasonably safe. Even if she didn't want to feel that way with him.

"Looking for something?"

Rayelle startled, drawn from her thoughts by a stranger's words. She did her best to school her reaction. The stranger had buttercream yellow skin with butterfly-like wings sprouting from the sides of their face and large pink eyes.

Other that those details, they seemed rather humanoid. Overall, they weren't the most outlandish extraterrestrial she had seen. In fact, they looked – and smelled, Rayelle realized – rather sweet.

Hesitating, she teetered behind saying she was fine and slinking back to Tai'dqei's ship or continuing her mission. What was the point of getting off his ship if she didn't take this first step? Tugging at the collar of her own jacket, Rayelle showed the butterfly-stranger the blinking collar latched around her neck. "Yeah, I need to get this off."

"Why're you wearing that?" Something changed in Butterfly's expression, translating to surprise to Rayelle. Although she couldn't pinpoint what exactly had changed. A widening of the eyes or perhaps the wings angling upward.

"My friend thought it'd be a funny prank." Her voice dripped with dry snark as she recited the lie she had come up with on the ship. It wasn't the best, but she couldn't be sure what would even land. A mischievous cohort with an ill-thought prank seemed like something that would be universal. Or intergalactic in this case.

Butterfly snorted, their face-wings fluttering. "Your friend is an ass."

"Don't I know it," Rayelle sighed, releasing her jacket's collar. "Got any recommendations?"

The extraterrestrial paused for half a breath, their eyes narrowing imperceptibly. "Why don't you have your *friend* remove it?"

"They took off this morning. They're supposed to be back tomorrow." Rayelle leaned into the second part of her lie, hoping it was believable to whatever Butterfly was. "Part of their prank."

"I see." Butterfly's lips scrunched together, their wings fluttering slowly as their feet shifted.

Apprehension rose in Rayelle's head. She didn't like the feeling radiating from Butterfly. If her own intuition was correct, it was either suspicion or some sort of calculation. Neither struck Rayelle as appropriate or heartening. "If you can't help, I'll keep look—"

"Wait up, wait up. I didn't say I couldn't help!" Holding up their hands while their wings fluttered nervously, Butterfly flashed Rayelle a mildly distressed expression.

Rayelle paused and the alien peered around, humming to themself. It seemed Butterfly was trying to decide something before they gave a resolute nod and turned back to Rayelle. "Follow me, I know a place."

They turned and trotted between two storefronts, through something that felt akin to an alleyway to Rayelle. In reality, it was just a smaller and slightly dimmer corridor. The warning bells in her head rang and she ran through her options. She could just not follow them. Turn around and head back to Tai'dqei's ship and wait for him to return. Allow this new norm to remain.

But if she followed the stranger, she might get the collar removed thus regaining her freedom. Tai'dqei wasn't about to give that to her. She wasn't sure if he would ever trust her enough to remove the collar. This seemed to be the only way.

Though she doubted Tai'dqei would offer her freedom easily, once she snagged it for herself — even if he caught her again — maybe he'd let her have what she managed to grasp. If she managed it once, she could do so again. And again, and again. Until he got the hint.

If she lived, a treacherous little voice said at the back of her head, but Rayelle steadfastly ignored it as she strode toward the smaller corridor.

CHAPTER 8

Okay, so following Butterfly had been a bad idea. A 100%—No! A *200%* bad idea.

Rayelle gasped for breath as she raced through the crowded corridor. Her pack thumped up and down on her back with every step she took. Even if she'd been in peak physical condition – which she wasn't, even before her abduction – the number of people milling about the station were numerous obstacles.

She constantly found herself ducking and dodging around bodies. Always adjusting her path to the one of least resistance as she hurried and scrambled through the throngs.

Behind her, a horde of fifty or so aliens pursued. Rayelle should have known when the longer and further she followed Butterfly, the more people Butterfly had shared a look or a few quiet words with.

At first, it hadn't seemed strange. Perhaps they were just amiable and had plenty of friends and connections. It was when some of these presumed friends started to accumulate that Rayelle worried. Some wandered next to Butterfly, some flanked Rayelle and made idle conversation with her, others tailed behind her. They all shared the same intent gaze. A pressure descended on her, the warning bells screamed louder in her head until she felt breathless.

Rayelle didn't remember how she got away. Maybe it was something that was said or the salacious timbre of the words or the looks that made her stomach churn. Or maybe she caught the concerned gaze of onlookers. She couldn't say.

She just suddenly stopped, pushed through a weak side of the group, and took off running. The pounding footfalls of pursuit soon followed behind her, along with a cacophony of shouts and even snarls. At points, it even seemed as if her pursuers fought with each other as meaty slams or shrieks of pain followed her.

A crackle of something like an intercom hissed overhead, but Rayelle couldn't make out the words. She just ran.

Occasionally, something would grab at her with a hand or tentacle or claw. She lost her rucksack and her jacket before she resorted to yanking away from the touches, slamming fists and elbows and feet into anyone that laid a hand on her.

She had just shoved off yet another stalker, when something big, heavy, *and invisible* landed behind her from above with a hard wham! The unseen thing made her and others in the crowd scream. Some turned tail and raced off. The floor vibrated intensely beneath her, making her very bones shudder and her feet stumble.

As she tumbled, the impact of her body meeting the floor bruised her hip and she heard the unseen thing give a familiar snarl. Meaty sounding thumps resounded as strikes landed. She managed to roll onto her back, pushing herself further away from the new danger. As her previous pursuers piled onto the thing, a faint outline of the invisible opponent glittered to life wherever hits landed.

Her eyes widened when – whether due to damage or voluntarily – the cloaking mechanism shut off.

Tai'dqei was there, various aliens barreled atop him as he flung them back. Attackers went flying across the corridor, slamming into walls or skidding across the floor. The sound of bones and cartilage cracking echoed in the air, followed by painful screams. It was like watching a pride of lions getting tossed by a battle-hungry rhino.

It hadn't taken him long to track down Rayelle. The fucking swarm of aliens running after her had been a decent hint. At the sight, rage instantly bubbled through him. Many would enjoy a human companion for various reasons and the longer that thought rotated in his head, the angrier he became.

Barely taking in another breath, he had clambered up a support beam and bounded his way toward the chase. He'd at least had the sense to trigger his cloaking mechanism in his angry haze. Metal creaked under his weight and lights flickered as his body passed in front of them, but everyone down below was too focused on the chaos in their midst.

The others were gaining on Rayelle, grabbing at her. Every hand that landed on her prickled through Tai'dqei's self-restraint. They yanked her rucksack from her back, but it was watching someone haul her jacket off her that made his rage flare. She had barely stumbled far enough ahead of her pursuers before he dropped between them.

His opponents didn't have time to readjust their pursuit mindset before Tai'dqei began thrashing them all. Satisfaction coursed through his blood with every impact of his fist, every foe fumbling to the ground. Some of the quicker enemies managed to reroute their thought processes, going on the attack or fleeing from the ja-tau newcomer.

By the time the last contender had been tossed aside, Tai'dqei's chest heaved with enraged breaths. At some point during the brawl, someone had managed to knock his helmet off. It lay yards away, none of the onlookers daring to touch or get close to it. His body remained in a fighting pose, feet planted and muscles tense. Readied for further fight, readied to strike anyone who dared to come close to his human charge.

Rayelle stared up at him, eyes wide and mouth agape. Self-preservation screamed at her to get up, to run. A sick fascination kept her staring, watching Tai'dqei's muscles flex as he fought and listening to his aggravated gnarls. As he stood over her, she could but help but admire how far his chest expanded with his breaths.

He slowly shifted backward, positioning Rayelle between his feet. At that point, she tore her gaze from him, half rolling to her side. She didn't trust her gaze to remain on polite areas.

A raspy hiss left him before a roar expelled from his chest. A cry caught in Rayelle's throat as she curled on the floor, partly around Tai'dqei's large foot. His bellow vibrated through her ears, through her skull, but her arms instinctively wrapped around his leg, hugging his familiarity close.

His roar rumbled through the corridor before dwindling into a clicking growl in his chest. Others in the crowd fell to their knees or scurried backward, if not outright fled. Some did linger, still watching with concerned expressions.

If the fight had not made his intentions clear, his bellow did: *This human was his.*

◊ ◊ ◊

A heart pounding stillness descended on the corridor. There were still bystanders watching Tai'dqei and Rayelle, though at a far greater distance than before.

When it appeared no one was going to challenge him further, Tai'dqei turned his attention to Rayelle. She still cowered at his feet, curled into a fetal position. With a gentle tug, he relinquished his foot from her grasp. As he crouched down, she looked up at him with features drained of color and a slight tremble to her lips.

Her gaze flickered along his face. He wore smears of bright green liquid and, upon further inspection, he had a small handful of cuts along his arms and legs between the plates of armor. All oozing bright green blood. Something uncomfortable shifted in her stomach, her eyes dragging back to his face.

Another series of memories danced along her mind's eye. Old conversations with Evan echoed in her head, angry and accusatory. Tiny little gremlins of fear and desperation clawed through her chest.

Before Tai'dqei could say anything, Rayelle blurted in a painfully hushed way, "Are you angry with me?"

His mandibles fidgeted around his maw as he stared at her. He wasn't sure how to respond, his brain was still full of triumphant battle frenzy and adrenaline. If he was honest, he wanted to haul her over his shoulder and drag her back to his ship. An almost silent rumble rattled in his chest, all the lurid things he could do to keep her from running away again flashing through his head.

Beyond the haze of hormones, he was a little annoyed. He had told her to stay put for her own safety and, even then, she couldn't listen. He couldn't blame her. She harbored little trust in him for good reasons.

Before Tai'dqei could answer Rayelle, or shake away the troublesome hormones plaguing his thoughts, a heavily armored Station Peacekeeper loomed over the both of them. "What's the problem here?"

Tai'dqei offered the Peacekeeper an annoyed glance before straightening from his slight hunch. He didn't feel like taking on an armored authority, especially when he could sense their disdain behind their helmet. "I'm her travel companion, officer."

Tai'dqei and this presumed station guard were of equal height, making Rayelle feel even tinier than she had moments earlier. Shakily, she pulled herself together and raised herself off the floor. Even as she peered between the two hulking figures, her eyes were drawn to Tai'dqei's bleeding injuries. Her stomach twisted with guilt.

"Is that so?" The officer turned to Rayelle. Though she couldn't see their expression beyond the smooth helmet, she thought she could hear their eyebrow equivalent raise with skepticism. They leaned a little closer to her. Faintly, Rayelle wondered if their helmet had some sort of scanning implement or if they were just peering very intensely at her.

"Yes, it is," Tai'dqei growled, crossing his arms over his chest. His heart pitched with aggravation, wanting nothing more than to push the officer away from her.

Ignoring the ja-tau's insistence, the Peacekeeper leaned even closer toward Rayelle. "Do you feel safe?"

She blinked, surprised at the question. She didn't look to Tai'dqei for guidance but she could see him stiffen from the corner of her eye. The inquiry was a loaded one. He knew it.

Did she feel safe with Tai'dqei? Well certainly safer than with the pursuers from earlier or her previous captors. She'd even hazard to say she felt relieved when he showed up, even if she was apprehensive about his reaction to her escape.

She could imagine how the situation looked, as well. A squishy dowdy human traveling with a ja-tau? Others must think they were an odd couple. After he went to the trouble of saving her, Rayelle didn't want to cause more problems for Tai'dqei. For now.

"Yes, I feel safe with him." The answer didn't seem to surprise the

Peacekeeper, though it certainly bewildered Tai'dqei. Rayelle felt the surprise emanating from him.

To his credit, Tai'dqei instantly hid his reaction as the officer turned back to him. There was a tense moment as the Peacekeeper surveyed the ja-tau, but the officer eventually gave him a terse nod before walking off down the corridor.

The public that had congregated around them appeared assuaged. A Peacekeeper had stepped up, interviewed the last two participants in that hectic frenzy, and deemed it a safe companionship.

All, apparently, was fine.

Tai'dqei watched the officer continue down the corridor until Rayelle spoke again. "What now?"

Turning his attention to her, she shifted awkwardly under his silent stare. It was hard to tell if he was angry with her or not considering his features seemed perpetually agitated. At least to her.

What now, indeed, Tai'dqei thought as he retrieved his fallen helmet and clipped it to his belt. He needed a moment to wrangle in his careening thoughts. Which was proving to be difficult.

He'd gotten his payment from Zav.

Rayelle said she felt safe with him.

The plan earlier was to retrieve a tech gauntlet, like his and Ah'ke's and the rest of spacefaring society possessed, so he could retire the collar.

Rayelle said she felt safe with him.

But she had left his ship after he explicitly said not to and she had nearly gotten swept off to stars know where and for what?

Rayelle said she felt safe with him.

He barely managed to keep from growling, knowing she would take the vocal frustration the wrong way. Taking a deep breath, letting his chest expand against his crossed arms, he steadied himself. This was no way for a full-grown ja-tau to act.

"We are going to the nearby gear shop," he finally said as he started walking. From his peripheral, he watched Rayelle startle to attention and rush after him.

Gear shop. Rayelle wasn't sure what that meant. It could have meant anything from ship parts to weaponry, she thought. Her eyes flickered to the still bleeding cuts, her eyebrows furrowing. "You should treat those cuts, first."

"Not necessary." Explaining how he got the injuries to Ah'ke and hearing her opinion of the whole fiasco was the absolute last thing he wanted to hear. She'd hear about it soon enough. Rumors involving a human being chased through the station and was, more or less, claimed by a ja-tau were probably already spreading. It would be easy enough for Ah'ke to put the pieces together. *Especially* if he arrived at her clinic, covered in cuts.

"Why not?" The furrow between her eyebrows deepened at his reaction as she continued to follow him at the brisk pace. She wished he'd take shorter strides to allow her to keep up.

Tai'dqei shook his head, "They are minor. I'll live."

"You can't walk around public, bleeding everywhere." Rayelle made a motion to the station at large. Both of them could tell they were still being watched. Her words were not help their attempts to *not* be a spectacle, especially as she added, "Bleeding over everything is a health hazard."

"No one's going to stop me." This time he finally looked at her, turning his head to glimpse her over his shoulder. He didn't stop walking nor slow his pace.

When he did glance back at her, Rayelle had to pause. He knew people wouldn't – couldn't – stop him and he was just flaunting it. She stared at his expansive back and the way his muscles shifted as he moved. It brought back mingled memories of big cat videos interspersed with memories of how he fought. None of his opponents were able to leave more than a laceration. Some of those people had been pretty beefy or massive themselves, but they were the exception.

Just looking around, she could tell the average spacefarer was not ja-tau built.

Fully stopping in the corridor and crossing her arms, she glared up at him. "Just because you're intimidating doesn't mean you get to do whatever you want."

With that acknowledgement, Tai'dqei spun on his heel and leaned over into her personal space. Rayelle didn't flinch, but her eyes followed his face. It took immense self-control for him to not let his hands on her cocked hips.

A soft guttural clicking entered his words as he strained against temptation. "Do I intimidate you?"

Her mouth popped open, ready to snap a negative retort at him but she paused. Something glinted in his eye. Her own gaze narrowed as her mouth snapped shut, wondering if he was amused with her. She couldn't decide if that was better or worse than him being angry. It didn't make her heart stutter any less.

When Rayelle didn't reply, a mixed sensation stirred in his chest. Disappointment and primal pride mingled with an unknown something else. Before he could name it, Tai'dqei turned around again and began walking once more. Prompted by that unnamed something else, he found himself calling over his shoulder, "I'm upgrading your tracker by the way."

"*Excuse me?*" Rayelle nearly shrieked, storming after him. It was instant realization, immediate rage. She hadn't even taken a moment to register what he said. Upgrading her tracker? Her imagination fed her a number of awful 'upgrades.'

Tai'dqei felt oddly pleased with her reaction, as he picked up the pace to a light jog and forced Rayelle to run after him.

◊ ◊ ◊

It wasn't long before they returned to his ship. Although, at Rayelle's insistence, Tai'dqei had gotten his own wounds treated while they were out. As expected, they weren't anything to be concerned about. Most had already begun healing but she wasn't going to stop complaining until he listened. In return for obeying her, she had flashed him a relieved smile that made his insides twist.

He mentally shook himself. There were things to do. He couldn't let himself simper over her smile or how she had said she trusted him.

It took an asinine amount of focus to not recall how she lay on the ground under him, staring up at him with wide eyes. Or forget how her soft warmth had curled around his foot as he roared a warning to would-be attackers.

He shook the thoughts from his head. They had retrieved her a tech gauntlet and now he needed to give her a basic lesson on using it. Tai'dqei was already considering which programs to highlight and which settings to alter.

As he considered what would be most beneficial to her, he removed his outermost layer of armor and set it aside to be put away later. "I should show you how to—"

"Wait."

He froze at her voice, glancing up from where he set his armor on the mess table. Conflict was evident on her face. She stood stiffly, shoulders tight and an air of electric discomfort around her. Her hand was on her wrist where the shiny new wrist device clasped.

Her eyebrows furrowed as she sorted through the sudden thoughts ricocheting around her head. She wasn't even looking at Tai'dqei. "I tried running away despite your warnings. I almost got you in big trouble. You've spent so much on me and I just..."

Rayelle struggled to sort through the emotions and thoughts rumbling about her head. She was fine until that moment. They had gone through the gear shop, got her fitted, and had even gotten his cuts treated. She had given input. She did all this and felt fine. Or she thought she felt fine.

Alone with Tai'dqei again, an inner turmoil roiled within Rayelle. Her hand tightened on the wrist gauntlet, the cool metal a salve against the sudden heat inside her. The collar had been removed, now inactive and hanging on his hip.

The wrist bracer was the upgrade Tai'dqei had been talking about. It allowed for two-way tracking, meaning he could track her location but she could also track his. A compromise, he had said, since she chafed so badly at her lack of freedom to the point it put her in danger.

The gauntlets were also a form of long-range communique. He always seemed to strive for clear communication..

The gesture seemed wrong to her. Or maybe it was better to say she wanted it to be wrong. Rayelle wanted to feel like he was trying to bribe her into obedience with the niceties and gifts. Or that he was trying to pull a Stockholm Syndrome on her, being nice while keeping her detained. She couldn't quite convince herself that was the case.

Stubbornness and uncertainty teamed up to build protective walls around her.

Leveling a hard look at the ja-tau, she ignored the frustrated tears pooling in her eyes. Her expression set firm, daring him to bristle at what she said, "Just so it's clear, I'm not thankful for any of it. I have no reason to be thankful for any of it."

Tai'dqei stayed in his spot, giving her that quiet look of his. It was an indiscernible resting bitch face in her mind. She wished he'd say something, do something, to make the nettles of anger in her worthwhile. If he'd just react poorly, it'd make this ever-present prickling rage make sense.

But he didn't.

Tai'dqei watched the expressions pass over Rayelle features. He couldn't name all of them and he couldn't say he related to what she was going through. The pain, the confusion, the uncertainty, the fear. They were on a level he hadn't experienced.

A distracting conflict stirred in his chest while he thought of what to say. He couldn't blame Rayelle, but he was having a hard time finding the right words to soothe the situation. Not that he needed to since after enough silence she continued to talk.

"I can't take out my anger on Evan or my human kidnappers or my alien abductors because they're dead. They're all dead." Before Rayelle even realized she was speaking, words were rambling out of her. Thoughts she had at the back of her brain during her dark moments in her room were surging forth. Sudden epiphanies took root and grew.

They pushed full throttle through her lips, hot tears slicing down her cheeks. She took a step toward Tai'dqei, uncertain of what the point was of closing the distance between them. "You're the only one I can be angry with, that the anger will even affect. And I am *so* mad. And frustrated. And little trinkets won't— I don't— I'm not—"

Unable to keep going, despising the burn of tears behind her eyes, Rayelle let out a frustrated snarl. She pressed her face into her hands, wetness dripping from her eyes and searing her palms.

Tai'dqei raised his hand, took a step closer to Rayelle. Even with the comfortable distance still between them, he watched her body stiffen from the sound of his footfall. He forced himself to stop and lower his hand.

He guessed everything she was feeling — the pain of losing everything she knew, the fear of where this unknown journey would take her, the frustration of being foisted into so many unknowns — easily morphed into anger. It was easier to be furious, to lash out, to strike and maintain distance, than to give in and get close. To risk getting hurt. He knew that feeling well right after he and Ah'ke separated.

Tai'dqei had known part of her anger stemmed from survival, from pain. He'd seen it in many of his own people. Knowing that didn't soothe his own hope she'd trust him, but what he wanted wasn't important.

"I appreciate you're in a difficult situation and I haven't made it easier," he started, his words slow and measured. Rayelle sniffed and her eyes appeared above her splayed fingers, her palms still covering the lower part of her face. Like many times before, Tai'dqei wanted to reach out and press a hand to her in an attempt to comfort her on a level that he felt his words lacked. He didn't reach out, he couldn't. "If my penance for what I did the first night is to be the target for your angry lashing out, I'll accept it. I can handle it."

After a beat of consideration, Tai'dqei crossed his arms and added, "Just don't run from me afterward."

Something eased in her as he accepted her rage. He didn't try to douse it or stifle it. He just said he'd bear the brunt of it. At the same time, him crossing his arms put her off. Or maybe it was the way a confusing heat curled in her chest as she watched his biceps flex.

He ruined that pleasant warmth with his demand she not run from him. As if he was in any position to give her orders! Pushing the comfortable warmth away, Rayelle balled her hands into fists and spat back, "I'll run from you if I want to run from you!"

"You've been told the possible consequences if that happens," Tai'dqei growled, his voice deep and guttural. While he wasn't saying he would fall to his instincts, he felt Rayelle needed a reminder of his inclinations.

If it was only an occasional thing, that was different. Her earliest stunts coupled with the constant grief she now gave him kept an ongoing frenzy roiling inside him.

Tai'dqei's friendly warning transformed into a threat to Rayelle. Her words were out of her mouth, her finger pointing savagely at his face before she could even censure herself. "How about you learn some self-control!"

Instead of a harsh snarl or retort in reply, Tai'dqei silently stared down at her. Her outburst sent a pang of heat through his core. One he needed to control before it consumed him.

She glared up at him, her finger still cocked at him and her shoulders stiff. The air between them grew hot and charged. Rayelle watched as his arms tightened harder across his chest, his claws digging into his own arm and his mandibles flexing. Pinpricks of green pooled up where his nails met flesh.

There was no way he could show her the new tech in this state, he decided.

"I'm going to go train." Once more, Tai'dqei made sure his words were level and measured but there was a slight strain. His actions were not as composed as he sharply turned away from Rayelle and forced his feet to move toward his training room, away from her. In his effort to do so, his footfalls were heavier than he intended.

With her anger scorching all other thoughts and feelings, Rayelle rode high on a wave of defiance. "You do that, you fucking perv!"

Her words made him stop. A low, clicking growl burbled in his chest, his slowly overheating brain supplying a different situation that would draw such crass words from her lips. At his sides, his hands flexed into fists as he strained against his own mental reins.

He couldn't deny her words. Around her, he was in a frequent struggle with his baser instincts. It frustrated Tai'dqei to no end. He was better than this. With nothing to say or do in return, he was about to force himself forward and lose himself in a grueling regimen. Which, yes, would require a damn long shower afterward.

Before he did, however, a memory came to him. Something he had seen other spacefaring humans do to one another in bouts of frustration or friendly jest. Something that Ah'ke had explained to him a long time ago.

Without turning around, Tai'dqei raised his arm and flashed his hand over his shoulder.

Rayelle's eyes widened at the gesture, her rage replaced with a cold rush of incredulity. "Did you just flip me off? How do you even know that gesture?"

Hearing her tonal shift was enough to cool the desirous heat in his lower abdomen. Though a new sort of delight took its place. Tai'dqei gave a chuff of a chuckle, continuing on his way to his training room.

As difficult as this situation was, he couldn't say he didn't enjoy her companionship.

CHAPTER 9

The training session had strenuous, with self-punishing extra sets every time his mind wandered into lewd territory. By the time he re-emerged, a good sheen of sweat coated his skin and he'd abandoned most articles of clothing, save for the barest necessity to keep modesty.

Tai'dqei had actually been tempted to strip that, but — despite believing Rayelle would be tired after the eventful day — he knew she inevitably defied expectations. So he had kept one scrap of cloth for modesty.

As he exited the training room, she stood in the corridor by her room's door. She rubbed sleep from her eyes, having just napped for a good hour or so. As she blearily paused in the hallway, debating on what to have for a snack, she froze upon seeing Tai'dqei.

The two stared at each other from opposite ends of the corridor, an indescribable sensation snapping through the air between them. Hot and biting and tingling.

Tai'dqei knew where the sudden heavy twist at his core originated from, but Rayelle was struggling to understand her own reaction.

It was the first time she had seen him with barely anything on. Well, in comparison to the partial armor with netting he tended to wear. Not to mention the sheen of sweat that coated him like a thin glaze, highlighted the curvatures of his muscles. Stirring sensations in Rayelle wobbled, warm and confusing and making her skin prickle.

Before she knew it, her eyes had slid down his form. So bare – with only a piece of fabric belted around his waist and tucked to keep everything private covered – she could pinpoint his color pattern even further.

Sandy-beige colored the highest peaks of his features, fading to the red-orange she was familiar with. That sandy color continued down the front center of his throat and along the underside of his arms and at his inner thighs. It continued down the underside of his legs to his large claw-tipped feet.

She tried to recall if Tai'dqei's palms were light-colored and wondered if the soles of his feet would mirror the coloration.

She also noticed a greater gamut of colors on Tai'dqei's body. Speckled from that sandy yellowish brown to burnt orange to rust red. Here and there, scars marred his body, including a curious pair on the underside of both his pecs. They tickled at some distant familiarity but Rayelle shoved it away. Finding anything familiar about Tai'dqei wasn't welcome in her head.

With a start, she realized she had been staring for longer than politeness allowed. Her eyes flickered back up to his face, making a minor detour to his black-to-red feathers tied back into a sort of flared ponytail. For the first time, she realized there were little metallic beads braided through his hair at certain points. She couldn't help wondering if there was a significance to them or if they were a simple fashion statement.

When Rayelle's eyes found his, she realized he had stood without moving. It was like he was conceding to being assessed for something. In his arms, the rest of his usual attire sat in a mound of metal and fabric.

Instinct had Tai'dqei holding still, allowing himself to be surveyed by a potential mate. That wasn't true, sense told him. She didn't want anything to do with him, regardless of how her body reacted in relation to his. Still, he waited until she said or did something. Even if she wasn't a possible mate, he had a hard time determining when she'd be skittish.

As he waited for her reaction, he couldn't help letting his eyes wander too. Her hair was mussed from sleep, her eyes a little red-rimmed from crying, but it was her clothing that held his attention.

Rayelle wore a fitted sweater dress — suggested by Khimiel — and leggings he'd bought for her. The fabrics clung to her form, highlighting her silhouette.

His gaze razed over her wide hips, the roundness of her breasts, the soft arc of her stomach, the curves of her thighs and calves. A stark contrast to the jeans, tank top, and baggy jacket she'd chosen to lounge around the ship in or runaway in. His palms tingled, remembering how soft and cushiony she felt under his touch, wondering if she felt plusher with the delicate fabrics enveloping her.

It wasn't something he realized he was doing until her eyes narrowed on him. As if she could sense the direction of his thoughts. Keeping her back pressed to the opposite side of the corridor, she slid toward the galley.

"You're sweaty," she observed, a petty bite to her words. A heady scent hit her nose, reminding her of their musk conversation from earlier. Heat crept up her body at the thought. Before she could consider the implications, she added, "And you smell."

"I was training." Tai'dqei mirrored Rayelle's movements, heading in the opposite direction toward his room. Cool metal bit into his back, distracting from the heat of his thoughts. The heap of clothes in his arms felt like a shield. Whether it protected him or her, Tai'dqei wasn't certain.

She slid further down the hall, her nose wrinkling. "Well, go take a shower."

"Planning to," he sighed, partly amused and partly exasperated. He continued to mirror her movements while heading the opposite way.

"Okay, well, good." Rayelle realized she really shouldn't have said anything. They could have passed each other in the hall, not even exchanging words or looking each other's way. No discussion was necessary. Why had she said anything to begin with?

As she ducked into the mess and he likewise disappeared into his room. Neither minded the words exchanged, though Rayelle had to ponder why she even initiated conversation. She had spent the last few days ignoring him, after all. It should have been easy to continue the cold shoulder.

She couldn't stop thinking about Tai'dqei slamming down in that corridor, fending off her pursuers, roaring at any would-be opponents while he stood over her. A conflicting muddle of heat and distress tangled in her stomach.

Dismissing her inner confusion as hunger, she shook the images from her head and rummaged around in search of something to eat.

◊ ◊ ◊

The shower had barely turned off when Tai'dqei's gauntlet notified him of an incoming message. He groaned as he groped for a towel, wicking away the moisture as he trod over to where he'd abandoned the tech earlier.

The communique was from Ah'ke. A coded warning that the rumor mill was churning, not just about Rayelle but about Zav's interest in her. The Florizian was also aware of Tai'dqei's involvement. Tai'dqei barely contained a hissing growl read over the message again and considered what to do.

He had hoped to stay in port another day or so, but it seemed a hasty retreat was necessary. Though powerful, Zav posed no threat to Ah'ke. Tai'dqei's main concern was keeping Rayelle safe. Considering her penchant for running, perhaps confining her to the ship via space travel would be a good option.

Or it would be the end of him, part of him mused, recalling the tension between them in the corridor.

Another sound rang out, this time through the ship's communication system. With a sigh, Tai'dqei rushed to dry and get dressed before heading to the cockpit. Along the way, he passed Rayelle reading one of her antique books in the mess, an empty plate peppered with crumbs sat by her elbow. She glanced up as he passed.

During his time in the shower, she had plenty of time to consider the potentially problematic shift in her attitude toward him. The situation felt like a continual seesaw. Through it all, though Tai'dqei made missteps he'd been reasonable. It chafed at Rayelle to admit it.

Where she felt like her feelings were swinging like an erratic pendulum, never giving her a chance to get her feet under her, Tai'dqei seemed assured. Even when giving her orders that agitated her, there was a sense of stability from him that part of her found comforting.

And she hated it. Or maybe she hated admitting it to herself.

Or maybe she just hated everything at the moment and just wanted her old life back.

Rayelle sighed to herself and rubbed the bridge of her nose, her fractured thoughts dragging at her energy levels.

Crossing into the cockpit, Tai'dqei's footsteps moved purposely to the front. He jabbed at a button on the main console, accepting the call that was, expectedly, from the Florizian. "Do you have another job for me already, Zav?"

Rayelle dawdled by the entryway, staring into the cockpit. Or whatever it was called. Considering Tai'dqei didn't have a crew, she assumed a little of everything was handled in this particular room. Which meant navigation, communication, piloting, perhaps weapons, and likely the main computer system was housed here. With the number of buttons, levers, and knobs available she could believe it.

What she didn't expect was a sort of cramped passenger area behind the piloting seat. Two rows bisected by the walkway with four seats in each row. It reminded her of a plane, she thought, as she stepped forward and plunked down in the closest chair.

"Are you still claiming to have found nothing on that bounty ship that would have interested me, Tai'dqei?" That voice drew her attention to the front. A holo-screen flickered with the image of a green alien with writhing tendrils and completely dark eyes. It took her brain a beat to register they'd been talking about the bounty ship she'd been aboard. Another microsecond to consider, perhaps, their words might have something to do with her.

Tai'dqei – fully aware of Rayelle's presence – kept his response level and short. "Yes."

"And what of the human?" The screen suddenly flickered. In place of the Florizian, security footage rolled displaying Tai'dqei, Rayelle, and the mob of others from earlier.

Her gaze jumped to Tai'dqei, but she could only see his broad back, darkened in shadows. He didn't appear particularly tense, but his default posture always seemed stiff to her.

Her eyes slid back to the green alien as they returned, abruptly wondering if her chances with them would be better than Tai'dqei. Doubt lurched in her stomach at the thought so perhaps not.

"I didn't find her on the bounty ship," Tai'dqei lied, hoping Zav couldn't see Rayelle in the background and that she'd have enough sense to stay hidden. He leaned into the falsehood, weaving a tale he had manufactured at the back of his head throughout the day. "I bought her at a spaceside rock to keep me warm on cold nights. Maybe they sold her off before I got to them."

Rayelle's attention flickered back to Tai'dqei, her eyebrows furrowing at the lie. Why didn't he want this Zav to know the truth? Was he saving his own skin or was the green extraterrestrial a threat to her?

A slow smile spread over Zav's face, flashing an array of large pointy teeth. Their tone oozed with menace, answering Rayelle's threat-level concern. "Oh really? Shall we check your ship's travel records?"

"If you want to try, go ahead." Tai'dqei crossed his arms, leaning his hip against his pilot's chair. His voice dipped with an aggressive, clicking growl as his mandibles flared, showing off his inner jagged teeth. "I'm not going to let you."

Zav slammed his hands down on whatever surface he sat behind, his tendrils writhing with rage. His lips pulled back with a snarl, anger crimping his otherwise smooth complexion. "I know you are lying! She was part of your mission, you oaf!"

Alarm piqued in Rayelle, betrayal heating her face as she turned an angry look on Tai'dqei's back. He *had* been paid to kidnap her, on top of murdering those other aliens! Her stomach lurched at the very thought. This betrayal didn't answer why he hadn't turned her over to his employer though.

Tai'dqei narrowed his eyes on Zav, his mandibles flickering with agitation. There it was. Zav paid well, but often expected more than what he negotiated. It also settled the fact that he saw Rayelle as cargo, a thing, rather than a sentient being. Stifling his ire, Tai'dqei gave the Florizian a careless one-shouldered shrug. "Wasn't part of the terms we discussed."

All at once, Zav went still. Tai'dqei's survival instincts prickled. Despite his former employer's rather calm expression, the tendrils whipped angrily, seeking flesh and blood. The Florizian gave a deceivingly sweet purr, "Such a pity when a good professional gets themselves killed over a wet slit."

The image flickered out, leaving behind status reports and communiques on the holo-screen. Apprehension tightened in Tai'dqei's stomach.

He had hoped Zav would believe him or, at the very least, drop the subject. Write off the human as a loss and move on. Surely, there were other humans the Florizian could get hold of. Maybe even one willing to accept his pollen or whatever his kind did to reproduce.

But no. He wanted Rayelle.

Zav had plenty of resources at his disposal. Deep pockets and an army of lackeys, ranging from grunts to specialized assassins. That wasn't even mentioning other bounty hunters he could hire on to take care of Tai'dqei. There were a few that might even take up Zav's offer for free if it meant taking down a ja-tau.

Stilling the sudden dread, he had to take it one step at a time. Firstly, they had to get out of port. Which may or may not entail an interstellar dogfight. Not exactly the preferred way to fight for the ja-tau, who preferred something more hand-to-hand, but doable. It wasn't as if he had a choice in the matter.

"Take a seat and get buckled in," Tai'dqei commanded as he sent the appropriate requests to disembark to the port's authorities. Silently, he hoped Zav didn't have those on duty on his payroll as well. Breaking out of a docking station on a spaceport wasn't something he was keen to do.

If it meant keeping Rayelle safe, he would, but he wasn't excited at the prospect.

Rayelle thankfully listened to his instructions. He heard her scooting into a seat behind him, fidgeting around. However after more rustling about and a long stretch of quiet, she eventually asked, "How?"

He turned to face her, watching as she held up an array of safety belts in confusion. The metal and fabric of the belt was torn and bent beyond safety standards.

"Shit." Tai'dqei's stomach lurched. He'd forgotten a prior patron – one he had to ferry from one planet to another – had broken the passenger safety belts. All of them due to their long writhing body and fear of space travel. Tai'dqei meant to get them fixed after his latest assignment, since he'd have the money. He never planned to have another person aboard in the meantime.

Consequently, there was only one working belt system.

His.

Which wasn't necessarily a problem when he was able to pilot slowly and safely. He'd brought Rayelle to the station without a bruise while she was in the brig. With Zav on his ass, slow and steady wasn't an option.

With no time to argue – and she would certainly argue – Tai'dqei turned and swept Rayelle up in his arms.

She yelped and squirmed as he made his way back to his pilot chair, demanding to know what the hell he was doing. As he lowered himself down into his chair, he dropped Rayelle between his widespread legs, her back to his chest.

"I'm sorry, but this will keep you safe." As soon as he had positioned her, she struggled against him. He tried his best to be gentle, yet he could not yield to her. The safety strap buckled in the middle of his chest and across his lap but making adjustments for Rayelle added to the aggravation. Staying composed was harder said than done when Tai'dqei just wanted to get out of the port.

Rayelle's brain struggled to keep pace. There had been another alien speaking to Tai'dqei, demanding he hand her over. She had tried to stay out of view during the call, but it had aroused other questions in her head. Questions she should have asked Tai'dqei earlier now that she was thinking about it.

Finding herself hauled between Tai'dqei's thighs wasn't helping the sudden chaos in her head or her heart. "That still doesn't explain what you're doing!"

"The other safety belts were damaged from a previous client." Tai'dqei rushed to explain as he tried to buckle the belts into place, in spite of her fighting. He choked down his own guilt over the less-than-acceptable answer, knowing it would be of no help in the present situation. "I was going to get them fixed, but all of this happened and…"

A new message chimed into his bracer. Quickly, he scanned it and a miniscule amount of tension eased from his shoulders. They were given permission to disembark. As soon as he finished reading it, he heard the mechanisms keeping his ship in place unlock.

Unaware of the entire exchange with port authorities, Rayelle gaped up at Tai'dqei, incredulity and skepticism coloring her words. "Your lap is the only safe place for me to sit?"

"*I'm sorry,*" he rasped, refusing to look down into her accusatory expression.

For the first time since she met him, his tone fractured. She wasn't even sure how the earworm managed to translate such a thing, from his hissing and warbles. A mixture of frustration and desperation and guilt bled into his voice, making Rayelle freeze. A chill settled in her stomach, realizing he was worried.

Tai'dqei finished strapping the two of them in before turning to ship's controls. He was thankful she hadn't continued to press the matter. He could fully focus without fighting her squirming form.

The holo-screen in front of him flickered to life once more, this time displaying the varying viewpoints outside his ship as he maneuvered them from the port and into open space.

CHAPTER 10

Fighting her own dread and mortification, Rayelle remained quiet as Tai'dqei piloted. It wasn't like she had a choice. The ship was moving and she was already strapped into the only available safe seat. Which consequently had Tai'dqei as a backrest. She tried not to think about it, but prickles coasted over her skin until she resorted to watching the holo-screen to distract herself.

As they moved out of the station, the array of different directions on the holo-screen shifted. It made her stomach churn. A large variety of spaceships – probably with classifications like freight and cargo and passenger – slid before her. Most were docked, kept in place by metal arms. A few hovered in mid-air, either arriving at or departing from the station. Rayelle couldn't even begin to imagine what mechanisms and science kept them afloat.

Tai'dqei felt tense and awkward behind her. She glanced up at him, finding his focus entirely on the ship's controls. Taking advantage of his distraction, she let her eyes trail over his face. It was the closest she'd been to it since the first night.

The sandy yellows of his face faded to a darker burnt orangey-red at the outermost parts. Those outer parts, up along the ridged head with the horn-like protrusions, looked sharp and hard. Her attention drew down to his mandibles, folded against the sides of his maw. Memories of them unfolding, the skin between them stretching as he roared fluttered through her head. The appendages moved subtly as he focused on piloting and it struck her like he was mumbling to himself, though he made no sound.

She was a little unsettled to realize the sight of him didn't disgust her or make uncertainty roil through her. He'd become familiar and she wasn't sure if she liked that. Much like she didn't enjoy her other changing feelings.

Tai'dqei could feel her eyes on him, distracting a small part of his brain as he monitored their escape. Up until that point, he'd been going through the motions, running on autopilot as he eased the ship from the port. It was doubtful Zav would do anything in-port, especially in the docking area. Too many combustible things. Too many bystanders. Say what he could about Zav, the Florizian at least kept things clean if savage.

Once they were out in open space, a few clicks away from the space station, Tai'dqei caught masked movement on his screens.

"Brace yourself." His sudden words jolted Rayelle from her quiet observation. Her eyes swung back to the holo-screen and her stomach lurched. Various directions of space displayed on the screen, split and moving in different directions. It took her a breath to realize they were all different angles from around the ship.

Tai'dqei hissed, suddenly jerking the steering. Rayelle squeaked, her stomach dropping as the whole ship tilted and lurched to the side. A booming sound thundered to her right and she could only imagine what sort of weapon it had been. Or if maybe another spaceship had tried ramming into them.

To make her motion sickness even worse, they continued moving erratically and in directions she was not accustomed to. Her brain couldn't even make sense of which direction they were moving in. Her stomach swayed, feeling like she was on a roller coaster that never ended.

They were already being followed by Zav's cronies, if Tai'dqei's curses and insulting snarls were correct. She wasn't sure how he could tell. There only seemed to be empty expanses of darkness, perhaps peppered with the odd asteroid or bystander ship going in the opposite direction.

Finally, she realized there was a radar, blipping quietly on the console itself. Presuming the middle was their ship, there were three other dots following behind them in an upside-down 'v' formation. When she looked back on the screen, trying to determine where they showed up, a chill soaked through her.

Whatever their ships were made of, whether mirrored material or perhaps some semi-cloaking panels, they melded with the darkness of space. It was only when Tai'dqei made the ship tilt a certain way – when a certain hit of light or strange shadow glittered on screen — Rayelle could partially spot the ships. Between mounting horror and the rocking of the world around her, she had to wrench her eyes shut.

She sat stiffly between his legs, enveloped by his limbs and feeling the subtle shift of muscles as he controlled the ship. Occasionally, he'd jerk suddenly, yanking levers or struggling to make the steering take a sharper maneuver.

Her lungs tightened around what little breaths she took, feeding off the tension he radiated. Around her, metal shuddered and creaked — occasionally something would ping off the hull — and her body would be tossed roughly. She felt like a bouncy ball, rollicking between the straps and Tai'dqei's solid form.

As if feeling his flexing muscles wasn't embarrassing enough, the rumble of his growls added a vibrato against her back. Rayelle swallowed, half-wondering if the heat consuming her was thanks to her own mortification or Tai'dqei's body. And if the sensations were heightened thanks to the adrenaline suffusing the situation.

It didn't escape her that Tai'dqei's snarls of frustration slowly became goading, delightful rumbles as he got better vantages and control of the field. She risked cracking her eyes open, finding other ships on the screen falling back or exploding from a disastrous run-in with a floating asteroid. "Yeah, that's right, scum suckers. Your little shit ships can't maneuver through this."

Needing a distraction, something else to fill her head other than observations that made her ignorance of the world around her even more apparent, Rayelle slid back into something comfortable.

With accusation thick on her tongue, she scoffed, "You seem like you're enjoying this."

She didn't even consider how ill-thought distracting him could end. The air was prickling with an unlabeled feeling and she couldn't help but let her mouth run off with her.

"The rush of victory over opponents can be intoxicating," he returned, easily splitting his attention between the woman in his lap and the remaining ship. The other two had been easy to lose, with one slamming into an asteroid and the other falling back only to be taken out by one of Tai'dqei's rear-weapons. He had the suspicion that Zav had sent less-experienced members as a means of testing his skills. Or maybe to cull his own ranks before sending in the ringers.

"Oh, yeah, *victory.*" Rayelle gave a sarcastic laugh, pressing back against him. Part of her had been aware of his growing erection against her back while another part struggled to avoid the realization. Now that it had been addressed, it was impossible to ignore the heat of his excitement against her lower back.

Her movement derailed Tai'dqei's thoughts concerning Zav. He grunted in return to her words, a roiling burn shooting through him. He subtly shifted to gain whatever tiny amount of distance he could, lest his hips returned her taunt.

A chime cut through the scalding air between them and Tai'dqei gave an abrupt curse. His focus snapped back to his controls and the ship lurched. Rayelle tensed, her hands braced against his thighs, fingernails digging into his skin. He jerked a control stick and flipped switches, but she had no clue what any of it would do.

On the split holo-screen before them, the pursuing ship kept pace as Tai'dqei navigated wildly around asteroids and through clouds of space dust. While the enemy ship was in one of those clouds, Tai'dqei's palm slammed on a button. Rayelle's eyes widened, watching a laser blast toward the ship.

A burst of something akin to electricity crawled over its exterior, then the enemy ship's power flickered before it fell dead dark in space. Effectively incapacitating the ship, the ja-tau gave a series of triumphant deep-chested croaking clicks.

His sounds quavered along her spine, forcing her thighs to clench tight as a whimper caught in her throat. Tingles spread out along her back, hot and like claws on her skin. Something in Tai'dqei seemed to go still at her reaction. Like he was suddenly careful about everything he did, including breathing.

It would be more accurate to say Tai'dqei was trying to not inhale too deeply. Her scent was beginning to change. Turning heady and tart, demanding his attention. Coupled with the whimper she had made, desire rolled at his core.

They both were very aware of every place they touched. Her hands on his thighs, her fingers finding their way between the netting to dig her nails directly into fleshy muscle. His chest to her back, the additional heat of his arousal pressed against her rear and lower back. The back of her head pressed to his chest, hearing the thump of his heart close to her ear. How her body shifted and moved against him with every little breath.

"A-are we safe now?" Rayelle wanted to bite her own tongue off for stuttering, but she had more pressing matters than punishing herself. "Can I move?"

It took Tai'dqei a moment to respond. He had to connect thoughts through the warm carnality inflaming his brain while also maintaining control of the ship and staying alert for other enemies. As enticing as it was to have her in this position, sense knew it was wrong to keep her there without good reason. But they were being pursued. Even if he had managed to shake them off for now.

"You should stay put," he finally said, after determining he wasn't caving into his own temptation.

She responded quickly with a tone that was equal parts frustrated and curious, "Why?"

"If you're not strapped down, you could get badly injured." He didn't like the idea of her trying to scramble back to him or ride out a fight elsewhere on the ship. She'd be flung around without proper safety. No matter how it annoyed her, he wasn't willing to put her in danger for her comfort.

"Uh-huh." She pursed her lips, knowing he was right. But this particular situation was absurd. Being stuck in between his legs because there were no other working safety belts? She made her own assessment known, scoffing a little as she shifted against him. "Has nothing to do with the fact my ass is warming your cock, huh?"

Her movement sent another strike of warm lightning through his body.

"*Careful*," he warned, his growl cautionary and playful. The fiery satisfaction of triumphing over three opponents, mid-space, hadn't dispersed. Confidence thrummed through him, making it hard to stay somber with Rayelle. Especially when the burn of her eyes still lingered on his skin.

She craned her neck, looking up at him. He didn't shift his gaze to her, but her lips curled into a wry smile as she challenged him, "Or what? Shove me out an airlock after going through all this trouble to help me?"

It was meant as a joke. An acknowledgment that he had, indeed, done a lot. To the point she didn't believe he'd let it go to waste.

All those words accomplished was dragging his gaze to her face. He appeared to glare down at her, probably not finding her joke funny. A small bead of worry bled through her thoughts. Maybe she had just given him an idea he hadn't considered. Tai'dqei probably would rather shove her out an airlock, be done with her, than running around the universe trying to help her.

Tai'dqei was struggling against a different sort of temptation, though. Her scent had sunk its claws into him, making lust scrape along his nerves. Deciding Rayelle would react best to a straightforward answer, he growled out, "I might use you as an actual cock warmer."

Hot sparking sensations slammed through Rayelle. Her fingers inadvertently tightened on his thighs. For a second, she found it difficult to breathe, struggling to not imagine the scenario while fighting against a growing curiosity about what it'd be like. "You wouldn't."

"I might," he answered, feeling bold when she didn't outright reject him. Her breathless words sounded more like she was arguing than telling him no. Given a chance, he certainly would use her as a cock warmer if she allowed it. The mental image of it made his hands tighten on the controls. "The scent of your own arousal is testing me."

Rayelle gaped up at him, her eyes wide and round and her face bleeding into a darker pink tinge. "I'm *not* aroused!"

"Aren't you?" He couldn't help himself. Her little squawk of embarrassment had cracked his resolve to be good. Besides, he was curious to confirm what it had been that had sparked the hormonal flame in her. Once more, clicks vibrated through his chest. Curious, testing, taunting.

Prickles exploded down Rayelle's spine, and she shivered. Heat spiked inside her lower stomach and, once more, her thighs clenched tight. She squirmed in her spot, breathing hitched. "Stop that!"

He gave a chuffing sort of chuckle, but at her demand he turned his attention back to the screens and controls. It took steely concentration to draw his focus away from her.

Rayelle's face burned with embarrassment and confusion. She didn't want to think about how her body reacted to him. It was one thing when she thought he was going to take her against her will. A body can react in protective ways not consistent with conscious wants. But he wasn't threatening her now.

Further, he'd noticed her reaction to his vocalizations. A dual realization smacked her across the face. She had been obvious enough to be caught, but he'd been paying enough attention during a space fight to notice. Rayelle slammed a mental shutter down against a wave of curious heat and flutters.

Absolutely fucking not.

He had tried to force himself on her that first night. He did apologize and explain his error, though, and took culpability for his actions. *But he had collared her! Restrained her freedom!* But when she ran, he found her and fought off a swarm of others. Tai'dqei wasn't even angry with her afterward. Just exasperated.

Something in her stomach flipped, realizing this line of thought was not helping. Rayelle turned her focus on another issue that struck her. The one she should have thought of earlier.

She stared at the holo-screen before her, eyebrows furrowed as only space and stars and far off planets peppered the screen. "So those ships were after me?"

Tai'dqei, though already silent, went still. He had forced himself to pilot the ship, to not think of her. Now a new slew of thoughts flooded his brain. Connected to Rayelle, but not quite drenched in the same hormones as earlier.

The way his body froze wasn't lost on Rayelle. It was strange that she was starting to understand his body language. Well, perhaps strange wasn't the right word. That sort of intimacy was learned from time spent together and it was an unwelcome element, everything considered.

"Do you know why all those aliens are after me?" She pushed, her tone even and intent. Surprising herself, she didn't even sound stressed, just exasperated and resigned. "I didn't ask earlier, because… well, emotions were weird. But do you?"

Aware of how awkward his earlier teasing and mild flirtation were going to look now, Tai'dqei braced himself. "I was hoping not to tell you why, in case you returned to your time."

There was another reason for his omission of information, other than anachronistic fears. More selfishly, he didn't want Rayelle to see him like the others. Like those who kept her captive and chased her for their own wants and desires.

Rayelle made a face at his words, clearly annoyed with the prospect of being kept ignorant. She craned her neck, glaring up at Tai'dqei.

Feeling her irritated gaze on him, his shoulders slumped in concession. "Humans have double helixes in their DNA, right?"

"Yes." She had no clue what this had to do with non-human species chasing her down, but she decided to humor Tai'dqei. It wasn't like she was particularly studied in biology or genetics beyond a high school level.

"Many alien species have three helices, which means humans are…" He groped for a word that wouldn't set here off. "*Compatible* with far more species than average."

His tact was only met with a disgusted snort from her. Of course that's what it boiled down to, she thought bitterly. Sex and breedability. "More sex-crazed assholes, but this time with a breeding fetish. Got it."

"There's many races who have a hard time procreating or who have been hit with tragedies that decimated their populations," Tai'dqei replied, his words a little chiding. There we're many reasons beyond 'sex crazed' for non-humans to seek out humans. Some reasons were understandable, in theory, though acted on in dishonorable ways. "Humans, by comparison, do not have a hard time reproducing and, due to lacking one DNA strand, the children often are more non-human than human."

The resonance of sympathy that echoed through Tai'dqei's words struck Rayelle as curious. It was as if he understood the plight. She gave a contemplative hum, her thoughts turning toward ja-tau and what little she knew or surmised from her interactions with Tai'dqei and Ah'ke. Admittedly, it wasn't a lot.

Catching her hum, he tilted his head toward her. "What?"

After a furtive glance up at him from the corner of her eye, Rayelle decided to satisfy a sudden curiosity. "Do ja-tau have a hard time having children?"

The question caught him off-guard, making his hands slip on the controls and causing the ship to shudder. Hurriedly, he grabbed the controls again, regaining control. "We're getting off-topic."

"Right, right." She didn't notice his flub as she considered her situation. "Whatever Zav is, do they have a hard time having children?"

"Yes. Florizians have suffered recent genetic illnesses and their populations have suffered. But it is not just Zav who is after you." Relieved, Tai'dqei leaned into being informative. Talking about others would keep him from talking about – and thinking about – mating with her. "There are races that have suffered like the Florizians and those that just generally have a hard time reproducing. Not to mention those who simply prefer humans as sexual partners for one reason or another."

The last category tended to be quite a lot. For whatever reason, humans seemed highly adaptable in many fields, including the reproductive acceptance of non-human anatomy and genes. he doubted she would ask for further details.

"Oh." Her attention flickered to the screen again, mulling over what he'd told her as she watched little pinpricks of light and swirling far-off galaxies pass by.

That would explain the multitude of aliens that had chased her. If Zav had been their boss, it was more likely he would have known about her sooner. So what had Butterfly's intentions been? Sell her to the highest bidder? Would she have become a babymaker for some hapless species? There were probably other reasons Tai'dqei wasn't revealing. An involuntary shudder coasted down her spine at the thought.

Her soft response and the way a tremble shot down her back vindicated Tai'dqei. Unable to keep the nettling tone from his voice, he asked, "See why I wanted you to stay on the ship now?"

His tone only sufficed in reigniting her agitation. She craned her neck again, glaring up at him. "If you explained this to me—"

"I said I was trying to keep you safe, didn't I?" Tai'dqei interrupted her with a flash of annoyance. It'd be nice if she could just admit he'd been trying to help. This whole ordeal had been a balancing act, figuring out what to tell her when considering her home time, her emotional stability, and more. After the chaos of the day, his patience was running on empty.

The aggravation was infectious. Rayelle mirrored his tone with her own ire, "Well, sorry if I had a hard time believing that, Mr. Gets-Turned-On-From-Violence."

"You really want to talk about arousal?" Tai'dqei's challenging question melted quickly into a clicking growl, resonating from his chest.

She gasped, sitting straighter though the action pushed her body harder against him. Each click was like a nail toying down her spine while the growl warbled through her lower stomach, sending heat along her limbs. Her fingers splayed out, feeling the warmth of his thigh under her palms, before curling again, dragging fingernails along the netting.

It was his smug chuff of a chuckle that piqued Rayelle's defiance. He was taunting her, knowing how he affected her. Knowing how he struggled against own instinct around her, she realized two could play that game.

CHAPTER 11

"Sure, let's talk about arousal," she hissed, arching her back and reaching into the space between herself and Tai'dqei with one hand. Her fingers homed in on his erection, grabbing at his girth through the fabric of the loincloth-like bottoms. The grunt he gave as her hand squeezed around him was gratifying to her ears. "Like how you've been sporting a huge boner since I sat down."

He had miscalculated terribly, he realized. In retrospect, he hadn't thought through his actions at all. Between his agitation and the growing heat in his lower stomach, he wanted to both silence her and hear those delicious little sounds.

And she had responded to his challenge. Tai'dqei only had himself to blame for his weakness.

He couldn't muster up any regret. Not with Rayelle's hand on his cock, kneading slowly along the underside with her thumb, exploring his length and ridges and lip of his cock's head.

"What about my dick do you want to discuss?" Tai'dqei shot back, an amused gnarl in his voice. With something new to hold his attention, he absentmindedly put the ship on autopilot and initiated cloaking. Considering how long ago the last enemy had accosted them, he doubted another assault would come soon. Zav's forces needed time to regroup and strategize, since the ja-tau was not going to easily hand over Rayelle.

Her hand paused, her flushed cheeks darkening as a frown twisted at her lips. "That's not what I said."

"It was more or less what you said, isn't it?" Tai'dqei's hands drifted from the controls to Rayelle's knees. Her free hand, still lingering at his thigh, gripped at his netting as his palms skirted up her legs. That sweet burn of excitement sunk into his hands and through his lungs. It skittered down the length of his body. Wordlessly, she tilted her knees wider the higher up his touch travelled and delight swelled in his chest.

"If we're talking about arousal that means my dick getting hard and your pussy getting wet," he said, his hips rolling gently against her hand. Instinctively, she squeezed as he did so. His cock flexed against her fingers. A small, delicious sound left her as his claws skimmed over where her thighs met her torso. His voice dipped lower, gravellier, as his finger grazed over the fabric covering her slit. Pleasure rumbled through him as he found her already moist and heated.

Once more, Rayelle felt like she couldn't breathe. The air around them both flickered with excited warmth and that made the sharp edge of fear tilt into her thoughts. "S-shouldn't you focus on piloting the ship?"

"We're on auto and cloaked." Tai'dqei hadn't caught the uncertainty sifting into her voice. His hips rolled against her hand again, the friction stoking the heat in his core. Absently, her hand moved again, fingers curling tight around the fabric of his bottoms and his girth. She pumped slowly, experimentally, up and down his length.

Tingles coursed up her arm. She didn't want this, but she didn't *not* want it either. It was annoying and bewildering as the burning hot sensations knifed through her. Her stomach spun with both excitement and disgust.

Tai'dqei couldn't have been more unaware. Her scent layered over him, lighting his brain aflame. He wanted to coax every little drop of pleasure from her until she was a quivering mess and begging for him.

One of his hands drifted further upward, stroking over the curves of her hip. His palm dallied along the softness of her stomach and breasts through the silky sweater dress.

Even the curviest of ja-tau didn't have Rayelle's sort of delicate pliability. She gave little gasps, back arching under his caresses. Burning intensity flared through him, the desire to touch her, to actually feel her skin-to-skin, clawed through his thoughts.

The warmth of his hands made her brain swirl with conflicting thoughts and feelings. She wanted to give in, to melt to his touch, to feel something other than conflict and anger and sadness. That part of her had both her hands behind her now, one atop the other, squeezing around his impossibly hot member. Matching the rhythmic rolls of his hips as he sought the friction as well.

At the same time, she didn't want any of it. The urge to jerk away, to run, to hide and forget any of this swelled in her head. It filled in the empty spaces between her hormonal haze with cold apprehension.

As Tai'dqei began undoing the safety harness, Rayelle's heart jerked. Mustering up as much petulance as she could, masking the turmoil within, she reminded him, "I thought I had to stay buckled for my safety."

"It's safe enough right now." As he unclasped the last fastener, the belts reeled back into the seat with a wild zipping hiss. A lump formed in her throat, her breaths becoming short and hitched.

Inadvertently, her grasp tightened on his cock. The thick rod flexed at the sudden pressure, making his hips jerk hard as he gave a low groan. He curled over her, excited breaths making his chest rise and fall and making her shift with his breathing.

One hand had fallen to her breast, his thumb toying with her hard nipple and his fingers squishing her tit through the fabric of her dress. An appreciative clicking left Tai'dqei as he continued to knead her, first one breast then the other. A keening left Rayelle, her back arching as she writhed under vibrations and his groping hand.

His other hand hiked her dress's hem over her hips, his clawed fingers sliding easily under the waistband of her leggings. Without much actual thought, her feet came up onto the seat and bracketed his legs, her toes nudging under the crook of his knees to help keep her stabilized.

Rayelle's breath caught in her throat, her attention tilting to his hand. That cold apprehension clawed into place against the sensual heat licking over her body.

Constant worries and concerns had tired her, making her resolve buckle. If Tai'dqei wanted to touch her, wanted gratification, fine. Let him have it. Maybe once it was over, the conflicting awkward heat would finally bleed entirely away.

The smallest movements, the tiniest sounds, the littlest movements from Rayelle sent heat and pressure pounding through Tai'dqei's body. The end in sight of a drawn-out, repeatedly triggered mating instinct coating his thoughts.

There was a brief, almost frantic, moment where he abandoned all his caresses. Lifting her up to reach under her, releasing the clasps on his protective gear to pull the belted fabric free. Released from its confines his dick stood tall, demanding attention while Tai'dqei adjusted how Rayelle sat on him.

When he set her back down, he sat her higher on his lap, her feet braced on his thighs and his cock nestled between her splayed legs.

Rayelle stared down at his member, pushed up between her thighs. The head was spear-shaped and the shaft ridged from what she could see. It looked so big, the heat so close, it made her insides pulse.

Her knees clamped tight and her thighs pressed around his hot hardness. A sudden hiss left Tai'dqei as her soft body melded around his cock and Rayelle shivered as the sound tickled the back of her neck.

He forced her knees apart again, the show of strength making searing pleasure shoot down Rayelle's spine. With a deft move, he yanked her leggings down and bared her to open air.

"I thought you wanted to talk," she gasped, her brain barely functioning enough to piece together the teasing sentence. Under the taunt, however, there was a small edge of apprehension. A small hope he'd hear it, but maybe that was her own imagination. Maybe she was hearing things that weren't there.

Despite the unsettled feelings, a small part of her was also excited and eager.

"You want to hear me talk about your cunt?" The scent of her arousal dizzied his senses, the sight of her slickened folds teased his anticipation. An excited snarl sounded through his chest as his hips bucked. He wanted to land his cock in that soft wet paradise but refused himself for now. "Want to hear how I can't wait to bury myself in you?"

Between the words and growl sluicing through Tai'dqei's chest, hot prickles of ecstasy jolted down her spine. A tremble worked its way down her body, her abdomen clenching hard. She barely had a chance to understand what was happening when his hand landed on her exposed pussy.

"How I want to feel your soft heat pulse around my cock?"

Careful with his claws, Tai'dqei's fore- and ring-finger parted her entry wide, the digits sinking into her soft flesh there. His thumb stroked at her swollen clit, making further tremors jolt through her as his middle finger carefully delved inside her. Electric heat pierced through her, her back arching and her hands grabbing at his arms.

She was surprised at how dexterous his fingers were and how thick just one felt inside her. Not to mention how well he angled his nails. The occasional graze of a sharp pinprick inside her sent searing delight through her, making her core clench excitedly.

"Feel you squeeze and writhe as I drill into you?"

Tai'dqei's other hand curled around her the front of her throat, not hard enough to choke but enough to keep her in place as his finger slowly slid deeper and deeper into her. The gesture simultaneously sent a hot-cold shot of pleasure and uncertainty through Rayelle. Only her heavy swallow showed he didn't constrain her at all, merely held her in place. Chasing the pleasure, her body rocked against his lower hand as her sounds became louder and obscenely breathier.

"Making you come, over and over, until you're pleading for my seed?"

His cock still stood fully erect between her thighs, flexing and bobbling and oozing with precum. Prompted by carnal whims, Rayelle reached down to stroke it. An almost purring delight reverberated from Tai'dqei, his member flexing to her touch. She couldn't keep a steady pace with her hand as he worked his finger in and out of her, sending fire through her veins. Her inner walls clenched desperately around him.

"Or should I talk about how I'm going to fill you up, cock and cum, until you can't take any more?"

She wasn't sure if it was his words, the image he painted, the way his hands moved on her, or just everything. The pressure spiked inside her, heat clawing at her bones. A sobbing cry escaped her as her body jerked hard, a wave of hot pleasure and a chilly pain crashed over her. Her hands found the wrist of the hand at her throat, her fingers curling tight around it and nails biting into his skin as she spasmed.

The way her body tensed and trembled sent a spark through Tai'dqei. Heat sliced down his body, making his cock jump against the plush softness of her thighs. His hips bucked, following the tempo of her thrashing as she came around his finger. His thumb pressed tight against her clit, rocking his thumbpad back and forth over the bundle of nerves.

When Rayelle finally fell slack in his arms, Tai'dqei gave her a moment to recuperate before they continued. Her chest heaved with heavy breaths and her body wracked with the occasional tremble. It was nothing out of the ordinary for a well-fucked partner.

Until he saw her tears hadn't stemmed. Pleasuring someone until the overwhelming delight brought tears to their eyes wasn't abnormal, in his experience. Once the climax ebbed so did the tears. Even her throat continued to flex under his palm as if fighting back louder sobs.

Slowly, he released her throat and he eased his finger from her still fluttering folds. His question was soft and careful, hesitant to hear the answer, "Are you okay?"

"I'm fine," she whimpered, her forced words just as shaky as her trembling body.

Suspicious of her tone, Tai'dqei pressed further with a softer voice, "Are you sure?"

There was a breath of silence. She debated how to answer him, but her brain was a flurry of aggravating thoughts and perplexities. Swallowing a lump in her throat, she simply asked, "Can I pull my leggings on now?"

Her dismal tone was the worst sort of knife to Tai'dqei's gut. After he gave an absent nod and she slid from his lap to pull up her leggings.

He quickly adjusted his own coverings, reorienting them as he was unable to look at her. Heavy dread and guilt hardened in his stomach.

It took him a moment to pull together the words, but Tai'dqei soon asked without looking at Rayelle, "Did I misunderstand again?"

The quiet that followed was another knife to his gut.

"No… maybe. I didn't exactly say yes or no, but I enjoyed it. I just… I also didn't enjoy it." The more Rayelle explained, the more the tears swelled in her eyes. She pressed her face into her hands as she started to cry. "I'm sorry. I'm not sure I even understand myself right now."

Tai'dqei fell quiet once more, watching how Rayelle's shoulders scrunched up toward her ears. His gaze fell to his hands in his lap. Flexing his hands, he felt that was all he could really do without making the situation worse. He felt frozen to his chair, unable to move lest he upset her further.

His thoughts took form before he could adjust his words, "What am I supposed to do?"

Had he really asked that? It took Rayelle a moment to parse his words. It sounded too much like sexual partners of the past. Those who were upset she didn't want to continue. Those who blamed her 'teasing' nature for their own erections and demanded gratification.

It wasn't even like she didn't want to make Tai'dqei come either! She did… but, well… she also didn't. Thinking about it made her head throb. She reverted to the path of least resistance.

When she lowered her hands and turned her eyes to him, his own gaze flickered to her face. His stomach fell further at her expression. Resignation, disappointment, sadness. It all crumpled her features as she said, "I guess I could finish you with my mouth or something. If you really—"

"That's not what I meant," he sharply interrupted her, offended she'd think that's what he meant. He risked shifting in the chair, sitting straighter and leaning toward her. "What should I do to help you?"

"I—" Rayelle was so close to saying she didn't know what he could do to help her. What could anyone do? Her reaction was a broken one. Both enjoying and not enjoying what had happened. Being conflicted about something she had, essentially, guided.

Her feelings were valid, she told herself. Even if they didn't make sense to her. She didn't exactly blame Tai'dqei either. She was too tired to continue her mental therapy session and ached for creature comforts she recognized.

"Do you have, like, a couch? Somewhere comfortable to sit." Rayelle surprised herself when she answered him. In the chaos of her current life, she had forgotten these familiarities even existed. She turned her eyes to him, feeling a little more comfortable even though she still sounded tired and almost expecting denial, "And a way to watch shows or something?"

Happy for the guidance, Tai'dqei motioned for Rayelle to give him space as he stood. Given directives, he was a ja-tau on a mission now. Instead of focusing on his own roiling inner turmoil, he headed toward the door and motioned for Rayelle. "Follow me."

She was hesitant, given everything that had happened, but it was short-lived as she fell in step behind him. It would be worth a shot if he could provide some semblance of a movie night.

He led her back to the mess, pausing to indicate a broad space of emptiness. She hadn't paid it much mind, in all honesty. Now Tai'dqei motioned to the ceiling, where a rectangle could be seen.

"Usually, I have a screen on display that slides down from the ceiling and comfortable seating arranged here," he explained, hoping to cut off any later suspicions when he told Rayelle her actual options. "My prior passenger not only damaged my safety belts but also did irreparable damage to a settee and some more comfortable chairs here."

"Oh," she mumbled, frowning a little at the inconvenience. All she really wanted was to curl up on a couch, put on some mind-numbing television, and bask in some characters' asinine drama instead of her own.

"You're free to bring out blankets and pillows to watch here but there is one other option." He didn't like the thought of her laying on the floor, especially if they got blindsided by an enemy. For now, while in the clear and with her obviously upset, Tai'dqei had to force himself to allow it as an option.

Without looking at her, mentally preparing for her distrust again, Tai'dqei strode away. He moved down the hall, back toward his quarters.

Rayelle's stomach dropped at that realization. Her other option was in his room. Residual heat from their recent escapade clawed across her cheeks. She dawdled by the open door, not looking into his quarters as she struggled with her own inner debate.

Maybe she should just choose the floor in the mess. Rayelle

pressed her lips together, not really pleased with that idea. Really, watching television in a bedroom sounded cozier and welcome than the hard floor.

Finally, she peeked into his room.

Inside was muggy and humid with walls in varying shades of desert rock coloration. A circle in the ceiling blared down warm yellow light over a bed, which was nothing more than an upraised dais covered in what appeared to be pelts. Plants flanked around the bed, some with broad flat leaves and some with spiky looking foliage that came in varying shades of all hues.

Taking a tentative step inside, Rayelle turned to Tai'dqei who stood in a space opposite the bed. It appeared to be a modest sitting area with a couch facing a screen embedded into the wall. As much as she hated to admit it, this area was what she had in mind. As he busied himself with a console panel on the wall, she sat down on the couch.

Firm yet comfortable, her body was already relaxing into the cushions. She drew her legs up onto the couch, folding them beneath her.

"I know my room isn't preferable," Tai'dqei started, not looking at her as he input commands into the panel. Rayelle noticed how tense his shoulders appeared.

Finally, he looked up and the room shifted. With wide eyes, she watched as the warm red-orange-yellows faded to purple-blue-pinks, the light dimming to something more akin to dusk. "But it *is* my room, so there are luxuries that other rooms on the ship don't have."

Rayelle pursed her lips, looking around in an exaggerated fashion. Luxuries was right, if the whole room shifted to fit one's preferences. She couldn't even begin to imagine how it worked or what other indulgences he had, but it was definitely better than the floor. With a glance to Tai'dqei, she shot him an awkward smile. "I don't suppose you have access to 20th and 21st century Earth movies?"

"I have an excessive catalog of content available," he answered, with a one-shouldered shrug. Though he looked toward her, she got the feeling he wasn't looking at her. "You should be able to access it via your wrist gauntlet. May I show you?"

She narrowed her eyes, realizing he was being careful. While it was appreciated, she couldn't deny a little bit of amusement at the prospect. He was a roughly eight-foot tall, muscular, capable killing machine that was wary of upsetting her.

Perhaps Ah'ke had threatened him if he messed up again. She struck Rayelle as someone capable of holding their own friend accountable.

With a nod, she held her gauntleted wrist up as he stepped closer. Tai'dqei knelt down at her knee. He showed her how to pull up the holo-screen that would give her access to programs. It reminded her of a desktop with icons except available in watch and with a screen that flickered to life in mid-air.

"I asked for 21st Century Human English, but translations may still be clunky." Tai'dqei motioned to the languages on the screen.

"Understood," she replied, giving a little snort as his claw hit an icon that read VidSight. She wasn't sure if that was the company or a mistranslation, but it bore too much of a similarity to the term 'television' for her to ignore the latter possibility.

He taught her how to access the human section of his entertainment database before further showing her how to search for particular eras. It was fairly straightforward, much to her relief.

Considering everything he had already told her, Tai'dqei had given up on sheltering her from information anachronistic with her time. It was easier that way. He wanted to give her the space she required, so anything that allowed him to retreat sooner was a better tactic.

After narrowing down of terms, Rayelle eventually found titles she began recognizing. She scrolled for a while, trying to decide what she felt in the mood for. Tai'dqei remained silent, still kneeling on the floor beside her. It was difficult to choose a movie with him right there, but she eventually settled on Pride and Prejudice.

It was nice to see Jane Austen's works had survived the test of time, to be saved into a depository of human entertainment that was available to aliens. Perhaps there were even new renditions she could enjoy.

Once she made her choice by tapping on the option, the misty green field opening flickered to life on the screen. The room around her shifted, meeting the same shades at the viewscreen. Twittering of birds and soft windchime-like notes filled the air around her. It was impressive immersion, she had to admit.

With Rayelle settled, Tai'dqei decided it was time to go. He still had to process what had happened and, to do that, his own distance was needed. He pitched his voice soft, though it still cut gruffly over the dialogue of the movie, "I'll leave you to this. If you need anything, let me know."

Her eyes followed him as he stood, making his skin itch.

She debated quickly to herself, before she said, "I wouldn't mind you staying."

That surprised him. Tai'dqei paused and squinted at the screen. He watched as a slim brunette woman passed through the scenes, walking around an apparent home. More humans were running about. One played something he recognized as a piano. An older couple spied through a window.

It appeared to be ancient Earth, if his middling knowledge of human history was accurate.

He looked back at Rayelle, trying to confirm whether he was truly welcome or not. Sometimes humans made offers they didn't really want to make. Her eyes shifted from the screen to his face, offering him a small uncertain smile.

Once more, she was of two minds about Tai'dqei. Conflicted over what happened, she didn't mind his presence. She didn't want to be alone with her thoughts, but she wouldn't put up a fight if he wanted to be alone too. Or just away from her. She wouldn't fault him for that either.

Quietly, to Rayelle's stifled delight, Tai'dqei lowered himself onto the couch. He sat a comfortable distance from her, but not on the completely opposite side. He couldn't force himself to move any further away.

Tai'dqei sat stiffly, silently watching the movie with Rayelle. It had to be a time before her own, he decided. Though his eyes narrowed when he finally parsed human courting rituals played into the story. He tried to avoid her gaze when he realized it. Too many questions and thoughts churned through his head.

Thankfully, Rayelle fell asleep midway through the movie. She had curled up against the arm of the couch, her arms pillowing her head. With slow care he got to his feet, doing his best not to disturb the sleeping human. After draping a blanket over her, he silently exited his quarters.

Over the duration of the vid, his mind had ambled. Partially paying attention to the movie while a greater portion of his processes gnawed on what had transpired with Rayelle.

His thoughts agonized over her earlier words. "*I didn't exactly say yes or no, but I enjoyed it. I just… I also didn't enjoy it.*"

It sent a rush of guilt and frustration through him. Was it human custom to act this way? Were human women not supposed to like sex and Rayelle struggled to accept pleasure? Or was it something else entirely?

Maybe he should have paid closer attention to her words. Tai'dqei narrowed his eyes, trying to understand. He played back her words, their movements, in his head.

"*S-shouldn't you focus on piloting the ship?*"

"*I thought I had to stay buckled for my safety.*"

"*I thought you wanted to talk.*"

In his lust-driven mind, he thought the words were just coy tactics. Something to further delay the climax, to put an edge to the swelling pleasure. Of course, it wasn't as if he needed that, but knowing Rayelle, she'd still make him suffer through it to test him.

Now he wasn't so sure.

Yet she said part of her wanted it while another part hadn't. His thoughts lit onto her abductors again. A deeper furrow carved between his eyebrow ridges. It wouldn't be unheard of to utilize aphrodisiacs or the like to get humans pliable to carnal desires. What if they had done something more than that? Something that had the potential to be permanent?

His mandibles joggled irately at the very thought, the tips clacking loudly together in anger.

With purpose, Tai'dqei strode back toward the main console in the cockpit. Gradients of agitation danced through his thoughts. Enraged at those who had kidnapped and stolen Rayelle. Infuriated that those others — Zav included — sought to steal Rayelle away. Mostly Tai'dqei was annoyed with himself for his missteps and inability to think straight around her.

His line of work was tenuous, always changing, always necessitating new angles. Getting all the information he could always worked in his favor, so he made a habit to upload any bounty's digital information when able. This last bounty was no exception.

Tai'dqei quietly cursed himself for not looking at the files sooner as he dropped into his pilot seat. It took him a few moments to set up the safety of a decoy virtual machine. A requirement unless he wanted his ship and all connected tech to get compromised.

Once he got the correct files loaded, it took him some time to scour the information. When the data registered, he continued to read with a growl vibrating in the depths of his throat the whole time.

CHAPTER 12

Three cycles passed before Rayelle had any meaningful conversation with Tai'dqei. Though they did exchange pleasantries they were empty. He did inform her they were heading to the nearest Temporal Authority Council office. However, due to the risk of being followed, Tai'dqei had chosen a roundabout route.

All said, the atmosphere on the ship was tense like waiting for long-anticipated news. Rayelle didn't have the nerve to break it.

Breaking the silence fell to Tai'dqei when he happened upon Rayelle after she'd eaten her mid-cycle meal in the mess. He took a seat across the table from her without announcement. As she tilted her eyes to him, he said softly, "I wish to speak to you about something."

Her stomach somersaulted under his words. She'd been waiting, of course, since she woke up in his quarters on the couch after the movie and scurried off to her bedroom. She'd even held onto the blanket he must have placed over her. It was a pelt, more than anything, but it had the faintest Tai'dqei scent on it.

Her gaze fell to the table, unable to meet his eyes as she thought of that stupid blanket. Every night had been spent with it since the movie. She picked at the smooth tabletop with a fingernail, pretending to scrape at a stain. "Does it have to do with what happened a few days ago?"

"It is connected, yes." he gave a partial nod, anxiety making the simple movement stiff.

That wording made her eyebrows raise with curiosity. Not a solid yes, but related to the events? Hesitantly, she looked up to Tai'dqei, catching his rigid posture. He leaned forward, shoulders hunched, and hands clasped together on the tabletop. Those unnerving pale-yellow eyes watched her dolefully. Everything about him gave off the impression of bad news about to be delivered.

When he spoke again, his voice was oddly gentle, though the gnarl in his tone was still there, "I don't want to upset you again so if you're still distressed, we can talk about this at a later time."

While still apprehensive about the subject, Rayelle found herself wanting to know what he had to say. Sidestepping the issue of her comfort, she asked, "What's this about?"

"Your abductors. The second ones..." Tai'dqei amended, his eyebrow ridges furrowing. His clarification made Rayelle's lips twist into an ironic smile. The fact he continued to acknowledge his technical status as her third abductor weirdly amused her. His next words, however, did not. "They kept you sedated, correct?"

"I think so," she responded, fighting a sudden wave of nausea. Brief snatches of her time with the other aliens flew through her brain. Little moments, barely coherent. Being fed or washed. Introductions to others that came and went. The memories were mottled with dark blank spots. "It's all muddled."

Tai'dqei nodded, his mandibles pulling tight to his maw. He already knew that and, even if he hadn't, it was in the medical records he found.

"I finally went through the files from the bounty's ship." Another rush of shame flooded Tai'dqei. He really should have looked at that information sooner, especially when Ah'ke had been around.

Masking blame, he busied himself by sending a translated copy of the records to Rayelle via their wrist gauntlets. "They had you medically altered which explains your sedation. I've consulted with Ah'ke, and she's explained some of the things they put you through. Her assessment is with the files I sent you."

Rayelle just stared at him for a breath, her eyes round and her features paling. When her wrist gauntlet pinged, her gaze slowly slid to it. A growing urge to retch climbed up her throat but she fought it down. She didn't move to open the communique. "What did they do to me?"

Another subject he wished Ah'ke was here for. She could explain this far better than him, but he tried. "As we've discussed, humans are compatible with other non-human races. Your aging reproductive system—"

"*Excuse me?*" Rayelle reeled back, as if struck by the words 'aging reproductive system.' A frown curved deep at her lips.

"Your reproductive system has been revitalized to the point of being like that of a human just beginning sexual maturity. Likely for anyone who wanted you for reproductive purposes." Tai'dqei held his hands up to pause any of Rayelle's inclinations to lash out as he rushed to clarify his wording. She relaxed, so he trudged forward to the point that concerned him the most. "The more prominent issues are your pheromones and hormones."

Rayelle leaned back in her chair as her lips twisted into an unamused grimace. "Let me guess. They supercharged them."

Tai'dqei nodded silently, the air around him cold and sober. "Your scent has been made extremely attractive to non-humans. Your own olfactory senses has been made more sensitive. All of this is affected by, or affects, your sexual drive."

Midway through his explanation, Rayelle groaned and pressed her face in her hands. Though she still listened. A flush had already started to crawl across her cheeks. This would explain most of the issues surrounding Tai'dqei and herself, she supposed. The conflicting push-pull she felt when interacting with him, especially as of late.

She had spent plenty of hours pondering his attraction to her. More than once, she had wondered if his instincts simply hinged strongly on her many attempts to escape him or if there was more to it.

She couldn't imagine he found her physically appealing, considering how different ja-tau and humans were. Sure, she was soft and squishy and warm but was that what ja-tau were attracted to?

That line of thought had led her to examine her own feelings concerning the alien. Did she find him attractive? That was harder for her to answer than she cared to admit.

He wasn't bad to look at. Just different. A swarm of memories descended on her at the thought.

The sensation of his body against hers, his touch, his warmth. The way he had slammed between her and her pursuers at the spaceport. The consistent attempts, successful or not, to be courteous of her feelings. Each recollection sent a not-unpleasant tingle through her body.

Luckily, Tai'dqei saved her from her own thoughts as he continued, "Knowing this, I will take greater care in our interactions. For the time being, it may be best to keep contact to a minimum."

Her eyes snapped to him, indescribably hating that idea. With his eyes cast down to the table, Tai'dqei missed the look she leveled at him. His posture was painfully straight, screaming awkwardness.

In recent days, Rayelle had avoided him, but it was only to get her head on straight. At least she knew, on some level, she could approach him if she wanted to. Albeit with a discussion about what had happened hanging over her head but still.

"I don't want that." Her words came out soft, like a hesitant confession muttered in a church.

It took all of Tai'dqei's self-restraint to refrain from looking at her, to not gauge her body language. Obviously, her alterations didn't help in this situation. Rayelle had been tampered with. Her mind, body, and feelings. Until they could know to what extent, any choice she made in terms of intimacy may later be regretted. He didn't want to make the situation any worse than it already was.

Ah'ke had warned him this might happen. Some humans bonded over intimacy. Some despised being told what to do. Still others would just cave to temptation. Overall, even if her feelings were genuine, had it not been for the medically boosted factors, she may have created an attachment unwillingly.

No, he doubted she felt anything for him, sexual or otherwise. That admission sent a frustrating ache through his chest, but he clamped down on the feeling and knocked it away. Even his own feelings on the matter weren't to be trusted.

"I won't force you to keep distant, but I might need to be more removed." He allowed himself to slump further against the table, arms crossed on the tabletop. This talk had sent an uncomfortable heat through him which the cool tabletop alleviated a little. He turned his gaze to her, voice steely with certainty. "For your sake."

Another cacophony of feelings slammed into Rayelle. She quietly stared back at Tai'dqei, suddenly aware of the great space the table settled between them.

Her hyped-up hormones explained her own hot-cold reactions to him. Wanting to touch him and wanting to be touched by him clashing with the ever-present swirl of discontent and resentment for everything. She wasn't entirely sure it covered all of it, but it certainly didn't help matters.

Rayelle couldn't forget the other player: Tai'dqei.

She wondered how different he was before her. Did he visit brothels on a regular basis? Or train and shower as much as he had since she showed up? Did he have similar problems around Ah'ke? Or other people he found sexually alluring? Rayelle couldn't answer those questions and couldn't ask them.

One worry blossomed in her head. Had it all been her fault? If she hadn't been altered, would he have shown any interest?

Beyond that, he'd done so much for her in a short amount of time. Even in spite of her less-than-delightful moments. After he let her use his own space for comfort, Rayelle had begun to believe he genuinely liked her beyond being something of sexual value.

Maybe he was only influenced by his instincts, reacting to her initial violence coupled with manipulative hormones. Which meant her response to him may just be chalked up to medical interference as well. A dangerous loop, just repeating itself with two unwilling players.

That wasn't fair to either of them.

In her lap, her hands balled into fists as a heaviness settled in her chest. "Maybe staying away from each other is a good idea."

Tai'dqei couldn't say it was the answer he wanted to hear from her. A small part of him had hoped she'd assuage his concerns and declare she wasn't so easily swayed by carnal chemicals. That was folly on his part. Of course, she'd choose the distance. It was the safest option and kept mistakes from happening. Like what happened in the cockpit.

"It will take a little less than a cycle to get to the temporal authority quadrant headquarters," Tai'dqei forced himself to say, pushing back from the table. His limbs felt heavy as he stood, as if his very body didn't want to move away from her. "Let me know if you need anything."

And that was it.

Casting her gaze into her lap where her hands had settled, Rayelle fought a new slew of emotions. Something heavy settled in her stomach. The room felt a little chillier than before. She listened to Tai'dqei move, to the chair being shoved back in place, and finally to his dwindling footfalls as he turned and left her behind.

CHAPTER 13

The remainder of the cycle was the absolute worst. Tai'dqei busied himself with maintenance. Most of the time was spent rummaging through the larger cargo hold for the old safety belt buckles he had stored there, then he replaced his pilot belt with the old one. That gave Rayelle a spot equipped with the newer safer belt, *not* in his lap, if they encountered enemies again.

Rayelle wondered when ja-tau slept and for how long they slept as she listened to his footfalls around the ship from her room. That thought brought other considerations to her mind, since she now knew his bedroom layout. She shook those thoughts away, returning to her book or watching a vid on her arm gauntlet. Staying in her room seemed the kindest course of action as Tai'dqei tromped about.

The two tried to forget the other existed in their small space of the universe.

Without incident, they arrived at TAC S7B. The S7B, Rayelle learned, meant Sector 7 of the universe. What *that* meant, she wasn't exactly sure. The B was also a mystery.

TAC S7B was a manufactured planet, teal green in color with silvery wisps of clouds when viewed from space. After a consultation at the main office – which was at the uppermost pole of the planet – Tai'dqei had to ferry Rayelle to a lower hemisphere.

For Rayelle's own understanding, she thought of the world in the same terms of continents, countries, and cities. Each continent had a headquarters that specialized in a particular planet, which was further segmented by eras – centuries, for humans – via massive countries, which were *further* divided into city-like areas. For Earth, the cities themselves were parsed into decades.

It wasn't just paperwork or files. It was *everything.* The layouts, the food, clothes. The style of the decade was reborn on the alien planet. Rayelle assumed, being the authority on time, this meant some of the employees of TAC actually traveled to their assigned periods. Whether to suss out crimes or, as the alien at the HQ explained, to examine the weight her own missing case had on the world.

Essentially, understanding how the day-to-day worked for the ancient Earth time of the 2020s made sense. Even if a bitter voice in Rayelle's head kept wondering why they couldn't just send her back. She still couldn't imagine her case having any bearing on anything or anyone. Well, other than her kids.

A dual sense of comfort and wariness etched into Rayelle's very bones as she walked through the 2020s Earth City. As accurate as the city was to her own time, it also felt like a farce. A movie set that, while it certainly had working restaurants and clothing stores and who-knew-what-else, had none of the feel of the 2020s.

"Are you doing alright?" Tai'dqei's sudden question drew Rayelle from her thoughts and observations of the city.

The two of them were sitting on a bench inside the city's "town hall." The facsimile town hall was basically an office where detectives and staff worked to deal with problems of the 2020s. Their bench sat outside the office of Detective Gorgiel, with enough space between them for a whole other person.

At least, according to what her earworm had translated, it was Detective Gorgiel. She wasn't sure if aliens used a term like 'detective' and she aggravatingly couldn't read the odd alien text on the walls and doors. However, as par for the course of replicas, they did have signs that rotated out different Earth languages on a screen.

"I'm fine," she answered without looking up at the ja-tau. Today, he'd chosen to wear his mask and heavier armor. It was useless for her to try to figure out his feelings through visual cues. After the scene she caused at the mall, and the following pursuit through space, she presumed he was just being prepared for anything by wearing it.

Which was true. Tai'dqei had considered the possibilities of Zav, or any other contender vying to possess Rayelle, attacking once they got to TAC S7B. Landing on one's destination tended to bring one's guards down. He didn't know what TAC security measures were like. Could they be overwhelmed with a contingent of attackers? Did they thoroughly check everyone who came on-planet?

He doubted they had necessary safety precautions and it paid to be careful.

As much as Tai'dqei had been operating on autopilot since landing, simply going through the motions while speaking with TAC officers, a part of his faculties kept an eye on Rayelle. Ever since they had agreed to keep their distance, things had grown heavy again.

Or maybe that was his interpretation. There was always an itch to touch her in his fingers. At random, memories of their moment in the cockpit would skitter across his thoughts like unwelcome flies flitting through his vision. Actively fighting against his wayward body and mind made him less than enjoyable company. Still, he wanted to make sure she was doing okay so he pressed further, "Are you certain?"

"Yes." She inclined her head to him, exasperation evident in her voice. Part of her wished he hadn't worn the mask today. Though she struggled with his facial tells and tics, she found herself wanting to see it.

That thought made her stomach lurch and she hurriedly looked away from him. Her eyes returned to the far wall, staring at the bulletin board on the other side. She wondered if it was simply a prop. Something to add to the immersion of this whole place. It was hard to imagine any actual important information still being in a hard format. Her own time had been transitioning away from papers, as well.

Tai'dqei fell silent, his mandibles writhing under his mask. His leg began to joggle, considering what he should do or say. When he stumbled on something, the question blurted out of him, "Is the city at all like your time?"

This time, Rayelle inhaled deeply at his question, her eyes closing. She had actually been avoiding that thought. When her eyes split open again, her head turned toward him. An angry and brittle smile carved at her lips. "On the surface, yes. Deeper down, it's missing the constant dread of pandemics and mass shootings and government corruption and police brutality that kind of coated my time."

Tai'dqei silently stared into her face, feeling he had again made a mistake. He didn't know what to say to her statements of her own time. In theory, he knew it was all terrible, but he hadn't experienced any of it himself. Anything he said would ring hollow and trite.

"It's fine. It doesn't matter now." The angry tension in Rayelle's shoulders eased with defeat. She sighed, her eyes tilting away from him again. That bitter smile made a reappearance as she muttered, "It's all in the past."

Another quiet fell between them. Tai'dqei felt as if the divide between them had grown even larger. Far off in other offices, he could hear others talking. His mask picked up several heat sources elsewhere in the building. All that ambient sound didn't seem to puncture the bubble around Rayelle and himself.

"Maybe we should get some food after this," he heard himself say, needing something to fill the silence. Though he added distractedly, "If they don't assign you to a handler."

Rayelle grunted an empty acknowledgement. A handler. She hadn't even considered she'd be trading in one alien for another. The thought just enhanced her desire to see Tai'dqei's face again, just in case they were indefinitely separated soon.

She was on the verge of saying "I don't want someone new," before she stopped herself. She and Tai'dqei had been avoiding each other up until this point. Wanting to stay with him couldn't be true and this whole ordeal was becoming too much for him. He should be able to wash his hands of her without guilt. It wasn't like he signed up for assisting a lost-in-space-and-time human nor all of her baggage, anyway.

Instead, Rayelle gave a one-shouldered shrug to Tai'dqei's suggestion. "Yeah, maybe we can."

Luckily, it was at that moment that the door to Detective Gorgiel's office fell open. Both Rayelle and Tai'dqei sat straighter on the bench, eyes turned expectantly to the doorway.

"Rayelle Carter?" The non-human that turned to them was bone-white with blue etchings on their skin. Their eyes – three of them, Rayelle noted – were the color of crystal and their mouth appeared like a jagged crevice in their face. She wondered if the rock-like appearance was an evolutionary mimic or if this alien – presumably Detective Gorgiel – was genuinely made of rock. Their button-up shirt and slacks looked out of place on their body.

"Yes," she responded, getting to her feet.

"I am Detective Gorgiel. Come this way," the rock alien said with a nod, standing to the side and motioning toward their office door. Rayelle was over the threshold when she heard the detective add to Tai'dqei, "You may come, as well. Any information will help."

"Of course," Tai'dqei grunted, getting to his feet and following at a safe distance behind Rayelle.

Inside the office looked like any other Rayelle could recall being in.

Two plush chairs sat across a desk from a single, larger chair. Papers riddled the desk, along with a familiar-looking computer. Rayelle assumed it was actually far higher tech than what she realized.

Delicately, she settled into one of the chairs. Tai'dqei dropped into the other. He crossed his arms, sitting ramrod straight. As Detective Gorgiel rounded the office to take his seat, Rayelle edged her own chair closer to the desk. She idly reached out to fiddle with a pen and, after that, a business card from a holder.

The interview took far longer than she anticipated. Detective Gorgiel squeezed every last drop of information from her. What exact year, month, day, hour did she come from? Who was president? What was her full address? Her full name? Her full maiden name? Children's names, her ex's full name, her parents, any pets she had, any possessions in her name, her friends, her kids' friends, her friends' kids, her hometown, and so on.

The worst was once again going over the events of The Night, when she was kidnapped and then abducted. A blunt pain edged through her retelling and brought on a sudden wave of exhaustion. She actually resorted to pulling out the fidget cube she had brought with her, expelling her nervous energy as she retold her story.

Tai'dqei noticed her distress and stepped in at one point, citing the alien races involved and forwarding Rayelle's medical records to the detective. The diversion gave her a little breather. He also explained to Gorgiel how the Straux earworm was his own doing so they could communicate. Though Rayelle noticed he didn't discuss *other* things that were his doing. Just scant facts of finding her, who was with her, and the records.

She supposed their personal interactions didn't have any bearing on her situation. His mistakes and her mistakes. It was like they existed in their own pocket of reality, totally separate from what was currently happening. Which was another wobbly thought that made her head swim.

"Well, Miss Brooks— you prefer Brooks, correct?" Detective Gorgiel surprised Rayelle by intuitively knowing she'd prefer her maiden name.

She nodded, still feeling a little woozy. "Yes, Brooks is my preferred surname."

"Miss Brooks, I know this wasn't easy for you. Even in less harrowing circumstances the trauma of time travel *and* space travel, for those unready, is difficult." Detective Gorgiel reached across their desk, gently patting her hand. She knew it was supposed to be comforting, but the tiny way Tai'dqei tensed in his chair was honestly more gratifying. "That said, it will regrettably take some time for us to investigate your case."

Rayelle blinked at that, her eyebrows furrowing. "Can't you just take all the time you need and then come back to this exact moment with the findings?"

A fleeting smile curled at Gorgiel's hard lips as they pulled their hand away. "This planet was specifically designed to halt temporal anomalies. Duplicates of ourselves, which would happen if a future me arrived here now, are not allowed."

"What about forwarding the information to someone else and have them do it?" She was pressing a topic she had little knowledge of, but she felt compelled to. It didn't make sense to her. If the Temporal Authority Council could travel through time, they could pop in and out whenever they wanted to. If staggered correctly, she thought it could be instantaneous.

"Rest assured, there will be many of us working on your case, but it will take time." To his credit, Detective Gorgiel didn't balk at her insistence.

She supposed he had been asked these things many times over. Rayelle still couldn't keep the disappointment from her tone as she gave a skeptical, "Hm."

Now Detective Gorgiel heaved a sigh, their shoulders rising and falling with their breath. "We will need time to investigate and untangle the web of contacts through the years. Direct, secondary, tertiary, and so on. Sometimes we discover important avenues we hadn't thought of before."

That made sense, she thought. She could imagine her connection to her kids, to Evan, to her family, to what few friends she had. There'd be police officers and detectives and true crime bloggers who spoke of her disappearance, as well. Her friends' families and their friends. People who stumbled on her case, completely detached from anything associated with her. Unraveling that web couldn't be easy and it couldn't be quick.

As if further sense was needed, the detective added as gently as they could, "Please remember, you're not our only case, Miss Brooks."

"Right, right. Sorry." Rayelle hung her head, her cheeks warming with embarrassment. Asking for more than they could give wasn't going to get her home any sooner. Ironically, if she just waited, it might expedite the process.

"It's perfectly fine. You're in a complicated situation and I'm sure you're looking forward to going home." Gorgiel paused and Rayelle could hear the wince in their voice as they added, "If possible, of course."

Rayelle gave a weak nod and a hum of acknowledgement but couldn't bring herself to say anything nor look up at the detective. *If that is possible.* Those words clanged around her head, making her stomach cramp unhappily.

"While you wait for our assessment, there is a resort we have set up on Rerli 3." Thankfully, Detective Gorgiel turned their gaze from her and addressed Tai'dqei. "I can provide coordinates if you could take her. We will provide compensation, of course."

"I can do that," Tai'dqei answered, meeting the detective's gaze. From the corner of his eye, he kept an eye on Rayelle. She slumped in her chair, hands drawn into her lap. A part of him was shamefully happy her hands weren't in reaching distance of the detective any longer. Another part of him worried she was mentally withdrawing. "What's this resort like?"

At the question, Rayelle peeked up again. First, to the ja-tau who'd asked a question she really should have asked herself, then to the detective.

"It's relatively new with a handful of humans there already. All from around Miss Brooks's time period." Whether the detective thought it was strange Tai'dqei asked the question, they made no indication.

Instead, they pulled a pamphlet out from a drawer and slid it across to Rayelle. "Entertainment and enrichment are provided. Cooking implements from the time period and kitchens. A pool, a gym, a spa. Anything and everything to keep a human busy."

Rayelle hummed once more as she tentatively grabbed the pamphlet. She didn't want to say she had no clue what was typical for a resort, having never been to one herself. The front page looked vaguely like what she expected. A large white building with bright adornments in a rainbow of colors, big windows, an abundance of flora — similar to Earth's catalog — and a blue ocean in the distance.

Once again, Tai'dqei focused in on Rayelle. He couldn't tell if she was excited for the resort or not. She just heavily scrutinized the front of the pamphlet but leafed no further into it. Maybe she was saving it for later, considering how tired she looked.

"First, we need to address the medical side of things." Detective Gorgiel pulled up the files Tai'dqei had sent them. There was a long moment of them eyeballing the alien words, nodding quietly to themself until they looked up at Rayelle and Tai'dqei. "We see these particular alterations a lot. Our clinic can reverse them, if desired. Miss Brooks can discuss more with one of our physicians."

That made her eyebrows shoot up. They'd reverse the changes if she desired. Were there humans that wanted to keep the changes? Things that had been done against their will? She supposed there had to be. Vaguely, she started to wonder if there was more done to her than becoming a "revitalized" baby machine.

As she considered the possibilities, and decided to discuss it more with the physicians, Detective Gorgiel and Tai'dqei hashed out the rest of the details. Coordinates and funding was exchanged. A few side questions answered.

Finally Detective Gorgiel stood from their desk, skirting around to be on the same side as Tai'dqei and Rayelle.

"If you have any questions, I've also sent my contact information to your gauntlets." As if on cue, Rayelle and Tai'dqei's gauntlets chimed with an incoming message. Not to be distracted, Detective Gorgiel opened the door and let it swing wide open. The detective stood beside it, obviously expecting the other two to leave. "Until we find out more, take care."

And like that, Tai'dqei and Rayelle found themselves ushered from the office. The walk through the halls was quiet as she mentally gnawed at the new information given to her. The pamphlet in her hand weighed with an unexpected heft.

Once they breached the threshold, out into the air of TAC S7B and down the sidewalk a bit, Tai'dqei broke the silence, "So, do you want to get something to eat? Or go to the clinic?"

At his question, Rayelle paused on the walkway. Her gaze flickered around their surroundings. There was an eerie sense of division to it all. The clothes, the vehicles, the signage. It was all familiar but there were non-humans milling about with familiar styles of dress tailored to their size or extra limbs.

It was also a lot cleaner and quieter, she realized. There was no litter blowing about the streets and, though dressed like gas guzzling cars, the vehicles didn't make any sound. No far-off trains or the sounds of planes, though spaceships that whizzed through the air gave a slight whum. No sirens of police cars or ambulances. No construction.

It was a facsimile of her time. A farce. Much like other things around her. Her eyes returned to Tai'dqei and her lips pressed tight together in thought. His emotionless mask stared back at her, patiently waiting for her decision. A nauseous feeling swam through her stomach, wondering where he truly fell on the gradient of genuine to false.

"The clinic," she finally said, heading to the garage where he had landed his ship. She straightened her spine and set her shoulders, the resort pamphlet crinkling in her fisted hand. "I want to get this over with already."

CHAPTER 14

Detective Gorgiel wasn't kidding when they said they had dealt with Rayelle's sort of alterations a lot. The clinic had perfected reversing the procedures in as short an amount of time as possible. Though she wondered if the swift operations were thanks to some sort of time manipulation, she didn't ask. She'd rather be ignorant of it, and not as angry, than know and be livid about the limitations put on her own goal of returning home.

After a private consultation with a physician, Rayelle had chosen to keep some of the alterations. Or at least tweak them to suit her needs.

Tai'dqei hadn't caught all the changes they made to her. Or maybe he simply highlighted the ones that caused the two of them problems when addressing it with her. Either way, some of the procedures had practical application beyond sex and breeding.

After about an hour and a half in the doctor's office and an equal time under surveillance, Tai'dqei and Rayelle were back out into the grand old city of 2020s Earth.

"If you need me to carry you—" Tai'dqei had been hovering over her the second they stepped out of the clinic. He followed more closely at her heels than earlier, seemingly prepared if she should swoon or trip. If she hadn't known better, she would have thought the physician made her pheromones worse.

"Oh my gosh, stop. I am fine." She paused on the walkway, planting her hands on her hips and turning to the ja-tau. He froze, making sure to keep a buffer of space between them. A little ironic, Rayelle considered, since he offered to carry her.

Surprisingly. she felt better than she had since the kidnapping and abduction. Discussing her options with the physicians gave her a sense of empowerment over her own self, something that she had lost. She had a say in what happened to her and she wasn't about to relinquish that.

It definitely made for a better mood.

Tai'dqei simply gave her a deepthroated, uncertain growl in response. His masked face tilted away from her. She fought down the familiar tingles that slid down her spine. Thankfully, they weren't as powerful likely due to the not-so-sexy circumstances.

Even though Tai'dqei's concern was obvious, there was an inner battle as to why he held such concern for her. Was it his own pride fueling the worry? She was officially his job now since Detective Gorgiel had paid him. Or was it genuine interest in her well-being? Which begged the question: how deep did that regard go?

Mentally shaking herself, Rayelle turned her thoughts to other things. Namely, food. "Earlier you wanted to get something to eat. Let's go."

Not one to give up easily, he jumped on the opening. "Because you need sustenance and rest after a surg—"

"It was literally an in-office procedure and they cleared me to leave after observation," she interrupted, waving her hand dismissively to which he crossed his arms and huffed even more moodily. Taking a few more steps down the walkway, she scanned the offerings that lined the street. "Stop pouting at me and let's decide what to eat."

As she turned away from him, she caught another little trilling huff and couldn't help but smile.

They settled on a recreation of one of the many relatively popular fast-food restaurants for the 2020s. After Rayelle ordered herself a burger with a large fry and milkshake, Tai'dqei ordered three specials. According to him, the portions were paltry for a grown ja-tau. She had to admit was probably right, taking his size into consideration.

"What do you think?" She asked, after they sat down and Tai'dqei sampled a variety of his meals. He'd removed his mask, placing it beside him in the booth they shared. Rayelle still failed to assess his reaction to the available foods.

While separated from her, Tai'dqei had done some research on her time period. The things she'd mentioned earlier had piqued his curiosity. He didn't know the circumstances, beyond personal, she had been snatched away from. Even on a cursory view, barely getting into the grittier aspects, it appeared to be a chaotic time on the verge of large social changes.

He wasn't sure even a lifetime of research would help him understand what she was normally used to.

"I understand that in your time, foods high in carbohydrates and fats were valued for energy. Especially for cheaper prices. These seem to cover that requirement." He shrugged after swallowing the lump of meat he'd been chewing. Plucking a fry from its pseudo archaic container, he popped it into his mouth. Chewing the strange food was awkward with her watching, but he tried to ignore the sensation.

Rayelle's lips twisted into an amused smirk. It sounded like a studied non-answer to her, on top of echoing the complaints many from her time had about fast food. After swallowing her own bunch of fries, she pressed further, "How do you like it though?"

"I am not a picky eater," he answered with a shrug of his massive shoulders. He'd eaten far worse when needing to survive, but she didn't need to know that. "This is satisfactory enough."

"Noted," She chuckled, leaning back in her chair while sipping at her drink. Her eyes trailed over the others in the restaurant. They all appeared to be staff of TAC, except for a select few which were other humans. She wondered if they were also stolen from their own times or if they had unique stories of their own.

Was there more genetic variance or illnesses floating around? Heck, if what Tai'dqei said was true about human compatibility with other DNA, were there fewer "pure" humans?

Tai'dqei noted how she looked around the eatery. He strained to find something reasonable to say, something that wouldn't send Rayelle spiraling if it nudged at the wrong nerves. At the same time, he was curious to know how accurate their surroundings were. "Is it the same as what you're used to?"

"More or less." Rayelle turned her attention back to him, a curl of a grin on her face. "Didn't have aliens, obviously."

He made a contemplative clicking hum as he chewed on his food. With her attention back on him, he suddenly felt a wave of nerves. Especially as her gaze fell on his face, watching his maw and mandibles and teeth.

"I never asked what you did on Earth," he said suddenly once he swallowed, needing her attention away from his mouth.

"Hm? Like my job?" Her gaze lazily flicked to his eyes. She was only slightly aware she had been staring at him. Her thoughts had been traversing along an array of imaginative scenarios involving his mandibles, like wondering how they grew or if they molted. She also wondered what parts of a human's everyday life would pose his mandibles issues.

Tai'dqei nodded in return, his body language sagging with relief as her gaze focused away from his mouth. There wasn't much human about him, but he knew his mandibles and maw were unsettling to others.

The slight shift in body language, coupled with his line of questioning, made a realization flash in Rayelle's thoughts. Not that she had a lot of experience, but this suddenly felt like a date. An awkward first date, she realized, as she took in Tai'dqei's hunched posture over the table.

Of course, he was bigger than the furniture allocated for so perhaps that was the reason for his positioning. She couldn't help but think of how the few boys she had dated in high school and college had similar postures. It was strangely cute, if one could use that term to describe a ja-tau.

"I was a housewife for a big chunk of time. Cooking, cleaning, errands, taking care of the kids." She tried to shoo away the thought of dates, focusing on her life before being thrust into space. Of course, turning her thoughts to that period of her life brought on sour thoughts. A bitter smile notched across her lips. "I actually just got a job to prepare myself for single life before this happened."

"What was it?" He tilted his head, curious to know what sort of occupation she had chosen.

"Cashiering and stocking shelves. Just something to pay the bills." She had tried for something above minimum wage, but when you had an employment gap for about eighteen years, you took what you could. Especially with the economy the way it was and trying to get out from under an ex's thumb. She had been so desperate, hoping for a decent occupation, but she had to settle.

She had done that a lot in life, she realized. Settling. Settling for a low-paying job. Settling for a man who demeaned her and who didn't like anything he deemed abnormal. Of course, Evan hadn't seemed cruel or bigoted at one point, but maybe she'd been seeing him through rose-tinted glasses. Or maybe she didn't thinks he deserved better. It wasn't like her life growing up had offered much better.

Not wanting to think about that, Rayelle refocused on Tai'dqei. A teasing smile tilted at her lips as her words took on a nettling tone, "And *you* are a glorified Uber that occasionally murders people."

His eyebrow ridges furrowed with lack of comprehension, even as his heartbeat tripped at her tone. "Uber?"

"Like a taxi. You ferry people to their destination and provide comfort during the trip. Although Ubers were usually for shorter trips," she explained, her smile growing as she considered the implications. "Admittedly, Uber drivers weren't supposed to kill people."

He chewed on a chicken nugget as he considered her words before giving a slow nod. "I do provide passenger support and the occasional killing, but I have other services."

Her eyebrows jumped up, her head cocking as she leaned forward. "Other services?"

She almost bit her tongue with how suggestive it sounded coming out of her mouth. He didn't mean it like that. And she wasn't even concerned or interested if he did provide such things to others. It was just curiosity and a sense of ease that allowed the teasing intrigue into her voice.

"I am more of a…" Tai'dqei considered the operative phrase, his large hand gesturing as if to find the word. Bounty hunter was just one thing he'd done. In truth, he bounced from job to job. Whatever caught his interest, he'd try. Though he was confident in his skills and abilities, which meant he could charge higher than fresh faces. Being a ja-tau helped in getting better payments, as well. "A general contractor, I guess?"

"*What?*" Delight cracked a smile across her lips as she immediately pictured Tai'dqei in dirty jeans and a toolbelt.

"I am hired to do what is needed," he replied, a heat rising in him. The choked laugh that came from Rayelle made his insides writhe. He wasn't sure if she was laughing at him or simply amused, but her giggles still affected him. Dutifully, he ignored the sensation. "I've helped shipyards, farms, construction, mining operations, and have done pest control."

Though Rayelle couldn't imagine what sort of pests would need a ja-tau's hand, she could picture him at a space shipyard or working construction or sweating away in a mineshaft. Trussed up in a work coverall, which just happened to be unzipped or folded down to his waist in her imagination. She'd noted how his muscles flexed many-a-time and had seen first-hand his strength at the port. Not to mention having felt that same strength on various occasions at this point.

She rushed the thought away with a roll of her eyes, though her tone still had its flirtatious teasing lilt, "Quite the resumé."

"I had a hard time settling after Ah'ke and I went separate ways." He gave a helpless shrug. The burning itch to fill the emptiness left by his former lover was seared into his memory. Some days, it had been unbearable. He'd thrown himself headlong into whatever assignments came his way, and sometimes into workers at brothels, trying to ease the ache. It was an erratic and chaotic time, but it had given him a variety of experiences and growth. Even if some of it was painful.

"What happened between you two anyway?" Rayelle asked before she realized just how sensitive of a topic it might be. Hurriedly, she added with an awkward wince, "If I may ask."

"We changed. *The* Change." Tai'dqei answered straight away, simply giving another helpless shrug. There was a time when talking about it hurt. At least, worse than it did now. It still panged at something in his chest, but Ah'ke's continued friendship — after the initial rough patch — had dimmed the bite of it.

When Rayelle shot him a confused look, he rubbed the back of his neck and stumbled through an explanation, "When we started our relationship, she was a man and I was a woman. Sometimes ja-tau hormones change suddenly and our bodies follow suit.

"My feelings for Ah'ke didn't change, but hers for me did." The familiar ache in Tai'dqei's chest throbbed as he described it as simply as possible. The pain was far blunter than he was used to.

"Oh, does that mean… The scars that were about here on you?" Rayelle motioned to her own chest, just below her breasts. Was that why she thought those scars had been familiar? Despite not totally being sure where he sat on the transgender spectrum, Elliot had talked to her about top surgery and even shown her photos of trans men who'd gone through the procedure.

"Yes, breast removal." Tai'dqei kept his gaze trained on Rayelle's face, not trusting his own eyes to wander to where she indicated.

"Oh!" Though Tai'dqei braced for a colder reception, Rayelle's smile brightened. Something in her eyes lit up and a fresh sense of camaraderie flared in her. Before she knew it, she found herself babbling, "My kids are the same. I mean, as much as humans can be.

Surgeries and medicines are needed, and for someone under eighteen to get hormone blockers for gender affirmation, both parents need to agree to them."

Tai'dqei warmed with appreciation at her sudden words, his head cocked to the side to drink in her smile and the way her hands moved as she spoke. When her slew of words stumbled a little, his mandibles twitched downward. Some little thought had cooled her sudden sunny burst.

It was the raincloud that always followed her. With a purse of her lips, she sighed, "That was part of the reason I was divorcing Evan. He didn't support our kids. I intended to get full custody so I could get them what they needed."

"And the other reason?" Tai'dqei asked quietly, finding his contempt growing for her former mate. Then again, the man didn't seem to have any redeemability. Unable to accept his children *and* playing a part in his ex's kidnapping? Certainly, no honor with this Evan.

"For myself. He wasn't good for me, if getting me kidnapped wasn't indication enough." Rayelle snorted even as a pang of hurt shot through her chest. She knew he wasn't her biggest fan, especially when the divorce proceedings began. At best, he ignored her kidnapping. At worst, he'd orchestrated it.

"He wasn't a nice person. Put me down a lot. Got mad if I did anything without him or he'd wield his position as breadwinner over me." Her hands busied themselves as she spoke, cleaning up their empty wrappers and unused napkins. She heard herself relaying the same things she had once told her therapist. This time, she wasn't trying to make excuses for Evan. "He got jealous if I hung out with anyone else, so I stopped having friends. But he went out a lot with co-workers and his own buddies."

Rayelle briefly glanced up Tai'dqei, expecting a bored expression or maybe even overplayed sympathy. There was an unexpected heat in his eyes that made her heart stutter. Unable to stay locked with his gaze, she drew hers to the nearby wall. "He had me so isolated, I can't imagine my disappearance made any difference to anyone. Other than my kids."

As Rayelle cleaned up their trash, wordlessly reaching over to grab his wrappers, Tai'dqei placed their empty cups onto the tray. When there was nothing else to gather, he quickly slid his mask on. "The more I hear of this Evan, the more I feel the urge to go on a Hunt."

It was, perhaps, an excessive thing to say. A sear of indignant and righteous rage flooded through his blood, seeking an outlet. Evan may not be worthy prey but the reason for such a hunt seemed admirable enough to Tai'dqei.

His little outburst made a half-chuckle fall from Rayelle's lips. Their gazes met across the table as she cast him a soft and oddly appreciative smile. "Can ja-tau even do that?"

To distract himself from that gentle look, he got to his feet and gathered up the now trash-laden tray. Rayelle followed suit, pushing in her chair before following him.

"Not through time. Limited species have the knowledge or capability to time travel," he confessed as he tossed their garbage into the indicated receptacle. After placing the tray on a return shelf, he turned to her. "But ja-tau can initiate a Hunt for personal reasons as they see fit."

"Interesting." Rayelle narrowed her eyes, though a smile still played across her lips. She leaned forward momentarily, head cocked to the side. "So how many people have you hunted?"

Something in Tai'dqei bristled at the question. She didn't say animals or quarry, but *people*. He was no stranger to this sort of goading. Plenty of others had nettled him on this topic in the past, from hunting in general to hunting peoples capable of defending themselves. Most of them painted ja-tau as a monolith, a singular culture with all clans sharing the same rules and traditions. Which wasn't true.

However, he had been raised valuing their hunts and Hunts, their searches for worthy prey. He couldn't deny part of him enjoyed the rituals, though some of his kind did get reckless or extreme on their own excursions.

Rayelle didn't wait for his answer as she spun on her heel, heading for the exit. As expected, she heard Tai'dqei's footfalls follow behind her. It sent a little satisfactory thrill through her knowing he'd follow her. It even sent a little wishful hope bouncing around her head.

As much as she was enjoying learning more about him, she was painfully aware that their time together was dwindling by the moment. Their next destination was the resort, allegedly tailor-made for humans in her situation. That meant she and Tai'dqei would soon go separate ways.

A silly part of her thought that, if she could make him follow now, maybe their time apart would be short.

"Why do you make it sound derogatory?" The question came off gruffer than Tai'dqei intended as he followed behind her. Wariness over a negative reaction from her left him feeling raw. Most of the time, when people snubbed his culture, he didn't care. Her opinion mattered to him though. If only so he'd know she felt safe around him.

"Humans had hunting too." Rayelle shrugged and a grin that made Tai'dqei even more cautious tilted at her lips. "I was never much of a fan, but I'm curious to know how inundated ja-tau life is with it."

"I've had been on more hunts than I can count," he admitted quickly, trying to absolve her curiosity without giving a hard answer. Despite being outside, he was beginning to feel a stuffy heat rise within his body.

Thankfully, the walk from the restaurant to the docking area wasn't far. It seemed fairly scant on bystanders, as well. Which he was thankful for, given the topic of their current discussion. He didn't want to feel the eyes of strangers on him as they overheard.

"Give me an estimate," Rayelle pressed as they strolled, side-by-side down the walk and turned into the hangar for spaceships. A wave of cool air slid over her. Docking areas, she had learned, were kept chilly to keep any delicate parts from overheating while ships were parked. The burst of cold also served to show her how warm she was feeling. It wasn't an unbearable or biting sizzle, as it had been before, but a pleasant heat was there.

To her undeterred suggestion, Tai'dqei glanced down at her as a leery gnarl bobbed in his chest. The cold of the hangar did little to assuage the burning in his body. Whether it was lust or annoyance, he wasn't entirely sure. It felt different than other times when Rayelle roused heat in him.

"Don't growl like that at me," she scoffed, resisting the urge to push on his arm. As light as she was feeling, as much as she teased him, she didn't feel they were exactly on friend level. She didn't know what they were to each other and focusing too long on it sent conflicting sensations through her. "It's not like you're going to hurt me."

Something in her tone, the mischievousness or maybe the familiarity edging between them, made him pause. He wasn't sure how to handle this situation. When she was quiet and obviously hurt, he struggled to maintain a level of sensitivity. Now he wasn't sure if she could handle it or expected more affability from him.

He wanted to find out.

Before he even realized it, his stance had shifted. Shoulders arched, knees bent, hands dropped to his thighs while his clawed fingers flexed. That posture, plus his armor, tended to send alarms along other people's survival instincts.

"There's always time to change that," Tai'dqei growled, with a gravellier rasp than usual.

Something pinged through the air, causing Rayelle – who had taken a few steps further even after he had stopped – to turn. Her eyes widened, her eyebrows raised. She took in the sight of the ja-tau, the darkness of the hangar working in his favor. Her heart did indeed suffer an uptick of pace, but she couldn't say it was entirely from fear.

Tai'dqei braced for a scream or some demand he stop or even a backpedaling apology. Something to show she still feared him.

Much to his surprise, a slow smile crept over her lips. The smile gave way to a snort of laughter as she rolled her eyes, one hand planting on her cocked hip. "Sure, there is, but you won't."

He didn't drop his stance. Instead, he slowly tilted his head to the side, much the way a larger predator does when prey does something interesting. When he spoke, the words came out slow and measured, "Why do you say that?"

"Precedent." Her response was quick and full of confidence. As if her reaction to him wasn't startling enough, she closed the distance between them with a few bold steps. Amusement buzzed along her body, catching the slightest indications of his surprise in his body language. She crossed her arms, fighting off the itch to prod him in the chest, and leaned forward. "If I'm wrong, prove it."

With that, she spun and regained the distance once more, heading for his familiar ship. The logical part of her knew she was egging him on. To what end, she wasn't admitting to herself.

Tai'dqei watched her walk off, a growl rumbling in his chest and his fingers flexing at his sides. Mental chaos reigned in his head. He had to talk himself down from the flare of heat inside him. A flare that was not anger but just as dangerous where Rayelle was concerned.

She was teasing. *Friendly* teasing. Not challenging him. Even though it certainly sounded like a fucking challenge. And she was walking away, which could be construed as running. That's what a sly inner voice said in his head. Tai'dqei mentally clamped down on the surge at his center, wondering if there were residual pheromones or if the physician hadn't completed the reversal entirely.

Shaking himself, he fell out of his stance and followed after her, soon clambering into the sanctity of his ship.

"Do you mind if I watch something in your room again?" Once the door shut behind them, she turned to smile up at him. The way she inclined her head to him made him wonder if she had something else planned. He wasn't sure if he should be apprehensive or excited about that prospect.

Before he could reasonably answer her, his curiosity needed to be satisfied. "If you don't mind me asking, what did the physicians do exactly?"

He hadn't moved far from the doorway of the ship while Rayelle had ventured further in. She turned to him, a curious look on her face. As if she wanted to know why he wanted to know. Tai'dqei tensed, prepared to be denied the answer. A beat passed and she seemed to decide he deserved to be informed.

"They reversed the pheromone and hormone issues. Well, put them to normal levels, I guess?" According to the TAC physician, it turned out the method used to alter her body wasn't entirely reversible and tied into her rejuvenated reproductive system. Essentially, her initial abductors turned back the clock to horny teenage years while adding her ability to pick up on extraterrestrial pheromones. Now her hormones were more manageable, but explaining everything in detail to Tai'dqei seemed a little tedious. "Oh, and they tied my tubes per my request."

They didn't completely remove the pheromone component, thought Tai'dqei. Just adjusted it so she'd be less affected but what about the reverse? Did she still affect others strongly? He would think a physician familiar with these situations would make sure that was corrected.

"I did keep the increased stamina and durability, revitalized joints, and rejuvenated flexibility." Those words startled Tai'dqei out of his thoughts, his gaze shifting to her. She flashed what he thought was a somewhat sly smile and gave a shrug. "Thought it'd come in handy, even if I head back home."

"I see," was all he could manage to say. His brain hinged on her increased stamina and durability, dragging it through the gutters of his mind. Was it coincidence that she had seemed more teasing then? Or did it mean something else?

Self-restraint halted the instantaneous fantasies that flooded his brain. No, her flirtatious teasing was likely just a result of her finally feeling autonomy since being stolen away. She still had to re-adjust to the changes. Besides, maybe she just naturally teased others. It meant nothing.

Rayelle could almost see Tai'dqei's thought processes chugging away from the subtle shifts in his expressions. She smiled to herself, admittedly amused by his deep focus on the subject. If she was being honest, she couldn't say what she hoped his response would be. Part of her still strangely ached for his touch. Not as large and hot and obsessive of a part as before, but it was there. Another part of her didn't want to assume that he even wanted that.

On top of all that, who could say there weren't going to be residual pheromones and hormones still causing havoc?

No, it was the best course of action to not make things worse for either of them. Which meant keeping their hands to their respective selves. That thought did make a small bubble of regret course through her, but she ignored it. Being responsible and making sure no one got hurt was important.

Of course, her own sense of temptation liked to challenge even Rayelle. Tilting her head at Tai'dqei, the safe distance still between the two of them, she rocked back on her feet. "So can I watch something in your room again or nah?"

"I suppose," he sighed as he moved further into his ship, which consequently placed him closer to her.

It couldn't hurt, he decided. So far, neither of them had overstepped a blatant line nor did their immediate situation call for awkward closeness where something might happen. While she enjoyed her entertainment, he could get some maintenance completed around the ship or clean his armor.

"Good, because I'm going to put you through a marathon." Rayelle closed the last bit of distance between herself and Tai'dqei, boldly wrapping her arm around his elbow.

Her sudden touch on his arm and the way she pulled herself against him sent a lightning bolt of heat through him. All at once, his brain registered her warm softness against him. *Oh*, he wanted to put her through a marathon, but one of an entirely different sort.

Confusion was the emotion that got to his vocal cords first, "What? Why?"

"I'm going to make you watch more of my awful movies with me."

"*Why?*" Tai'dqei repeated desperately as his brain tried to shake off the satisfaction her words instilled.

Rayelle puckered her lips, narrowing her eyes as she tilted her face up at him. She waited a beat, pretending to consider the options, before answering with a cheeky smile, "Because you're not going to say no."

If Tai'dqei was human, she thought she could picture his eyes flying wide and, perhaps, a flush flooding on his cheeks. As he was an alien, his flustered expression wasn't as blatant. She couldn't explain how she knew it, but it was there.

Heat clawed up his back at her assertion. As true as it was, her confidence in that fact somehow felt shameful for him. "That's not a—"

"You deal with taking off, I'm going to put together a watchlist!" She wasn't going to give him a chance to argue. Spinning on her heel, she jogged down the hall toward his room. The sensation of his eyes – curious and confused and maybe a little frustrated – following her burned at her back the whole way.

Tai'dqei did indeed watch her go and disappear into his room, agonizingly delighted at the sight. Conflicting feelings warred in his chest. This new facet of Rayelle was relieving to see. A softer, sweeter sort of stubbornness. Although she still seemed evasive but less apologetic about it.

He heaved a sigh, his mandibles fidgeting as he thought. This didn't really change anything, did it? The pheromone issue was allegedly handled. It wasn't as if he hadn't sat with her before to watch a movie, even if he had left partway through.

Shaking his head to himself, Tai'dqei treaded to the cockpit, allowing his own mental autopilot to take over as he got them free of TAC S7B.

CHAPTER 15

It took more time than Tai'dqei appreciated to get clearance to disembark. As soon as he was cleared, he pulled out of the planet's orbit. With no foreseeable issues making themselves known, he settled his ship on autopilot and headed back to his quarters.

Part of him considered not going back there. He could try to explain his absence as unavoidable, an issue with the route or computer. His pride was the only thing keeping his feet moving. Rayelle shouldn't scare him. Any potential happenings between them shouldn't fill him with uncertainty.

Yet there he was, standing outside the door to his own quarters and staring at the metal but not entering. A wave of memories fluttered through him when he'd been met with similar apprehension. Tense moments between himself and Ah'ke during and after their respective Changes. Dread swelled up as the memories stirred residual grief and pain.

Rayelle was like Ah'ke in a way. At least to him. Neither were going to stay with him. He should enjoy the time he had left with Rayelle and cherish the experience, just as he held his time with Ah'ke so dear.

That thought sent a pang through him, but he urged himself to enter his room.

Inside, Rayelle sat on his couch, her teeth sunk into her bottom lip as she scrolled through the options. She had a list of five movies that she thought Tai'dqei may enjoy with her. Of course, she didn't expect to get through them all. Although maybe they could. According to the detective, it was roughly a two-cycle trip to the resort. There could be issues like ion storms or electricity fields or something that could delay their trip too. Maybe by just an extra day?

Feeling pathetic, she shoved that little inkling of hope away. No, that was asinine. They were going to get to the resort without issue. In her chest, there was a resigned certainty about it. There wasn't going to be any silly sci fi bullshit that would extend her time with the ja-tau bounty hunter.

Pushing away the surprising disappointment, Rayelle looked up as Tai'dqei entered. "Finally! You took forever."

He grunted in return but didn't come close to her immediately. Instead, he crossed the room and pointedly removed his helmet. It was a bid for time on his part. Removing his helmet followed by the pieces of protective plating, left behind the thermal netting and a pair of tight black shorts that he had worn under his full armor. He placed each piece carefully into his wardrobe, struggling to get ahold of himself.

It didn't work. Especially as Rayelle watched him intently, that small eager smile on her lips.

He wished she'd stop staring at him like that. The itch to touch her, the heat at his core, started to rise again.

Turning as the wall to his wardrobe shutting behind him, his feet felt clumsy and heavy as he trod closer to her. Irritation with himself and his own cowardice reared up. With mandibles fidgeting in agitation, Tai'dqei motioned to the screen. "Why did you want to do this with me?"

"Because…" Rayelle started to say 'because I want to spend time with you' or 'because, despite everything, I do like you' but she stopped. The instance of vulnerability she had been tempted to open clamped shut. This was silly she realized. She was acting like a teenager, testing the waters of a close friend-that-was-secretly-a-crush.

She bit her bottom lip, her eyes drifting away from Tai'dqei. It was nice to realize her own feelings were genuine but was she just riding that high of *knowing* it was her and not some over-hyped hormones? When she glanced back up at him, she shrugged and offered an awkward smile, her voice soft. "I don't know. It just sounded fun."

The shift in the air around her didn't go unnoticed by Tai'dqei. Contrition fluttered through him, realizing his question had dulled her excitement. This wasn't about him, he reminded himself. She deserved whatever little delight she garnered in their time together, if only to create positive memories they both could look back on when the two of them were inevitably separated.

"I don't understand," he sighed, coming around the couch to sit. Sense told him to sit at the far end, but his body ignored it. He plopped down next to Rayelle, who also sat in the center of the couch. "However, if it makes you happy, I'll do it."

The cushions on the couch sank down under his weight, adding to the mischievous temptation roiling in Rayelle. Once more, she felt like a teenager testing the waters with a crush. Not that she had a crush on Tai'dqei, certainly not. He had been kind, beyond kind. The times when he *did* mess up, he did his best to rectify the situation. At the very least, he made her feel safe and comfortable.

She also couldn't deny being physically fascinated with him. It was no longer an aching burn to touch him, but more of a keen curiosity. Her brain swarmed with questions. How would those mandibles feel on her? And how would he feel atop her? Or holding her? How would his claws feel, grazing over her back or thighs?

Spurred on by her brazen inquisitiveness, Rayelle scooted closer to him. Situating herself against his side in a way that wordlessly prompted him to drape an arm over her shoulders. She angled her face up at him with a grin. "Told you, you weren't going to say no."

Once more, she surprised him. She cuddled close to his side as she selected a movie via her gauntlet and he absentmindedly curled an arm over the back of her shoulders. He had barely realized he'd done it until she shifted a little while tucked under the limb. He stared at her, painfully aware of his breathing and where they made contact.

Her body heat, her softness, the scent of her. It didn't dizzy him as it had, but it still made his heart pound and bring tempting thoughts to mind.

A pensive rumble resonated through his chest before turning into a deeper, more guttural clicking gnarl. She was testing his limits, he thought. Toeing the edge of an ocean that was liable to swallow her up. He was on-so tempted to pull her under.

His growl teased Rayelle's nerves, bringing a sharp gasp to her lips. Her back arching and her hand – where it had absently rested on his leg – curled into his thigh. Sudden flashes filled her thoughts. Of them sharing the pilot seat, of Tai'dqei's hands on her, his finger *in her.* Rayelle's throat felt thick, a sear of excitement and uncertainty razing through her.

Self-discipline clamped down on Tai'dqei's throat when he saw her reaction, cutting his soft clicking off. It was probably best if he didn't instigate her any further with his snarls. Last time he fell to the temptation of her bodily reaction to his sounds, it ended with her upset. He didn't want that again.

Thankfully, the movie tilted into full swing. Both Tai'dqei and Rayelle turned to the screen, attempting to focus on it while being painfully aware of each other's presence. Though if asked, neither would be able to explain what was happening on-screen. They quietly basked in each other's heat, his thumb gently stroking her far shoulder and her fingertips absently feeling the texture of his thigh.

Their time together was growing shorter by the second. Though both would be hard pressed to admit it, neither wanted to reintroduce distance any sooner than necessary.

◊ ◊ ◊

The time spent on Tai'dqei's ship passed by with agonizing swiftness. Rayelle couldn't help but wonder if there was yet another time anomaly happening, but she knew the truth. She was actually enjoying her last cycles with him. Now that the heightened hormones that caused such a burning need were under control, they weren't struggling nearly as badly.

Well, she wasn't struggling. Whether Tai'dqei was feeling differently was another issue. She still couldn't help but tease and mildly flirt with him, especially whenever he seemed tense or awkward. It was kind of cute how the massive, beefy killing machine could be undone by a suggestive word or innuendo from her.

She also supposed that her renewed sense of control helped the situation. Before the visit to the clinic, she felt like she was being pulled along by the nose. Now she felt as if she held the reins.

In the scant time they had together, Rayelle jam-packed it with as much as she could. They watched movies and conversed and played a few games. At one point, she had a sudden hankering for pancakes to which he humored her with some basic supplies available onboard. Even though he ate what she made and said he enjoyed it, she wasn't entirely certain he was being sincere.

Just as she wasn't certain about leaving him.

Sitting in the passenger row behind Tai'dqei, Rayelle stared at the incoming space station floating mid-screen. A little off center and behind the station, a blue and green planet hovered. Apparently, they couldn't land directly on the resort planet.

The sudden realization set in that their time was up. That thought sent a nervous prickle through her body.

In an attempt to ignore the sensation, she focused on the station in the holo-screen. It was a large spherical structure with an outer ring. A ship left the far-right side of the ring as they approached. Other than that, it seemed fairly low traffic. Well, as low traffic as she could infer.

She wasn't sure why they couldn't land on the planet, but Tai'dqei didn't seem confused about being restricted to the station. Rayelle tried to convince herself there wasn't anything to worry about. She presumed the resort simply didn't want humans — unused to space travel and ships crisscrossing the sky — to be continuously bombarded with unfamiliar sights. Other humans could be struggling more than she was.

This place was designed to be an oasis of familiarity, an effort to shield time-displaced humans from too much novelty, advanced technology, or non-human interaction. Any alien presence was probably restricted for that very reason.

It made sense, but she obviously wasn't a usual case. She had spent plenty of time with a non-Terran species and it hadn't completely devastated her senses. Hopefully, Detective Gorgiel had relayed that information to the counselors on Rerli 3. *Hopefully,* they understood that Tai'dqei had been one of the only constants and her protector during her time-space jaunt.

The hopes smacked of wishful thinking. Realistically, or pessimistically, this was it. She and Tai'dqei were going to part ways by the end of the day, if not sooner.

The mounting agitation over her inevitable separation from Tai'dqei clung to the back of her thoughts. It was like a tick, burrowing deeper and deeper into her synapses.

Phantom tears burned the back of her eyes, but she took a deep breath, trying to alleviate the pressure. While the immense sadness sunk deeper in her, an irritation flared at herself. This was silly. *She* was being silly. In the grand scheme of everything, she barely knew Tai'dqei and was only clinging to him because he'd become someone familiar.

They both were going to easily move on with their lives once they parted ways.

Rayelle jolted as the metallic sound of something clamping, of gears whirring, of hydraulics hissing echoed around the ship. Tai'dqei stood, drawing her eye to him at his pilot's chair. Her teeth sunk into her lower lip as he stretched his arms over his head, his full armor glinting in the lights. Even though this was heavier armor than his usual, his skin peeked out between the plates and pieces.

Rayelle's fingers itched to touch him, to feel the thick leathery skin under her fingertips. Time was running out to solidify the sensation in her head. Then her attention flicked to the chair, faint memories tickled her thoughts. His hands on her. His fingers inside her. The growling, clicking vibrations that sunk to her bone marrow.

Good luck forgetting any of that, she told herself as she fought down a shiver.

Abruptly, she unbuckled and stood before her imagination could marinate too long in the recollections.

Tai'dqei watched as Rayelle fled the bridge, his mandibles barely flickering. He was trying to rely on emotional autopilot to get him through these final moments. It was becoming increasingly hard though. As it had over the last cycles with her, the desire to touch her crept over his hands. Now his skin burned with the *need* to touch her. A hug, a brush of his fingers over her cheek, any physical touch to memorialize.

He refused himself the nicety. The fewer sweet memories he could dwell on, the less it would hurt. Or so he hoped.

They moved to the mess — which was really a lounge, she thought, since it had a couch and screen — when a counselor from Rerli 3 boarded. Introductions flew around, and Rayelle couldn't help but brood over how tooth-achingly sweet the counselor's tone sounded.

Jezika appeared as a human with neon blue hair cut in a bob and wide brown eyes. Her bright blue lipstick accentuated her unwavering smile. There was something about her that seemed off to Rayelle. Skin that was too smooth, with little to no flaws. Eyes that didn't blink quite enough. A stiffness to her movements that seemed awkward.

Or maybe Rayelle just wanted something to be off with Jezika. She was looking for any reason to fight leaving the comfort of her known companion for an unknown.

216

"You will love it at Rerli 3's resort, Miss Brooks," Jezika chirped while rocking on her heels. Her hands gesticulated as she spoke and even that seemed more performance than natural. A sudden flash of memory, of old animatronics at eateries and amusement parks, tumbled through Rayelle's thoughts. "We have everything you could ever need."

Having perused the pamphlet during moments when Tai'dqei was busy with piloting or training, Rayelle knew almost all of the amenities. She didn't doubt Jezika's claims. The enormous resort had different areas, separated by decade. Each wing had their own community kitchen, equipped with appliances and available foods of the time; a library with books from their era and an area to do crafts; pool and gymnasium, again with equipment from the time; and other period-appropriate entertainments.

For Rayelle, 2020s entertainments meant a theater-style area to watch movies or having 'streaming services' in her personal room. Also, she would have access to a computer that somehow accessed her era's Internet, though she couldn't post, share, or comment on anything. Just scroll and play some 'ancient' games.

Rayelle still had a question. She motioned to Tai'dqei, who resided on the far side of the room from her. "Can he come down with me until I get settled?"

Tai'dqei stood stiff and straight, ignoring how his heart jumped as Rayelle asked a question he'd been struggling to breach. He had chosen to wear his full armor today. The helmet obscured his face, and the armor mostly obscured his form, which meant humans unfamiliar with his kind might overlook him. The fledgling hope that he would be able to grab a little more time with her flared in his chest.

"I am very sorry." A frown flashed across Jezika's lips as she tilted her gaze to Tai'dqei before looking back to Rayelle. "Many of our guests are humans from eras ignorant of non-Terran life and culture. Those who are familiar with non-human life have minimal and unsavory knowledge of the ja-tau."

At that, Rayelle raised her eyebrows and shot Tai'dqei a questioning look. What kind of experiences had transgressed between humans and the ja-tau? If Tai'dqei knew, his body language didn't betray it.

He did know, but only in rumors and stories. Ironically, the ja-tau and humans had a score of interactions recorded in their respective histories. He didn't really want to discuss any of that if this was going to be his last moments with her.

Thankfully, Jezika continued with a renewed smile. She seemed intent on barreling over any curiosity in Rayelle. "We strive to cause as little conflict as possible within our patrons."

"I see," Rayelle replied as she grudgingly shelved her curiosity over prior interactions between the ja-tau and humans. There was no time to discuss past transgressions or diplomacies.

She didn't like how Rerli's strict 'no outsiders' policy made sense either. The ache to spend more time with Tai'dqei distractingly burned within her. She had hoped to blunt it by weaseling a few more hours of time with him.

She wasn't ready to admit that to anyone. she was barely ready to admit it to herself. The entirety of their time together had been one miscommunication and misstep after another, dolloped with a helping of confusion and conflicting baggage. Untangling the threads of how she felt took time.

There wasn't any more time for that now.

"I suppose this is it." She turned to him, her limbs both heavy and twitchy with anxiety. In an effort to stop the sensation, she clasped one hand to her opposite wrist and let her hands hang in front of her thighs. A small voice at the back of her head held its breath, hoping he'd say or do something to prolong their companionship.

Tai'dqei disappointed her by giving a nod and affirmative grunt.

Her lips pressed tight together, trying to find any small sign he didn't want her to go. Reading his face was hard enough, the mask made it impossible. Rayelle couldn't fathom why he had worn all his armor today.

A part of her mused he was going to fight to keep her aboard. Or maybe he was anticipating having to protect her from hordes of other aliens once more.

Or maybe he had a new assignment already lined up. That thought made her stomach twist and she wondered how much of his time she had wasted, how many potential assignments he'd missed due to her.

At the same time, a flare of mournful annoyance nipped at her thoughts. Rayelle felt as if she was about to be crossed off his To Do List and completely forgotten. He had only done all of this — from carting her around space to providing her the ear worm and gauntlet – out of a sense of duty. She couldn't really ask for any more from him.

Trying to keep that in mind, she forced a smile to her lips. It wasn't an insincere smile, but she fought to hide the wave of sadness that lapped inside her. "Thank you for everything."

Rayelle's heart stuttered as Tai'dqei suddenly lumbered toward her. Disappointment bloomed in her chest when he stopped an arm's length away. He reached a large hand out, palm up as if he was expecting some sort of payment from her.

Oh. The gauntlet, she realized, suddenly feeling the metallic heaviness on her wrist. Not entirely sure how to remove it, she held her wrist out to him. Her free hand clutched at the hem of her shirt as her bottom lip was worried by her teeth. She tried not to think how this was yet another thing taken from her, on top of everything else that was happening.

Instead of hitting a button and the gauntlet falling free of her, Tai'dqei took another step closer. Rayelle tensed, his body heat sinking into her as he stooped over her. A small part of her mind dedicated it to further memory. His grip firm and gentle as he tapped through the settings and options with is free hand.

Quietly, under the counselor's gaze, he instructed her how to remove the gauntlet – something he had avoided telling her when she had a habit of running off into danger – and how to send him a general communique.

"Contact me if you need anything. If it's urgent, press this here." He tapped another button, and his own gauntlet gave a continuous repetitive alarm. Tai'dqei released her arm to silence the message on his own gauntlet. Then he tilted his face toward her, his expression unreadable beneath the mask. "I will find you no matter what."

Heat snapped across Rayelle's face as she registered the words, her heart stuttering. She averted her gaze, her gauntleted wrist held against her chest. He didn't mean that, she thought to herself. An uproar of thoughts churned through her head, rippling through her. He was just being polite. They barely knew each other.

Still, it was a nice thought and she couldn't keep the slight smile from her lips. "Thank you again."

Tai'dqei gave a terse nod, posture painfully straight and stiff. Inside, he felt as if something was cracking. It was all he could do to keep his tone level. "Take care. I hope you can see your kids again."

At the mention of her Elliot and Skylar, Rayelle's heart lurched. Here she was, wanting to prolong her time with Tai'dqei despite what he wanted and what her children needed. She was being selfish, said that little inner voice too similar to Evan's own.

Her words stuck in her throat and a pang in her chest threatened to spill tears from her eyes.

Struck by an urge to do something, to convey the mess of emotions, Rayelle suddenly grabbed for his wrist. He allowed her to move his arm, probably struck by curiosity or surprise. She turned his hand over, bringing his bare palm to her lips and pressing a kiss to the center. His fingers twitched, and she felt the tension coiled up his arm.

Unbeknownst to Rayelle, a prickling sensation knifed through Tai'dqei's body, landing deep inside him. Breath caught in his lungs, his eyes widening at the affectionate display. It threatened to completely upend his tattered calm.

As hurriedly as she grabbed him, she released his hand and turned away. Snatching up her backpack and duffel bag, both stuffed with things he'd bought her, she reminded herself of what she could keep from their time together. Admittedly, it was a lot of little things. Books and clothes and fidget toys. Plenty to remind her of Tai'dqei.

None of it was him though.

"Goodbye, Tai'dqei." She couldn't force herself to turn and face him. To be met with that blank mask, to not be able to discern what he felt, wasn't something she wanted to confront.

Consequently, Rayelle didn't see how motionless Tai'dqei stood. Nor how his masked face inclined to his hand still frozen in the spot she had held it. Savoring the small action.

If Jezika thought anything of the interaction, she did not make it apparent. She followed Rayelle out of the ship, after beckoning a chipper thank you and goodbye to Tai'dqei. The two women traipsed out the ship and into the docking port before the door closed behind them.

It wasn't until the two were well gone that Tai'dqei realized he hadn't said goodbye. All the better, he thought, as he fisted the hand Rayelle had kissed and allowed it to drop.

His other hand reached up to wrench off his helmet as he headed to the cockpit. A spark of unaddressed frustration had him flinging the helmet into a passenger seat where it bounced down the row. Thankfully, it didn't clatter to the floor, though he was only half-aware of that fortune.

His mind focused on other things. Namely leaving before he did something ill-thought and ridiculous.

If he lingered too long, he feared he'd go after her. The burn to touch her still seared through him, made worse by her kiss. Dropping down in front of his console, he scanned the area for any points of interest. Thankfully, a bounty outpost wasn't far. There, he could find his next job, restock supplies, and maybe have a destined-to-be-unsatisfactory stop at a brothel. His mind sloppily listed several to-dos while trying shove thoughts of Rayelle further away.

She got to where she needed to go. The proper authorities would handle it from here, whether that meant sending her back to her time or finding her a nice human settlement to live in or sending her back to Earth. Tai'dqei honestly didn't know what the protocol would entail if a human *couldn't* be sent back to their time.

There was never going to be a message from her. No matter her flirtations or friendliness over their last hours together.

Tai'dqei's mandibles flexed with agitation. No, this was only a short eventful chapter that was now closed. He steeled himself until he received clearance to leave. A swell of something leaden and heavy settled in his chest as he maneuvered away from the docking station, away from the planet.

Away from Rayelle.

CHAPTER 16

From the jump ship, while in-transit from dock station to resort while disguised as a cloud, Rayelle watched a light flash from the suspended station and disappear into the atmosphere. She presumed it was Tai'dqei's ship. Something in her chest twisted, thinking of how he left so quickly.

Looking away from the sky, she turned her gaze to the gauntlet still on her wrist. The sensible part of her told her to remove it. She didn't need it any longer.

Another part of her wanted to test his claim. Would he really come if she sent an urgent message? Even if they had just parted? Her fingers hovered over the contact button.

"You will absolutely love it here, Miss Brooks!" The counselor twittered, seated beside Rayelle. She ticked off what Rerli 3's resort had to offer, all of it simple repetition from what Rayelle had read. "We have all sorts of fun things to do. Books to read, old media to view, kitchens to cook, a spa and pool to relax in. And so much, much more!"

"Sounds wonderful," Rayelle replied, feeling as hollow as her words. She closed out the communication program, forcing herself to forget about messaging him. At least, not urgently. She had already taken up so much of his time. Maybe in a week or a month or a year, she'd reach out to him. See how he was doing and reconnect, if she was lucky.

If she was still in this time, she added to herself. Rayelle wondered if the gauntlets would work out-of-time. If she sent a message from 2024, would it bounce around the universe until he received it in this time? Her lips pressed tight together at the unlikely scenario.

"Oh, it *is* wonderful!" By this point, Rayelle felt like Jezika was a broken record. She suspected the woman did, have more in common with technology than with herself. Unaware of Rayelle's thoughts, the counselor continued on, "It will be so nice after space-hopping with a ja-tau. They can be particularly difficult."

Rayelle offered a half-laugh at that, unable to deny that sentiment while not liking her tone. Again, her heart twisted. She wasn't sure if Tai'dqei was necessarily more difficult between the two of them.

As Rerli 3 came closer into view out her window, Rayelle picked out trees, hills, rivers, and buildings. It looked so much like Earth she was surprised. Either this planet was specifically chosen due to the very similarities or it was manufactured. She still couldn't believe man-made planets were an actuality here. It seemed so absurd.

She pondered what the resort was like, if she'd be the only human in the 2020s wing, and other inane little details. Meanwhile, the other half of her brain fought between the pros and cons of reaching out to Tai'dqei, how soon, how often, if she ever should.

Frustration mounted the longer her mind split her attention. With fists clenching in her lap, Rayelle glared out the window, not really seeing Rerli 3.

She was not going to live each day, pining away for an alien that couldn't wait to leave her behind. Not to fault him, of course. She had put him through the hormonal ringer while he tried to tiptoe around her emotional baggage.

It was just obvious, with how fast he left, how eager he was to be done with her.

Firmly deciding she wasn't going to waste any more of his time, Rayelle forced her thoughts on Rerli 3 and hopefully returning to her home time.

◊ ◊ ◊

Five cycles passed.

Tai'dqei languished an outpost on Vh'oi for three of those cycles. He replenished his supplies, had regular ship maintenance performed, and experienced an extremely unsatisfactory visit to the local brothel. All the while, quiet thoughts of Rayelle bubbled at the back of his mind.

How was she doing? Had she befriended anyone? Had she gone beyond friendliness? Was she already back home, in her time with her kids? Was she safe? Did she ever think of him?

The thoughts got louder and the crowds on Vh'oi became harder to stand. On the fourth cycle, he decided to take off to a nearby planet rife with wilderness to camp and hunt. To be within the quiet embrace of nature would hopefully settle his thoughts.

It didn't do much good. Much of the fauna on the planet was small, unchallenging, and sought to flee rather than fight. In the end, Tai'dqei hunted for sustenance and not glory. Which was fine. There was a pit in his chest that made it hard to even imagine celebrating a good hunt well commenced.

Sitting half-dressed in the balmy light of day, his ship nearby and the sun high, Tai'dqei stared out over the expanse of flora from his spot on a cliff. He was avoiding thinking since the effort tended to roll around to Rayelle.

A comm chimed on his gauntlet and he glanced at it. He'd kept Ah'ke apprised of the situation. Aware or simply intuitive, she had uncovered his own conflicting emotions easily. Likely, she was checking up on him and making sure he hadn't done something erratic and ill-thought.

Tai'dqei's eyes widened when he realized it wasn't from Ah'ke.

His mandibles flickered with sudden unrest as he opened Rayelle's message.

◊ ◊ ◊

I'm sorry to be contacting you so soon. It's probably my imagination but…

Something doesn't feel right.

I think most of the staff are androids, made to look human. But there are other staff. Alien staff, which strikes me as strange, since you weren't allowed on planet.

I also see non-humans late at night, after staff SUGGESTS we get some rest. I don't know if they're staff or visitors. They don't wear Rerli uniforms.

But I'm catching sight of more of them at random intervals. There's a buzz in the air, like something big is going to happen, too. Like an event or something.

Something FEELS wrong. I don't know how to explain it.

It's probably nothing. I'm sorry. I'm probably bothering you. Maybe I'm just having a hard time adjusting.

I hope you're doing well, wherever your line of work has taken you. Sorry, again, for bothering you.

~ Rayelle.

With a heavy sigh, Rayelle threw her arm over her face and sunk deeper into her bed. There, she sent it. And she felt like an awkward teenager for it.

Her mind was probably playing tricks on her, making her see

228

concerning things that weren't there because she was desperate for a reason to contact Tai'dqei.

But, this *was* a genuine issue causing her concern.

Rerli Resort had provided everything it said it would, including personal rooms for individuals.

Rayelle's own room was currently a gentle blue. She could change the color with the console on the wall, which was anachronistic for the 2020s but she wasn't going to complain. Overall, it was like a hotel room.

A large plush bed sat against one wall. A white desk equipped with a computer and a desk chair took up another wall. In one corner, there was an extra chair and a table, presumably so one could read or write. She even had her own attached bathroom with a shower.

The first morning she had woken up there, she almost thought her whole excursion with Tai'dqei had been a dream. A very vivid and oddly detailed dream. Then Jezika popped her head in, offering their newest resident a cheerful 'good morning' and all of Rayelle's dream assumptions fled.

"Finally wrote him, eh?" From the floor at the foot of Rayelle's bed, Lisa laughed around her gum. It was hard to acknowledge that, by all technicalities, the young woman – with her cherry red hair and studded denim jacket and fishnets – was older than Rayelle. At least in the respect that Lisa grew up in the late 70s and had been a teenager to young adult in the 80s in the United States.

Another thing Rayelle had learned while residing in the massive resort was the fact all the humans – men, women, and non-binary people – had come from some stage of the United States. Whether it was the pre-colonial Indigenous land, the Colonies, her US, or a later iteration of the country.

Theories had flown around as to why that was, but no one really knew. It seemed the resort was made for many more people, but fewer than one hundred had arrived. Rerli was a new establishment, so perhaps that was the reason for the scant number of guests.

Rayelle had a growing paranoia that the reason why they were all from the US had to do with who had been snatching them all, though. She worried their captors shared more than just a proclivity for kidnapping.

From the desk chair, which had been turned to face the others in the room, Sandra chuckled. She was a housewife abducted from 1956. Her era showed with carefully coiffed hair and a penchant for blouses paired with long skirts. A light floral scent always wafted from her.

In Sandra's hands, she worked a piece of knitting with her clicking needles. "You have certainly agonized over that missive since you arrived!"

"It's difficult. He's probably halfway across the universe," Rayelle groused, faint heat nudging at her cheeks but not quite coming to the surface yet. It was a little aggravating to be teased so relentlessly from a housewife and a mallrat punk, but that was her life at the moment.

At least she wasn't the only human any longer.

Though she did want to message Tai'dqei since setting foot at the resort, her reasons for doing so expanded the longer she stayed. It wasn't simply her missing him, but a gut feeling that something was wrong. Part of her still struggled against that instinct, believing she was just looking for any reason to reach out to him.

Before the other two could reply, one of the android staff poked their head into the room. A quizzical look passed over their features after a beat of observing the three women. "What are you three doing here together? You're from highly disparate decades."

Rayelle frowned, being reminded of one of the few guidelines of Rerli 3: Stick to your era.

It was a rule few abided by, much to the staff's chagrin. Some decades had far fewer people. It was unfair to isolate the few from socialization, simply due to potential anachronisms.

Besides, it didn't seem there had been any successful return stories from what Rayelle managed to dredge up. Which meant no one returning to their home could blab about the 'wonders of the future,' whether near or distant.

Again, Rayelle reminded herself this resort was new. Maybe there were successful stories of return trips elsewhere.

"What do you need, Jane?" Lisa's nose wrinkled as she popped her bubble gum. Her cherry red lips curved down into a harsh frown.

Forgetting the transgression or simply not caring — as far as an android could care — Jane made a delighted sound and clapped her hands together once. "There are guests who wish to make your acquaintance."

"Guests? Are they non-humans?" Rayelle pushed herself into a sitting position, trying to stifle the way her heart jumped. There was no way Tai'dqei could have gotten there so soon, right? It had to be someone else. That itch of concern started to weasel its way into her thoughts again.

"Yes, isn't that exciting?" Jane's smile didn't falter. Her gaze was far more unblinking than the suddenly missing Jezika's ever was.

Rayelle narrowed her eyes. The other two human women in the room exchanged glances, apparently already aware where she'd go with this. "What happened to disallowing non-humans here?"

"I haven't the slightest what you mean, Miss Brooks," Jane replied, no hint of deception in her voice or her features. Maybe she was programmed not to show such negative emotion. Jane folded her hands in front of herself, primly, still sporting that spotless smile on her pink lips. "We hope to facilitate strong bonds with non-humans here, in case our residents cannot go home."

Residents. Not guests. Rayelle narrowed her eyes, not really enjoying how her mind gnawed on the distinction of those two words. Sandra shifted in her chair and Lisa snorted, both swathed in the same aura of uncertainty that Rayelle felt.

"What kind of aliens are there?" Sandra was the one to ask, slowing as she said 'aliens' as if she couldn't believe it was coming out of her own mouth.

Rayelle didn't know if it was a novel word or simply personal experiences making it taste bad on Sandra's tongue.

Not picking up on Sandra's distaste, Jane twittered excitedly, "Oh, there are many esteemed guests of all sorts to meet!"

"Ja-tau?" Rayelle asked, unable to stop herself. Maybe Tai'dqei had gotten into the heads of the androids and altered their programming.

Maybe he petitioned whoever ran Rerli 3 for access. Maybe, maybe, maybe. A billion wishful thoughts spun about Rayelle's head, knowing they were all unlikely.

"Of course not!" If it wasn't for their situation, Rayelle would have found Jane's scandalized tone and expression funny. "They're too much for delicate human sensibilities."

Rayelle sucked on her teeth, before hazarding a tentative guess. "Florizian?"

"What a good guess!" Jane's delighted expression felt like a punch to Rayelle's gut. She wished the android had visited before she sent the message to Tai'dqei. Then she could warned him what was going on with more evidence and not just her silly gut feeling.

"Tell 'em to come back later." Lisa's brusque voice caught Jane's attention, the android turning a perturbed look to the red-headed punk. Waving her hand, her plastic bracelets rattling on her wrist, Lisa added with no less bite, "I don't feel like meeting anyone new today."

Jane seemed about to say something when Sandra, with her working knitting needles jittering a little more than earlier, sighed, "Neither do I, I'm afraid."

"Me either," Rayelle chimed in, leaning back on her hands on the bed and crossing her legs. She and Jane locked gazes across the small distance between bed and entryway. Calculations, considerations, and – perhaps – a fight between original programming versus new flickered behind Jane's eyes. Rayelle waited quietly, hoping she'd be proven wrong.

"I'm afraid you don't have a choice in the matter. Our guests are sizable investors to our organization," Jane finally answered with a sigh.

She stepped to the side, motioning to the hallway where two aliens emerged. One had long, wiggling tendrils like Zav and the other had four multi-faceted eyes and strange solid-looking growths from their cheeks. Both were built like tanks.

The air in the room stilled. One side, thick with distrust. The other firm in their sense of complete control. Only Jane appeared unaware of the quiet clashing of forces. The android made a gesture to the two aliens as she continued to speak to the humans, "You will be escorted to the assembly hall with everyone else. Please, come along."

With that, Jane happily flounced from the room, leaving humans and aliens to leer at one another. Rayelle considered refusing to move but Sandra sighed and put her knitting away into her bag. The housewife stood, dusting off her skirt.

Sandra shot Rayelle and Lisa a look that read 'let's get this over with.' Rayelle and Lisa exchanged a look, before quietly following Sandra and the unknown aliens from the room.

◊ ◊ ◊

Apprehension lit hot and heavy in the air of the assembly hall. As per everything else in the resort, each decade had its own auditorium to keep decade mingling to a minimum. Unexpectedly, it seemed the forces in charge funneled all available humans into the 2070s hall. Most likely due to the heightened tech and plush seating available in that particular auditorium.

Jane gathered more humans since retrieving Rayelle, Sandra, and Lisa. It seemed as if she was just going door to door, herding in who-so-ever was around. With the number of humans, the number of non-human escorts also expanded.

By the time they made it to the assembly hall, there were six non-humans and nearly twenty-five humans. No one spoke since every time they did, one of their escorts would gargle or growl or snarl at them.

An alien that reminded Rayelle of a cross between an octopus and a shark stopped Jane's troupe near the entryway. They regarded a holo-screen in tentacled hands. "Do you have guests TDA2G, TDA3K, and TDC8P?"

Rayelle thought she could hear the whirring of mechanics in Jane's head before she eventually affirmed, "Yes, I do."

"Those're Zav's dibs," the alien gurgled before rushing to intercept another group. Another non-human shuffled into the spot Octo-Arms had left empty. This one was purple with blue flowers blossoming at their temples and vine-like hair pulled back into an elaborate pile atop their head.

"What an honor!" Jane turned to her group of humans, clapping her hands with manufactured excitement. She pointed out the three humans, bouncing on her heels with delight. "Bette, Rayelle, and Mizan, you'll be going with this lovely Florizian gentleperson."

The two others — Bette, a 1940s factory worker, and Mizan, a young scholar from the 2050s — dawdled in the safety of the group until Rayelle stepped toward their new escort. Bette and Mizan followed her, both staying behind Rayelle as the Florizian led them away. Rayelle tried to shoot the two assured glances, but Bette's features remained stony and Mizan looked about ready to faint.

The walk wasn't a long one, but it did lead them to a more secluded area of the resort. The wing they were led housed basic administration offices. As Rayelle traversed the corridor, she realized the area had changed since her last visit five days ago. Cubicles had been torn out and desks shoved to the far walls. A number of aliens lingered about, some lollygagging as others moved purposefully.

Into one of the larger offices, the three humans were led. Other humans were corralled in, as well. Rayelle wondered what they were intending to do with the humans left behind in the assembly hall. Her mind took her thoughts to places too grim to focus on with the present danger before her.

Instead she turned her attention to the desk, behind which a nauseatingly familiar person stood.

"Ah, good, my darlings have arrived," Zav said when one of the lackeys turned his attention toward the humans. He turned, all smiles and charm while the vine-tendril hair wiggled with excitement. He stood tall and lithe, dressed in a nice enough octarine-colored suit. Rayelle couldn't help but picture how that smile could easily turn into a toothy snarl.

"Let me take a look at you all." He rounded the desk and approached the roughly twelve humans in attendance, an appraising look in his eyes.

All of them stood to attention as Zav approached, noticeably uncertain but spines straight. He tilted his head this way and that, drinking in the details of each person and occasionally touching them with a hair vine. He'd mutter instructions to another Florizian, a smaller one that tailed at his heel but Rayelle couldn't catch whatever he said.

The longer the inspection went on, the more her peers lost their cool exteriors. Mizan's shoulders arched to their ears, their lips pressed together with anxiety, while Bette glowered with her arms crossed over her chest. Others fidgeted or tugged on their clothes. Rayelle schooled her expression into neutrality, to hide any inkling of recognition in her eye when Zav stared at her.

His hair wavered atop his head, before he traced a single tendril down the curve of Rayelle's jaw. It felt velvety soft and pliable, but cold. She braced against the vine, waiting to feel a thorny bite as he asked, "And you are the one who'd been traveling with a ja-tau, yes?"

"That's right," she answered, forcing herself to remain still under the touch. Her eyes angled toward Zav's face, hating that she had to look up into their features.

Their dark eyes surveyed her for a moment, but they were unreadable to her. She couldn't begin to imagine what Zav saw in her, what he thought of her.

"I do hope he didn't tarnish you," he finally said, another brush of the vine coasted over her cheek to her chin and down her neck. It was a normally gentle action that felt like spiders crawling over her skin.

Her brows furrowed at the assertion, a frown threatening to tilt at her lips. "What do you mean?"

"Well, your importance to me is for the revitalization of the Florizian population." He patted her cheek as he gave her a narrow-eyed, double-edged smile. "Can't do that if you're carrying a litter of ja-tau spawn, can you?"

A litter. That was curious wording. Rayelle stowed that away for later contemplation and perhaps to ask Tai'dqei if she ever saw him again.

Otherwise, she chose not to focus on the implication of those words. Still clinging to her sense of calm since she suspected it wouldn't last, Rayelle managed to evenly reply, "If you're asking if I had relations with my traveling partner, I did not."

"That is good to hear!" That edged smile softened into one of actual delight on Zav's features. Pity that he was a piece of shit, Rayelle realized, since the expression was actually almost sweet.

"I also don't intend to be a Florizian broodmare," she added, squaring her shoulders and raising her chin. At her sides, her fists clenched and her fingernails dug into her palm to keep her from trembling.

The Florizian before her blinked owlishly. Behind him, others shifted awkwardly, aware of how the air around their boss dipped dangerously. Zav's delighted smile was short-lived as a colder grin took its place. "You won't be a broodmare. More like a greenhouse."

Rayelle rolled her eyes at the wordplay. As if he could turn this into a cutesy exchange when he was about to force the humans into a state of perpetual parental servitude. "My tubes are tied. No babies for me."

Before she could register the movement, one of Zav's hands whipped out and grabbed her forcefully by the chin. His fingertips held tight, the throb of bruises already forming. A startled sound choked in her throat as his other arm looped around her back, pulling her closer to him.

"Do you really think we can't reverse that?" Zav sneered down at her, vines waggling in cruel amusement. A long green tongue flickered out wetting his lips as he stared down at her, his teeth glinting in the brief moment his mouth opened. "Pity about the pheromones though. That was more for your pleasure than anything else, but we'll make do. Won't we?"

He squeezed her cheeks, demanding a reaction or answer. A dull throb ached through her jaw as her heart pounded. Rayelle shot him a squinty-eyed, sarcastic smile as her hand moved carefully to her hoodie pocket.

It hadn't taken a rocket scientist to feel the shift in the resort's atmosphere over the last two days. Nearly every human noticed it. A few had mentioned the androids acting strange as well. Others had actually seen unfamiliar non-humans loping about. Two humans had gone completely missing and the staff had been unable to account for them, even in their own records.

Suspicious, Rayelle had spoken to others, revealing to them what Tai'dqei had told her about human breedability. As the word spread, more and more humans came to her. Even if the chance was slim, even if they were simply being paranoid, they decided to prepare for the worst.

Anything that could be used as a stabbing or bludgeoning weapon, that wouldn't immediately be noticed as missing, was gathered. Knives and meat tenderizers from the kitchens. Scissors, knitting needles, and woodcarving implements from the craft areas. The gardens provided the most fearsome would-be weapons with three-pronged cultivators, sharp edged trowels, shears, clippers, and scythes.

As far as anyone could tell, the staff hadn't noticed at all, which led to the bolder thefts. Shovels and automated knives and saws and anything that could feasibly have a use to protect themselves. Larger items were hidden around the resort, in places they could flee to. Smaller items were kept on their persons. Such as the hand cultivator in Rayelle's hoodie pocket.

Zav was too intent on snarling into her face to realize her movement. She quickly withdrew the three-pronged weapon from her pocket and swung it up, into the side of the Florizian's face.

The Florizian let out a shriek of shock and pain as the satisfying squish of metal sunk into his flesh and eye. He shoved her away and Rayelle kept a tight hold on her weapon. It *shlucked* free of the side of his face and sticky dark green liquid spurted from the injury. An overwhelming scent like cut grass but headier filled Rayelle's nostrils as she stumbled back.

Taking her lead, the other humans instantly followed suit by bludgeoning and stabbing any alien who had the misfortune of being close enough. Bette, armed with a knife and a metal pan — wherever the hell she managed to conceal that — as a shield, slammed two Florizians away. Mizan, with their taser in one hand and a knife in the other, fell a surprised four-armed alien.

The room erupted into chaos and screams. Rayelle hoped the others could hear back in the assembly hall or that they had already begun their own escape attempts. It hadn't been a perfect plan. Optimistically, the others figured out what was up and used their stolen goods to start their own escapes.

The stunned guards took a moment to react before rushing toward the sharps and electricity. Green and red blood splattered, though more of the former spilled than the latter. Rayelle spun toward the door, finding Mizan struggling against a Florizian with their knife. Launching herself at the alien, she slammed the cultivator into the back of its head before it even spun to face her.

"Let's go!" Someone headed for the hall, slamming through the door and into the corridor. High on adrenaline and taking advantage of the shock, all the humans rushed from the room, scattering into the hallway. As Rayelle raced with Bette and Mizan, others in similar states of bruised and bloody disarray met up with them.

She thought to do a headcount, but there was no time. They had to get to the 1950s bomb shelter or to the 2170s radioactivity shelter. There were a number of smaller holdout spaces but most of the supplies like first aid kits, weaponry, and communication tech had been stored in those two places.

The longer Rayelle ran, the more shrieks and screams she heard. Alarms started blaring through the resort, flashing red and angry, as the far-off sounds of booted footfalls and barking orders echoed.

Trash cans and laundry carts and supply stations were

overturned to hinder alien pursuers. Anything that couldn't be nailed down was thrown in the way.

Ungodly howls swelled up behind Rayelle and she couldn't help but look back. Zav was there.

Or she thought it was Zav. It was hard to tell. He'd grown larger and his tendrils had overtaken his body. He was a writhing mass of teeth and vines, one eye glowing and the other a bloody hole. Judging from the hate-filled glare pinned to her form, it was definitely Zav.

Her legs carried her faster, her heart stuttering as her lungs ached for more breath. The mental map in her head knew she was close to safety. Just one more skidding turn down a hall and…

Others were already in the shelter, waving other runners in and screaming for laggers to hurry up.

Rayelle's heart twisted. They had all agreed, if necessary, the doors would shut even if some were locked out. There was hope they could flee to a smaller hidey hole or into the vents or even to the outside.

They were banking on the fact their reproductive capabilities were too valuable to destroy. But they all knew it was a gamble.

Rayelle hurtled over the threshold with two others before the door slammed shut. Spinning around as the locks chunked into place, she peered through the porthole — heavy glass that would deflect bullets or maybe even lasers — and the solid door vibrated with impact. Something big and angry and vicious pounded at the door. It shook in its frame, but the metal held firm.

She stood, staring at it as her chest heaved with panting breaths. Her lungs ached and her legs twinged. The place where

Zav had gripped her along her jaw throbbed with heat. She was definitely bruised.

But they had done it! At least for the moment, they had managed to rebel and get away from the aliens. These alleged investors of Rerli 3. They were likely also the aliens that had funded so many lives being ripped away from home to begin with. It hadn't just been Florizians, Rayelle absently realized. There had been other non-humans, ones she didn't have names for.

Shaking her analytical thoughts away, she turned to the innards of the bunker while ignoring the angry howls on the other side of the door. "Was that everyone?"

"No one was locked out if that's what you mean," replied Abe, an older man who Rayelle suspected was from the 1930s from his typical attire and accent. Those particular clothes were ripped and bloody now and his words strained.

Initially, it had been surprising to find people typically incapable of pregnancy at Rerli 3. After some thought, Rayelle guessed there were aliens out there needing sperm just as much as eggs and incubators. Or maybe there were aliens that incubated via any kind of human. Whatever the case, that was a consideration for a time when a threat didn't loom so close.

She nodded and muttered thanks to Abe before glancing over the assembled people, crammed into the room. Not everyone got away in one piece. Quite a few bloodied people sat on the floor as others tended to their medical needs. Quiet sobbing and whimpering filled the room.

Rayelle tried not to fret or worry about familiar faces she didn't find among the masses.

Even if everyone couldn't get to the bunkers, they had mapped out a number of other decent hiding places. She just had to hope everyone had gotten somewhere safe. Even if those other areas weren't stocked with as much food or intense weaponry, it was better than in the hands of the enemy aliens.

With her heart still pounding, she glanced at her wrist gauntlet. Her fingers shook as she pulled up the communication app, the one she had sent a message through to Tai'dqei earlier.

Had he seen her message?

Had he replied?

Was he coming?

Her stomach sank as a '*No Satellite Connection*' error flashed on the holo-screen.

CHAPTER 17

It was always easier to covertly sneak into a place when chaos consumed it. Everyone else was too focused on solving the more dire problem, they didn't remain alert to new unseen threats that may creep up. Not that Tai'dqei wasn't proficient in sneaking. His thermal netting masked his exterior as the ambient temperature while retaining hist heat on the inside. Not to mention the ja-tau cloaking tech he carried. Even the wariest observer would find it hard to pinpoint him.

Luckily, chaotic was how he found Rerli 3 after his long trek from the isolated place where he had landed his cloaked ship. It took no effort to sneak through the doors as random aliens darted in and out. It was easier to hide his footfalls under the shouting as the other aliens sought something. Or someone.

Like a phantom, Tai'dqei scouted out the resort, sidestepping rushing bodies and slinking into opened rooms. It didn't take him long to find out

Rayelle's worries had been on the mark.

After stumbling into a tech repair bay, he realized the staff mostly consisted of androids. Blank replacement faces and detached limbs lined the shelves as he crept through the bay.

He hadn't read the pamphlet nor had he done extra research on Rerli 3. Now he could have kicked himself for not being more thorough. Androids were not a foolproof method of security. He was willing to bet their programming had been hacked by the very alien forces filling the rest of the resort. That or the whole resort was a front. A growl threatened to spill from his throat at that thought, but he clamped down on it.

The agitation churning through the resort didn't feel anticipatory or excited. There was a sharper edge to the air, a sense of fright and chaos, of surprise and rage. Which soothed Tai'dqei's concerns a little. Even if the resort was a front, their plans had gone awry. He faintly wondered if it was Rayelle's doing but shoved the thought away as the bay opened up to another corridor.

He'd find out what happened to her. If he didn't like what he found — or if he failed to find anything at all — then these intruders would have another problem on their hands.

The building rage twanging through his body barely remained contained as he silently trailed another small group of aliens. It would have been so easy to take their distracted little heads off with a swipe of a blade, but he needed to shadow. When he finally did slip into a security office, he got some of the answers he sought.

Various parts of the resort reflected on an array of holo-screens. However, there were two channels enlarged and eagerly being watched by the two Canoid guards seated in front of the console.

"They seriously disconnected it from the systems?" One barked a laugh, apparently having just sat down since the chair creaked beneath his muscular bulk.

"Yeah, apparently there's a mechanical override mechanism on the door. They can still open and close it themselves, but outsiders can't do shit." The other Canoid was smaller and lither, but their muscles flexed as they motioned to a particular video rectangle. They grinned at the screen, showing off sharp teeth in their canine-like maw.

Tai'dqei edged closer, taking care to remain silent. One wrong step and the sensitive hearing of the Canoids may alert them to his presence. He peered at the indicated screen, attempting to spot Rayelle. All he saw were fuzzy images of humanoid figures.

"Stars above, these humans really planned, huh? Thought they were completely clueless." The first one chuckled, throwing an arm behind their chair as they settled. Their flung arm barely missing striking the invisible mass of Tai'dqei, causing the ja-tau to tense.

The other chortled an uncharacteristically deep laugh for such a small frame. With a clawed finger, they pointed to a smaller screen labeled 'Exterior 1950s Bunker' in a lower corner. "Yeah, well, y'see the angry mess of tentacles there?"

Their claw clinked against a splotch on the screen. Ice slid through Tai'dqei's veins as he recognized the writhing blob. Under the writhing mass of vines and thorns, Zav raged.

The other guard leaned forward, squinting at the poor quality vid. He leaned back after a few seconds and yelped, "Is that bossman?"

"Yeah," snickered the other, their lips crooked in a smirk. "I heard he went full aggro mode after one of the tits carved his face up with a knife or some shit."

Tai'dqei's attention spun toward the gossiping Canoid, his eyes widening. Was that something Rayelle would do? Her immediate response to meeting an intimidating ja-tau *was* to attack and run. The deduction wouldn't be too unwarranted.

The two guards laughed together for a moment, still unaware of Tai'dqei's presence. He was beginning to consider killing the two in order to get further with his own investigation when a disembodied voice crackled from the guards' own gauntlets. "Hey, you two. You're needed out by the 1970s kitchen. We think someone's holed up in the vent there."

Both Canoids sighed and rose from their chairs, making their way to the door. One of them issued back a reply, "Right, right. Heading there now."

Just like that, the two left their post. Leaving the security office completely unlocked.

Tai'dqei watched them go, mentally haranguing them for lacking awareness. If they hadn't been so terrible at their job, he wouldn't have gotten the answers he needed. Turning back to the security footage, he crept closer to the screens.

He stared at the image of Zav in full offensive mode. Tai'dqei rarely saw a Florizian in full attack mode, but he recognized the spiky vines and massive growth of the body well enough. It appeared Zav was snarling at a door or wall.

Whatever, or whoever, on the other side likely wasn't opening up any time soon.

Next to the screen displaying Zav, another screen showed a room tightly packed with humans. 'Interior 1950s Bunker' flashed in the corner. None of the humans looked toward the camera. Tai'dqei wasn't even sure they knew a camera was there.

He frantically scanned, seeking Rayelle. In the far edges of the screen, he found other humans leaning over prone companions. Faintly, he wondered if she had been hurt. Was she among those lying recumbent, needing more medical help than what an aid kit could provide? Or worse?

The very idea she was worse off than the injured made his heart give a violent twist. He continued to carefully scan the security footage.

Finally, his eyes found her crouched in the corner of the room nearest the door and he involuntarily gave a relieved chuff. The quality of the vid didn't allow him to gauge her expression. Her body language, on the other hand, appeared tired and strained. Of course, that was only to be expected if she took part in or even orchestrated this chaos.

His main concern assuaged a fraction, Tai'dqei raised his wrist gauntlet. Despite whatever communication jamming tech the enemy had initiated, he located a satellite signal. It took him longer to ping a comm off his gauntlet on a frequency no one would notice. As soon as his encrypted communique shot into space, calling in reinforcements with an explanation of the circumstances, he turned back to the security console.

A number of options spun about his head, but it didn't take long to choose one. He needed to ruin the system, make it impossible for the enemy to utilize security capabilities.

Removing a gadget from his belt, Tai'dqei slapped it to the side of the computer. Released from their container, the nanobots ate into the metal of the console and were soon on their way to destroying the system from the inside out. He cast one more look at the screens, dedicating the mental map to memory while locating the power grid and generators.

Once sufficiently prepared, he was going to rain hell on anyone non-human. *Then*, with the immediate dangers taken care of, he'd find Rayelle. He just had to hope she – and the door – could hold out until then.

Tai'dqei slid from the security office, purpose and plan in place.

A ja-tau's fury was something to behold. And these fuckers were about to beholden it.

◊ ◊ ◊

At first, Rayelle thought they were trying to smoke out the AWOL humans. Everyone in the bunker tensed as lights flickered and dimmed. A cacophony of different alarms sounded before draining away, as if their batteries had died over the course of a few minutes. More frantic panic bled into the bunker from the halls. Screams and trotting feet, most of it leading away from their shelter.

Then more shouts as bodies and footfalls rushed the other way, past the door to the bunker. Some of the hollering ended abruptly, but Rayelle couldn't determine if it was due to voluntary or involuntary means.

Glancing around at the others assembled with her, everyone seemed to wear a similar concerned expression.

Something was wrong.

Well, something *else* was wrong.

Nervousness skittered across her skin, forcing her to rise from her crouch. Fright jolted through her when the lights fully gave up, plunging everything into darkness. Slow blinking emergency lights, charged by a generator somewhere, illuminated the world. The red hues, fading in and out of the dark, weren't helping the general anxiety.

"What the fuck is going on?" Abe's voice warbled between a concerned whisper and a brusque snarl.

"I think something is happening," she answered, cutting through the hushed theories. At the awkward quiet that hung in the air after her words, she sighed and amended, "Other than our rebellion."

A hesitantly hopeful question came from Lisa, "Do you think someone's alien-in-shining-armor answered the calls?"

As it turned out, Rayelle wasn't the only human who had been brought to the resort by an alien. Hell, some of the others had done *more* with their traveling companions than she even thought about with Tai'dqei. If she was being honest, she didn't even understand why some had parted ways.

Trying to shove the small envious whispers in her head aside, Rayelle shrugged. "Don't know. When I got here, I couldn't send a message out, so it would've had to get to him before everything blew up here."

Whatever anyone else was going to say in reply was interrupted as a scream sliced through the air. It was very, *very* close.

Something slammed bodily against the door. More cries and shrieks tore through the air, making many of the people in the bunker give responding screams or cover their own ears. It was a good thing many covered their ears, as she thought she heard the *schluck* of metal slicing flesh and the spill of copious amounts of blood. Rayelle strained her ears to hear that much and it could have been paranoia playing tricks on her.

Carefully, she crept closer to the door again.

Zav, who apparently hadn't abandoned the viewport as others fled, dodged when a body thumped against the door. He swung around, his tendrils riled and flexing along his body like enraged worms. Rayelle pressed her face to the glass, straining her eyes to see what – or who – Zav addressed, but she saw nothing in the red-black darkness.

Something tickled at the back of her memories. It wanted attention, but for the life of her she couldn't grasp it. She was too focused on what was happening in the hall to give the needling little recollection any notice.

252

With unfair speed, Zav threw himself at the invisible foe.

Abe hovered behind her shoulder, squinting into the darkness. "Was there a gas leak or something? He went off after thin air, it looks like."

Rayelle narrowed her eyes, focusing on the vague shape of Zav scrambling and flailing down the hall. She angled her vantage point to continue watching him. Judging from his movements, he was attempting to fight something. His tendrils shot out with intention, slapped in an intentional direction. Huge thorns shot across the corridor, spraying across something that seemed to glitter in the shadows.

"I don't think so," she said as scanned the area around Zav.

His writhing vines whipped around faster, seeking and striking something in the shadows. In the dark and in the throbbing red light, Rayelle had a hard time seeing anything, but she saw his tentacles connect. A spray of that glitter pulsed in the dark before darkness filled in again.

Finally, Zav seemed assured of his opponent's location. He charged across the corridor and…

Out of Rayelle's line of sight.

For a long breath, she stood at the door, struggling to see or hear anything. The shape of a shadow. The faint footfalls beyond. She closed her eyes, trying to pinpoint any sound outside the shelter. Every breath, every fidget, every shift inside the bunker irritated her as she focused.

There was nothing. Or she just couldn't hear anything.

Then, faintly, there was a shriek. Enraged, angry.

And another faint sound.

So faint, her mind could be playing tricks.

She willed herself to home in it, to *hear* it through the heavy walls. Something caught her ear and her eyes flew open. She thought she heard a familiar clicking gnarl.

◊ ◊ ◊

After arguing with the others, they finally allowed Rayelle to poke her head outside and around the door. The silence in the corridor was even eerier after all the commotion. She took a tentative step out, armed with a fire extinguisher.

Her nostrils flared and caught the mingling scents of bitterness and copper tinging the air. Something wet and sticky slicked against her shoes and she forced herself not to look. Goosebumps lit across her flesh as she took another quiet step.

Slowly, she edged down the hall in the direction Zav had gone. Tension wrought along her muscles, moving at a snail's pace in the alternating black-red world.

Her mind twirled with a billion different explanations for what happened. An asteroid shower, an attack from another alien race, a natural disaster outside. None of it really answered why Zav acted the way he had or the screams or the—

"I'll enjoy bending your little whore under me, Tai'dqei."

Rayelle froze, hearing the Florizian's voice about fifty feet around the corner. His tone wasn't the smooth and languid as before. Like his physical form, his voice had deepened and become thornier, filled with rage. Her grip tightened on the fire extinguisher as she edged closer to the corner to peer around the bend.

"I should have guessed she'd have a bit more bite, tagging along with you," snarled a writhing dark mass, hatred dripping from every syllable like a poison.

It took her a moment to make sense of the forms in the lighting. Zav thankfully stood with his back to her. She glanced over the Florizian, seeing what he had become.

His lithe body was still there but entangled in a mass of swollen tendrils. Spiky vines whipped around, as if in a frenzy that sought flesh and blood. She noticed there was some bright green liquid dripping from some of the appendages, but not enough for her to believe it was actual poison.

From the dark shadows near the ceiling, a warbling growl was all the response Zav received. The sound sent a flash of electricity down her spine. Rayelle hazarded a glance to the dark, trying to make out the glint of armor or a telltale silhouette.

In her distraction, Zav inhaled deeply and spun toward her. "Speaking of your little slut."

Tai'dqei hissed a curse to himself, his eyes darting to Rayelle's heat signature on his helmet's visor. Why did she have to come out now? That made dispatching Zav harder, since the Florizian had a faint ability to sense another's presence. It likely had something to do with breathing, but Tai'dqei wasn't entirely sure.

His stomach twisted, seeing how small the human was compared to the mass of alien vines.

Rayelle's eyes widened as she took in the Zav's large eyes, black as death and reflecting the fading red light. Dark ooze escaped between his serrated teeth. Was that blood? Or did he emit a viscous poison from his maw? She stumbled back a few steps, receiving an amused chortle from the dangerous alien.

"If you won't come out to play, Tai'dqei, I'll play with her instead." Zav launched himself at her, hands and tendrils extended.

Tai'dqei let loose a snarl, heart thrumming as he ricocheted down from the rafters. He knew he couldn't reach the two before they collided. And he'd already used up so many of his projectile weapons from culling the others.

Frozen, Rayelle watched as the writhing mass of rage closed the distance at a breakneck speed. A wicked smile spread over his features and a delighted cruelty lit up in his eyes. She didn't react until she could feel his balmy heat upon her. Her instincts blazed to the forefront as she registered a snarl from above.

Just as Zav was about to encapsulate her in vines and hands and teeth – Tai'dqei's stomach lurching at the preemptive image – she smashed the extinguisher against the side of his face, a primal scream erupting from her lips. The extinguisher made a deep *twung* on contact, metal slamming into flesh. Vibrations rolled up her arms, making her bones shudder.

Zav let loose a shrieky squawk, surprised by the sudden retaliation. His trajectory veered and slowed from instinct, recalibrating his tactic.

Rayelle wasn't about to give him a chance to recover.

With another feral scream, she slammed the butt of the extinguisher into his head over and over. When the metal became slick in her hands, she resorted to lengthwise bashing again. She ignored the vines that tried to wrap around her weapon, her arms, her body.

Equally struck by Rayelle's retaliation, Tai'dqei had to force himself to keep moving. It was no time to become a breathless whelp, admiring her beautiful savagery. He aided her with silent redirection of Zav's attacking tentacles as she carried on her assault. Even as he helped her, his thoughts burned with that familiar ache to have her be his.

In her periphery, Rayelle realized something invisible was intercepting the entangling appendages as she struck Zav continuously. Vines halted in mid-air, before an unseen force sliced them and threw them to the floor. Otherwise, she was too incensed to notice as the sound of metal crunched soggily against cartilage and bone and flesh and whatever else made up a Florizian's face.

As Zav crumpled lower and lower to the floor, her strikes followed him. Her thoughts swarmed with fury over her own circumstances, over the muddied situations of others, over how many lives had been affected by this revolting selfish bastard.

Warm blood splattered over her clothes, her arms, her face. Thankfully, none of it felt caustic and burning. She didn't stop until her arms ached and trembled. Unable to continue, she let her arms drop, staring at Zav hunched over on the ground. Taking a step back, her breaths heaved as she took a look at her work.

Liquid pooled around her feet, the scent of cut grass filling her nose. Detached vines, some wiggling and some still, covered the tiles. Rayelle had just lowered the extinguisher and stepped back once more when Zav jerked upright suddenly. He gave a strange tri-toned hissing shriek as he lunged.

She should have known he'd be as sturdy as a weed. Even with his face mangled, teeth chipped, and edges jutting in painful angles, hatred burned in what was left of his eyes.

Whatever he was intending to do, whatever her instincts braced for, nothing came. Her eyes widened as Zav's face split in two, before she realized an invisible blade had cleaved the Florizian's head in twain. Unseeable heft slammed into Zav, grappling the alien down to the floor.

With wide-eyed horror, she watched as the Florizian's torso split open on its own. More dark blood sprayed and oozed across the floor. He howled and gurgled and retched before suddenly seizing. The edges of his tendril hair seemed to wither as Zav took one last wheezing breath and fell still.

There was another hiss of unseen metal on flesh and Zav's head toppled from the stump of his neck.

Instinct, fear, adrenaline. It all pumped through Rayelle as she wildly trying to register what had just happened. The air shifted in front of her. She didn't know how she knew. Maybe it was lighting or shadow, but it reared up her fight or flee instinct.

With a surprised half-scream, she slammed the extinguisher into the invisible force even as her muscles protested. A grunt sounded on impact before a cascade of flickering lights revealed who she had hit. As the slow blinking red lights illuminated his helmet, her eyes widened.

Tai'dqei.

Something was wrong. Rayelle sensed Tai'dqei glowered at her behind his visor, his shoulders stiff. Her gaze flicked over his body, wondering if it wasn't him. Had she mistaken a different ja-tau for her former traveling companion? For the most part, his form felt familiar. If only the damned lights weren't red and blinking, she could tell for certain.

"Tai'dqei?" She gasped softly, hoping for confirmation while her heart still pounded. Was this actuality? Or had she suffered from so much stress, she was imagining things? Though fluorescent green blood oozed from various points on his face and body, the amount of other unidentified liquid – presumably enemy blood – far exceeded his own.

It took all of Tai'dqei's willpower to not pounce on the woman, especially as she said his name so breathlessly. Two streams of thought diverged on what they'd do to her. One side just wanted to hold her close, check her over for injuries. The other wanted to tear her clothes off and feel her soft heat under him as he plunged into her. He couldn't stop his low gurgling growl as it resonated in his chest.

Rayelle's eyes wheeled back to his face, hearing more than seeing how his mandibles flexed. His low snarl made her stomach dip with a tingling sensation she couldn't concentrate on. Now, she was more than certain it was her companion. She took a wobbly step toward him, fire extinguisher still gripped in hand. Her free hand rose, intending to touch his arm. "What's wrong?"

Rayelle froze in place as he snarled a singular word. "Run."

Confusion settled over her thoughts at his single command. Run? Why? There wasn't any danger any longer.

"Why? Zav's taken care of and no one else is—" Rayelle cast a wary look around, wondering if there were other dangers lurking in the shadows. Dangers that would make the ja-tau tell her to flee.

Tai'dqei took a step forward, barely restraining himself. A strong urge to grab her, drag her close to him, bit into his arms. Under that urge, the desire to lose himself in her churned hot and hard. To hear her sounds while she was caught in the throes of pleasure. To feel her clench around him as her nails raked over his skin. Searing claws of instinct sunk into him, threatening to tear his self-control apart.

"You. *Hit.* Me." He bit out each word, trying to put meaning into every syllable. Please let her remember. Let her understand. Between the adrenaline of the fight and dispatching an untold number of enemies, his urges were riding hard in his head. Like rivers of sparking electricity, sinking deep into his muscles.

Her striking him, after *everything*, didn't help his self-control.

"It was an accide—!" Rayelle started to snap, before a memory of his own words ricocheted through her head.

"One ja-tau mating ritual is meant to assess the capabilities of a mate by gaining their attention and then running. Challenging them to a different sort of hunt."

She wheeled her attention back to him, her heart skipping at the realization. He stood stiff, fighting something inside himself. Like a dog trying so hard to be good and not gobble up a treat. Heat flared up her body and warmed her face as all she could do was stare at him in the fading in-and-out light.

She realized he was *covered* in blood of various hues, including his own. Scratches and dents marred his armor. Before he even intercepted Zav, Tai'dqei had engaged with who-knew-how-many others.

How many had he dispatched or incapacitated? How many had he tied up for others to deal with? How much victory had he witnessed and how did that play into whatever thrummed through him now?

Her mouth snapped closed before opening again to say something. Before she could piece together words, a small contingent of humans scurried around the corner. Each was armed with some sort of makeshift weapon.

"Rayelle! What's going on?" Lisa demanded, hoisting a crowbar swiped from the tech bay. Her eyes wheeled around, seeking immediate dangers while overlooking the hulking armored alien and the dead Florizian in the red-black lighting.

Before Rayelle could answer, Abe noticed Zav's decimated form. His free hand half-covered his mouth as the shovel he held drooped in his other hand. "Oh lord, *what's that?*"

"Forget that, who're *they?*" Bette pointed her rolling pin at Tai'dqei, suspicion painted across her features. She looked ready to attack if Rayelle said the word.

With eyes so wide they nearly popped out of their face, a pallid Mizan softly gasped from behind Abe, "Is that a ja-tau?"

The appearance of the others eased the tension in Tai'dqei. Good. Their human audience dampened the carnal hunger burning inside him. Not entirely, but enough to keep him from straining against his own self-control.

"Are you all done now?" Rayelle planted her hands on her hips when there was a lull in the rapid-fire questions. When everyone remained silent, she pointed to the ja-tau with her thumb. "That is Tai'dqei. The ja-tau that ferried me here."

"Him?" Sandra's eyes grew wide. Her expression couldn't exactly be considered fearful, Rayelle thought, as the housewife's eyes dipped down and up Tai'dqei's armored form.

Easing from her offensive stance, Bette copied Sandra's assessing look before giving an appreciative hum.

Tai'dqei's mandibles flexed as they spoke, not noticing how the others stared at him. He was used to most humans fearing him, given history. If these were time-displaced humans, their attention was going to be apprehensive no matter the situation.

No, his mind gnawed on the fact Rayelle had told other humans about him. The only question was whether it had been good or bad gossip. Likely both, he decided in an attempt to neither get too hopeful or too dire.

"What's going on, Tai'dqei?" Rayelle's question shook him from his thoughts.

He glanced up to find she hadn't moved any closer to her human companions. She stayed rooted in the spot she'd been when they arrived, between him and her peers. Though her outstretched hand, previously intent to touch him, now dangled at her side. A part of him wished she had managed to touch him before the interruption, but he knew that would have spelled disaster for his restraint.

He trilled a frustrated clicking sound – though Rayelle doubted it was due to her question – before replying to her. "You messaged me, so I came."

"What about the others?" She motioned to Zav, highlighting the implication she was talking about the other aliens. She struggled to ignore the pleasant heat his answer stoked inside her. She voiced her worries and he came running.

"Many are dead. Others incapacitated." Tai'dqei rolled his shoulders absentmindedly as he glanced around the corridor. Rayelle didn't miss how, even clad in his armor, the movement highlighted his musculature. It made the corners of her lips threaten to split into a smile, wondering if he had done that intentionally or without thinking.

It was her ghost of a smile that made Tai'dqei realize what he was doing. He forced his body to still, even as the inclination to move, to do particularly unspeakable things with Rayelle, made him fidgety. "Reinforcements will be here soon. I apprised them of the situation in a transmission."

"Other ja-tau?" She ignored Mizan's slight whimper at her words. They had told her their stories of the ja-tau and it was apparent the memories were strong and fresh in their mind.

Tai'dqei ignored how one of the humans whined. "Yes."

"Okay." The tension in her shoulders eased. She didn't want to say it out loud, considering the stories she had heard from later generations of humans, but her trust was low for other non-humans. Even if Tai'dqei was an exception, she still felt better knowing it was only ja-tau coming. Other humans present likely didn't hold the same relief.

Turning to the thankfully silent humans, she nodded back down the hall toward the direction of the bunker. "You all go back to the shelter."

"What about you?" Bette raised her eyebrows, simultaneously curious and critical. The woman's expression made Rayelle feel like a teenager again, being silently chided for being in a closed room alone with her boyfriend.

"Tai'dqei and I have some things to discuss." A blush flared over her cheeks as she explained, hoping her expression would silence Bette. Rayelle ignored how Lisa snorted at her answer or the looks the others gave her.

"*Now?*" Sandra wrinkled her nose, though it was hard to miss the amusement curling at her lips.

Taking a deep breath, Rayelle closed her eyes and attempted to sound calm with her own people. "Remember what I said of ja-tau rituals? I accidentally hit him with the extinguisher."

Rayelle opened her eyes just in time to see Sandra's lips form an 'o' before she nodded and scurried off. If it wasn't for the red light, she would have guessed the other woman blushed fiercely. The others soon followed after, save for Lisa who lingered with a shit-eating grin on her lips. "So, if you scream, should we—"

"Lisa, I swear to fuck! Just go!" Rayelle snarled, jabbing a finger down the hall. At that, Lisa cackled and trotted off.

Glaring after the insufferable punk, Rayelle was grateful Lisa hadn't decided to dawdle or try to eavesdrop on them. With the entourage gone, silence slipped between Rayelle and Tai'dqei. It weighed heavily over both of them as the lights faded through a handful of red-black cycles. When her attention turned back to him, she realized this 'talk' should wait.

Both of them were covered in blood and her clothing was ripped in places. Scratches and cuts littered her body. The blood-encrusted fire extinguisher weighed heavily in her hands, which also were caked in viscera.

Tai'dqei appeared in worse condition. Parts of his netting were ripped or completely missing and armor was dented and scraped. Large smears of blood coated him like a messy fingerpainting project. She wasn't even sure if he was badly injured or not. If he was, he didn't act like it but Rayelle suspected that no ja-tau would kneel to pain easily. Especially when high on battle fervor.

"You should go. Whatever needs to be discussed can be addressed later," he finally growled, still not stepping closer to her, not trusting himself. He had to fight himself just to say those words. Her departure was the last thing he wanted. Her excuse to the others had stirred wonderful carnal heat in him, but he stuffed it down. She wasn't going to humor his instincts, wasn't going to let him rut her right there. Not in the state either of them were in.

She looked up at him, her expression appraising and

unreadable. He stiffened as she stepped closer, the muscles tightening down his back. Intuitively, he was preparing for something. What it was, however, he couldn't bring himself to label it. He didn't want to be disappointed.

Whatever considerations Rayelle held about holding off dissipated into thin air. Between her surgeries and arriving at the resort, she had stalled enough while trying to make sense of her feelings toward Tai'dqei, someone so capable and comfortable with killing. Their time apart had given her a new perspective, a new understanding.

In this moment, they were here. Together. The danger — according to him — was handled for the moment. Zav, the likeliest ringleader, was dead. Their little audience had finally retreated to safety. The calvary was on the way.

Rayelle took another step closer to him and had to bite down a laugh as Tai'dqei seemed ready to stumble backward. A killing machine so scared of her or, more accurately, scared of what he wanted to do to her. Tilting her chin up and narrowing her eyes while she still smiled. "Why?"

"You know why," he growled, clearly frustrated. The frayed ropes of his restraint were ready to snap as she took another step closer.

Rayelle's smile widened further. He was trying so hard to be good, trying not to touch her, that he completely overlooked her signals. Then again, maybe her signals were foreign to him, considering they were different species.

She tilted her head to the side, licking her lips before pressing further, "Do I?"

"Ye—" A sudden *splurt* of foam from the extinguisher caught him in the face. An annoyed rumble vibrated from his chest as he reached up and swiped the mess from his mask's smooth visor. Doing so only revealed the sight of Rayelle dropping the extinguisher, turning, and running.

She was running.

CHAPTER 18

Tai'dqei didn't even get a chance to stop himself. No thought fired off between his brain and feet as he took off after her. With a snarl, he charged and gained ground.

The second she heard him start rushing after her, excitement prickled through her veins. Excitement sparked as she sensed, more than felt, a hand reaching for her jacket's hood. A bead of mild disappointment at the game being short-lived pulsed through her but it didn't have to be that way, she realized.

As Tai'dqei triumphantly closed his clawed fingers around her hood and prepared to yank her back against his chest, Rayelle writhed out of the jacket. She slipped from one sleeve and spun, sharply turning to free herself from the other sleeve.

A half-snarl half-hiss left the ja-tau as he instantly dropped the hoodie, wasting no time to lunge for the woman. He barely missed snagging her as she turned a corner. A pool of blood caught his boots, making Tai'dqei lose traction.

There was a second of confusion as the sound of his footfalls faltered and skidded, a dull thump against a solid surface. Glancing over her shoulder, Rayelle had to bite back a laugh. Even in the fading red light, she could see him push off the wall he had slid into. A telltale smear of blood trailed from a puddle, evidence of his fumble.

Was he so focused on her, he wasn't paying attention to his surroundings? Flattered delight jolted high and sudden in her chest, making it hard to breathe momentarily.

Ducking and dodging through the war-torn Rerli 3 resort, Rayelle only caught glimpses of disaster between bumbling through the darkness. Heavy carts turned over around large fallen foes. The underside of vents and wires torn from the ceiling and walls. Large claw marks adorned much of the damage, indicating it wasn't all her rebellion. Tai'dqei had certainly done a number on the place if that was all his doing.

Some of the damage had to be from other humans, fighting to survive. Part of her knew that. But that part was quickly shoved to the wayside as her delight and hormones took control. There'd be time to worry and fret and grieve later.

Right now, she just wanted to steal some time with Tai'dqei. Even if running away from him appeared counter-intuitive to that. More than once, she stumbled and gasped, sure that he would descend on her in her mistake.

Being larger, Tai'dqei was forced to take more care moving around a building made for human-sized entities. The bulk of his armor slowed him down, catching on debris or bodies skewered to walls or the ceiling. It was utterly infuriating. Whatever Rayelle had sprayed at him was playing havoc with his helmet's thermal sensor. He supposed running into that wall hadn't helped the damage either. A background thought noted he'd have to get it repaired.

Whatever the case, the damaged sensor made following her movements in the emergency lighting aggravating. Even as she staggered on occasion, whatever ground he gained was lost as the world habitually plunged into darkness. Without his thermal visor, the shadows forced him to slow lest he make another ill-thought mistake and lose her completely.

The longer he followed her, the worse the heat in him grew. As frustrating as the situation was, as ridiculous as he felt for blundering, Tai'dqei was determined to finally alleviate this pressure. It had gnawed at him for too long. The hunger for her cleaved through him, spraying fire over his nerves and making it difficult to think logically, to plan, to defend against Rayelle's own tricks.

His thoughts whorled around her. How she'd feel under his hands, under him. The sounds she'd make as he drew her body to the highest peaks of pleasure. An excited growl perpetually caught in his throat as he plunged on, this time not slowing as the lights dimmed.

Rayelle's desperate feet wove their way back to the 1990s and 2000s areas, trying to recall the mental map she had of Rerli resort. She nearly ran by the door she sought, but she thankfully saw it in the last second of red light.

Ducking through it, she found herself in the strangely quiet and seemingly untouched library. Once the lights bathed the world in red again, she picked up her pace. Racing through the stacks, she tried to remain silent on her feet and attempted not to drip any gore on the library's offerings.

She wasn't exactly sure where to go, just yet. For now, she was just leading Tai'dqei on a chase. That seemed the important part. It got the blood pumping, the heart racing, anticipation rising. At least, that's what it was doing for her. Excitement skittered across her skin, already eager for the end of the game but not ready to give in.

Her more forward thoughts tried to find the next obstacle to make the chase satisfying. Meanwhile, her under-thoughts were distractingly plagued with scenes of what would happen when he finally got his hands on her.

The door slammed open as she made it three-quarters of the way across the library, toward a door on the opposite side of the room. Slapping a hand over her mouth to stifle her gasp, Rayelle ducked down. In a crouch, she moved silently until the bulk of a desk shielded her.

"Rayelle!" Tai'dqei's snarl sent a shiver down her spine and his authoritative tone rattled her bones.

His own pace slowed as he peered around. The room appeared to be a cache for books in tall shelving units. So tall, they easily hid her from view. Further frustration pulled a growl from his throat.

Coming up to a shelf, he eyed the books. Flashes of memory flickered from his time with Rayelle, watching her bent over a book and reading. He gave a thoughtful click as an idea struck him. Working off a theory, he snatched a book off its shelf and flipped it open. After one last glance around, finding no hint of Rayelle, he experimentally tore a few pages.

For a wild second, Rayelle tried to make sense of the hissing sound. It sounded familiar, but not dangerous. Realization struck her like a truck and her eyes widened. Was he tearing pages out of the book?

Forgetting herself, she jumped up and lost the protection of the desk. "Tai'dqei, don't you dare!"

She realized her mistake instantly. His attention snapped toward the movement before she had even called out. Tai'dqei chittered with satisfaction. Already forgetting the book, he carelessly dropped it to the carpet as he bolted toward her.

A yelp squeezed through her lips as she darted the final feet toward the door. Bounding over the threshold and slamming the barrier shut behind her, she knew the ja-tau would not cause further destruction in the library. There was no doubt in her mind that he'd only damaged the book to rile her.

Rayelle only hoped it wasn't something valuable or irreplaceable. If so, Tai'dqei was going to get a tongue lashing after this was all over.

She had barely stepped out into the hall when the doorknob rattled behind her. Her heart leapt in her throat as her feet carried her fast down the hall, not caring how heavy her footsteps thudded against the tiles. Desperately, she looked around for another destination. There would be little obstruction for Tai'dqei's pursuit in the hallway.

Relief swelled as her eyes landed on the kitchen's swinging doors. Swerving toward the entryway, she pushed through while listening to Tai'dqei gaining behind her. An excited apprehension nipped across her nerves once more. The sensation dropping deep into her center.

Rayelle careened into the community kitchen, skirting the large island in the middle of the room. Tai'dqei burst in before the kitchen doors even closed after her and she turned to face him. Adrenaline clawed through her, focusing on her core.

"Got you," Tai'dqei growled with pride, hands flexing at his sides as his steps slowed. Now he walked like a big cat, eyeing its prey. And he was going to enjoy eating her up. Even now, he imagined he could taste her sweetness on his tongue.

Rayelle's heart thrummed in her chest, the blush worsening across her cheeks. Her chest rose and fell with deep breaths, but delight burned through her. Even if she wanted to, even if she hadn't been running, she wasn't sure she could calm her breathing. It felt like electricity snapped through the air around her, both tempting her to give in and continue running.

Tipping her chin up, she tried to sound firm despite the teasing half-smile crooked at her lips. "I don't think I'll let you catch me just yet."

A chuff of a laugh left the ja-tau and he moved further into the room, his steps measured and precise. He let loose another growl, his mandibles flexing. He wondered how he should go about this as a litany of raunchy scenarios played out in his mind's eye.

As his brain fed him hormone-drenched thoughts, Rayelle's mind noticed his growl didn't possess an undertone of irritation or anger like when he was fighting Zav. This growl felt playful, somehow. A cascade of quivering sensations slid down her spine, just like when he taunted her in the seat.

Her thoughts stuttered to a halt as Tai'dqei skillfully hopped up onto the island in one jump. His weight thumped hard on the counter. With an alarmed curse, she pushed back into the far corner while her eyes remained on his form.

Her surprise turned into a cackle of amusement as, in his intense focus on getting to her, he hadn't noticed the ceiling rack of dangling pots. The lips of metal pots caught onto the edges between his plates of armor, making him hiss and spit with displeasure. Once he was free of one implement, three more would tangle or bang noisily against him.

Thanking her lucky stars, Rayelle wasted no time racing around the island and the entangled ja-tau. His frustrated snarls followed her through yet another door and into a new hall. Her laughter, trailing behind her, sent a stab of impatient fire through Tai'dqei. With an annoyed howl, he grabbed the rack itself and yanked hard.

Parts of plaster and ceiling rained down as he broke the rack free. A cacophony filled the air as pans and pots and metal utensils clattered across the floor. He didn't notice any of it. His fiery gaze turned in the direction Rayelle had gone as he tossed the rack against a far wall. Before the rack made an intimate impact with the wall, Tai'dqei launched himself off the island and raced after her.

He was making ill-thought mistakes. Part of him was frustrated at his inability to think critically, too distracted by Rayelle to focus, but another part of him enjoyed the chase, her laughter and amusement. It incensed something deep inside him, promising to make the rutting she was about to receive unforgettable.

The longer the wait, the sweeter the end result. And he had waited so long already.

After the clatter – and that howl that churned at her insides – Rayelle heard those familiar impatient footfalls behind her once more. She barely kept from looking back. The worry she'd just stop and let him finish the game clashed against the continuously building desire within her.

Now, she had an idea of where she wished to lead him.

A sharp turn ended in a dead end with no apparent exits. Rayelle spun on her heel, walking backward as Tai'dqei's steps slowed behind her.

His growl smugly, goading her as his head cocked to the side. "Dead end."

"That doesn't sound very sexy." She wrinkled her nose as her back nudged against a wall. Reaching behind her, her fingers looked for the console inlaid into the wall. It had to be there, she thought. Unless she got turned around, which was a possibility. Either result would end the same way, but her mistake end the game sooner.

Tai'dqei's response was only a growl as he took more steps toward her, closing the distance. Part of him waited to see what she would do. Would she submit? Would she fight? Or did she have an aggravating trick up her sleeve?

Her fingertips finally found the screen and she flashed Tai'dqei a cheeky smile. "Let's try once more."

His confusion morphed into complete surprise as she slipped back into the wall. Timed well, her escape coincided with the lights fading to black.

◊ ◊ ◊

In mapping out the resort, Rayelle's recon squad had found the laundry chutes were surprisingly large. Whatever alien entity that had designed the chutes thought the whole laundry cart should fit. It turned out that the chute doors were only a stylistic choice. In actuality, the 'doors' housed a control panel that opened up the wall so a whole cart could slip down a metal slide-like structure.

They'd had a good laugh about that. Of all things, these high-tech aliens had gotten the laundry chutes wrong! Now it seemed like a desperate reprieve within the dismal knowledge that something bad was about to happen.

Either way, Rayelle slipped into the chute, managing to turn in time to slide down frontways. She left a dumbfounded Tai'dqei staring after her.

Though large, the chute was not big enough to accommodate a ja-tau, especially one sheathed in full armor. In fact, she was a little grateful he hadn't immediately followed her. Whether or not the chute would have held his weight and hers was another question entirely, she realized as she slid down the slide-like feature.

Tai'dqei's sense kicked in and, with a gnarl of frustration mingling with grudging amusement, he cast a look around. The exit point she had disappeared through was too small for him so he needed another way down. There was a stairwell not far and, on further inspection, he realized the placard hanging above the chute bore the same unintelligible human language as the sign just outside the door to the stairs. Hopefully, his assumption that they lead to the same place was correct.

Bursting into the stairwell, Tai'dqei didn't race down the flights. Instead, he jumped over the railing and leapt from level to level, grappling onto the railings as he made his way down. When he spotted the ground, he bound from his perch and landed with a loud *wham* on the concrete. The vibration tore up his legs, metal ringing out at his impact. Off to his left, he caught a familiar gasp of surprise.

He turned slowly toward Rayelle, already moving toward her. She stared at him, wide-eyed from her place near yet another door, one she was about to slip through. A survival instinct in her brain flared as she slammed the door open, this time leaving it wide open as she ran through it.

Tai'dqei shot after her, eating up the distance between them as she ran in a straight shot.

It took his brain a long second to realize they were outside now. Since his sneaky entry into the resort hours earlier, night had fallen. A blue-blackness blanketed the world. Stars sprayed the inky expanse overhead and a large moon hung in the air, providing further illumination. He only vaguely realized poles with rope strung between them stood off to his right, some lines still holding clothes.

All of that was ancillary to chasing Rayelle down. In the fresh light, she wasn't bathed in fading hues of red or swathed in black light. Her shirt was rumpled and stained from Zav's blood. Her jeans had fared a little better, less rumpled and less dirtied. A smaller part of him surveyed her, looking for obvious injuries and thankfully finding none.

Rayelle gulped down deep breaths of outside air. For a moment, she could almost believe she was back on Earth and in North America. Hell, with the temperate climate and types of trees nearby, it could have been near her home. That was the point of Rerli 3.

A stick snapped awfully close and her attention flickered to the alien behind her. Tai'dqei was not factored into what Rerli 3 offered. So alien, so unlike anything on Earth. The thought of him, of what they were about to do, made her heart skip.

"Wait!" Wildly, Rayelle spun to face him and threw her hands up. To his credit, he managed to stop right away despite the carnal intuition chomping at his insides. He loomed over her, so *so* close to having her in his clutches. An annoyed but curious growl rattled from him, the muscles in his arms flexing.

Rayelle offered him an apologetic smile and bashfully replied, "I like these jeans and bra and I don't want them ripped."

Tense, he gave a singular nod and waited as she hastily slid off her lower garments – her socks and shoes and jeans – before wiggling from her bra. That left her shirt and panties.

Some part of his brain still functioned, at least. Following her lead, he wrenched his helmet off and hit a command on his gauntlet that let the rest of his armor drop to the ground. Anything to streamline the process.

With the armor off, the blessedly cooler air breezed over him. Tai'dqei hadn't even realized how hot he'd become until that moment. It was hard to focus on anything but Rayelle. Even now, his eyes remained glued to her, gauging her reaction to the sight of him, ready to bound after her if she ran.

Heavy breaths had her chest noticeably rising and falling. Her eyes bored into him, trailing from his face and down his body. The path her eyes took made his skin tingle hotly and made his cock bob against the fabric of his loincloth. A small sound echoed from deep in her throat, her attention flickering back to his face.

She was grateful for the better, less inconsistent, lighting.

Tai'dqei wanted to say he saw desire in her eyes. Especially as her teeth sunk into her bottom lip, making him think how her blunt teeth would feel on his thick hide. But his brain was too caught up in arousal to make any coherent thought. His attention only heightened as she flashed him a smile, turning to take off through a grove of trees nearby.

"No," he rumbled, low and deep. A shiver shot through Rayelle as the reverberation echoed down her body, making her stumble.

Two of his strides was all it took. His senses homed in on her warmth and he thought he could smell her arousal tinting the air around her. A predatory sense of delight swept over him as he descended on her. His hands clamped onto her sides, his claws pricking at her plush skin.

Rayelle's immediate scream of surprise devolved to laughter as he yanked her close to his chest and purred against her ear.

CHAPTER 19

She continued to wiggle in his arms, legs and hands flailing as he pulled her to the ground. Heat bled from his body and into hers. The way his muscles shifted against her teased her senses. His weight forced her legs to spread, her thighs acting as cushioning for him to lean over her.

He barely registered her fighting, but she still tried to twist and yank from his grip. His strong unwavering grip on her only made her heart pound harder. Especially as those hands traced up her arm, finding one wrist before easily capturing the other.

Soon enough, Tai'dqei had her pinned to the ground. Not that it stopped her writhing or the way her back bowed up and down as if she were trying to displace him. She had no interest in actually breaking free, but she still tried her hardest. It wasn't as if Tai'dqei was going to budge.

Every little move, every failed attempt of hers to escape, incited further prickling need through him. He stared down at her, mandibles flexing as memories of their first interaction flickered under the present.

It was so similar. Her state of dress, the chase, even the position they were in now. The feeling of the whole experience was monumentally different. Her unwavering grin tilted up toward him, her eyes flickered over his face, his mandibles, his feather-like hair. There was no screaming or terror or tears.

It was like her eyes couldn't get enough of him. As if she enjoyed the gregarious differences between them, when before the smallest alien features unsettled her.

He couldn't help the low and slow purr that vibrated through him, aware of how heavily his own heart throbbed in his chest. Rayelle's breath caught in her throat as his growl echoed from him and into her, the resonance making jittery excitement sink to her bones. A shudder unabatedly slid through her, her eyes fluttering momentarily shut.

The hiss of fabric being shredded made her eyes pop open, her body jerk. A gasp burst from her lips as Tai'dqei tore the front of her shirt with his claws. Cool night air licked over her chest as the material fell away. She gave another gasp as he bent down, catching one of her breasts in the grips of his mandibles. The sharp tips squished into her tit, his closed teeth teasing along her nipple until the heat of his mouth opening washed over her.

It was a diversion, she soon realized. As her back arched, her own fingers curling tight into fists where his hand still grasped her wrist firmly. Tai'dqei's free hand snagged her panties by the crotch, ripping them clean from her body. Another excited jolt shot through her. Instinctively, her legs jerked, muscles tensing as her knees attempted to lock together, to cover herself. Impossible with the heated heft of a ja-tau between her thighs.

After a quick adjustment, Tai'dqei's last remaining article of clothing was torn away. Rayelle couldn't see his cock from her angle, but she definitely felt it nudge against her thigh. The soft heat of heavy testicles pressed against her. The warmth alone was enough to make a small mewl curl from the back of her throat, coaxed into a moan as his forked tongue flickered over her nipple.

Running on carnal instinct, her thighs clenched at his sides as she arched, seeking any heat, any friction from his still-to-be-seen dick. Intuitively, she could tell he was big. The humid heat and weight of his dick made sizing clear.

When she had stroked him in the cockpit, her fingers had felt ribbed ridges along the length of his shaft. Now her mind couldn't stop wondering if they were hard or soft and how they'd feel inside her. The very thought made anticipation sear at her center.

He lightly chuffed against her breast as he pulled back, amused by her need. After all the hassle she put him through, she hadn't earned a look yet. Tai'dqei shifted to her other breast, going through the same motions and earning the same whimpers and gasps as before. His uncharacteristic patience created a dizzying uptick in her arousal.

Every sound, every reaction milked from her made his cock bob and his sack tighten. Temptation tore into him, wanting to bury himself deep. He would do that soon, he told himself. He just wanted to revel in the moment, draw it out a little since it may be his only chance. The heat *was* going to consume him and he *was* going to get lost in it, but he could taunt her in his victory lap.

The teasing of his hard cock being so close, but not inside her, was driving Rayelle equally wild. Her pussy clenched around air, slick with excitement. She needed to have something in her. There was a throb deep at her center that demanded satisfaction. Craving rigid heat drilled hard into her and a pleasurable assault on her senses.

"Tai'dqei, please." The words escaped her lips, unthinkingly.

That was it. That's all it took for what little restraint he managed to stitch together to completely fall apart.

Tai'dqei drew away from her breasts, making the woman whimper before he flipped her bodily onto her hands and knees. She had only barely registered he'd released her wrists when she felt him hoist her hips high and plow into her. A wordless cry left her lips, her back arching and fingers digging hard into the ground beneath her. Hard heat split her, stretched her, filled her. With her lips stretched wide, her clit bared and his balls grazed against the sensitive bundle of nerves.

Back on Earth, size was something Rayelle was always quietly chasing. Nothing filled her, lengthwise or widthwise, *enough*. Nothing hit all of those places that yearned to be touched simultaneously. And in one fell swoop, Tai'dqei had shattered that quiet decades-long need. Providing a fulfilling experience in all manner as her pussy stretched and clenched around his cock.

He had more yet to give her.

She wasn't given a chance to regain her breath as Tai'dqei gave a low growl, her soft heat ensnaring him. The instinctive need that had simmered for so long in her presence burst forward. His claws dug into her hips and his hips snapped back before plunging forward again. Intent, hard, unstoppable, his thrusts came fast and without any build-up, without any slowing. Each one pushed him deeper and deeper into her.

Rayelle's whole body quaked with each stroke. Her inner nerves sang as friction ground against them. The smack of his sack against her clit becoming mind-numbingly sharper, hotter the deeper he drove his cock.

A gasp, a moan, a cry left her lips with every impact. In between strokes, the woman was left gasping down air, suffocating humidity filling every inch of her insides. All of her reactions only goaded Tai'dqei on harder, faster, deeper. Her body clenched around him, filling the spaces between the ridges on his shaft. The friction of every ridge teasing, pulling, razing across the soft wetness of her core. Pleasure tangled and knotted inside her, coalescing at one spot deep at her core.

Her fingers tangled in grass, her toes curled against the ground, as she mindlessly tried to raise her rear higher, meet his thrusts, get Tai'dqei even deeper than she ever imagined was possible. Every twitch and throb of his cock sent an electric tingle through her. Pain and pleasure pounded in her lower stomach, her muscles flexing hard.

Embarrassment and delight rose high within her as she caught the obscene sounds of his hips slapping against her ass and upper thighs. The sloppy noise of his cock cleaving in and out of her drenched folds.

The small part of her sense that remained mused how fortunate it was they'd gone outside. Their sounds would undoubtedly have echoed throughout the resort. The heat pitched higher in her, just imagining the others overhearing them.

Her muscles suddenly tightened until the pressure exploded. Rayelle tossed her head back, a sobbing cry torn from her lips as her thighs quivered. Tai'dqei grunted, her body coiling tight around his cock, pulsing hard around him. He didn't stop.

After a momentary slowing as her body tried to squeeze him tight, he continued his unrelenting pace. He watched, enthralled, as the woman beneath him gasped and writhed again.

Heat fluttered inside her, her muscles trembling around his dick. Her fingers clawed at the dirt beneath her, her back arched and bowed beneath him. There was no pause in her sounds. A litany of mewls and moans and gasps fell from her, each breath razing his center.

Two more times, he milked a loud cry from her lips, her body seizing around his member each time, until Rayelle's arms gave out. Her chest dropped down, helpless panting echoing from her lips. With a snarl, Tai'dqei released her hips, his upper body curving forward to blanket her back. A whimper rose from her throat, the feel of him all around her and inside her making the tired muscles clench with delight.

With one elbow braced on the ground, his other hand cradled her throat, his rut didn't falter. The shift in position roused the animal in him, his strokes uneven and short. Desire and need to fill his mate with seed blossomed hotly. Desperation clawed at his insides as her tight walls continued to squeeze, harder and harder.

Slightly renewed strength made Rayelle reach up and behind her. One hand sifted through Tai'dqei's plumage, the other on the back of his neck, her fingernails digging in hard. Delight seared through him, feeling her groping hands touching him.

His hand on her throat shifted until one of his fingers brushed the corner of her mouth.

Later, Rayelle wouldn't be able to explain the sudden thought that struck her. Maybe there wasn't any thought involved, only pure instinct. Her mouth turned toward his finger, her panting gasps hot on his flesh. Then her teeth sunk into the thick flesh along the length of his digit, tasting salt on his skin.

The sensation of her teeth sparked through Tai'dqei's brain. His clicking and grunts choked as a hissing snarl left his mouth. A shock clawed down his spine, his cock jerking as his ridges swelled. The new sensation, the further sense of being filled, made her gasp and whimper, her back once more arching. This time, her muscles compressed around him tighter than before. As if they were knotted and frayed and this was the final tension before they snapped fully.

With a roar, Tai'dqei threw his head back, her grip on his hair tightening as his orgasm crashed through him. His hips continued to work their short rough strokes as ropes of white-hot seed spilled into her.

A scream breached Rayelle's lips. Tremors raked along her body, making her shake intensely under him. Overwhelmed tears swelled at the corner of her eyes as the sense of satisfaction and pleasure and ecstasy swirled at her core and spidered out through her body. Liquid heat filled her, pooled in her. Rivulets streamed down her thighs, tickling at her nerves.

After a few more short jerks of his hips, a final twitch of his cock as the last of his seed spilled into her, Tai'dqei's form relaxed above her. His chest pressed into her back with every deep rasp he took, as she realized her own breathing was equalizing too. Her eyes cracked open – unsure of when she even wrenched them shut – as her senses returned.

Tai'dqei didn't move to free himself, happily buried deep in her still fluttering heat. The drive to procreate wanted to give her body time to absorb his seed, though he wasn't even sure that was possible between a ja-tau and human. Regardless, he enjoyed how soft and wet and warm she still was. He faintly mused how enjoyable it'd be to fall asleep with her speared on his cock.

Eventually, he softened – not entirely flaccid – and Rayelle squirmed beneath him. Slowly, he pulled free of her, her little gasping whimper almost convincing him to delve back in. Her body clenched around the emptiness, suddenly very cold. The shifting made the thick globules of his cum spill from her.

Tai'dqei didn't move off of Rayelle nor did he fling himself to his back beside her, to enjoy the cool grass on his back and leave her shivering. He kept his body curled protectively around her, even as she shifted and squirmed her way to her back.

Once she had adjusted, however, he dropped on top of her. A grunt left her lips, her hands braced against his shoulders and her knees bracketing his hips before surprise hissed from her lips. He buried his face against her throat, his mandibles splayed and his sharp teeth teasing at her flesh. Light clicking left him like a sigh of contentment.

Absently, one of her hands slid down from his shoulders, feeling the bulge of his muscles under her palm. The other toyed with a hanging lock of feather-hair, catching it between her fingers and sliding down the length. She enjoyed the smooth texture against her skin. The motion brought a purr from Tai'dqei's chest, which caused her to pause.

She tried to catch his eye, tried to suss out what exactly he was feeling. He had his eyes closed, swathed in the enjoyment of after-sex basking. The sense this was suddenly more intimate than just sex roused in her thoughts. Which brought a slew of other concerns warbling through her hormonal haze.

"Tai'dqei," she gently whispered, just in case the ja-tau was actually asleep. She couldn't recall a moment when she caught him slumbering. He grunted in acknowledgement but did little else. Fighting her own desire to stay put, she forced her words out, "We should probably get back to the others."

The way his shoulders flexed as he sighed brought an amused smile to her lips. She could just imagine his thoughts. Oh, yes, saving a whole resort of people was such a tedious chore. And it was so nice and comfy and warm here atop this squishy human.

"Fine," he grumbled, pushing himself up to his knees. Rayelle remained on the ground for a beat, staring up at the ja-tau before her. She swallowed, heat dipping into her center as her eyes trailed up his body. Apparently, when not in use or fully aroused, his cock slid back into his body through a slit. Though the ja-tau had exterior testes like humans. Her toes curled, memories of the weight of those gonads taunting her clit whenever he'd thrust into her razing her thoughts.

She bit her lip, averting her gaze as he gave a smug chitter at her surveyance of him. A familiar flush crawled across her cheeks as pleasant heat began to churn once more. Rayelle didn't have a chance to wonder about her quickly renewed libido as Tai'dqei dipped down and scooped her up in his arms.

"I can walk!" She instantly twisted in his hold, the turned-on blush tilting towards embarrassment.

"You cannot," he firmly retorted as he traversed the expanse of forest and grass. Even in the black-blue dark, the moon gave enough light for Rayelle to see. He was dutifully returning them to the resort the way they came, picking up their discarded wardrobe along the way.

Though she knew he was right, it didn't stop the petulant pout from puckering her lips. "What makes you say that?"

Tai'dqei gave a snort, which drew her eyes up to his face. His light yellow gaze caught hers, his mandibles pulled upwards a little in what was equivalent to a human smirk. "You're still trembling."

Another searing flame of embarrassment shot through her when she realized he was right. Her thighs still quivered and the occasional uncontrollable tremble coasted over her body. She still let out an annoyed huff, crossing her arms and looking away from his face. The way he had purred and nuzzled against her throat was still bright in her head, making a confusing and uncertain emotion coil at her center.

The chuffing laugh he gave in response to her didn't ease the feeling either.

CHAPTER 20

When Rayelle was able to walk again, she was thankful for her prior intuitive decision when it came to her clothes. If she hadn't stopped to strip off a few key articles, she had no doubt Tai'dqei would have utterly decimated her hoodie and jeans. She would have had to resort to fashioning a makeshift dress from one of the many sheets in the laundry area, which would have made the smirks and grins from her human peers all the more mortifying.

For the return trip into the resort, Tai'dqei opted for partial armor along with his mask. Arrogant as it was, he *had* taken care of the bulk of the enemy forces alone. If any such enemies tried their luck after his pleasant romp, they would be throttled within an inch of their life. Especially if they threatened Rayelle.

The other reason, the one he didn't fully admit to himself, was the scent. He didn't know how strong human olfactory senses were, but most non-humans — especially his fellow ja-tau — would know and notice his scent was all over Rayelle and hers all over him. It would be clear what activities they had very recently partook in. He wasn't keen on covering that up.

Thankfully, by the time they returned inside the reinforcements had arrived. Albeit to varying degrees of diplomatic success. There were behemoth ja-tau rounding up and hauling around struggling, screaming, crying humans. Other humans were still wielding their stolen weapons, racing around this new threat.

Rayelle had little time to feel embarrassed about her activities with Tai'dqei as she ran the gamut of calming down others and explaining the ja-tau were there to help. Their reactions varied greatly, from light curiosity to full-on admiration. She was just thankful that the ja-tau that came to Tai'dqei's call were as patient as he, at least from what she saw.

Just like the humans present, the ja-tau's reactions varied. From equal curiosity to annoyance and frustration to intrigue. Rayelle couldn't shake the feeling of being caught between kids at a dance, interested parties on all sides but no one was quite certain how to go about breaking the ice.

All through the chaos, Tai'dqei was at her elbow. He'd further explain details to those ja-tau who couldn't understand the humans or give suggestions, if not outright commands, for what the others should do. More than once a dissenting opinion had been met with a quiet growl from him and a threatening step forward as he nudged Rayelle behind him.

He'd remind them that *he* had done most of the hard work,

clearing out the resort. To which the other would eye Tai'dqei, sizing him up before backing down. With shoulders hunched, they'd scurry off to do whatever was asked of them.

And there was so much to do.

Rewiring the power grid. Cleaning up dead bodies and repairing damage. Tending to the wounded. Attempting to fix the android staff. Smoking out any enemy survivors and detaining them. After some discussion, the ja-tau offered to hold the enemies in their ships' brigs, under watchful surveillance and away from humans.

In one of the lulls, Rayelle flopped into a chair in the 2070s conference room. Previously, when the humans had been herded into this very area, the apparent plan was to auction them off to tables of bidders.

Now the room housed humans and ja-tau – with the occasional other race traveling with the latter – tending to the wounded, eating food, and trying to relax. Tables and chairs splayed across the room with little rhyme or reason.

Their repair efforts had returned the regular lights, temperature control, and PA system. It made for a far more pleasant atmosphere than the red-tinted world of emergency. Every so often, an announcement would come on over the stereos, spoken once in every necessary human language and then ja-tau.

Leaning back in her chair, Rayelle sighed and accepted a water bottle from a green ja-tau who quickly bustled off afterward. She had just unscrewed the lid and took a gulp when she found herself swarmed by some familiar faces.

"Hey Resistance Leader, how's it going?" Lisa slammed her hand down on the table by Rayelle, grinning into her face. Behind Lisa, Bette and Sandra drew closer.

Rayelle threw Lisa a cross look, not really in the mood for her teasing nicknames. Waving a hand at the activity around them, she muttered, "Pretty busy."

That made Lisa laugh and waggle her eyebrows suggestively. "Oh, yeah, *busy*."

"Lisa, quit being so… uncouth," sniffed Sandra as she carefully dropped into a chair across the table from Rayelle. The woman must have had a chance to actually change, thought Rayelle as she noticed the clean shirt and skirt. Not a fleck of viscera in sight.

"Oh, don't get on me, Sandy." Lisa rolled her eyes as she crossed her arms and flopped in a chair near Rayelle. "I saw how you were looking at that big blue fella earlier."

"Do not call me Sandy," Sandra gave an uncharacteristic hiss, frowning deeply. In return, Lisa flashed a mock look of horror before sticking her tongue out at the housewife.

Before Rayelle could press Sandra about which big blue fella she was allegedly taken with, Bette elbowed into the conversation in her quiet and firm way. "Ignore them. We came over here to ask how it went."

Rayelle blinked, a little lost and feeling ambushed by her friends. "How what went?"

The other three women exchanged looks before Sandra hedged in with an awkward whisper, "The courting ritual."

While Sandra attempted to be delicate, Lisa threw her hands into the air. "Just ask if she and her boytoy fucked."

Embarrassed heat flooded through Rayelle as she inadvertently straightened from her tired slump. She fought her deepening blush as amusement bubbled up from those around her. Their reaction made her frown, a furrow cutting between her eyebrows. "How is that any of your business?"

"Well, you already heard about Sandra and Big Blue. Bette's been making eyes at curvy green thing too." Lisa was eating up the turn of events, Rayelle thought as she eyed the delighted twinkle in the other woman's eyes. Novel experiences seemed to be Lisa's bread and butter, which lined her up perfectly for alien matchmaking.

Pulling up a seat next to Rayelle, Lisa leaned over and motioned to the room with a wave of her arm. "Seems like it's a benefit to human-alien relations to discuss this stuff, yeah?"

"Oh." Rayelle stared at the women flocked around her, their expressions ranging from bashful to eager. It made sense they'd come to her about this. Especially considering how she talked about Tai'dqei and how she shooed them away earlier. The understanding didn't help the heat sinking deeper into her cheeks.

Hesitantly, she glanced around the room, seeing if they were being eavesdropped on. The assembled ja-tau weren't paying them any mind, or it at least seemed that way. Tai'dqei was on the other side of the room, speaking with a small team about needed medical supplies.

"Well, uh, it was fine," Rayelle said, half-distractedly. As if sensing her gaze from across the room, Tai'dqei glanced up. He cocked his head toward her, his mask shielding whatever expression he shot her way. In return, she offered him an awkward smile before quickly turning back to her small audience. "Tai'dqei got his chase and, uh, we did the thing."

"How scandalous." Bette snorted, a smile tugging at her lips. The smug good-humored expression was mirrored on the faces of the other women at the table.

"Look, I don't usually talk about stuff like this." Giving an aggrieved groan, Rayelle pressed her face into her hands. With her cool palms against her warming cheeks, she took a deep breath. This wasn't a big deal. They all were adults and it would be better if they went into any seduction with some knowledge.

Not that Rayelle was supporting any of them actually taking on a ja-tau lover, but it wasn't like she could stop them if they really wanted one. "The chase was heart-pounding and kind of fun. He was so intent on getting to me he ran into some stuff along the way. Make sure you remove any clothes you like or they might get torn off."

Another round of snorts from Lisa *and* Bette made Rayelle's cheeks burn a little. It had been so long since she talked about sexual encounters with anyone who could remotely be considered friends, she'd almost forgotten how mortifying it was.

What else could she tell them to slake their curiosity? Her hands slipped down her face, her fingers resting lightly on her lips. She found the words hard to say, stumbling over herself as she continued, "He was pretty big, but I was already sopping wet so we managed and there were these ridges."

"Ridges?" That got a curious, almost worrisome, gasp from Sandra.

She leaned forward, her hands folded tightly atop her thighs as she pitched her voice to a whisper, "Did they hurt?"

"No, they were spongy and when he came, some of them swelled. I think to, like, make sure the cum stayed inside." Just explaining it made Rayelle's thighs clench tight, even as her hands made motions to indicate what she meant.

"Was it just mating? Or is he interested in more?" Bette surprised Rayelle with the particularly sentimental question, but after an exchanged look with Sandra she realized other women had similar curiosities.

Rayelle gave a helpless shrug, uncertain how to answer the question. "I don't know."

She and Tai'dqei had gone from wild sex and back to serious work quickly. Neither had a chance to pursue further conversation on the matter. Rayelle wasn't even sure there was anything to talk about, even if the thought of it being a one-time occurrence made her insides crimp unhappily. Having those stolen moments with him was better than never going through with it.

A beat of contemplative silence weaved through the group before Sandra asked, "Do you want more?"

"I don't know," she confessed, a wretched feeling swelling up inside her again. She'd been holding the question off, trying to focus on what needed to be accomplished in the here and now. Faced with it head-on, something in her chest went tight and the back of her eyes burned.

Of course she wanted something deeper, something that lasted, but she didn't know if Tai'dqei was seeking the same. Nor could she shake her other responsibilities still waiting for her. "I have kids back in my time that need me."

That little reminder of the reality of the situation quieted the other women. They all had families, somewhere in time. Rayelle was certain a few of the humans could get away with traveling the wild interstellar yonder with little to no cares about the life they left behind, but so many others had friends and family to consider.

Rayelle cast a glance at the other human women present. Faintly, she wondered what they'd choose. She didn't exactly know all the nuances of their stories, just the basics.

"Can they kiss?" Lisa's sudden question derailed Rayelle's saddened thoughts.

At this point, Rayelle was beginning to feel useless. Another shrug, another sigh. "I don't know, we never did that."

Not that she would have minded if they had bumbled through a kiss, but intense need and desperation hadn't allowed them to stop and try. Figuring out the best meeting of lips and mandibles wasn't really high on their lust-consumed minds. Without thought, her teeth sunk into her bottom lip, considering the possibilities of kissing Tai'dqei.

She had been so deep in conversation she didn't hear or notice the hulking ja-tau sidle up beside her. "Is something wrong?"

Rayelle's eyes wheeled up to him and the urge to die, right there and then, rose up in her thoughts. He stood right next to her, his fishnets highlighting the curvatures of his build while his partial armor barely made him decent. Once more, his infuriating helmet obscured his expression, but at least his body language was free. His head tilted and the smooth visor angled at her in a curious way.

With her cheeks still burning from the conversation, the last thing Rayelle wanted was him to see her all flustered like a schoolgirl. Thankfully – or perhaps horribly – Lisa piped up with one of her incessantly direct questions. "Do ja-tau know how to kiss?"

"Kiss? What do you mean?" His head swiveled toward the inquisitive human. From the corner of his eye, he saw Rayelle tense and the color in her cheeks deepen. Was she mad that another human was asking him this? Was it something intimate? His curiosity heightened at the thought.

"With humans, we press our lips together, like this." To illustrate what she meant, Lisa grabbed Sandra and mashed their lips together. The other woman squeaked but didn't pull away as Rayelle would have expected. She merely stared wide-eyed at Lisa. The red-haired firecracker pulled away quick, leaving the housewife more than a little flushed and dazed. "Do ja-tau have a similar sign of affection?"

"In a way. We flare our mandibles and put our mouths together. Sometimes there is tongue included in the action." Unruffled, Tai'dqei explained the mechanics of a ja-tau kiss, sliding his hands together and interlocking the space between the forefingers and thumbs to demonstrate.

Plenty of ja-tau pups and other species had similar questions. Though Tai'dqei wore his helmet, there were plenty of his kind wandering around bare faced, so he assumed even humans unfamiliar with the ja-tau would note the mandibles.

If he was being honest, he only answered since Rayelle was right there. Her knowing was all that mattered to him, on the off chance she too was curious.

With large round eyes, a woman seated stiff and wearing clothing that had to hamper her movement, leaned toward Tai'dqei. "Can you show us?"

"Sandra!" Of all the people, Rayelle didn't expect *her* to ask.

The red-headed woman pointed a finger toward Rayelle, her gleeful smile so broad it made Tai'dqei's own jaw ache. "Kiss Rayelle right now!"

"*Lisa!*" Rayelle's voice cracked, her blush eating away at her cheeks. She leveled a glare at the other woman. The last thing she needed was someone being her wingwoman, especially with a man she'd already bedded.

Even under the glower, Lisa didn't wilt. She just grinned and shrugged without concern. "Hey, it doesn't hurt to ask."

Tai'dqei tilted his mask off his face and cast Rayelle a curious look. She weakly smiled up at him, hating the way the soft expression in his eyes made her melt inside. "It seems some of my fellow humans are intrigued by the ja-tau."

The way his mandibles seemed to flex in amusement just enhanced her own mortification.

She wondered if he had to field any similar questions from any of the ja-tau. It was hard to say whether any of them were interested in humans presently. Though that may have been thanks to Tai'dqei dousing any desires of pursuit with threats of violence.

There was also the snag of human and ja-tau relations being tense, given the history between them.

"Ah, well, would you like a kiss?" He settled his mask on an empty chair as he asked. It seemed a fair question to throw out there. They hadn't exactly locked faces when they were together earlier, but it appeared other humans found the action an important subject to breach with him. Kissing could very well matter to Rayelle.

He couldn't help but notice how she sat stiffer in her chair, unable to meet his eyes. A small chill dipped in his chest, wondering if she wasn't interested. Her soft reply presented a different message. "I am curious to know how well it'd work between us."

Tai'dqei gave that amused chuff that made her insides squirm before he stooped over her. Instead of laying one on her, as she braced herself for, he scooped her up into his arms. She gave a little squeak as he positioned her legs around his sides, her thighs squeezing. He held her high up against him, almost eye-to-eye. Not quite, but almost.

Rayelle's teeth sunk into her lower lip, already aware of others taking an interest in the proceedings. It was like searing tar, scorching her back. Plus, the width and heat of Tai'dqei's torso between her legs ignited those tingling sensations in her core. She wondered, if it wasn't for his armor, if she'd feel the nudge of his excitement against her.

It took her a moment to realize he was waiting for her to make the first move. The thought of being the one to initiate made even further heat bleed across her cheeks, but she was also thankful for his consideration. Bracing her hands against his chest, her fingers curled around the edge of his chest armor and she leaned forward.

His mandibles splayed wide and the wet fleshy interior of his maw spread out around her. The sharp tips of his mandibles were gentle, almost like fingertips as they slid along her cheeks. Her eyes fluttered shut as her lips pressed to his slightly parted interior mouth. The heat and moisture of his maw pressed around her as his mandibles enclosed gingerly around her face.

Her tongue traced over his large, pointed teeth, tentatively tasting before breaching into his jaws opened wider. Rayelle's tongue explored, making sense of Tai'dqei's mouth as his own tongue did the same to her.

A deep-chested purr echoed through his chest as he considered her flat, soft, spongy tongue. His own was more cylindrical and firmer with a bisected end. If the way her tongue writhed against his was any indication, Rayelle didn't seem off-put.

When she experimentally sucked on his tongue and squeezed the back of his neck, pleasure sparked down his body and spiked through his center. Forced to end the gently end the kiss, lest he ravaged the woman in front of their audience, he pulled back. It wasn't easy to reel himself in. An instinct still simmered in him, wanting to wordlessly assert his position with her to any gawking ja-tau.

The way her mouth briefly followed his sent an appreciative flare of delight through him. As he leaned back, Rayelle's eyes fluttered open and he thought he caught the faint embers of lust in her gaze.

302

"Thoughts?" He had to say something to distract himself from how her thighs flexed around him and how her fingers brushed along his neck.

Rayelle was still trying to process the sensations. It was an odd kiss, but she was more than willing to repeat it. She suspected sucking on his tongue had excited him too much, causing him to cut the kiss short, and she wanted to explore that further. Maybe not with such a plentiful crowd watching… Maybe.

But there was moisture on her face, cooling against her flush. Bashfully, she brushed the back of her hand against both her cheeks, wicking away the saliva. "Kind of wet."

"I'm sorry. It is an odd configuration." His shoulders sagged a little under the observation as he huffed a sigh. There were bound to be things that didn't quite match up between them. Still, it sent a pang of disappointment through him.

"I'm not complaining," Rayelle reassured him, momentarily forgetting the audience they had and pressing her cheek to his shoulder. "I wouldn't say no to it happening again."

"Good to know." He shifted on his feet, painfully aware of the human women eagerly watching them. It reminded him of the groups of ja-tau circling and eyeing potential sires. A mild embarrassment crawled up his back at that thought. To make matters worse, humans weren't the only curious eyes on them. Other ja-tau were eyeballing Rayelle and himself.

He barely swallowed down an agitated chitter. As if reading his irritability in the air, many ja-tau turned away and busied themselves.

Though their shoulders hunched as they went about assigned duties. Not for the first time since returning from outside, Tai'dqei wished he and Rayelle could have some privacy.

Rayelle had just begun to let her eyes close, comfortable in his arms to the point that previously ignored exhaustion coaxed her toward slumber. Then she heard a giggle to her left. Her eyes snapped wide as she remembered the peanut gallery watching the whole spectacle. Immediately, she sat straighter in Tai'dqei's arms, swinging a glare at Lisa – the presumed giggler – and the others.

The women straightened under Rayelle's leer and her lips pressed tight together in amusement as they all averted their gazes. They acted like school children caught being naughty. Only Tai'dqei's contemplative growl dragged Rayelle's attention back to him.

He considered his words carefully, mandibles wriggling before inquiring, "The situation is stable and trustworthy authority should be here soon. Would you like to rest with me on my ship?"

A smile curved at her lips, recognizing the mindful and deliberate tone in his words. Unable to help herself, she rocked against him in his hold, her arms tightening around his neck and her legs pressed firmly to his sides. She was rewarded with an almost silent grunt from him and his fingers tightened on her.

"Please, take me away from all these nosy biddybodies!" Pressing her face dramatically against his neck, his plumage of hair settled around her head as if to shield her. Her friends sputtered mock outrage behind her, but it didn't matter. Tai'dqei, unaccustomed or uncaring to human departure conventions, already turned toward the exit. He only paused to swipe up his helmet, clipping it to his hip at his belt before retreating entirely.

CHAPTER 21

His long strides made short work of the distance and soon the two were in a comparably quieter hall. With far fewer eyes on them, Rayelle thought felt tension leaving his body. She certainly eased, but the ja-tau's warm body and the bob of his steps lulled her.

Both of them were silent for a long time. She listened as other ja-tau regarded him and felt how he returned recognition through a nod. A few asked if something was wrong with her, but they were easily dismissed by a curt word or throaty growl from Tai'dqei.

In his head, a mess of thoughts and feelings whorled. It had been easier to ignore the concerns when there were other, more dire, issues to distract him. Organizing which ships housed the captured enemies. Providing guidance on how to approach humans. Delegating repair teams and cleaning crews to get the resort to a somewhat livable state again. There had always been an itch, a consideration he should untangle, but he shoved it away.

How he felt, what he wanted, didn't matter in the moment. Rayelle had suffered yet another strenuous, traumatic upheaval. Worst of all, it happened in a place that was supposed to be safe. He could only imagine how she'd feel once everything settled and she rested.

Absently, his grip on her flexed.

Though her eyelids drooped, she watched the ja-tau's features from where her head rested on his shoulder. The way his eyebrow ridges dipped in thought. How his mandibles flexed, like someone mouthing something to themselves. Something was on his mind. Likely the same things that lurked at the back of her thoughts.

When the air around them began to grow noticeably cooler and somewhat humid, Rayelle realized they were heading into the laundry area. Another second later, she realized he was walking the same path he'd chased her down earlier. Her lips twisted into a wry smile, a teasing tone bleeding into her voice as she said, "Why do I get the feeling you have something on your mind?"

He froze on one of the stairwell landings, shoulders hunching under her observation. "I moved my ship closer when you went to talk down some humans earlier."

"You moved your ship to the laundry room?" Her smile broadened, her teasing tone weaving through her voice. She knew he couldn't have moved the ship to the laundry room. It was too big. But she wanted to hear him say he just *happened* to move his ship to where they'd laid.

Her tone raised something hot and prickly along his skin. He continued down the stairs, his body heat rising for reasons other than the natural humidity. "No, to the forest. Past those poles with the ropes. There was a clearing I noticed. Earlier."

The best course of action was to ignore her expression and the mocking suggestion in her voice as he answered. He already knew what she was thinking and how it reflected on him. Sentimental fool, that he was.

She made another amused sound, as if she didn't quite believe him. Absently, she reached out to stroke along a feather of his plumage, tracing the gradient of colors. There was a texture there, though she couldn't quite explain. While soft, it was a little thicker and firmer than the fluff of an Earthen feather. The touch sent another flash of heat down Tai'dqei's back, but he focused on continuing to move. Her finger caught on one of the metal beads just as he stepped down into the laundry area.

"What are other ja-tau mating rituals like?" The question came suddenly to Rayelle's lips before she could even consider it. She blinked, realizing there was a curiosity burrowed deep in her thoughts. Though she couldn't look directly at it. It slid away, shy and protective of itself.

The evenness in her tone told Tai'dqei this wasn't a sensual sort of teasing. He inclined his head to her, eyebrow ridges raised. "Hm?"

"A while ago, you told me the hit-and-dash was just one mating ritual which implies there's other methods," she explained slowly, her eyes still on the lock of feather-hair she idly stroked. She couldn't bring herself to look closer at Tai'dqei, especially when she herself was unsure where she was headed with this conversation.

"Well, yes. Different ja-tau cultures vary a bit." Dragging his attention away from Rayelle, he let his eyes draw over the laundry area. It seemed a tidy ja-tau had cleaned most of the strewn fabrics up, piling the dirty ones up near the cleaning machines.

Rayelle gave an acknowledging hum, carefully feeling her way through the conversation. "What does yours do then?"

Tai'dqei's footfalls echoed through the cavernous laundry area as he thought how to answer. To Rayelle's credit, she quietly waited.

"Other than the hit-and-dash, as you put it, my people have an annual festival." Tai'dqei finally made it to the door that led outside. He shouldered his way through it, still holding Rayelle against his chest. Once more, she had her face tilted toward him with an intense gaze on his. He couldn't begin to imagine what sort of thoughts ricocheted through her brain. "There are three days of events. Ja-tau show off their strength, intellect, leadership capabilities, talents, and so on. Anything that we might want to pass to the later generations."

Each year was different, concerning what was considered desirable. The universe's current events – with its wars and technological advances and so on – often played into what the ja-tau sought for later generations. In the past, the most sought-after traits were strength, stamina, and leadership. As time went on, there was a larger splay of desire for a multitude of traits.

"Every adult can participate in the events, though the events are mostly for the virile to show off so the fertile will choose them." The festival was rather chaotic. Events were staggered at intervals, overlapping contests going on, vendors hawking goods, and the general uproar of exuberant crowds. The scents of food and excitement hung heavy in the air and chatter vibrated around the crowds.

He wasn't sure he could explain the vibrancy and energy well enough for Rayelle to understand. Tai'dqei wasn't sure she'd ever want to go to such an event, but he couldn't stop imagining her there, in the familiar crowds. "Throughout the day, adult ja-tau will flirt, gaining one another's attention one way or another before running off. Pursuit doesn't happen until after the last day's evening meal. Then…"

Rayelle's attention had wandered to the clotheslines, conflicting feelings churning inside her. The sun was high in the sky, indicating just how long they'd been cooped up inside the resort while trying to get things in working order. It felt like days had passed since she and Tai'dqei had last been in this area. That course of thought invariably led to memories of their heated chase.

She could easily make conversation something sexy and flirty, but she just wanted to understand. Even if she didn't exactly know what or why she wanted to understand. "Then what happens?"

He adjusted his hold on her, his large hands cupping her ass and bodily raising her higher on his abdomen as if she had slid down a little. Casting her a sidelong glance, he felt like he was stepping into a minefield. While he was incensed by their kiss, he couldn't ignore the pensive tone to her line of questioning. Just as he had thought earlier, they had some things to discuss.

"The Hunt to Begin All Hunts." It was an old nickname for fornication. In order to have a hunt, hunters needed to exist, to be born. The Hunt to Begin All Hunts set the stage for hunters to be born.

A little crass, but it was a well-known saying among ja-tau.

"What?" That brought her attention back to his face. Rayelle's lips tilted in an amused smile, presuming she already knew what he meant but wanting clarification regardless.

"It's an old name for the next part," he chuffed, half-shrugging. The knowing amusement in her eyes sent a needle of heat threading up his spine. "Those hoping to get pregnant slip away during the meal, the ceremonial horn sounds, and it is up to those who caught their eye to find them."

"The one who finds them first gets to mate with them," she guessed, her eyebrows knitting together as the cool shade of the forest trees dipped over them.

"No." Tai'dqei shook his head, trying not to roll his eyes at human possessiveness. "Any they deemed desirable may mate with them. If they are able."

Ability was another issue as well. Some seeking to become pregnant put up quite a fight, desiring further evidence of a mate's potential. Others were less of a struggle.

"Oh," Rayelle breathed, considering the scenarios that nugget of information led to. Were ja-tau more selective in who they mated with? She imagined they would be if the festival was for procreation. However, Tai'dqei's answer indicated a ridiculous amount of stamina if the ja-tau weren't particularly choosy. She chuckled a little, pressing her cheek back to his shoulder. "That sounds like it could be exhausting."

A chuff of a laugh left Tai'dqei as her soft words registered.

For a long moment, she was quiet while considering what he had told her. On the surface, it almost sounded like something humans would do, except there was no singular mating season for humans. Although, she knew sex – and probably pregnancy – happened at other times for the ja-tau beyond the festival. Like Tai'dqei's moments with her, anomalous mating events were likely normal.

Thinking back to her first meeting with him, she tilted her face to him once again. "What if someone wasn't deemed desirable but wants to mate with them?"

By that point, the ship was in sight. Tai'dqei adjusted the woman in his arms again, unlocking the ship via his tech gauntlet from the distance.

"That's up to the one getting pregnant. It's not rare for last minute entries to be added to the roster, so to speak." Another shrug came from him, but Tai'dqei's thoughts also curled around the first night with her. A pang of familiar guilt bounced through him. "If the one getting pregnant doesn't want them and a progenitor still pursues, usually the progenitor gets killed."

Rayelle hummed, also remembering their first night. A small part of her was shamefully thankful no other ja-tau were around to enact vengeance for her. Turning away from the possible retribution, she followed another line of thought, "How do you know who the sires are? When the kid is born."

Tai'dqei couldn't help the way his mandibles pulled up a bit, amused by her endless questions. Why she wanted to know so much about ja-tau, he could only guess. But his guesses did warm him with an indescribable feeling. "All who mated with a particular fertile ja-tau are considered the children's parents."

"What?" That answer surprised her. People willing to parent children that may or may not be theirs? There had been plenty of instances where Evan lobbed the 'are they even my kids' bullshit her way during fights.

"Ja-tau are prone to having multiples. Two or three on average," Tai'dqei continued, unaware of the faint memories playing across Rayelle's mind. "It can be obvious which progenitor sired which child, but traits do mix in-utero and multiple sires are responsible for the same litter. Though many sires have multiple broods at the same time."

Now that this can of worms was open, Rayelle couldn't let it go. She didn't even notice that Tai'dqei had brought her onto the ship until her ears registered his footfalls on the metal. "How does parenting work?"

"The ones who become pregnant often raise the children in the community. Everyone – including those uninterested in parenthood, the elderly, and the older broods that haven't reached adulthood – assists in some way." He settled Rayelle down on the floor as the ship's door closed behind them. The amused pull of his mandibles hadn't disappeared. Though it always felt a little strange explaining a norm he had grown up with, this wasn't the first time he'd spoken of this to a non-ja-tau.

"Sometimes the pregnant ja-tau have their children and return to doing something else, leaving the rearing to the community.

Usually a family member, if not the sire."

Rayelle took a moment to look around his ship as Tai'dqei fed her answers. She didn't dally far and still listened to him as he stopped by the mess table to offload his gear. Without thinking, she reached her hand out to touch one of the walls. The gentle thrum of the ship, the systems, buzzed under her hand. She hadn't realized she missed that constant, ambient sound. Nor had she realized how much she missed the scent of his ship. A light tang of metal and oil and something faintly like Tai'dqei's aroma.

For the most part, the vessel was as she left it. No television in the lounge. The safety belts were still intact since he had intently replaced them. That meant there had been no missions involving flight-averse patrons. She wasn't sure what she expected. Cloying scent of perfume from sex workers? Dirty lingerie strewn about? Empty bottles of drink? Dirty clothes and the stellar version of take-out containers left everywhere?

None of that seemed particularly like Tai'dqei. Or, if it was, he cleaned up after himself. Rayelle didn't care much if he'd visited someone to scratch whatever carnal itch she'd awoken in him. It wasn't as if either one of them thought they'd see each other again.

It *did* appear as if Tai'dqei had been in the middle of making what looked like necklaces from various bones, considering what supplies were spilled over the table. That was something that nudged Rayelle's curiosity.

As Tai'dqei removed his armor, he continued his explanation, "Sires can be part of the childrearing communities or they can go off – hunting or working – to bring something back into the community."

Rayelle paused at that part of his answer, glancing at Tai'dqei as she was unsure of how to feel about it.

On the one hand, it sounded like there was a lot of wiggle room for different situations. If a pregnant ja-tau decided to return to whatever spacefaring adventures they had, the progenitor was there to be the parent, and vice versa. If neither stayed, then the community would care for the children, probably in a way that meshed broods with broods. If both stayed, they would likely care for more than their own progeny.

Parental-ish figures, always around to help you. Multiple lovers to shoulder the parental load. On the surface, it appeared all well and good. Rayelle couldn't help but wonder if she had grown up with such a system, would it actually seem as nice?

While Tai'dqei removed what little armor he had on, her eyes narrowed on him as a sudden question popped into her head, "How many broods have you had?"

"I was never interested in being pregnant, so none from before the change. After it, though, hard to say." If the question bothered Tai'dqei, he didn't show it. Rayelle was beginning to think he didn't have too many children, but after a moment's thought as he scratched the back of his neck, he said, "Perhaps seven broods?"

That answer made her heart stutter and her eyes widen, a strange awkward warmth rushed over her body. "You could have twenty-one children?"

"Ah, pups. There's twenty-four of them actually," he replied, with ease, piling his armor onto the table and offering her a shrug. While there was an amount of hilarity in watching her eyes grow wider, there was a small bead of apprehension. This was a ja-tau norm and having a human react to it made prickly uncertainty settle in his stomach. "One litter had four pups and then two were adopted after their parents passed in a hunt."

Twenty. Four. That was a lot. *To humans* it was a lot, Rayelle reminded herself. Considering how Tai'dqei had described the mating ceremonies, she wondered if it was a low amount to ja-tau.

She rubbed a hand down her face, flopping into an available chair. Her brain sputtered at that amount. Tai'dqei had sired twenty-four children. It seemed absurd. Besides, he'd never discussed it with her before!

Further than the children, that meant he'd had up to seven lovers he was still entwined with. Were they his spouses? Or was mating something totally separate from relationships? He had never had children before his change, so did that mean he and Ah'ke never had kids together?

So many questions spun around her head.

"What do you bring to the community?" Rayelle crossed her arms, her lips puckering as she tried to decide if she she'd be ambivalent about his answer or not. Or perhaps she was concerned with what emotions his answer would awaken in her. At the very least, he didn't appear perturbed with her line of questions.

Part of Tai'dqei had decided this was another form of a mating ritual. His people already knew how this worked. Humans in Rayelle's time and place usually had one partner. Having a singular partner was as instinctive for her as the 'hit-and-dash' was for him.

Tai'dqei sat down next to her, angling his chair to face her. "I provide money and, when asked, supplies. If they need something off-planet, I can retrieve it for them. And if they need to get off-planet for some reason, I can ferry them around."

He was an errand runner and chauffeur. If needed. Leaning toward Tai'dqei, her elbows on her knees, she asked, "Do you spend time with your kids?"

"When I visit, if they want to spend time with me they can and do." He shrugged and, once more, Rayelle wasn't sure how to feel about the ja-tau arrangements. "But there are other sires that are always on-planet. Their bonds with the children are usually stronger, as expected."

While he was always given a warm welcome by the pups, Tai'dqei was no fool. He knew there were other parents his children were more attached to. He held no resentment for that fact. Some were simply better with kids than others were. At the very least, he provided what was asked of him, whether that was money, transportation, or teachings.

Mirroring her pose, he head cocked to the side. Rayelle could be assessing his capabilities as a mate or going through the questions to assuage some inner concern. However, there was another worrisome angle that might be feeding her inquiries. "Are you thinking about your children?"

"A bit," she sighed, smiling weakly up into his face. Briefly, she considered how easy it would be to forget these more difficult thoughts. To lean up and bring her lips close to his mandibles, wrap her arms around his neck. Get lost in his heat and firmness.

Guilt flickered through her at the thought. Her attention dropped to the floor, a small frown creasing her lips.

Tai'dqei gave a thoughtful clicking noise, which Rayelle took as the ja-tau version of a hum.

"I'm also trying to figure something out." Suddenly Rayelle was on her feet, pacing the length of the mess. "What we did. The stuff before your reinforcements arrived…"

She trailed off, struggling with the shy words lodged in her throat. They felt presumptuous and unnecessary. Her heart thundered in her chest as a burn bit at the back of her eyes.

"Go on," Tai'dqei prompted, watching her move with his own quiet apprehension growing.

"I don't really know how to process it." A jittery feeling coursed through her body. She couldn't stay still, especially knowing he carefully watched her.

He straightened in his chair, scooting it to face her again so he could give Rayelle his full attention. The fact he did that, and that she understood his reasons for the movement, sent another wave of emotion through Rayelle. "You and Ah'ke seemed so close, but the way you talk about mating and parenting makes me wonder how ja-tau see relationships."

Rayelle made a third pass by him. Tai'dqei noticed one hand was held in the other, just about at her chest's level, and she pressed her thumb into her palm. He wondered if this was a new type of nervousness for her. He focused back on her face, watching small changes in her expression.

"Was what happened an instinctual misfire for you? I happened to hit all the triggers, so the cave-ja-tau in your brain went off? Was it that, coupled with a sense of fun?" On her fourth circuit, she paused right in front of him. Her heart pitched itself into overdrive, her eyebrows pinched upward with worry.

The words continued to spill from her, even as something in her screamed at her to stop. Her thoughts swung on a seesaw of debate. If she stopped to think, she doubted any of this would come into the clear and she needed a direct answer.

Staring at Tai'dqei, her chest rose and fell as her breathing became shaky. Swallowing down uncertainty, Rayelle forced out her ultimate question, "Is there more to it? For you and me?"

CHAPTER 22

There was a long stretch of time when Tai'dqei simply stared at Rayelle, his eyebrow ridges raised. A mental scale tipped in his mind's eye as understanding landed. Could he risk allowing more to develop when she could leave somewhere, sometime, he couldn't reach?

There was also the question about whether she'd feel obligated to stay with him if something more built between them. He had no doubt she'd, ultimately, choose her kids. How badly she would agonize over that decision bothered him.

In the silence that followed her question, Rayelle waited. With his elbows braced on his knees and his hands dangling, he looked like a man mulling over a sobering topic. So still, like a statue. Her teeth worried at her lower lip, realizing not even his mandibles fidgeted. The air around both of them felt like placid water, cold and dark. She wasn't sure how to feel about that.

The longer the silence lasted, the more she was sure he was going to confirm she was a casual mating urge. That he'd had many before her and planned to have many after her. That the bond he and Ah'ke had was different, more special, from whatever was happening between her and him.

Those thoughts made an uncomfortable heat flare in Rayelle's chest as her eyes flickered to the floor.

"When it first happened, that first night," he started and she had to stifle her flinch. His tone was somber and soft, making her brace herself for something she didn't want to hear.

Navigating between being 'too stoic' and 'too vulnerable,' he chose his words with the utmost care. "It was a combination of my own victory and adrenaline plus you inadvertently going through motions that certainly stoked my instincts.

"This time," he paused, heaving another heavy breath. His chest felt tight and hot, his heart thrumming a little too hard for a normal conversation. Rayelle dared to glance up at him, finding his gaze turned toward a wall.

His mandibles flexed as he chose what to say. Embarrassed warmth bled into his face, though Tai'dqei doubted she would notice. "This time I came back to help you, because you asked me to come. My prerogative was you and your safety."

Another heavy gnarl of a sigh left him as he reached up to rub the back of his neck. The line of 'too vulnerable' skirted rather close to his words, but he pushed on.

"There is a protectiveness ja-tau feel for potential mates. I hadn't completely ignored the thought that we might end up having sex."

This was true, whether it was reproductive mates – the parents of one's children – or the more romantic and intimate mates. The only relationship it could be untrue for were the casual affairs, but that varied from individual to individual. He wasn't sure how she wanted to be seen by him.

That fluttery heat tickled her chest. Carefully, she watched him while she parsed his words. What did it mean to be a mate? She needed clarification on what *he* wanted. What he hoped for.

She couldn't bring herself to be direct. A laugh trickled from her throat, tasting slightly bitter on her tongue. "You could say I'm a tedious charge that you need to nanny and us fucking was a benefit."

"No, I wouldn't say that." Tai'dqei didn't even stop to consider his answer. Heat flared through her at his certainty, her blush deepening as he stood.

She hadn't realized standing over the ja-tau had given her some sense of confidence, a sense of control over the situation. That sense of strength dwindled as he gently took her hand, enclosing it between both of his warm palms. "I enjoy your company and I wouldn't be averse to spending more time with you. A long time if you so choose."

If she chose. A lump formed in her throat, the realization landing in her brain again. She couldn't, wouldn't, choose Tai'dqei over her kids. If there was a chance she could be sent back to her time, she'd follow through. No matter how badly her chest ached at the thought or how horridly her eyes burned with unshed tears.

"What would that even look like, though?" Rayelle gave another semi-bitter laugh, ignoring how her voice cracked. She had tried wildly to *not* entertain the thought of being anything more than a fuckbuddy to Tai'dqei. It wasn't fair to her or him.

Without thinking, she slid her hand away from his grip, waving the hand at him. "You're a bounty-hunting, general contracting, hitman-for-hire. I'm a human with barely any skills in the here-and-now."

Tai'dqei flinched at her words, presuming she wasn't able to meld his work with her morals. Rayelle surprised him by pinning him with a pained expression, her hand pressed to her own chest. "I'd just be a liability, wouldn't I?"

While it was a justified concern, her words also stoked a little bit of ego in him. In a roundabout way, she acknowledged his skills and capability.

"It's a big universe. There are plenty of jobs that don't entail killing others. Those just pay the most." He inclined his head to her, his mandibles pulling up a little on one side. Almost like a smug half-smile, Rayelle thought.

A contemplative hum left her lips as she considered his words. She couldn't fault him for choosing the best job for his skills, especially with twenty-four children to provide for. Even if he wasn't the only one responsible for providing for them, was it too much to ask him to take poorer paying jobs? If only for his safety? Or so she could travel with him on missions without feeling like a hindrance?

Her brain still hadn't fully gripped the whole *Tai'dqei is a father* fact. She had presumed, since he traveled alone and only really mentioned Ah'ke, he wasn't romantically close with any of his seven former mates. Though she wasn't ready to delve further into that curiosity.

"If you're looking for something grounded, I do have a home."

"What?" With those few words, he made her brain spin in a radically different direction. He had a house? It was probably on his home planet, but what did that look like? How would she be treated? With a motion to the ship around them, she asked, "This isn't your home?"

"It is, but I have a place on my world. My mother is looking after it for me." His mother looked after his home? Another indication he wasn't close to those he had kids with if one of those past mates wasn't watching his house, Rayelle supposed.

He gave another awkward shrug, not sure what cultural differences stunned her this time. "Of course, she might have let it out to a sibling while I've been away."

Reality in Rayelle's thoughts rippled, her eyes flickering from Tai'dqei to the floor. Mother. Sibling. Ja-tau had multiples, two or three per litter. Of course, he'd have siblings. She pressed her lips together, the enormity of the situation pressing down on her.

She was far in the future, talking to an alien about where their whatever-it-could-be-called was heading. And he had a mother and multiple siblings and former lovers and kids. It made perfect sense. Tai'dqei didn't just pop into existence to help her. He had a life before her, with family — or families — and lovers and…

Sudden dizziness slammed into her, making her sway. She brought a hand to her forehead, inhaling sharply as an ache stabbed at her temples.

She heard more than saw Tai'dqei's step forward. A concerned lilt tightened his voice, "Are you okay?"

"It's just a lot to digest." She took a deep breath to steady herself, feeling the air fill her lungs before exhaling slowly. Tilting her head to him, she offered him a little smile upon finding his hands outstretched but not touching her. He still wasn't sure of the edges of their relationship either.

"Decisions don't have to be made right now." His hands fell from their mid-air position, choosing to trust Rayelle's own assessment of how she felt. Edging into 'too-vulnerable' territory again, his hands clenched tightly at his sides and he quietly added, "I'm happy you're safe and I can spend more time with you."

"Are you, really? Even if I choose to go back to my kids and not stay here?" The words were out of Rayelle's mouth before she could think about it. She blinked rapidly against the growing heat behind her eyelids. Desperation had her seeking any excuse to keep her crumbling walls solidly in place.

"Yes."

Another answer he said with so much confidence and without the need for thought. She swallowed down a whimper, tears threatening to spill. This situation was so unfair. So very unfair. It made her heart hurt as if it was being squeezed too tightly on all sides.

Her stifled whimper rose higher as Tai'dqei gently pulled her close, his hand splayed on her back. His other hand went to her cheek, coaxing her to tilt her head back as he stooped, pressing his forehead to hers. His eyes closed before he could look too deeply into her eyes. "I know your children come first, Rayelle. I will enjoy whatever time together we have."

Pain twisted through her as a sob burbled up her lips. She shook her head, dislodging Tai'dqei's hand from her cheek before pressing her face against his chest. Her hands gripped at his sides, fingers threading through the fishnet he wore.

The carefully constructed emotional walls buckled as relief and anger and sadness tore through her. Though she still swallowed down her cries, the tears flowed over her cheeks in unrelenting streams.

Tai'dqei stood quietly as Rayelle cried against him, rubbing his hand up and down her back as his other arm looped around her. When her quiet crying lulled, he tried to softly redirect her focus. "Rest is in order, I think."

Wiping away tears with the heel of her hand, and ignoring how she sniffled, Rayelle tried to rally herself. She shot him a vaguely cheeky – if watery – smile. "Oh, I am sure that was your original plan."

"It was actually." He said, a touch of reproach in his exasperated tone. As she took a step away from him, he crossed his arms over his chest. The ache of exhaustion gnawed at his bones as the adrenaline-drain squared up to knock him out. "As enticing as you are, I am tired."

Rayelle grinned, almost tempted to say something about the mighty ja-tau needing a nap but she feared that would go down a less wholesome path. She still couldn't help nudging Tai'dqei with her shoulder as she passed him. "Think you can keep your hands to yourself, if we share your bed?"

"No," he answered, easily coming up beside her. She shot him a wide-eyed look, a blush biting across her cheeks as she tried to decide whether to be aroused or annoyed. He didn't give her a chance to settle, as his arm reached around her back, his hand falling on her hip. Tai'dqei gave her a playful squeeze. "You are too soft not to pull close."

"Let me rephrase," she laughed, shoving his hand away and turning, dancing back to keep her distance. Tai'dqei watched her, head cocked as he respected the distance she set forth. She continued walking backward toward his quarters as she teasingly asked, "Think you can keep your dick to yourself if we share a bed?"

Ah, that's what she meant. Tai'dqei gave a nod just as they breached the threshold of his bedroom. "That, I can do. You have my word."

"Good," she replied, giving an encouraging nod as she kicked off her shoes. He followed her lead, removing his boots and fishnets. He chose to leave his lower garment intact, noticing how she had only stripped to her hoodie and underwear. She was probably more comfortable with some layers between them, he guessed.

Trying to ignore the excited patter of her own heart, Rayelle advanced on the raised dais where the bed sat. She crawled under the pelt-like covers before she could think for too long about all the things Tai'dqei had done in that bed. To himself or others. Her own censorship didn't keep her imagination from leaking the odd thought into the back of her head.

Before he crawled under the covers, Tai'dqei locked the ship and dimmed the lights from his gauntlet. He was painfully aware of the additional body in his bed, just as she was aware of how his heavier form made the mattress dip.

Even if they had wanted to sleep on separate sides of the mattress – which they hadn't – it was impossible. As soon as Tai'dqei settled, Rayelle found herself slipping toward him. Which was fine, she told herself, as nerves bolted through her. They turned to face each other and her hands slid to his chest.

Under her palm, he was as firm and warm as he always was. With the knowledge they were already sharing a bed, and they'd been far more intimate than *this* in recent memory, Rayelle curled against his chest. Other than the time she caught him leaving the shower, she wasn't sure she ever saw him without the fishnet-like fabric.

Closing his eyes, Tai'dqei allowed his hand land on her hip. Though he fought against the temptation of toying with the fabric beneath his fingers, unsure if it was her underwear or her hoodie.

While it was one thing to say he simply wanted rest, it was another thing to keep his body in check. With her so close, her scent wafting up in his face and her cushiony soft heat pressed against him, urges started to stir at his center.

It wasn't exactly the urge to rut her, though he wouldn't say no to it, but simply to touch her. To hear the small sighs of contentment. To feel her under his palm, his claws. To see what sounds he could draw out of her with slow gentle touches. Beneath those thoughts, the memories of being on top of her, in her, danced around his head.

"You're very warm," she sighed, absentmindedly hooking her leg over his hip, pulling his heat closer to her.

He shifted, making sure his traitorous growing arousal didn't nudge against her. Softly joking, he grunted, "You are testing me."

"Am I?" Faux innocence painted Rayelle's words, even though it truly hadn't been her intention to tempt his resolve. Now that he mentioned it, she realized how her cuddling could be construed.

It was better to act like she was trying to seduce him or else she'd cave to the squirming heat at her core and the desire to touch him more.

"Certainly, seems like it." His eyes cracked open, tracing the curve of her silhouette in the dark.

She pressed further against his chest, close enough for him to feel her smile against his skin and for her to hear the increasing thrum of his heart. "Maybe you're just weak-willed."

Rayelle was testing him, but two could play that game. Tai'dqei growled, the vibrations emanated out from his chest and into her bones. He knew exactly what he was doing, she realized, as he hunched further around her, keeping her squirming body from wriggling away.

The heat of his body bled into hers. One arm wrapped around her, his claws dragging down the fabric of her hoodie. Not hard enough to tear the material, but barely bridging the barrier. A shudder and embarrassing whimper left her as her breaths caught in her throat.

"If I was weak-willed, you'd already be pinned to this mattress and pumped full of my seed again," Tai'dqei hissed in her ear, causing her fingernails to dig into his chest. Trickles of pleasure slid down her spine at his words. Her back arched, inadvertently pressing his claws harder into her.

"I thought you were tired." She ignored the hint of breathlessness in her voice as she angled her head to look up at him. She couldn't see anything, except his silhouette in the dark. Even then, it was hard to get a clear idea of where he was looking. Half-unaware she was doing it, both her legs hooked around one of his thighs, seeking pressure against her the needy throb of her center.

"I am, but that doesn't mean my libido is tired." To make his point clear, Tai'dqei shifted his hips and allowed his semi-arousal to grind against her inner thigh. Her soft warmth teamed up with her little gasp, sending sharp temptation knifing through him. He was about ready to say screw sleep just to bury himself in her once more, but the sensible part of him knew rest was needed. They both needed it. Especially Rayelle, given how frustrated and concerned she sounded earlier.

"Okay, okay," she laughed, her cheeks warm with excitement and a bit of shame. Tai'dqei had been restraining himself for much longer than tonight. Not to mention he literally tore up a whole resort to help her. He deserved the rest without her taunting making it – *ahem* – hard.

Reaching up to grab his shoulders, she pulled herself a little higher along his body. Feeling her slide against him, it almost made him groan. Pressing her face into the crook of his neck, she sighed against his throat. "I'll be good."

"Good," he grumbled, though the movement of her lips against his skin did little to ease the fire and pressure throbbing inside him. At least, her change in position gave his erection wide berth. Though he wasn't sure if he liked that or not, it was safer.

Other than the occasional movement of her lips against his shoulder – half-drowsy kisses – and the slow stroke of his hand down her back, the two fell still. Sleep claimed them quickly after that. The promise of waking up in each other's arms when they next roused was an incentive to actually rest.

CHAPTER 23

When Rayelle next woke, sleep valiantly clung to her and attempted to drag her down again. Sheer exhaustion had succeeded against her in two earlier attempts to rouse. The bed was too comfortable and cozy. The companion she curled against was too warm to pull herself away. This time, she was able to shake off the dozy feeling and crack her eyes open.

It was still dark, but they seemed to be in the same position as earlier with her curled against his chest. Turned toward her, one of Tai'dqei's arms rested heavily on her side, the other cushioned her head. The low illumination from the lights wasn't enough for Rayelle to see clearly, but she felt the shift of Tai'dqei's chest as he breathed, deep and even. Without thinking, she ran her fingers traced along the scars under his pecs and the subtle dips of his front. Under her fingertips, she thought she felt a subtle texture difference in his pattern, but without light it was too difficult to know if it was scars or a physical difference in his very body.

At the very back of her head, worries and concerns still lingered. Eventually, she was going to have to decide. Her hopes for the end-result were fractured. She wanted to be with her children, but she also wanted to stay with Tai'dqei.

Something in her ached, thinking of Skylar and Elliot living with their unyielding cold father. A father that watched the mother of his children being kidnapped without batting an eye. Of course, if he did orchestrate it, that would explain his lack of surprise. Perhaps he even planned her potential murder if it had gotten that far.

There was no denying she wanted to stay with Tai'dqei. To make a life in the future, away from the hassles and tribulations of her time. To explore whatever this little pocket of the universe had in store. The possibilities made long-forgotten excitement swell in her chest.

The easiest course was being denied the chance to return home. If the temporal authorities said she couldn't go back, that would be it. Unless she fought it.

Whether she would or not was a question for a later time. For now, she would bask in this comfortable bubble of cozy warmth and explore what the universe had already dropped into her life.

Namely Tai'dqei.

She shifted her leg from around his side as her fingertips brushed against the border of skin and cloth, where his loincloth remained snuggly fastened. She considered letting her hand wander further along the fabric to palm at him. Not exactly a sexual touch, but simply wishing to feel the comforting heat and firmness of him.

Since they hadn't discussed or consented to intimate touches while either of them slept, her hand retreated back up along his side. There were other places to touch. Lightly, her fingertips caressed along his side, feeling along the grooves of old scars and that texture of leathery skin.

One of her hands detoured to his back while the one sandwiched between their bodies splayed over his chest. Beneath her palm, she could feel his heart thrum. He let out a huff threaded with a sigh as he shifted minutely under her touch.

"What are you doing?" Sleep still clung to Tai'dqei's throat, making his words deep and garbled. The question was intertwined with light amusement as he registered her hand rubbing along his back.

She pressed her face closer to his chest, as if it would hide the sudden heat burning her cheeks. The way his words sounded, deep and guttural, sent that delightful tingle down her back. She tried not to think about it — nor think how juvenile she was, reacting that strongly to the sound of his voice — as she softly replied, "Just touching you."

A series of thoughtful clicks left him as his own hand traced down her back, over her hoodie and to the edge of her underwear. He vaguely regretted retrieving her fresh clothes from the ship after moving it. If he hadn't, she might be far more undressed.

He paused his caresses as her deft fingers dug into his back muscles. Just barely, he swallowed a groan before asking, "And why are you just touching me?"

The gentle teasing in his tone made her lips pucker and her cheeks become hotter. Shifting from using fingertips to fingernails, Rayelle pressed a little harder along the seam of Tai'dqei's shoulder blade. Another sound, deeper than the previous one he had muffled, rumbled from his chest.

"Should I not be touching you?" She filled her voice with mock concern as she withdrew her hand from his back.

"Not saying that," he chuckled, catching her wrist at his side. He was tempted to lead her hand to exactly where she could touch him but decided to simply use his words. "There's places to touch other than my chest or back."

"I considered it, but I wasn't sure if I should," she admitted, clearly reading the suggestion in his voice. Pushing against his side, she propped herself higher up on her other arm and nudged his side.

Obeying her wordless request, Tai'dqei rolled over on his back, curious to see where she'd lead. "Why not?"

"Not everyone likes being touched like that when they're asleep." She shrugged as she moved to straddle him. Her legs spread to bracket the large alien's torso, stretching the muscles at the juncture of her inner thigh and trunk. A subtle tingle started at the base of her spine, spreading heat to her center.

"I'm not asleep now." In the dark, he watched and felt Rayelle settle on top of him. Her fleshy thighs pressed to his sides and her cushiony rear found somewhere preferable to settle. If she had eased lower on him, she'd feel his excitement rising. His hands found their way to her legs, palms skirting from her knees to her outer thighs, enjoying her supple warm flesh giving under his touch.

"That you aren't, but I realized something." She grinned down at him, her body buzzing where he touched. Rayelle wasn't entirely sure if Tai'dqei had better sight than her in the dark or not. Either way, she brought the room's system up on her gauntlet. The lights slowly brightened just enough for her to see him.

His hands coasted up her hips, giving Rayelle's love-handles an appreciative squeeze. "Yes?"

Leaning forward, she extended her arms out to brush his shoulders as her chest met his. She gave a little groan and arched her back in her stretch, feeling Tai'dqei's body react to her little sound. Once satisfied, she folded her arms over his chest, pressing her chin down while allowing her bottom to remain propped up. "I haven't actually seen your dick yet."

"Ah," he replied, his eyes narrowing and mandibles pulling up to 'smile' lazily at her. Though not entirely sure, he thought she was purposely teasing him with her movements and sounds. If so, it was working. If not, she was a natural at riling him up. Unable to help himself, his hands skimmed over the round curve of her ass, only the fabric of her panties warding off skin-to-skin contact. "Going to fix that?"

"Yes, if you're amenable to it," she answered, a sigh in her words as she pressed back into his touch.

"*Very* amenable." A playful growl edged his tone, making Rayelle noticeably shiver beneath his palm. Still not able to help himself, he traced his claws along the back of her thighs and Rayelle gave a throaty whimper in return.

Without another word, she languidly slid down his front. It was a slow movement that dragged her soft body along his firm one, the friction lighting fire in both their veins. The only thing that would have made it better, in Tai'dqei's mind, was if she hadn't kept on her hoodie.

Her lips grazed over his chest, tracing the scars under his pecs as her hands stroked his arms, then his sides. Rayelle seemed to explore every little dip and curve with her fingertips.

Each touch threaded anticipation through him, letting her explore at her leisure. Now that he'd answered the mating call, the desperation and need wasn't quite so urgent. With the way excitement pulsed through him, rippling through his center, that newfound ease wasn't going to last forever.

Closing her eyes, Rayelle relished all the small reactions she received. Under her touch, his muscles flexed and hisses or clicks left his maw. When she passed his chest, she began to nip and suckle down his abdomen. Tasting his skin on her tongue, silently enjoying the sharp intake of breath and the way Tai'dqei arched suddenly, needily. Her fingers crooked a little harder against his sides, digging her nails roughly against his tough hide.

Heat razed at his nerves, pressure clenching tighter as — after Rayelle's teeth grazed over his skin — he felt her lips twist into a smile against him. He watched her make her way down his body, murmuring approvingly with every nip and kiss.

At the juncture of his legs, his excitement betrayed him. Hard and straining against the loincloth, his erection begged for attention. For the touch of hands or the soft heat of a mouth. It would flex as stray imaginings taunted his libido.

It was only when her mouth had gotten to the barrier of his loincloth that Rayelle's eyes opened. She had settled herself between his legs, his knees bent. Her gaze trailed up the large expanse of Tai'dqei to his face. Propped up on his elbows, he watched her with a hungry expression, his mandibles moving. Her tongue flicked out over her lips, delight piquing in her as his eyes followed the movement.

Now that she thought about it, what sort of people did he have experience with? Faint recollections of Ah'ke mentioning a brothel danced in her head. Enjoying the intimate company with non-ja-tau wasn't something new to him, but did she offer anything novel for him?

It was just a meandering curiosity, distracting her from moving too fast. Just to antagonize the ja-tau already wrought with anticipation. Her eyes didn't leave Tai'dqei as her fingers explored his loincloth, finding the fasteners and undoing them.

A perpetual rumble, low and soft, vibrated through him as she shoved his final covering aside. She watched his fingers flex on the bed, claws digging into the sheets as if he wanted to grab her by the face. The thought sent a sinful shudder down her spine.

Finally, she tilted her eyes to his erection. Rayelle hid her surprise at it being so close, so tall. His tip brushed her jaw, flexing at the sensation of her gaze. A little sound caught in the back of her throat, realizing just how large he was.

She had managed to fit that – *all of that* – inside her? She couldn't even come up with an accurate comparison. Everything she could think of was too smooth, too skinny, too short.

Besides the sheer size, he had a multitude of ridges starting from the base of his arrowhead tip and noticeably growing thicker at the base. Her insides squirmed, remembering how it felt like those last few ribs enlarged before he came. Like Tai'dqei, his cock was a combination of rusty reds and oranges with his tip and the edges of his ridges fading to a deeper red. Her mouth watered, wanting to taste him on her tongue.

Tai'dqei watched her expressions pass over her face. From the slight surprise of her widening eyes to her half-lidded consideration, bottom-lip-nibbling. He felt he could see the direction her thoughts fell and it made his insides twist excitedly.

As Rayelle drew her lips closer to his flexing member, he swallowed a whine with impatience. Her movements were still slow, still exploratory. Entirely agonizing. She must have caught the hint from his sound, for her eyes flicked back up to his face. A smirk curved over her lips before she dipped lower along his shaft.

Her tongue, flat and warm, caught the underside of his dick and gave him a languid lick, dipping between every ridge. He didn't even realize he was growling, low and continuously, as the pleasure bounced from cock, to core, and then to the rest of his body.

The taste of him made her tongue tingle, heady and indescribably Tai'dqei. Earthy and warm, the scent of him dizzied her senses, making something sharpen within her.

By the time, she made it to his tip, his chest heaved, eyes wide, mandibles flickering. Rayelle's smile grew, pleased by his reactions as a throb of pride pulsed through her. His attention was so intense, it made all of her movements sear with need.

Without more teasing or fanfare, she drew his tip into her mouth. Rayelle closed her eyes, giving a contented hum as he weighed hot and heavy on her tongue. She tested the firm but spongy head with a swirling swipe before moving over one ribbed layer to the next.

"Fuck," Tai'dqei hissed, letting his head fall back to the bed, enjoying the wet hot heaven enveloping his cock. That singular word made Rayelle's insides jump and sizzle.

Muscles twitched along his body, taunted by the pleasure pinging along his nerves. Her tongue continued a slow examination of his member, tasting his every ridge and massaging along long stretches of his shaft. His hands flexed into the bed as every instinct in him was snarling to grab her, rut her, fuck her so hard there was a permanent imprint of her body on the bed.

Rayelle made a questioning sound, pausing her ministrations. She knew why he hissed and strained but teasing him while he was so strung out was too good to pass up. She paused in enveloping more of his length, tilting her attention to his face even though he couldn't see her.

When it became clear she wasn't going to move until he answered, he managed to grunt, "Your mouth… feels good."

The laugh she gave around his cock made ecstasy crackle through him. Tai'dqei couldn't even feel embarrassed for his lack of a refined answer. His brain didn't have the capacity.

And she wasn't about to let him scrabble his way back to sensible thought. Rayelle closed her eyes, focused on unraveling the ja-tau even further. Her hand coiled around his base, unable to fully encircle it. Tracing along the valleys and hills of his length, she stroked up until her hand met her lips.

Her hand and mouth worked in tandem, sometimes falling into opposing rhythms and sometimes synchronized. She drew out every needy sound from Tai'dqei, her own body responding with twinges of pleasure and growing wet between her thighs.

He bowed and twisted, clicked and growled beneath Rayelle's touch. Her hand gripped him tightly as her tongue exploring every crevice, both winding desire tighter through his loins. She'd suck and squeeze and somehow take more of him into her mouth, as if she were so determined to fit him down her throat. Involuntarily, his hips jerked and forced her to still for a second until he growled in frustration.

"I'm close," he snarled, his back arching as he tried his best not to thrust, not to force his excitement further down her flexing throat. Molten heat and pressure knotted tight inside him. His muscles flexed and relaxed, pleasure ebbing and flowing in a taunting balance as his hitched breathing burned his lungs.

A whimper almost tore from his chest as she pulled her delicious warm mouth off him, open air cooling the heat of his pleasure. "Is that so?"

Tai'dqei didn't even get a chance to voice his discontent of his cock missing her mouth before Rayelle swallowed him up again.

Clawed toes curled into the bed as he choked on a groan. Her head bobbed along his length, her hands wringing his shaft as his pulse beat at her fingertips.

If his sounds drove Rayelle wild, the sounds she made while on his cock did the same to him. Little whimpers and gasps combined with how her whole body moved, rollicking as her mouth sped up and down his shaft. The sight was as pleasurable as the act felt.

The addition of her hands, with her deft fingers massaging and squeezing every ounce of pleasure from him, made intelligible thought impossible.

It wasn't long before Tai'dqei seized, a clicking snarl falling loose from him. In that second, any sense shattered as red-hot heat pierced his core, flooding into her mouth. Both his hands grabbed at the back of her head, keeping her in place. His hips moved, jerking at every pulsing release. Lock by his hold, Rayelle was too far gone in lust to do anything other than attempt to swallow the ropes of cum blasted into her mouth.

Even when he was done, it took effort to uncurl his fingers from her hair. Heavy breaths huffed from him as he watched Rayelle sit back on her heels. The sight of her body bared further thrilled his senses as she casually unzipped her hoodie. The additional sight of his seed coating her chin and dribbling down her chest sent another bolt of urgency through him.

Before Rayelle knew it, Tai'dqei had snatched her and pinned her to the bed, somehow tearing off her underwear in the same movement. The scent of her arousal sent another stab of desire through him. His fingers brushed against her folds, a satisfied clicking as he found her sopping wet.

She whimpered and curved eagerly under his touch, her lower tummy flexing. Something other than excitement swelled in Tai'dqei, finding out she had enjoyed playing with him as much as he enjoyed her.

"Need." That singular word was all his hormone-ravaged brain could manage. Even then, it was heavy with a clicking gnarl.

"Please," she immediately responded with a gasp, angling her hips welcomingly. Throughout working Tai'dqei up, she had inadvertently steeped herself in desire. Her own body felt aflame, inner muscles clenching around an aching emptiness that had to be filled. Heat and fullness, her body keened for it.

No further instruction was needed. With a snap of his hips, his cock plunged through her folds and sunk deep into her center. She was already so wet, so ready, her slit took him readily. His own body surged with satisfaction even as the demand for more clawed through him.

A cry broke from Rayelle's lips as her knees clamped against his sides, her hands wrapping under his arms. Her fingernails dug into his back, pressing harder than she would have dared with a human lover. Tai'dqei snarled loudly, each thrust hard and fast and deep.

With ragged panting, she curved under him, arching her neck to watch his mandibles flex. The delirious concentration of pleasure flickered over his features, intensity making his gaze burn. It made his thrusts hit hotter, sending fire through her every nerve. Her fingernails crooked into his back, raking along his skin, not afraid of hurting him if she managed to pierce his skin.

Her whole body jerked with every impact, sending stars and sharp delight biting deep at her insides. Seeking purchase, her heels dug into his lower back and her body rollicked rhythmically against his. Muscles throbbed and her body clung tightly around his penetration.

Rayelle only faintly felt one of his clawed hands grab her hair before he tilted her head. Tai'dqei arched over her, capturing her face in his outstretched mandibles. With her eyes clenched tight, she only had instinct guiding her. She kissed him eagerly, sloppily. One hand slid from his back, grabbing a fistful of his feather-like hair to pull his mouth closer to hers. A rough growl vibrated through his body, sending reverberations through her as his thrusts became harsher.

Their universe dwindled to the sound of their moans and groans, the flexing of muscles, the feel of their skin against one another, the digging of claws and fingernails. Nothing else existed outside of this moment, outside of them. Just the burn of their bodies, the friction and sweat between them, slaking the ache for one another.

Rayelle was the first to break under pleasure. Her body jerked and trembled, a hiccupping cry stuttered from her lips as her toes and fingers curled. Muscles coiled tight and her mouth parted from his but her face was still held by his mandibles.

Tai'dqei's pace didn't falter, didn't stop. He simply growled and continued his jerky thrusts in and out. He wanted her sobbing and screaming, wracked with such decimating pleasure it'd put supernovas to shame. Fighting against her inner walls pulsing around him, trying to milk his own release from him, he dragged her from one orgasm to the next.

He had lost count of how many times her body seized or how loud her cries became. Her nails and heels dug into him, threatening to leave a mark or a bruise. Rayelle's body was an unending twist of muscles as her body quavered with every release. She sobbed, tears drawn from pleasure in the corner of her eyes, throat raw with ecstasy-fueled screams.

With a surge of energy, Rayelle's arms slid around his neck and she pulled him close to deepen a fresh kiss. The touch of her mouth against his sent Tai'dqei's urgency spiraling, overwhelming him. With one last sharp snap of his hips, his cock thickened and bobbed before letting loose his spend. He bore down on her, snarling and moaning into her mouth, answered by her gasps and reedy whimpers. White-hot heat flooded into her, licking at her innermost nerves and slickening her already drenched thighs.

As if she needed him even closer, her heels dug into his back and pressed him into her. Her fingers crooked against his scalp, carding through his plumage. Even as her body quaked, she held tightly onto him. It was as if he were the only solid thing as one last tsunami of pleasure blasted through her.

They stayed like that for a long time, breathing in each other's gasps as their bodies slowly loosened. Rayelle was the first to completely fall lax, her feet falling to the bed with her knees bent at his sides.

Tai'dqei carefully released his mandibles from around her face before rolling over, hauling Rayelle with him. A tired groan left her as she ended up atop him, her thighs straddling him as his cock remained firmly inside her. Still, her tired pussy throbbed in a rhythm around him.

Unable to get enough, his hands grazed up and down her back. She melted further against his front, little pleasant sighs escaping her. She never moved to free his cock from her nor did she say anything about the still hard member inside her.

It was only when she shifted, angling her face to look up at him, that Tai'dqei chuckled, "So go again in five minutes?"

"Are you trying to make me pass out?" She cushioned her chin on his chest with her crossed arms, a giggle tinging her incredulous question.

"Yes." His answer came out smug and teasing.

This time, his hands slid over the curve of her ass, giving her cheeks a taunting squeeze. Near his fingertips, he could feel the humid heat of their joining. It was only some modicum of self-control that kept him from pushing down on her ass, forcing her lower on his dick once more.

A soft hum escaped her, a contented smile curving at her lips. "I'd like to see you try."

Even as the threat of aching exhaustion nipped at her body, she hungered for more of him. Every last bit he would give her, she'd accept. She nipped at his chest and his cock jumped inside her with every graze of her teeth.

"You asked for it," he chuckled, grabbing her by the hips to hoist her up along his cock and unceremoniously drop her down. The singular movement made her jerk up with a sharp inhale, her breasts bouncing. Tai'dqei gave her little chance to respond as his hands engulfed her breasts, his hips already rocking a slow and easy pace.

Closing her eyes with a moan, she leaned into his touch as her body rolled with his pace. Pressure already built at her core, flexing excitedly for her next series of orgasms.

Just a little while like this, she told herself, before having to think about more difficult things.

CHAPTER 24

The next time Rayelle roused, it had to be the next morning. Late morning. Maybe afternoon, she thought, as she lay in bed. Tai'dqei was gone. Most likely, he let her sleep since he'd put her through the ringer yesterday. Multiple times.

She wasn't even sure if their continuous sex had really only been a day. They had stopped to eat or wash at intervals but would invariably succumb to their happy hormones and be tangled up in each other again.

Rayelle couldn't help but wonder if their sex drive stemmed from uncertainty. How long did they really have to be together? Would they soon be separated by time and space? Or was their eagerness born from sexual tension and, in her case, a blessed stamina boost from some futuristic rejuvenation process?

Whatever it was, they had gotten the bulk of it out of their systems. Or so she thought.

Sitting up in bed, she winced as her abdominals twinged with the pain of exertion. A sweet, delicious pain, but still a little uncomfortable. The door to the room slid open and Tai'dqei's familiar footfalls announced his entry before his soft words broke the quiet. "Rayelle, are you awake?"

"I just woke up." She flashed him a smile, but something in his demeanor made her sit straighter. Even as he neared her, she sensed an apprehension int eh air around him. Clashing thoughts of hope and dread hurtled through her head. "What's wrong?"

A pang shot through his chest, hearing his own feelings mirrored in her voice. He paused a little way from the bed, giving her ample space to get to her feet if she so chose. Even as the lump formed in his throat, threatening to make the words dissipate, he answered her, "The Temporal Authority Council wishes to speak with you."

As he expected, she scrambled off the bed. "Am I going to be told if I can go back?"

Tai'dqei swallowed down unfair bitter feelings at seeing her so excited. Now wasn't the time. He tried to stow the hurt as far down as he could, imagining it taking residence beside the now dulled pain of losing Ah'ke. "They didn't say. They just asked for your presence as soon as you're available."

Rayelle nodded, trying to restrain the hope building in her chest. With the excitement, another emotion swelled. It was a feeling that would make her cry if she stopped and focused on it for too long. That very feeling kept her from looking too closely at Tai'dqei, from brushing up against him. If she touched him, she thought she'd break down into tears all the same.

Too many thoughts, too many feelings, careened around her head. Taking a deep breath, she tilted her gaze up to him, forcing herself to look at him. "I'll shower and get dressed, then we can eat before going to see the Council?"

There was half a beat before Tai'dqei could answer her. He was too tempted to ask hard questions, too sobered by the potential of losing her to tease about joining her in the shower. An uncertainty wavered in the air around both of them, weighing on their shoulders. Right now, he needed to give her some inkling of support without making the pain worse for himself.

Instead of offering to join her, he simply nodded and chose an alternative. "I'll cook something up while you get ready."

Rayelle said a weak thanks before watching Tai'dqei turn and leave the room. She fought back a burn at the back of her eyes and forced herself to gather clean clothes. Movement was key, she had to keep moving forward. Focusing on her forward motion, she headed out of the bedroom and into the bathroom.

In the transit from bedroom to bathroom, she caught the sound of Tai'dqei moving implements in the galley, muttering to himself about what to cook. Or maybe he was on a comm with Ah'ke, talking about how Rayelle could soon go home. She ducked into the bathroom before she could hear more.

It was difficult to focus as she started up the shower. Her thoughts chased and tumbled over each other. She might be able to go home and see Elliot and Skylar again. If that was the case, what was she going to do?

How was she going to make sure Evan wasn't going to hurt them? Or stop him if he tried to hurt her again?

While part of her mind raced through options, trying to remember the restrictions of the past, another part of her thoughts lolled over Tai'dqei.

They both knew this announcement would come.

She was just glad Ah'ke had showed up soon after the liberation of the resort. Ah'ke said she was there to tend to the wounded, but Rayelle was pretty sure she was there for Tai'dqei. He probably told her what was going on between them. What would happen when the TAC got back to her about the possible options.

Scrubbing at her face, Rayelle wicked away moisture and tried to convince herself the warm droplets *weren't* from the few tears that had crested from her lashes.

She wasn't even sure if she was going home! For all she knew the Temporal Authorities would decline her and then… She'd have to live with knowing she could never return. Or she'd fight and find a way back to her children.

With a harsh shake of her head, she focused on taking one step at a time. First, finish her shower. Second, go eat. Third, head to the temporary offices TAC agents had set up on Rerli 3. Any plans beyond that would have to wait until she knew what was going to be allowed.

Another twenty minutes passed before Rayelle emerged from the shower. Dressed in a fresh outfit and with hair slightly damp, she headed into the mess area. Tai'dqei turned at her entry, as if he'd been listening for her. "Good timing, I just finished some *oatmeal.*"

Rayelle couldn't stop the smile that curved over her lips. During their brief reunion, they talked about a number of things including food. She couldn't recall how oatmeal came up – perhaps some teasing remark about something that was good on a cold day – but it had. It seemed he had endeavored to make some, probably with the guidance and resources from the humans on Rerli 3.

"Thank you," she said, as she accepted a bowl from a rather large pot of the still simmering food. The spicy sweet scent of cinnamon and sugar drifted up on the steam. He definitely had help, she mused with a smile.

The gesture made something in her chest twinge. Ignoring it, she took the warm bowl to the table, Tai'dqei followed with his own serving. Sitting down, side-by-side, the two ate quietly. Neither really tasted the food with their minds focused on other things.

Each bite, every passing second, got them closer to a possible end. What were they going to do? Both of their minds prepared for the worst. For the sad and lonely path, for the aching and the pain.

"Tai'dqei?" Rayelle finally piped up, placing her spoon at the edge of the bowl.

Her eyes didn't tilt toward him, he realized, as his attention focused on her. "Yes?"

A lump formed in her throat, a tangle of words that she wanted to say but was having a hard time getting out. She couldn't bring her eyes to meet his. Even as he shifted in his seat, giving her his full attention.

"No matter what happens... I... I am glad, you know. That we..." Despite her mental grip on herself, she couldn't stop the tears or the way her voice cracked. Her shoulders hunched and shook, quiet tears slipping down her cheeks.

It only took a single hiccup of her voice for Tai'dqei to slowly, softly, lean over to her. Rayelle turned her head toward him, about to apologize, but quieted as he gathered her up in his arms, pressing his forehead gently to hers. In silence, she stared up at him, finding the weight and texture of his forehead against hers both enjoyable but heart-wrenching.

She realized it took him a long breath before he said something in a painfully even voice. "I understand."

Those two words hung heavy in his mouth and struck her hard in the chest.

As true as they were, his heart ached. Something in his bones told him she was leaving. She would be returning to her time, her world. He tried to shrug it off as paranoia or just being prepared for the pain of losing her, but his intuition braced for her departure. Their time together was dwindling so fast now.

As much as Rayelle didn't want to admit it, she felt the same sense of an end coming. Perhaps that's why she threw herself against Tai'dqei, wrapped her arms tight around his neck as she quietly cried.

They sat like that for a little while, both memorizing how the other felt. Tai'dqei committed to memory her plush softness, her warmth, the scent of her, the feel of her smaller body shifting minutely against his. Rayelle basked in his arms, his body heat, the certain solidity of him wrapped around her.

It wasn't until she carefully disentangled herself from him, wiping at her tear-streaked face, that Tai'dqei spoke once more. "Are you ready to go?"

"No, but I don't think I ever will be," she mumbled, turning doleful eyes up to him. It was silly to already be crying, to already feel as if they were saying good-bye. Still, she offered a watery smile while giving her head a shake. "But I have to know if I can go back."

He nodded, his mandibles pulling upward in a reciprocating smile. Like hers, it didn't reach his eyes.

Once Rayelle dried her tears, she pushed back in her chair and stood. He followed her lead, feeling slow and heavy despite his lack of armor. Tentatively, she held out her hand to him, half-expecting a gentle wave-away the longer he stared. But his hand soon encompassed hers. He swallowed down the premature grief as he burned the memory of her palm in his into a permanent place in his brain.

Together Tai'dqei and Rayelle left his ship, hand in hand, enjoying whatever time they had left to touch.

◊ ◊ ◊

It took far shorter for the Temporal Authority Council agents to call on Rayelle than she expected. With Tai'dqei by her side, the two were led into an auditorium that had been converted into a sort of hearing room for the head committee. It was a huge room, filled with rows of chairs and a stage. People bustled in and out, carrying stacks of papers and holo-pads, addressing one of the five non-humans sitting at a long table on the stage floor.

As chaotic as it was, it somehow reminded Rayelle of a high school during some big function. There was a method to the madness. She just didn't know what it was. From the way Tai'dqei held tightly onto her hand, he didn't seem to know either.

"Ah, you must be Miss Brooks, yes?" One of the five obvious leaders looked up, offering Rayelle what she hoped was a friendly smile. It was hard to tell since their form seemed to constantly shift. Not that Rayelle could put a finger on how. It just seemed they were in a constant state of flux. Her mind turned to aliens capable of dimension hopping and time travel, wondering if they were one such alien.

What she did manage to register was blue skin and six glowing eyes and two smiling mouths, one atop the other. Or maybe that's how they wished to be perceived. She shook her head, dislodging the complicated thoughts concerning dimensional transmission.

"Yes, I am. I'm supposed to meet with the Temporal Authority Council," she said, diverting toward the stage stairs as the alien waved her in that direction.

Tai'dqei followed her, if only thanks to the fact she still grasped onto his hand. Or maybe he was holding onto her for dear life. That sense of instinctive dread swelled in him. On top of the misery he was doing his best to keep at bay, the busy nature of the area grated on his nerves. His shoulders hunched, tension winding down his back.

The blue shifting alien abruptly nodded before turning to one of their colleagues. "Sh'thal, I believe you were handling the progress of this case?"

"Which case?" Across the stage, another alien looked up. Their skin shone like purple glass, little specks of light flickering beneath the surface. Crystalline eyes turned to the blue energy alien, blinking owlishly as if they were readjusting their thought process from one task to another completely unrelated chore. Even as they tilted their attention to their co-worker and Rayelle, four of their six hands continued to presumably sort through holo-pads.

"The temporally displaced human, Rayelle Brooks of 2024, Missouri, United States," the blue alien answered. Sh'thal still stared, not replying. Tai'dqei and Rayelle exchanged a look. The first alien sighed, crossing their noodle arms as they said, in an almost deadpan voice, "The one a ja-tau brought in."

"Oh!" Tai'dqei's stomach dropped and Rayelle's heart twisted as recognition struck the crystalline alien. Sh'thal turned to one of their six wrists, inputting data and pulling up a holoscreen. "One second!"

Rayelle glanced up at Tai'dqei, who had at some point released her hand. The sudden realization sent a chill through her, but she shoved it away. It didn't mean anything. That was just some attempt to build a new wall between herself and him. Instead, she focused on Tai'dqei in the moment. The physicality of him. The way the lights of the room played off his skin and the metal adornments in his feather-hair, the barely-there scars that ticked along his arms and knuckles.

Tai'dqei had been staring off into space, watching the crystalline alien – a Corizite – scrolling through files and messages. He wondered if they were delaying bad news. Guilty hope fluttered through him at the mere idea of it. Feeling Rayelle's eyes on him, he tilted his attention down toward her and raised his eyebrow ridges with curiosity.

"I just enjoy looking at you," she answered softly, so low that no one else could hear her comment.

To that, Tai'dqei made a scoffing grunt and playfully pushed at her but couldn't help the way his mandibles quirked upward. They'd come so far, she realized, to the point she could catch such expression changes.

Returning the gesture, she nudged back at him, giving a short laugh before leaning against his side. Tai'dqei didn't fight it. His arm came around his shoulders, hand resting on her far hip as he relaxed against her.

For a brief moment, the hustle and bustle around them died away. It was just the two of them again.

Until the Corizite turned toward them with a triumphant trill.

"It has been decided that Miss Brooks may return to her time, if she so chooses." Sh'thal looked up, their countenance beaming as they closed out of the file. They clapped two pairs of their hands together, giving off guidance counselor energy as they chirped, "Isn't that *exciting?*"

CHAPTER 25

Silence filled the air between Rayelle and Tai'dqei as the bustle of bureaucracy continued around them. Rayelle stared at Sh'thal, excitement and relief clashing against dread and disappointment. The pressure of the conflicting emotions almost made her want to throw up. "I can?"

"Yes, whether you are gone or present, your being in the past makes no major changes." Unaware of the implications of her own words, Sh'thal smiled brightly at Rayelle.

To be told your presence – or lack thereof – makes no difference was both a slap in the face and a comfort. There were two people her presence made the difference for: Skylar and Elliot. The relief made her heart swell, excited to see her children once more after what felt ages of being apart.

Turning to Tai'dqei, Rayelle's delight diminished a little. He didn't move. He just stared at the Corizite, trying to maintain a handle on the inner roil of emotions threatening to burst forth. Even Rayelle could sense the tension in his limbs, the awful way his mandibles remained still and pulled tight.

"I-I have to go back. Elliot and Skylar need me." She reached out, her fingers shaking as her hand stroked down his arm. He jerked at the sudden contact, his head swiveling to meet her gaze. A guilty twinge twisted in her chest as he acted so struck by the mere graze of her fingers. Tears of frustration were again threatening to spill from her eyes. With a shake of her head, she forced the words out, "If Evan can do what he did to me, what's to stop him from—"

Her words halted as he turned to face her, his large hands moving to her shoulders. For a breath, both stared at one another in silence again. There were so many things he wanted to say, but the weight of the eyes around them clamped his throat shut. Instead, he leaned into the tried and true. "I understand."

Rayelle frowned at those two annoying *awful* words. She was growing to hate them, hate how calm and collected he seemed after the news. Her insides felt like they were being shredded, her heart tripping back and forth between happiness and woe. It had to be painted on her face, in her crumpling body language. The conflict and the pain.

And there Tai'dqei was, standing straight and tall with a firm set to his shoulders. Immovable, steadfast, strong. As if she was just the weak one, the one who was going to be upset *and* happy regardless of what the answer had been.

Rayelle shrugged off his hands, her voice cracking as she burst out, "Why though? Why do you understand *so easily?*"

It was hard to say how she even wanted him to react. Did she want him to throw a fit? Demand she stay? Or maybe wholeheartedly tell her to go? Either way would have made the decision easier. In the former, he would be too selfish to consider staying with. In the latter, it would be obvious he couldn't wait to get rid of her.

The reaction Tai'dqei was giving her somehow made everything so much harder. The longer his silence went on the more her chest ached, clearly feeling his struggle beneath his seemingly unflappable demeanor.

"It's *not* easy. I want you to stay here with me, but you wouldn't be happy. Not knowing what would happen to your kids would eat at you." When he spoke, his voice was soft and strained. His tone hardened his agitation as he shook his head, his fists clenched at his sides. A tremor arched along one of his arms, as if the tension of his muscles burdened his body. "You didn't ask to come here. It's unfair of me to ask you to stay, knowing what – and who – you might be sacrificing."

At a loss for what to say, Rayelle simply stared at him as frustrated tears brimmed in her eyes. On some level, she knew that would be his answer, knew that he was as struck as she was. It was just easier to believe he wasn't. It made her inevitable choice simpler to swallow.

But the choice wasn't going to be easy. Ever since she got closer to him, it was never going to be easy.

"You may take some time to decide or to find a way to remember one another, if you so choose." Sh'thal interrupted the tense moment with an almost sweet, yet matter-of-fact tone.

"Ideally, we wish you to return to your proper time as soon as possible, but there is some leeway."

Rayelle's attention flickered to Sh'thal, ideas careening suddenly through her brain. That was right. The Temporal Authority Council had plenty of time, didn't they? "How long may I have?"

Sh'thal hummed, looking over data on their holo screen. They seemed to tally something in their head before answering, "A few days, at most. We risk you looking too different from when you left if we wait too long."

"Thank you," Rayelle hurriedly said as she turned on her heel. She grabbed Tai'dqei by his wrist and led him from the temporary TAC office, immensely thankful that he offered little resistance.

In truth, Tai'dqei was weak to any time he could snatch away with her. Wherever she would lead, he'd follow until their last moment. He couldn't imagine being in her position, making the same choices. His chest hurt thinking about it. Still, it didn't explain why she was dallying. "Where are we going?"

Her mind spun out with ideas and thoughts. Last minute things to do. Last minute things to say. Last minute goodbyes. They all clattered through her head, clogging her throat with answers. She waited until they were outside of the auditorium and in the hall before settling on a direction. "I want to visit the others before I go."

He grunted, nodding in understanding. Of course, she would want to let the others know her news. Perhaps give a little hope to others who sought to return home to their planet and time. That made sense.

"And I want something to remember you by," Rayelle added quickly, fighting down the embarrassment such sentimentality roused. Her shoulders hunched and a flush crawled over her cheeks, feeling his gaze burn into her back.

Something in Tai'dqei perked up at her words. Something to remember him by? His mind filed through a list of gifts, of trophies, of things he could do for her. Quietly, he let his mind gnaw on possibilities as she led him through the corridors.

◊ ◊ ◊

It took the better part of an hour, but Rayelle and Tai'dqei managed to gather up a gallery of friends and companions. The little contingent of human freedom fighters — Sandra, Lisa, Abe, Mizan, and Bette — were joined by Ah'ke and Big Blue. Humans and ja-tau alike clustered around tables in one of the many community halls.

At Rayelle's initial announcement, informing them all of her intentions to return home, an awkward cacophony of congratulations for her and sympathies for Tai'dqei resounded. She couldn't stop her own conflicted expression from crimping her features. Even people who had barely known them could sense the heaviness in the air.

Leaning back precariously in a chair, Lisa broke the diametrically opposed joy-and-woe in the air. "No one would blame you if you stayed, y'know."

"Lisa!" Sandra swatted the other woman on the shoulder. Lisa yelped at the reprimand, shooting Sandra a dirty look.

Ignoring the dagger-filled glares, Rayelle sighed. "I'd blame myself. I know it's hard to understand, but I can't just leave them if I can go back."

It wasn't like she hadn't thought about staying. She was here now and, had the TAC not given her the go ahead to return home she wouldn't know the difference. But they did give her the okay and she couldn't just abandon her kids.

It was out of the question to ask Tai'dqei to go with her, as well. There was no life for him on Earth and she couldn't force her kids to be on the intergalactic run with an alien out of his time and his sector of space.

There was only one option for Rayelle.

"Since I'm leaving, I do want something to remember him by." Her eyes trailed to Tai'dqei, sitting beside her in a much-too-small human chair. He'd been rather quiet and introspective as they rounded everyone up. Without realizing she was doing it, she reached out to his hand resting in his lap. He looked up at the touch, the distant look softening as his eyes came to her face.

Lisa made a scoffing sound but everyone else exchanged glances, looking for the answer to Rayelle's question. Or maybe considering solutions that would leave the well-known couple together.

"How about a ray gun for Evan's face?" Mizan slumped against the table, chin cushioned by their crossed arms. A few chuckles rose up from the group, though the mood didn't lighten entirely.

The suggestion made Rayelle smile a little, unsure if ray guns were a thing in Mizan's time or still a thing of fiction. Regardless, ray guns certainly weren't a real thing in her time and she doubted TAC would let her take one with her. No matter her reasoning. "Something that's not anachronistic. Preferably easy to hide and not able to be taken from me."

"Did you consider a blooding ritual?" Big Blue – whose name was actually Ad'tuan but didn't seem to mind the nickname – spoke up from where he sat at the table next to Sandra. His bulk was even more at odds in the human-sized chair compared to Tai'dqei.

"A blooding ritual?" Rayelle inclined her head to Big Blue, raising her eyebrows.

"They are traditional ja-tau rituals that have fallen out of fashion. There are different rites for different events that vary from between cultures, but they all tend to leave a mark on the body," Ad'tuan explained, his voice deep and resonant and his tone pragmatic.

"It often requires something to cause a scar and a particular symbol, pending on the meaning." Ah'ke further explained as she shrugged her shoulders. Turning to Tai'dqei, she added, "You could use the acid of the tsai'tse flower. It is strong enough to mark humans, but easy for them to heal from. Many humans use it for cosmetic scarification."

This was apparently a common enough occurrence for Ah'ke to know that little nugget of information, Rayelle thought as she mulled over the information.

"And you could mark him in return!" Sandra flashed a smile to

Rayelle, clapping her hands together as if they were about to embark on a cute craft project.

"Like couple's tattoos?" Rayelle's nose scrunched at the thought, but she turned a questioning look up at Tai'dqei and tried to gauge his interest. He still kept his expression carefully masked and, in a bid to connect, she asked, "What symbol would we even use?"

She was sure there were plenty of Earth or ja-tau symbols to choose from but it felt unbalanced to choose a mark that was particular to her people or his. As for something that represented both of them, she drew a blank. Nothing she could think of could be condensed to a picture or word suitable for a tattoo.

"It does not have to be a symbol." Tai'dqei spoke slowly, still piecing together his own feelings on the option. Whether Rayelle wanted such a mark was her choice. Not wishing to admit it, he had considered blooding rituals in the hour it took to gather everyone. There was only one thing he wanted, one place he wanted it.

"I would like your handprint here." His hand rose to his chest, fingers pressing lightly over his heart. Before Rayelle could even open her mouth to argue or question it, he continued, "I can cover your hand with my blood – that should neutralize the tsai'tse acid against your skin – so you may mark me without getting hurt."

"But why my handprint?" Her eyebrows furrowed, trying to imagine the large swath of her own skin stained with his handprint. It would not be subtle. Was that what Tai'dqei wanted for her, in exchange for her hand on him?

"Even after you go back to your time, I want... I want..." He looked away, the words crackling and trailing off. Though unable to meet anyone's eye, his hand motioned to his chest, fingers curling against the very spot he mentioned earlier.

The motion reminded Rayelle of holding hands, sending a new swirl of painful emotion through her. She inhaled deeply, swallowing down the tears as she grabbed for his arm. When he did turn to look at her again, she offered him an encouraging smile. "Okay, that's what we'll do."

CHAPTER 26

One day. Twenty-four hours. That was all Rayelle allowed herself. Too much longer and she risked never leaving Tai'dqei's side. Together they got their corresponding marks and Ah'ke shortened the recovery time with an extra strength med-spray.

Tai'dqei now sported her handprint as a pale-yellow scar over his heart, as he wanted. She had already caught him touching it multiple times while quietly staring off into the distance. It made the cracks in her heart deepen every time. Instead of dwelling on it, she would just kiss him or snuggle closer or distract him with something to do.

He appreciated her attempts to lift his spirits. This was their last cycle of shared smiles and quiet words and lingering touches. His thoughts always swung back to how temporary, how fleeting, their time together had been. Every time, the thought sent an ache through him, but there was nothing he could do.

Soon enough, she was going to be gone. Wishful thinking clung to past precedent, hoping that would be a lie. They had already parted when he dropped her off at the resort and, yesterday, he had been sure she'd leave as soon as she was told the news.

Though he greatly enjoyed her presence, part of him almost wished she had left right after the news. Lingering in this state was tortuous. As the time drew nearer for her to go home, he could feel the necessary emotional wedge between them growing.

Unable to get his handprint over her heart, due to the sheer size difference, Rayelle settled for something else. Five lines, his claw tips, splayed apart and drawn together at a point above her heart. It wasn't until she was walking back into the temporary TAC set-up that she understood why Tai'dqei had been touching his chest so often. She couldn't stop doing the same.

Ah'ke hadn't managed to heal the marks entirely. The area was still tender. Pressing on it sent a slight hint of pain through Rayelle's skin, enough to distract her from the misery building in her chest. At the same time, she was comforted to have a piece of Tai'dqei right there.

Once they made it through the doors of the makeshift office, everything sped up. TAC agents guided the two of them from the office to a kitchen that had been modified into a science lab with a portable time doorway set up. It honestly looked rather unimpressive, Rayelle thought. An empty rectangle of a metal doorway displayed on a platform hooked up to a litany of boxy-looking power supplies and computers.

The words hit Tai'dqei like a punch. Then light flashed bright, blinding him though he made no move to back away. Looking to the spot Rayelle had last been, he found emptiness in her place. Much like the hollow spot growing in his chest.

His hands clenched tight until his claws dug into his palms and prickled through his skin, causing drops of blood to ooze out. A torrent of emotions swarmed him.

Around him, the technicians busied themselves with shutting down the doorway. Each in their own world of numbers and readings and settings. They didn't give the ja-tau in their midst another thought.

Numbly, Tai'dqei brought his hands in front of him and stared at his bleeding palms. Anger and despair roiled through him. He didn't even have the chance or strength, despite the drawn-out time, to tell Rayelle he loved her before she was gone.

◊ ◊ ◊

The world whorled around Rayelle in a sea of colors and lines and speed. Her brain scrambled to make sense of what was happening around her, trying to latch onto anything. Brief snippets and sounds of events flashed and echoed around her. Some of it in English, some of it in an entirely different – though recognizable – language. Occasionally, a scent wafted through her nose, familiar and unfamiliar and coating the back of her tongue. Through the chaos, she couldn't make heads or tails of anything thought.

Just as quick as the light, the sounds, the tastes had descended on her, it all lifted with a deafening boom. An unrelenting keening flatlined in her ears until it faded. Blinking her eyes rapidly, Rayelle tried to make sense of the world around her, desperate to gain her bearings.

It was night, she realized with a start. Darkness swathed the area, save for a few streetlights in the restaurant parking lot. Cicadas and crickets sang a noisome chorus around her. She was kneeling by her car, her door still open and her purse not far off.

Apparently, no one had noticed her abduction. Bitterness weighed against sensibility, deciding whether that was just human nature or if the Temporal Authorities had something to do with that. The less alarm around her disappearance, the less of a historical wave it made, didn't it?

Rayelle battled the sense of surreality as she stood.

She was back on Earth, back in her time. Back home. It didn't feel like home. Her hand pressed to her chest — over her heart, over Tai'dqei's mark — and she swallowed heavily. She couldn't help but feel her home was somewhere else in space, in the future.

That didn't matter, she told herself as she steeled against an onslaught of sudden emotions. Numbly, she grabbed her purse from where it had fallen — been thrown, she reminded herself — and climbed into her car.

It took her a few moments and a few deep breaths before she managed to jam her keys into the ignition and pull out of the parking lot. Thankfully, driving came back to her quickly. On autopilot, she made her way back to her house, her children, her life before Tai'dqei.

◊ ◊ ◊

The first few days back were eventful. In his miserable attempt to seem conscientious, Evan called the cops on Rayelle's home for a wellness check. Gratifyingly, the officers seemed annoyed when she explained the caller was her ex and they were in the process of a divorce. Seeing the confusion, shock, and rage mingling on Evan's face when she next met him was also satisfying. Although, not satisfying enough to make losing Tai'dqei hurt any less.

The following months passed, both a slog and at great speed. People around Rayelle noticed she was acting differently. A few even said she looked different, sounded different, acted different. For the most part, she didn't agree with them but she did have a new fire burning within her.

She was determined to give Evan absolute hell during court proceedings, the loss of Tai'dqei driving her to be ruthless. And she did give the damned man hell. Despite the dirty punches he pulled and the attempts to get a less progressive judge, Rayelle prevailed.

She was awarded full custody and hefty child support. Evan was granted visitation every other weekend, to facilitate bonding between father and children.

Elliot never wanted to go, but he did for Skylar's safety. There had been plenty of discussions between Rayelle and her kids concerning self-defense and what major issues to look out for, what to tell her.

Eventually, they fell into a comfortable routine.

And everything was good. Well, as good as it was in the daily grind. Elliot wore a tux to prom and, gradually, he became more confident in presenting as a boy. Skylar still shifted between various genders, rotating between pronouns. The only consistent thing for them was 'they' and their love of technology and games.

There were still struggles, still those difficult days. On the whole, Rayelle didn't regret her choice. She'd find herself sitting with her kids, in the living room or the kitchen or in the car, relieved and happy. Listening to their trials and tribulations and delights. Something twinged in her, imagining missing out on these moments.

On occasions, she would find her hand drifting to her heart her fingertips running over the scar beneath her shirt. The raised edges of the scar tissue was a solid reminder that it had happened. It wasn't just a delusion or daydream. No matter how much time passed, no matter how foggy the memories became.

She would remember Tai'dqei – be enormously thankful for what they had – until her life on Earth ended.

CHAPTER 27

The rest of Rayelle's life came sooner than expected. She should have known Evan wasn't going to take his losses well. To his credit, he bid his time with a fake smile on his lips and even seemed to move on with a girlfriend. Rayelle hoped everything boded well.

She should have known better. That was all she thought when she saw the truck speeding toward her. Absently, registered Skylar and Elliot screaming in the backseat, but it was too late. A second later, the shrieking crunch of metal filled the air around them.

They had just pulled into the truck stop, a location that she and Evan had agreed upon. It was completely neutral ground, midway between their respective homes. The truck stop was also very much closed on this day of all days.

"—hey were supposed to wait until it was just her. Get in my car!" Blearily, she heard Evan snarling as he yanked one of the back doors open. A little farther off, she heard the squeal of tires as the truck drove off. There was more scuffling closer by as she realized Elliot and Skylar were getting ushered out of her vehicle.

"What about mom?" Skylar asked, their tone wobbling. "We gotta take her to the hospital!"

There was a pause. A hissed expletive. Then she heard gravel crunching away before her door suddenly yanked open. She felt herself lifted, smelled the sickeningly familiar aroma of Evan's cologne and smoke-stained breath.

With her head still spinning, she struggled in his hold but he quickly threw her in the back of his car. Both kids crowded around her, asking her questions. Her head swam, unable to focus on any of their words. There was a sense of movement, a faint register of turn signals clicking and the roar of the car speeding up.

Rayelle's brain didn't make sense of anything until Skylar nervously said, "Dad, this isn't the way to the hospital."

"You wanna tell 'em about the men y'sent after me?" Rayelle pushed herself upright, words slurred in spite of her best effort. The world spun at the edges of her vision. She knew she shouldn't open this can of words, but rage had control of her tongue.

Evan remained still, ice emanating from his snappy answer, "I have no clue what you mean."

"You remember. It was the last dinner I agreed to with you alone." She waved her hand, shooting him a look in the rearview mirror. Part of her knew she was traveling down the worst avenue of discussion in this circumstance, but something in her wanted to needle at him. Maybe it was head trauma, making Rayelle reckless.

Or maybe, given how he'd paid someone to run them off the road, she was ready to let her kids see his colors fully. "You waved as they shoved me into a van."

"I have no *fucking* clue what you're saying, Rayelle," Evan savagely spat, turning briefly from the road to glare at her. He whipped back around a second later, after the kids screamed at him for taking his eyes off the road.

Her expression darkened just as a rumble of thunder sounded overhead. Vibrations rattled the car and she realized just how jumpy, how shaky Evan appeared. Looking in the rearview mirror, she spotted deep dark bags under his bloodshot eyes.

Flanking Rayelle, her children remained quiet and tense. Something beyond the usual wasn't right with their father. Elliot asked, with a shaking voice, "Where are you taking us?"

Evan didn't even look back at his children, didn't calm them. He just growled, "Somewhere. Let me focus, sweetie."

Beside Rayelle, Skylar whimpered and Elliot shakily reached for her hand. Rayelle's expression pinched, attention flickering from one child to the other. She looped an arm around both of them, pulling them close to her side.

They both were deathly pale, Skylar trembling and Elliot on the brink of tears. Neither understood what was happening. Thankfully, neither seemed physically hurt from the literal car crash that Evan had staged.

Taking a deep breath, Rayelle tried to remain calm. Her kids needed her to be strong and unwavering in the face of this disastrous turn. A brief thought of textured red-orange skin and mandibles flared through her mind. Determination solidified inside her as her eyes drew to the front, to the rain pelting the windshield.

Attacking him as he drove would do no good. They'd all end up in an accident, possibly dying. She just had to find an opening and take advantage after he stopped.

It wasn't long until Evan was driving them off the highway and through rural town streets. Rayelle's stomach flipped when she noticed he'd driven into a nature park. On a stormy day, it was guaranteed to be empty.

Rayelle and the kids braced themselves as the car raced through the parking lot, hopping a curb to barrel down a bike trail. The sounds of rocks and sticks pinged off the car's hull. The chugging of the engine roared around them as the car shuddered from being forced off-road. Rain continued to patter over the car, loud and incessant. The patter of the rain was joined by the shrieking scraping of branches along all sides of the vehicle.

By the time the car stopped, Rayelle wasn't sure if it was by Evan's design or whether it couldn't go further. Either way, he grabbed something from the other seat and slammed his car door open.

"Out," he barked on the other side of the back seat's door, waving a gun to emphasize his authority. Slowly, all three clambered out. Elliot, then Rayelle, and finally Skylar. The car had stopped in a clearing, a yard or two away from the edge of a cliffside drop-off.

With the firearm acting as a guiding force, Evan motioned for his hostages to stand between himself and the cliff's edge. While he waved the gun, he continued talking. His tone was one of pained sensibility, verging on breakdown. "It didn't have to be like this, Ray. We didn't have to divorce or go through court or any of that! We could've been together and happy."

She positioned herself between her children and her ex-husband, too apprehensive to do anything with that gun pointed at them. Her expression and tone hardened, eyes narrowing as she shot back, "Was I supposed to be happy when you hired those men to kidnap me?"

Evan's features darkened, pinched as he scowled. "What does that *fucking* matter? They didn't do their job."

"Dad?" Skylar's uncertain voice barely sounded over another roll of thunder overhead. Rayelle almost flinched, listening to her child's image of their father start to fracture.

Evan ignored them, opting to wave his ex-wife closer once more with his gun. "Come here, Rayelle."

With no other course of action, she obeyed. As she took a few steps forward, Elliot whipped his stricken attention to her, immediately grabbing for her arm. "Mom!"

"It'll be alright. Just stay close to your sibling." She shot him a smile, though she herself knew she couldn't make that promise. Gingerly, she pried her son's fingers from her arm before continuing toward Evan. Elliot listened to her directions and sidled closer to Skylar, though his expression remained warily on both parents.

"On your knees," Evan sneered, once again motioning with the gun. She couldn't help but feel he radiated some malicious smugness under his bitter exterior. He was going to get "the bitch" on her knees, one last time. Anger clawed in her stomach at that very thought.

Just as slowly as she approached, Rayelle began lowering to her knees with her hands still raised. Evan scoffed, oozing disdain as she got halfway. That small sound razed over her, igniting her growing fury.

With her left hand, she grabbed at his gun-wielding hand and twisted his wrist – away from her kids – just as her right fist slammed into his groin. The impact sent a rush of gratification through her. The gun clattered away, sliding across pebbles, as Evan crumpled with a pained groan, doubling Rayelle's satisfaction.

Before she could dive for the gun, Elliot rushed in. Quick as he was, he snatched up the weapon. Before she could praise him for helping, he threw the gun over the edge of the cliff's edge.

"No!" Thunder rumbled overhead as Rayelle screamed, taking a step toward him while watching the gun arc through the air. Dread sunk through her as she whipped around to face Evan again, putting herself between her child and her ex-husband once more. Evan was already on his feet, reaching for something inside his jacket pocket, which only made Rayelle's stomach lurch.

Oh no.

Above the thunder, Elliot sobbed with tears streaming down his cheeks. "*Can't we just talk?*"

"We're already past that point. Your mom has already poisoned you enough with this gender confusion bullshit, Emma." Evan growled as he whipped out a second gun. Rayelle flinched, hearing him say what had – thus far – remained in a court setting. Behind her, she heard Elliot exhale sharply, struck by the emotional hit. He'd been so careful, waffling for a long time between presentations. With the divorce settling down, with the talks he'd had with Evan, Rayelle knew he'd gotten his hopes up.

There was no time to think about that as Evan cocked the gun, the click clear despite the pattering rain. "Maybe I can save Austin, but you two are too far gone."

"Dad!" Together, Elliot and Skylar screamed, the former a watery cry and the latter a shriek of horror.

"Get down!" Rayelle waved behind her, motioning for her eldest to drop.

The gun went off a deafening boom. The world slowed as Rayelle's mind raced for options. Duck, dodge, drop. She didn't have the time. Bracing herself, she waited for the pain of the bullet to rend through her, hoping it didn't hit anything vital nor cleave through her to Elliot.

In midair, the bullet stopped. It didn't simply freeze. It hit something, crumpling in on itself as the sound of impact echoed through the air.

Everyone froze and Rayelle's brain fritzed for a second before she realized something else. Where the bullet stopped, where it hit something, rain was not falling. The air in front of Rayelle flickered like a glitched artefact as her eyes slid upward.

An organic clicking mixed with a warble before the cloaking flickered out. A black-armored back, large and broad, stood between Rayelle and Evan. Her breath caught as her brain tried to shake off the delusion.

There was no way. There was absolutely no way.

Even as she denied it, her eyes caught sight of red-orange textured skin between the plates of armor and long red-black plumage, pulled back into a sort of ponytail.

Her heart thundered in her chest, throbbing in time with her heightened pulse.

"You!" That singular word shrieked from Evan. That caught Rayelle's attention and her eyes swung toward her ex-husband, her eyebrows furrowing. How the hell did *he* know about Tai'dqei?

"I knew you were real!" Evan's scream sounded unhinged and deranged as he took a step toward the alien. The gun in his hand shook, but Rayelle wasn't sure if it was from fear or rage. "Everyone said I was just stressed but you've been tailing me, haven't you?"

Tai'dqei angled his masked face at the human and, despite months apart, Rayelle thought she could feel smugness radiating off him. Even as she blinked back tears, amusement huffed from her lips.

"And *you*," Evan hissed, turning his attention to Rayelle. Even as she turned her attention to her ex, she noticed a growl rise, slow and quiet from Tai'dqei. In her peripheral, she saw him tense, ready to throw himself at Evan.

The human man was oblivious to the danger standing right before him. His hateful focus was entirely on Rayelle. "You have something to do with him, don't you? You weren't happy ruining my life and my children. Oh no, you had to keep tormenting me!"

Whatever he was about to do was interrupted as Tai'dqei charged at him. Evan howled as a crushing grip snatched up his arm, the firearm yanked from his hand. Not one to be taken so easily, Evan jerked and struggled. Beneath the two tussling opponents, mud gave way and their footing slid.

Where Tai'dqei remained upright, Evan slipped and fell into the wet dirt. That was enough to make inspiration strike as Evan hefted a glob and hurled it at Tai'dqei's face. It landed with a smack, causing the alien to pause. A very loud snarl rumbled out of Tai'dqei as he wrenched his mask off. He latched the mask to his hip belt, the angry guttural clicks echoed through the rain and trees.

"What the fuck, *what* the *fuck*," breathed Evan, scrambling backward on the ground when he caught sight of the alien features. A low growl continued to emanate from Tai'dqei as he slowly followed Evan, like a jaguar stalking their next lunch. His mandibles flexed and, from the way he walked, Rayelle got the feeling he was playing with her ex. Evan was no actual threat to him and he was broadcasting that fact.

Quick like a viper, Tai'dqei lunged and snatched Evan's ankle. A surprised yelp burst from the human man as Tai'dqei hauled him up upside down, holding him at arm's length. With a few heavy squelching steps in the mud, the alien headed toward the cliff's edge.

Tai'dqei dangled Evan over the ledge, his eyes broadcasting the silent threat. Evan's hollering turned to begging, his voice tinged with further terror as he stared at the ground far below.

"Wait, don't!" Now it was Skylar's turn to rush in. They grabbed at Tai'dqei's free arm, but flinched away when the ja-tau turned his gaze on them. Skylar's lips trembled, blinking back tears as they weakly said, "H-he's still my dad. *Please*."

Tai'dqei glanced up to Rayelle, tone soft though he still held Evan over the precipice. "What are they saying?"

Oh right, she straightened as she remembered the translator nano worm. Of course, Tai'dqei couldn't understand her kids.

"They don't want to see their dad dropped to his death." With a wave of her hand, she edged closer to the car. She sighed as if resigning herself to taking the higher road. Ignoring the confused and curious looks her kids shot her, she waved Tai'dqei over. "Bring him over here."

Tai'dqei's eyes narrowed, his mandibles twitching with amusement. There was something in her stance that made him believe she had something else up her sleeve. Something she deemed less gruesome for her kids to view rather than their father splattered on the rocks below. So he obliged.

As soon as he was set down, Evan scrambled to his feet, moving toward Rayelle as if to hug her. "Thank you, Ra—"

Whatever gratitude he was about to show her was cut off as she grabbed his collar, her other hand reaching for his head. Using her pent-up rage, she forced Evan's face toward the car. Surprised, the man barely even had a chance to resist as his face kissed the hood.

"Never. Threaten. My children. Again!" Punctuating every syllable, Rayelle slammed Evan's face into the car. The sound of flesh hitting metal echoed through the air between the raindrops. Once finished, she released him and, with a groan, he slumped against the car. Blood smeared along the metal, his face, her shirt.

With her shoulders still tense, she turned to her children and Tai'dqei. All three watched her quietly. She waited for her kids to say something, to voice their dissent.

"Is dad going to be okay?" Skylar piped up, their eyes shifting from Rayelle to Evan. They didn't exactly move to help their fallen father, but there was concern woven into their tone.

From the ground, the aforementioned man groaned.

"He's alive, at least," Rayelle scoffed, fighting the urge to kick Evan while he was down. She knew she'd have to have a long and difficult talk with Skylar and Elliot — likely two different sorts of conversations - about what just happened. Those talks could be had later. There were more pressing matters on her mind. Turning to Tai'dqei, she demanded, "Why are you here?"

"It's a long story." Tai'dqei's fingers flexed as he considered what to tell her. There really wasn't time. Depending on what she chose, there was a lot to do. "We should get go—"

"No, TAC told us you couldn't come here. What's going on?" Rayelle took a step closer to him, her finger jabbing him in the chest plate. It was easier for her to hang on to suspicion and anger, than let herself believe their story could have a happier ending. She'd already gotten used to bittersweetness.

Her mind flew wildly with questions and accusations, her eyes widening as one potentiality settled. "You didn't *steal* the time machine thing did you?"

"I did not," was all Tai'dqei managed to say before Elliot grabbed his mom's arm.

Her attention wheeled to her son, finding his expression curious but conflicted. "Mom? How can you understand them?"

She opened her mouth but closed it when she realized she didn't have a good answer. At least, not an answer that would be accepted quickly. Despite how the phrase echoed in her head, considering Tai'dqei had just used it on her, she muttered, "It's a long story."

"No, seriously. What the fuck is going on?" Elliot released his mother as he ran his hands through his short hair. It was seemingly easier for him to focus on the absurd, rather than the family trauma that had just passed. "A time machine? And them, are they an alien?"

As Elliot paced away, Skylar intercepted him. They pressed a hand to his arm, as if the touch could calm their brother down. Looking up to Rayelle, their own expression a mirror of conflict and pain and uncertainty as their brother's face, Skylar asked, "Can we get out of the rain at least?"

Taking a deep breath, Rayelle turned her attention back to the patiently waiting Tai'dqei. "We need to get out of the rain. Somewhere dry."

He nodded, inputting a command onto his gauntlet. His ship uncloaked itself, hovering right at the edge of the cliffside in open air. With a motion of his arm, he wordlessly told Rayelle and her children to follow as the boarding gangway lowered.

No end to the surprises, Elliot grudgingly trudged forward as he yelled, "How long has this been here?!"

CHAPTER 28

The conversation with her children went about as well as Rayelle expected it would. Once she was finished with her grand tale of space adventures, occasionally interrupted by Tai'dqei clarifying something that only she could understand, she gave her kids time to process. There was about seven seconds of silence before Elliot and Skylar both began speaking over each other. "You were in the future? In space?!"

Elliot gaped, eyes wide. "*For months?*"

"And they saved you?" Skylar motioned toward Tai'dqei with a sweep of their arm.

"It was touch-and-go, but yes he did." Rayelle nodded, hands on her hips as she remained standing through the conversation. Overall, she thought they both were taking her revelation well. Of course, having a literal alien and sitting on a spaceship helped to smooth the understanding and veracity of her story.

Even now, Skylar was eyeing the walls and casting dubious glances toward the bridge, either assessing the equipment or trying to spot the candid camera crew. Rayelle faintly wondered if he could make sense of the technology just by looking at it.

Elliot still seemed engaged with the discussion at hand, his eyes flicking to Tai'dqei. The ja-tau had seated himself in a chair, hoping to appear less imposing. Though it only brought his unreal features closer to the kids' line of view. Elliot seemed to assess the alien quietly before he mumbled, "And then he came for us when we were all in trouble."

Rayelle only managed to nod before her other child interrupted.

"This is so weird." Skylar nudged their glasses up, rubbing the bridge of their nose. They had somehow managed to tear their attention away from their surroundings, which apparently allowed the oddity of the situation to sink in.

After a glance from the imposing alien to their mom, they asked, "Can me and Elliot go talk by ourselves for a bit?"

"Sure, I'll take you to some guest quarters," Rayelle said after an exchange with Tai'dqei. She led them down the hall toward her old room. It was odd to think of a room on a spacefaring ship as her 'old room,' but she stowed the thought away for later.

In his attempts to clarify things, Tai'dqei had leaked new information. Information that Rayelle needed to address.

If he was being honest, Tai'dqei found everything hard to process much the same way as the youngsters. Rayelle was near him again. He'd met her kids and, while it wasn't a warm welcome, it wasn't terrified screaming. Which gave him a strange sense of optimism.

The brief reprieve while Rayelle showed them a separate room was almost surreal. For a moment, he thought he'd fallen to a hallucination and that everything that transpired through the day hadn't actually happened.

It wasn't long until Rayelle re-emerged from the room, after a few more exchanged words between herself and her kids. Tai'dqei straightened from his slump, where his elbows had braced on his knees and he'd been staring at the floor. Her residual maternal softness sifted away as she neared him. Tension wrought up his spine, bracing for an inevitable impact.

With her children out of earshot, Rayelle stormed up to Tai'dqei's seated form. She barely resisted the urge to grab him by the collar. "*Seven years?* What do you mean you waited seven years for me?"

She had barely managed to keep her cool during Elliot and Skylar's interrogation when Tai'dqei told her that new nugget of information. It was a wonder she managed to delay her reaction in front of her kids. With them out of the room, she could press more information from Tai'dqei.

He was prepared for this reaction, though he couldn't figure out if she was angry or shocked. Ah'ke had counseled him on this very discussion, highlighting all the reasons she could have found his choice a poor one. Trying not to dwell on those discussions, he simply nodded. "Yes."

Rayelle wanted to cry as something in her chest twinged. That damned, steadfast, certain 'yes' of his. Guilt warred with sentimentality, making her heart ache. "You could have done something else! Moved on or found someone or—"

"I could have, but I didn't," he cut in, before she could ramble on about other options. There were many things he could have done throughout those seven years. The fact of the matter was he chose this route, there was no reversing that. Besides, he had good reason. "In order to get the time travel technology, TAC needed to know they could trust me. I opted to do jobs for them."

"You worked for the Temporal Authority Council *for seven years* to get me?" Another bout between guilt and sentimentality made Rayelle's words catch. "You don't even look any older!"

At that, Tai'dqei rubbed the back of his neck. This was something they neglected to talk about last time. "My people do age differently than yours."

Something else she hadn't considered, she realized. As familiar as he was, there were still things she had to learn about him. Rayelle hastily stowed the wild chaos the new information stoked, trying to focus on the here and now.

Ever-present paranoia flinched at being excited for his return in her life. Being back on Earth had reminded her how men often did good deeds in exchange for something. Her arms crossed protectively over her chest as she pinned the alien with a look. "What if I didn't want to come back with you?"

He fell silent, considering he had worried about that very prospect for the whole seven years they'd been separated. Only months had passed for her, but that could have been enough time for her to move on, to find a new lover. Ah'ke had drilled that possibility into him. The cautious distance between himself and Rayelle ate at his insides, even knowing that. "That was a risk I was willing to take."

"Why?" Her voice hardened, eyebrows furrowing as her heart skipped.

"Because…" His mandibles fidgeted as he trailed off. Rayelle fought down a wave of fondness, watching those alien features move nervously. Her intense look burned into him, waiting. Unable to take the tension, Tai'dqei abruptly stood, towering over the her. His shoulders braced tight for embarrassment or rejection, the muscles knotting down his arms. "I love you, Rayelle."

She stared up at him, her eyes widening as pink bled across her cheeks. He rushed to continue before she could interrupt his flow, "I held my tongue, because I wasn't sure the depths of your feelings or if saying it would make you question returning home. Then you said you loved me right before leaving and I hated myself for not telling you the same."

Rayelle continued to stare up at him, eyes still wide. He wasn't sure how to parse her reaction, but it didn't matter. His words continued to spill as his own heart slammed against his ribcage.

"I worked for seven years to prove myself to TAC just to tell you that. They were the ones who chose when." One of his hands nervously ran through his feather-hair, momentarily getting caught by the ponytail.

He avoided mentioning how they'd given him guidelines and an array of scenarios. Or how one of the options entailed how Evan was allegedly tormented by an unknown creature for a week before he kidnapped Rayelle and her kids.

He didn't even think twice about that route or the fact the creature might have been a driving factor in Evan's dwindling mental health. At the very least, it wasn't the sole reason for the man's attempted murder. And he wanted to destroy the man who had caused Rayelle so much suffering and pain.

When he held the wretched little man over the cliffside and saw the dread and fear in Skylar's face, guilt had washed over Tai'dqei. He didn't want to see that expression mirrored in Rayelle's own features.

That didn't matter right now. What mattered was letting her know she still had choices. "You don't have to return with me to my time if you do not wish. There are other options in place."

"What other options?" Rayelle nearly shrieked. She had already subconsciously come to terms with not being able to go back. What did he mean there were options? Did he not understand her situation? "I left Evan bloodied at his own car in the middle of the forest! I'll be the first suspect!"

"The Temporal Authorities had other lives set up for you," he solemnly informed her, hoping to cut through her spinning reality to steady her.

For the span of a breath, she stared at him, comprehension dawning behind her eyes but skepticism keeping her expression hard. Her attention flickered away from him as her thoughts slowed from their wild ricocheting. Taking a deep breath, Rayelle centered herself.

Tai'dqei had come back for her. It had been his choice to use seven years of his life for the endeavor.

Evan had tried to kill her. Again. Between Tai'dqei's intervention and her own brute force, he was currently sitting bloody by his abandoned car. He might have died, but he might not either.

So where did that leave herself and her kids? Her eyes drifted down the hall, where her kids were talking behind closed doors.

From what Tai'dqei said, the authorities seemed to have new lives already set up for them. Rayelle didn't know what that meant. Maybe there were slightly different timelines they could step into or maybe TAC had false families scattered about. Or maybe it was something like a temporal witness protection program.

Did she really need to spend time thinking about that? She knew what she really truly wanted. Wasting time assessing all the options seemed silly. When she turned back to Tai'dqei, she caught a slight jolt through him as if he was bracing himself.

"Why is it always like this?" She kept her expression carefully schooled as she grabbed at the lip of his chest plate, pulling him down. Even though she knew he was humoring her, it was gratifying to have him bend to her wordless demand. "Why does everything seem to fall into place when you're around?"

Tai'dqei didn't get a chance to respond before she pulled him in for a kiss. His mandibles instantly flared from instinct as her arms wrapped around his neck, her lips pressed to maw.

A tidal wave of relief crashed through him, melting away years of stomach-churning uncertainty as he kissed her back. His mandibles held her gingerly, preciously. An ache shot through him, realizing how much he missed this form of affection, the press of her body against him, the softness of her.

Rayelle's arms tightened as her own thoughts steered down similar paths as his. His familiar sturdiness, his warmth, the texture of his skin and the feel of his mandibles. Being able to kiss him again made happy tears burn at the back of her eyes.

They didn't get a chance to deepen the kiss as Skylar's hushed voice broke the moment. "This is really weird."

As one, Tai'dqei and Rayelle parted from the kiss and caught the two kids standing in the hallway. There was a tense moment of silence as both adults struggled to say anything.

It was Elliot, wrinkling his nose, who broke the silence. "Is he our new stepdad?"

"If he's our new stepdad, are we moving to space?" Skylar's eyes grew wide as they pointed upward.

Not for the first time, Rayelle felt the rug yanked from under her feet. The amount of options piling before her was dizzying. Though she wanted to be with Tai'dqei, the mother in her knew she had to consider her children.

This was their future too and they deserved a say.

She hazarded a look at Tai'dqei, whose expression held the same daunted look she was feeling. Reading the concerns painted over her features, his mandibles pulled up in an attempt to reassure her. "There are options for all possible outcomes on Earth, in space, with me, and otherwise."

Rayelle sighed, shoulders slumping as she realized that she would have to consider the available options. It was already making her tired. Turning to her kids, their expectant stares reminded her they couldn't understand Tai'dqei.

Despite the embarrassment of being caught in a make-out sesh with an alien, Rayelle smiled. "It seems like we have some choices to make, kids."

◊ ◊ ◊

In the end, Skylar and Elliot were amenable to the idea of the literal future in space. Despite the tough decision of leaving other family and friends behind, neither kid looked forward to suffering through the politically charged atmosphere that targeted LGBTQ+ folks in their era. After the divorce – and the last-minute fright of Evan's abduction – they just wanted to be left alone.

There was a short stop by their house, gathering what items they wanted to bring before they all blasted off into the galaxy. Rayelle didn't know if the temporal authorities had any qualms about that, but she wasn't going to force her kids to give up whatever possessions they deemed worth the trip.

After the rushed packing and jolt into space, they hurtled into a sort of portable time wormhole that TAC had allowed Tai'dqei to use. The portal was hard to describe and made Rayelle's brain warble, but Skylar looked enraptured, watching unnamed colors and lights and images flicker by. Elliot, on the other hand, suffered the time travel equivalent of motion sickness.

Once they hit Tai'dqei's timeline, a wild whiplash of events followed. A stop at the Temporal Authority Counsel headquarters relinquished Tai'dqei of his time-hopping tech. At the same time, the kids got their own earworms and a check-up by Ah'ke, who had stayed at TAC awaiting Tai'dqei's return. After being told of the car accident, Ah'ke demanded to give Rayelle a once over as well.

When they left TAC, with Ah'ke in tow, they headed off to their next destination: Yatou, one of the ja-tau home worlds.

According to Tai'dqei, Rayelle learned her little contingent of peers from Rerli 3 — and then some — had relocated to the ja-tau homeworld. Some had settled with the fearsome aliens. Others had gone to explore space, taken under the protective wing of the ja-tau. A lucky few returned to their home time.

It was still a trek that equated to roughly three days for Rayelle and her kids. Which meant plenty of time for Skylar, Elliot, and Tai'dqei to awkwardly dance around each other.

It was amusing from Rayelle's point of view. Sometimes she'd catch Elliot or Skylar looking at Tai'dqei, ducking their head down when the alien glanced at them. To his credit, Tai'dqei stayed approachable and helped them adjust the best he could. Though he was also awkward. Adorably so.

It was near the beginning of the third cycle when Ah'ke invited Elliot and Skylar to watch her and Tai'dqei train. Rayelle had given them the okay as long as the training stuck to observation. She knew she might have to eventually let Tai'dqei train them, but she wanted to limit grievous injury to a minimum for now.

Nearly two hours later, the four emerged from the training room.

"Damn, you two have, like, fucking 20-packs." Skylar's voice rang out through the corridor as the four exited the training room. Rayelle glanced up from where she read her book in the lounge area, finding both ja-tau in their partial armor with the thermal netting encasing them.

Ah'ke and Tai'dqei, sweaty from their sparring, laughed as all four trooped to the mess area.

"I didn't get to ask this earlier, but Tai'dqei," Elliot cut in, waiting until the alien looked at him before nodding to the alien's chest. "What're those from?"

Rayelle already knew what her son referred to. The obvious half-moon scars below Tai'dqei's pecs, the ones she had noticed so long ago.

Despite being an entirely different species *and* having all manner of futuristic healing at his disposal, Tai'dqei had chosen to keep the scars of his mastectomy. A sort of blooding ritual of his own, Rayelle had thought in one of the many lonely nights back on Earth.

"Sometimes individuals of my species have hormonal changes that result in many physical changes. Ah'ke and I both went through the Change." Tai'dqei nodded to Ah'ke, who returned the gesture with a nod and her own mandibles arching upward. With a motion to his own chest, Tai'dqei explicitly elaborated, "The scars are from my mammaries being removed."

"Wait, wait, wait." Skylar leaned over a counter, opposite of the aliens. Their eyes jumped back and forth between Ah'ke and Tai'dqei. "You're both trans?"

Ah'ke fielded the question with a casual shrug. "From how your mother explains it, by 2020s Earth standards we are."

"So our stepdad is a trans alien man," Skylar hummed contemplatively, eyes still jumping back and forth between the two ja-tau. Rayelle couldn't begin to guess what was going on in their head, but they eventually broke into a wide grin. "We're just a big ole queer space family."

From beside their sibling, Elliot winced at Skylar's words. They appeared braced for something. "That's not weird for you, right? Having us as kids?"

After a swig of water from a bottle, Tai'dqei shook his head. "No, you're about as energetic as my other children."

"Wait, you have other kids?" Skylar's tone brightened with a new eagerness. Rayelle fought hard to keep from smiling, waiting for Tai'dqei to reveal just how many kids he had.

"Yes, you will meet some of them when we arrive on Yatou." Tai'dqei tried to mask his own amusement, addressing the ongoing questions the two shot his way.

"Some? How many do you have?" Elliot asked, awkward uncertainty bleeding into their voice.

Again, Tai'dqei answered without hesitation. "Twenty-four."

"What?!" Elliot and Skylar shrieked in unison.

At that point, Rayelle couldn't help the laughter that spilled from her. It was nice to hear the excitement returning to her children's voices. Even on Earth, both had become quiet and a little withdrawn from ostracization due to their gender identities to life changes and the divorce. Now it felt like they were slipping out of their protective shells. Being the loud and exuberant kids from her earlier memories of them.

It also didn't escape Rayelle's attention that Tai'dqei hadn't added more numbers to his brood, despite the seven-year gap.

Maybe spurred on by the fact Tai'dqei was a parent as well – a fact neither child had apparently considered – Elliot suddenly asked, "Do you think our dad was a bad person?"

"Yes." The answer came quickly from Tai'dqei, without any hemming or hawing. It was Rayelle's turn to wince at her counterpart's lack of tact. She moved to rise from her spot in the lounge, ready to soothe her children. A heavy sensation fell to her shoulder and she started, not even realizing Ah'ke had crept close as Tai'dqei and her children conversed.

"Give him a shot," was all Ah'ke said with a wink. Grudgingly, Rayelle eased and sat back down with Ah'ke following suit.

"Oh," Skylar deflated a little, their shoulders hunched to their ears at the brusque reply. Elliot placed a consoling hand on their shoulder but didn't defy Tai'dqei's assessment. In fact, his face creased with his own slew of feelings about Evan.

Tai'dqei tilted his head, observing the crestfallen two. Just as he answered their question about Evan with precision, he pinpointed the source of awkward unhappiness in the air. They were still Evan's children, they still had memories and feelings they couldn't control. Tai'dqei understood those kinds of feelings.

Leaning against the counter opposite of the two kids, Tai'dqei's voice came out gentle yet firm. "You are not bad for still loving him or having complicated feelings about him. Your feelings show you did not fail him. He failed you."

Both kids glanced up at Tai'dqei, a shine to their eyes that betrayed tears that had yet to fall. Despite the glumness wrapped around them, Skylar and Elliot smiled a little at the ja-tau's words. They weren't dazzling smiles, but at least they were there, waiting to grow as time healed their wounds.

Elliot and Skylar fell back into jabbering again, shooting off questions about Yatou, about Tai'dqei's kids, about whatever thought that happened to wander into their minds.

Rayelle snorted as she and Ah'ke shared a look. It was a relief to see her kids rebounding from a discussion about their father with bright-eyed curiosity concerning the unknown. They had a whole new universe to explore and they weren't looking back on what was lost. Again, she was struck by how vibrant Elliot and Skylar had grown in a short amount of time as she settled back to read once more.

◊ ◊ ◊

It took a full day and a half before Skylar and Elliot bounded off — under the "supervision" of Lisa and the guidance of Blue and Sandra — to explore what their new city had to offer. Rayelle could only hope they wouldn't get in trouble. With Lisa tagging along, she wasn't certain if that was a possibility.

Sitting in Tai'dqei's home, she still hadn't come completely to terms with reality. Yatou had proven to be a pleasant planet, with the ja-tau spread across varying biomes. Tai'dqei's home — and many of his families' homes — centered in what Rayelle would have called a tropical, jungle-like environment.

Huge plants in various colors clustered around the homes, their scents unmistakably floral. A red sun hung in a brilliant blue sky always seemed orange at the horizon. Even the animals, at least the domestic ones she'd met, had a familiar sort of dog-like and cat-like quality to them.

There were so many things so similar, but so foreign. Even the domiciles and buildings had an uncanny familiar-yet-strange sensation to them. In part, it was thanks to humans incorporating themselves into ja-tau life.

Tai'dqei's own home — rough on the outside but full of futuristic luxuries — didn't help matters. It was relatively small compared to other homes she'd spotted and it was a little further away from the bustling city. Understandable, since he avoided crowds most of the time.

His place had been built into a cliffside and Rayelle found that traversing through the home brought one to the opposite side of the rock formation. The room she currently sat in overlooked blue waves crashing into the blood-red rock.

"This feels strange," she admitted, glancing at Tai'dqei.

"What does?" He sat next to her on the settee, a careful distance still between the two of them. Other than the impromptu kiss they shared days ago, nothing further had happened.

He had been too nervous with Elliot and Skylar close by, but the two were now off exploring under Ah'ke's supervision. Tai'dqei was suddenly painfully aware of his limited intimate time with Rayelle. As if reminded they hadn't properly been intimate in years, yearning sliced through him.

He couldn't bring himself to close the distance. Nervousness gripped him in its clutches again.

"*Everything.* Usually there's something happening or about to happen. Being abducted, other aliens, you, Zav. Even on Earth, there was Evan." Despite the exhaustive list, Rayelle's lips curled into a smile, a strange sort of joy in her words. "I think this is the first time in a long time I feel an ongoing sense of safety."

A surge of instinct swelled in him. Tai'dqei reached out to her, carefully laying a hand on her shoulder. "I will always strive to protect you, Rayelle."

"Even when I'm old and decrepit and you still look like this?" She shot him a wry grin, making a sweeping motion to his large buff form.

"Yes, but there *are* ways to slow human aging to match ja-tau." This was another discussion they'd had over their three-day trek to his home. Along with his confession about choosing to torment Evan.

Thankfully, she had taken the latter discussion with ease.

"I remember you saying so." Her grin curled a little further, recalling the key ingredient to extending her life. "Literal Bloody Marys. Except with a green glow."

"My blood can also be added to baked goods," he added a touch defensively. It was a reiteration from their prior conversation but one he felt important to repeat.

Blue and Sandra had experimented with ja-tau blood in brownies and it seemed to be working from Ah'ke's assessments. It was hard to tell since only seven years had passed, but humans healed quicker and had increased stamina after ingesting the goodies.

And maybe he was just being a hopeful fool, wishing to extend his time with Rayelle to as long as possible. It'd have to be her decision, of course, but he couldn't stop himself from hoping.

Rayelle suddenly swung into his lap with her eyes narrowed but a mischievous lightness to her gaze. The atmosphere had gotten too heavy and she wanted to lighten the mood. Playfulness teased through her thoughts, piecing together one last way to torment the poor alien who had gone to great lengths just for her. "One more question."

He seriously doubted she'd limit herself to one question, especially after spending time with not just Rayelle but her own inquisitive offspring. He didn't dwell on that with her seated on him, however. His hands slid to her hips, gently pressing his palms to her sides. Anticipation burned up his arms and he barely refrained from crushing her in a hug. "Yes?"

She leaned close to him, a cheeky smile still on her lips. His heart stuttered in his chest, a flair of excitement weaving up his spine as he considered the last time she'd gotten so close. The anticipation deflated as she asked, "On those TAC missions, how many people did you save showed their gratitude by fucking you?"

A groan rumbled from Tai'dqei as he tossed his head back with frustration. Embarrassment clawed up his spine as he heard her laugh at him. Of course, she was going to hint at their first meeting, his first huge misunderstanding with her. "It's been seven years!"

"Only been a few months for me, big guy!" She jeered as she smacked him with one of the settee's pillows. At his startled growl, she scrambled off his lap and fled further into his home. He bounded after her so fast, he only realized it once he was already across the room.

Rayelle's heart skipped to a familiar beat as her ears caught the pounding rhythm of his footfalls.

It wasn't long before Tai'dqei snatched her up midway down a corridor. Her surprised shriek devolved into laughter as she squirmed and struggled against him. Where he touched her, prickles of excitement bloomed.

Tai'dqei hauled her the opposite direction down the hall, throwing her over his shoulder as an amused clicking escaped him. Those sounds resonated through him, pleasingly rippling into Rayelle's core. She'd missed those sounds.

Turning into his room, similar to what he had on his ship, he closed the distance from entryway to bed before swinging Rayelle onto the sleeping pad. Seeing her splayed on his bed sent a flutter of heat through him. Tai'dqei pinned her down, pressing her into the sheets, delighting in her plushness, the soft heat of her body caressed against his. Her arms looped around his neck and she tugged him closer, her legs hooking around his sides.

Contentment thrilled through her, feeling his heavy wholeness pressed against her. She still hadn't shaken the surreal feeling of being in the future again, of being with him. It'd take time for her brain to accept the fact. With Tai'dqei so close, especially after the last few days of careful distance, a warm earnestness rooted further within her.

Burrowing his face against her neck, he inhaled her scent and his tongue flickered against her flesh. He wanted to burn every sensation of her into his brain. He never wanted to forget the sound of her voice, the way she laughed, how her heartbeat thrummed against him. Rayelle shivered as his mandibles splayed so his teeth could scrape against her neck, eliciting a keening sound from the back of her throat.

From the reverent way his body moved against her, how his hands stroked down her arms and felt her sides, she knew he was enjoying reacquainting himself with her. Much like how her hands skirted over him, fingertips digging into muscle or tangled in the plumage of hair. Everything the same, but with different feelings.

In the increasingly warm bubble of just them, Rayelle's emotions spilled out, "I love you, Tai'dqei."

Pulling up from the crook of her neck and shoulder, he blinked down at her. Roughly seven years and three days since he last heard those words and they still struck him. breathless She quietly waited, watching him with an amused grin on her face.

Both of Tai'dqei's large hands slid to her face, cradling her head in his palms as he pressed his forehead to hers. His mandibles flexed briefly before he quietly breathed, "I love you too, Rayelle."

Her grin took on a sharper tilt, provocation clear in her next words. "Good, it didn't take you seven years to respond this ti—"

Tai'dqei growled, cutting her teasing off with a fervent kiss. Her smile only grew against his maw. She matched his fierce affection, returning the kiss as her legs locked around his hips.

He had been patient, torn time and space apart just to make sure she ended up happy and safe. Without even a guarantee she'd choose him. Rayelle was determined to return the sentiment and give Tai'dqei the lifelong love and care he deserved.

Even if it meant eating blood-filled baked goods someday.

ACKNOWLEDGEMENTS

Well, this has been one heck of an adventure!

The Unexpected Human Problem began life as a fanfiction. Through much deviation of canon and editing, it now sits in your hands as an original work! I hope you enjoyed it.

When I began this story, I didn't anticipate weaving some elements so close with some of my life experiences. (No, I've never been abducted by aliens or traveled through time.) As such, I hope The Unexpected Human Problem can brighten the day of anyone in or leaving similar circumstances.

Thanks to my readers on Tumblr and other sites, whose continual excitement, delight, and key-smashes kept me motivated. While the bulk of the recognition belongs with my readers and followers, I'd be remiss if I didn't thank my partner.

So thank you Valerie, for your continued support in all avenues of life. Without my partner, I wouldn't have found the confidence and drive to continue pursuing a serious career in writing.

Also thanks to writing aspirations and inspirations: Vivian Vande

Velde, Terry Pratchett, Neil Gaiman, Guillermo del Toro, Jane Austen, Ruby Dixon, Marissa Meyer, all the differing renditions of Beauty and the Beast, and any other monster x human media — whether direct or tangentially related — I've consumed over my lifetime before I even had the terms for it.

Thanks to you as well, dear reader. I hope you enjoyed the story and will continue to peruse my available catalog!

Eruden Edure (she/they) is a Midwest Millennial that — like many others — never got over the Beast becoming human again. While her lifelong passion for writing has not solely revolved around monster romance, she has recently taken to giving all manner of beasts their Happily Ever Afters.

When not writing, Eruden enjoys drawing, reading, listening to an eclectic array of YouTubers. Her time is limited, since she also manages a household of five plus two dogs and more-than-the-reasonable-amount of cats.

Feel free to follow Eruden online at:
Tumblr @ eruden-writes
Tumblr (again) @ eruden-archives
Facebook @ Eruden Edure
Twitter @ erudenedure
Patreon @ erudenedure